Praise for Catherine Bybee

Wife by Wednesday

"A fun and sizzling romance, great characters that trade verbal spars like fist punches, and the dream of your own royal wedding!"

—Sizzling Hot Book Reviews (5 stars)

"A great story that I hope is the start of a new series."

—The Romance Studio (4½ hearts)

Married by Monday

"If I hadn't already added Ms. Catherine Bybee to my list of favorite authors, after reading this book I would have been compelled to. This is a book *nobody* should miss, because the magic it contains is awesome."

—Booked Up Reviews (5 stars)

"Ms. Bybee writes authentic situations and expresses the good and the bad in such an equal way . . . Keeps the reader on the edge of her seat."

—Reading Between the Wines (5 stars)

"*Married by Monday* was a refreshing read and one I couldn't possibly put down."

—The Romance Studio (4½ hearts)

Fiancé by Friday

"Bybee knows exactly how to keep readers happy . . . A thrilling pursuit and enough passion to stuff in your back pocket to last for the next few lifetimes . . . The hero and heroine come to life with each flip of the page and will linger long after readers cross the finish line."

—*RT Book Reviews* (4½ stars, top pick [hot])

"A tale full of danger and sexual tension . . . the intriguing characters add emotional depth, ensuring readers will race to the perfectly fitting finish."

—*Publishers Weekly*

"Hot romance, a mystery assassin, British royalty, and an alpha Marine . . . this story has it all!"

—*Harlequin Junkie*

Single by Saturday

"Captures readers' hearts and keeps them glued to the pages until the fascinating finish . . . romance lovers will feel the sparks fly . . . almost instantaneously."

—*RT Book Reviews* (4½ stars, top pick)

"[A] wonderfully exciting plot, lots of desire, and some sassy attitude thrown in for good measure!"

—*Harlequin Junkie*

Taken by Tuesday

"[Bybee] knows exactly how to get bookworms sucked into the perfect storyline; then she casts her spell upon them so they don't escape until they reach the 'Holy Cow!' ending."

—*RT Book Reviews* (4½ stars, top pick)

Seduced by Sunday

"You simply can't miss [this novel]. It contains everything a romance reader loves—clever dialogue, three-dimensional characters, and just the right amount of steam to go with that heartwarming love story."

—Brenda Novak, *New York Times* bestselling author

"Bybee hits the mark . . . providing readers with a smart, sophisticated romance between a spirited heroine and a prim hero . . . Passionate and intelligent characters [are] at the heart of this entertaining read."

—*Publishers Weekly*

Treasured by Thursday

"The Weekday Brides never disappoint and this final installment is by far Bybee's best work to date."

—*RT Book Reviews* (4½ stars, top pick)

"An exquisitely written and complex story brimming with pride, passion, and pulse-pounding danger . . . Readers will gladly make time to savor this winning finale to a wonderful series."

—*Publishers Weekly* (starred review)

Not Quite Dating

"It's refreshing to read about a man who isn't afraid to fall in love . . . [Jack and Jessie] fit together as a couple and as a family."

—*RT Book Reviews* (3 stars [hot])

"*Not Quite Dating* offers a sweet and satisfying Cinderella fantasy that will keep you smiling long after you've finished reading."

—Kathy Altman, *USA Today*, *Happy Ever After* blog

"The perfect rags to riches romance . . . The dialogue is inventive and witty, the characters are well drawn out. The storyline is superb and really shines . . . I highly recommend this standout romance! Catherine Bybee is an automatic buy for me."

—*Harlequin Junkie* (4½ hearts)

Not Quite Enough

"Bybee's gift for creating unforgettable romances cannot be ignored. The third book in the Not Quite series will sweep readers away to a paradise, and they will be intrigued by the thrilling story that accompanies their literary vacation."

—*RT Book Reviews* (4½ stars, top pick)

Not Quite Forever

"Full of classic Bybee humor, steamy romance, and enough plot twists and turns to keep readers entertained all the way to the very last page."

—Tracy Brogan, bestselling author of the Bell Harbor series

"Magnetic . . . The love scenes are sizzling and the multi-dimensional characters make this a page-turner. Readers will look for earlier installments and eagerly anticipate new ones."

—*Publishers Weekly*

Not Quite Perfect

"This novel flows extremely well and readers will find themselves consuming the witty dialogue and strong imagery in one sitting."

—*RT Book Reviews*

"Don't let the title fool you. *Not Quite Perfect* [is] actually the perfect story to sweep you away and take you on a pleasant adventure. So sit back, relax, maybe pour a glass of wine, and let Catherine Bybee entertain you with Glen and Mary's playful East Coast–West Coast romance. You won't regret it for a moment."

—*Harlequin Junkie* (4½ stars)

Not Quite Crazy

"This fast-paced story features credible characters whose appealing relationship is built upon friendship, mutual respect, and sizzling chemistry."

—*Publishers Weekly*

"The plot is filled with twists and turns, but instead of feeling like a never-ending roller coaster, the story maintains a quiet flow. The slow buildup of a romance allows readers to get to know the main characters as individuals and makes the romantic element more organic."

—*RT Book Reviews*

Doing It Over

"The romance between fiercely independent Melanie and charming Wyatt heats up even as outsiders threaten to derail their newfound happiness. This novel will hook readers with its warm, inviting characters and the promise for similar future installments."

—*Publishers Weekly*

"This brand-new trilogy, Most Likely To, based on yearbook superlatives, kicks off with a novel that will encourage you to root for the incredibly likable Melanie. Her friends are hilarious and readers will swoon over Wyatt, who is charming and strong. Even Melanie's daughter, Hope, is a hoot! This romance is jam-packed with animated characters, and Bybee displays her creative writing talent wonderfully."

—*RT Book Reviews* (4 stars)

"With a dialogue full of energy and depth, and a twisting storyline that captured my attention, I would say that *Doing It Over* was a great way to start off a new series. (And look at that gorgeous book cover!) I can't wait to visit River Bend again and see who else gets to find their HEA."

—*Harlequin Junkie* (4½ stars)

Staying For Good

"Bybee's skillfully crafted second Most Likely To contemporary (after *Doing It Over*) brings together former sweethearts who have not forgotten each other in the eleven years since high school. A cast of multidimensional characters brings the story to life and promises enticing future installments."

—*Publishers Weekly*

"Romance fans will be sure to cheer on former high school sweethearts Zoe and Luke right away in *Staying For Good*. Just wait until you see what passion, laughter, reconciliations, and mischief (can you say Vegas?) awaits readers this time around. Highly recommended."

—*Harlequin Junkie* (4½ stars)

Making It Right

"Intense suspense heightens the scorching romance at the heart of Bybee's outstanding third Most Likely To contemporary (after *Staying For Good*). Sizzling sensual scenes are coupled with scary suspense in this winning novel."

—*Publishers Weekly* (starred review)

Fool Me Once

"A marvelous portrait of friendship among women who have been bonded by fire."

—*Library Journal* (best of the year 2017)

"Bybee still delivers a story that her die-hard readers will enjoy."

—*Publishers Weekly*

Half Empty

"Wade and Trina here in *Half Empty* just might be one of my favorite couples Catherine Bybee has gifted us fans with so far. Captivating, engaging, lively, and dreamy, I simply could not get enough of this book."

—*Harlequin Junkie* (5 stars)

Faking Forever

"A charming contemporary with surprising depth . . . Bybee perfectly portrays a woman trying to hold out for Mr. Right despite the pressures of time. A pitch-perfect plot and a cast of sympathetic and lovable supporting characters make this book one to add to the keeper shelf."

—*Publishers Weekly*

"Catherine Bybee can do no wrong as far as I'm concerned . . . Passionate, sultry, and filled with genuine emotions that ran the gamut, *Faking Forever* was a journey of self-discovery and of a love that was truly meant to be. Highly recommended."

—*Harlequin Junkie*

Say It Again

"Steamy, fast-paced, and consistently surprising, with a large cast of feisty supporting characters, this suspenseful roller-coaster ride will keep both series fans and new readers on the edge of their seats."

—*Publishers Weekly*

My Way to You

"A fascinating novel that aptly balances disastrous circumstances."

—*Kirkus Reviews*

"*My Way to You* is an unforgettable book fueled by Catherine Bybee's own life, along with the dynamic cast she created that will capture your heart."

—*Harlequin Junkie*

Home to Me

"Bybee skillfully avoids both melodrama and melancholy by grounding her characters in genuine emotion . . . This is Bybee in top form."

—*Publishers Weekly* (starred review)

Everything Changes

"This sweet, sexy book is just the escapism many people are looking for right now."

—*Kirkus Reviews*

The Whole Time

"Adorable. Sweet. Sparky. Sexy. Full of good food and wine and family and friends and all the things! I so need to see this series on TV one day! *The Whole Time* was such an adorable + fun + sweet + sparky + just beautiful romance—I loved it! Run to your nearest book dealer for your own Ryan—this one is mine!"

—*BJ's Book Blog*

All Our Tomorrows

"I love a good billionaire story. *All Our Tomorrows* reminds me of a good drama series like *Dallas* or *Dynasty*. I love the dynamics of the storyline and all the characters, so many of whom are not to be trusted. I'm counting down the days to the second book in the series to see what happens to all that money!"

—*Glamour*

"The stuff of which Hallmark Movies are made, *All Our Tomorrows* is an impressive crafted and original novel that is especially recommended . . ."

—*Midwest Book Review*

Lead Me Home

OTHER TITLES BY CATHERINE BYBEE

Contemporary Romance

Weekday Brides Series

Wife by Wednesday
Married by Monday
Fiancé by Friday
Single by Saturday
Taken by Tuesday
Seduced by Sunday
Treasured by Thursday

Not Quite Series

Not Quite Dating
Not Quite Mine
Not Quite Enough
Not Quite Forever
Not Quite Perfect
Not Quite Crazy

Most Likely To Series

Doing It Over
Staying For Good
Making It Right

First Wives Series

Fool Me Once

Half Empty

Chasing Shadows

Faking Forever

Say It Again

Creek Canyon Series

My Way to You

Home to Me

Everything Changes

Richter Series

Changing the Rules

A Thin Disguise

An Unexpected Distraction

The D'Angelos Series

When It Falls Apart

Be Your Everything

Beginning of Forever

The Whole Time

Maybe One Day

The Heirs Series

All Our Tomorrows

The Forgotten One

No More Yesterdays

Paranormal Romance

MacCoinnich Time Travels

Binding Vows

Silent Vows

Redeeming Vows

Highland Shifter

Highland Protector

The Ritter Werewolves Series

Before the Moon Rises

Embracing the Wolf

Novellas

Soul Mate

Possessive

Erotica

Kilt Worthy

Kilt-A-Licious

Lead Me Home

A Novel

CATHERINE BYBEE

This is a work of fiction. Names, characters, organizations, places, events, and incidents are either products of the author's imagination or are used fictitiously. Otherwise, any resemblance to actual persons, living or dead, is purely coincidental.

Published by Montlake, Seattle

www.apub.com

EU product safety contact:
Amazon Media EU S. à r.l.
38, avenue John F. Kennedy, L-1855 Luxembourg
amazonpublishing-gpsr@amazon.com

ISBN-13: 9781662517297 (paperback)
ISBN-13: 9781662517280 (digital)

Cover design by Caroline Johnson
Cover image: © simonkr, © Dimitris66, © DrPixel / Getty

Printed in the United States of America

This one is for Rachel.
Thank you for helping me get my life back.

CHAPTER ONE

The bell on the door chimed as Luna entered the coffee shop. The sweet scent of roasted sunshine in the form of coffee beans met her senses and put an instant smile on her lips. There was something about coffee that someone else made that just makes it taste better.

The line nearly reaching the door, on the other hand, was worse.

She glanced at her watch to check the time, then counted the people in line in front of her. There were three baristas and two cashiers. Assuming that the twelve people in front of her ordered anything ranging from a shot of espresso, to a drink with steamed milk, say, a latte or cappuccino. And the baristas took anywhere between one minute to two and a half minutes per drink, it should only take six to eight minutes to get her drinks and get out of there. With twenty minutes to work with, Luna was certain she'd make it to her meeting on time.

In fact, she should have a couple of minutes to spare, which put an idea in her head.

Luna pulled her cell phone out of her purse, found a picture of her sister, and tapped on it.

"Hey, you," Harper's joyful voice sang over the line.

"Hey. I'm downstairs at Starbucks; do you want me to get you something?"

"I didn't know you were coming in today."

"I'm not. Not for you guys anyway. Peterson is running the numbers for one of his clients, he asked me to come in and meet with a new

PI he's working with. I have just enough time to drop a latte off for you like the good little sister I am."

"Ahh, what did I do to deserve you?"

Luna smiled into the phone. "Nothing. I was born this way."

"A double shot latte would be great. Almond milk."

The line inched forward while several people came in to stand behind her.

"You got it."

"Do you think you'll be around for lunch?"

"God, I hope not. Peterson is long-winded but this shouldn't take longer than an hour, two at the most," Luna said.

"If the meeting takes two hours, I can try and get out for an early lunch."

"Sorry, I wish I could. I'm meeting a roof guy at the house between twelve and three. You know what that means."

"Yeah," her sister laughed. "He'll show up at three."

"Exactly."

"What's wrong with the roof?" Harper asked.

"Another leak. The last storm blew off a few shingles. Luckily, I needed to get something from the attic and noticed before the water soaked through into the house." That was the problem with old homes . . . they had old roofs and notoriously bad plumbing and electrical. All of which needed attention. "I'm just hoping it can be patched. The furnace needs an overhaul first. I don't have money for both."

"I can help," Harper offered.

"No."

"It's the *family* home."

"That only *this* member of the family is living in."

The line inched forward, so far Luna's calculations were working and none of the baristas were taking a break.

"Still . . ."

"Not happening. I don't have a mortgage or pay rent."

"Yeah, but the bills on that place are double mine and Jerry's. The property tax alone is—"

"Paid in part by my roommate. I got this, Harper. One emergency at a time is all I ask."

The old Victorian home sat on Queen Anne Hill with a partial view of the sound. It had belonged to their maternal grandmother, who left it to the three of them.

Luna was the youngest of the three at thirty-five. Harper just turned thirty-nine, their brother Ash was thirty-seven.

Since Harper lived with her husband on the opposite side of Lake Union, and Ash was a police officer in Portland, Luna was the logical choice to live in the house.

Ash had a few personal items in a room he called his, even though he only stayed the night a handful of times a year. Luna's roommate Miley lived in the second largest bedroom in the house, and there were still three bedrooms to spare. Two, since Luna used one as a home office. It was a big house that collected big bills.

But Luna wouldn't change it for the world.

"I'm about to order. See you in a few," Luna told her sister.

"Okay."

She disconnected the call.

There were two customers in front of her now, a man in a suit and a girl who couldn't decide if she wanted blue hair or green.

Blue, Luna decided. The green didn't match her skin tone.

The voice of the man caught Luna's attention, the one in the suit. "Large coffee," she heard him say.

"What kind of coffee."

"Regular."

"Dark roast, light roast . . ." the barista prodded.

"Dark."

"Grande, venti?"

The man looked up at the menu as if it just now occurred to him that he needed details.

It was Starbucks, for God's sake. There was one on every corner in Seattle. How did he not know how to order coffee in a Starbucks?

"Venti."

Luna looked at her watch.

She caught the man's profile after he paid and moved to the other end of the counter to wait for his drink. Strong jawline, tan skin, which stuck out since it was late January in Seattle. They hadn't seen the sun since October.

The girl ordered a mocha frappe, too much chocolate with whipped cream that made it just one hair short of ice cream. That drink would take them at least three minutes to make.

With her phone in her hand, ready to pay, Luna quickly gave her order and stood aside in less than a minute.

At the end of the counter, she pulled a couple of napkins from where sugar, cream, and cinnamon lived and waited for her name to be called.

Milkshake girl looked up at the same time Luna did. She couldn't be a day over eighteen.

She offered a smile.

Luna smiled back. "Blue hair looks good on you," she told her.

"You think so?" She fiddled with the ends of said hair.

"Absolutely. The darker the better."

Her shoulders slumped. "It fades too fast."

"Then just do the ends."

"That's not a bad idea. Thanks."

Someone moved between them to retrieve their coffee.

One by one names were called and drinks were picked up.

Venti dark roast man kept looking at his watch.

Luna's ears tuned in when she heard her name. At the same time, the girl she'd been talking to moved forward to grab her cup.

"Thanks for the hair tips."

"No problem." Luna smiled at the girl as she pushed down on the lids of the coffee to make sure they were tight, then put two sleeves on them so she wouldn't burn her hands.

Outside the rain had started to fall.

Thankfully, the coffee shop was only steps away from the building that housed the offices she was going to.

Luna tightened the belt on her jacket and picked up both coffees.

The line to order would have extended past the door if not for the rain. Instead, patrons crowded at the entry, making it difficult to jockey her way out.

Free of the crowd in the doorway, Luna doubled her steps to avoid being drenched. As she did, her purse started to slide off her shoulder. She stopped walking and lifted her elbow in an effort to correct the strap of her bag.

The person walking behind her rammed straight into Luna's arm.

Luna lunged forward to keep her balance, but the cup in her hand didn't survive the encounter.

Hot coffee splashed on her hand, causing her to drop it completely.

Luna sprang back to avoid being bathed in java.

Most of it missed her.

Most. Not all.

"What the . . ." the man who bumped into her said.

"Damn it." Luna looked at her feet and the sad and empty cup that sat there. Cold rain hit the hot coffee with a splash of mist. "Watch where you're walking," she chided.

She looked over to find dark roast venti man staring at her.

He had hazel eyes, or were they green with flecks of gold? Whatever the color, they met hers and held.

"You stopped" was all he said.

Luna shook off the way he looked at her and bent down to pick up the cup. "You weren't watching where you were going."

She glanced over her shoulder, looked at the line in the coffee shop, and knew she'd have to settle for whatever mud came out of the office break room.

"I'll buy you another—"

"I don't have the time. I'm going to be late as it is." And wet . . . very wet.

Without saying more, she hustled toward the door where they were both obviously headed.

She dropped the empty cup in the closest bin and headed toward the elevators.

"I am sorry."

"No one died," she said. *They drowned.* Luna couldn't tell if her pants caught some of the coffee, or the wet was only from the rain.

Inside the elevator, she pressed her sister's floor and stood back while several people pushed in.

She felt the weight of dark roast venti guy's gaze and glanced over to meet it.

He quickly looked away to study the ceiling.

When her stop came, she didn't need to look to prove the man watched her walk away.

She felt his eyes with every step.

Luna walked into the law offices where her sister worked and breezed past the receptionist.

Harper sat in a small space she shared with another paralegal.

"Here you go," she said as she sat the coffee on Harper's desk.

Her sister pulled her gaze away from her computer with her fingers still covering her keyboard and looked at Luna. "It must be coming down out there," she said.

Luna shook her arms; water splattered in all directions. "You think."

Harper reached for her coffee and laughed. "Wait, where's yours?"

"Long story, I'm going to be late." She turned to walk away.

"I'll call you later."

Luna lifted a hand in the air indicating she'd heard her sister, then hustled to the elevators once again.

Five minutes past nine, Luna walked into the law offices of Allen and Associates. She paused at the reception desk and started to unbutton her coat. "Hi, Melinda."

"Hi."

"Marcus is expecting me. Is he in his office or the conference room?"

"They're in the conference room," she said.

They? Great . . . nothing like being late for more than one person.

Luna shrugged out of her coat.

Melinda stepped around the desk to take it. "No need to stress."

"I hate being late. This jerk bumped into me, my coffee ended up on the street . . ." Luna pulled in a deep breath, stood tall, and pasted on a smile she didn't feel.

Melinda laughed. "I'll bring coffee to the room."

Luna sighed. "I could kiss you."

"Not in the office," Melinda teased.

Swiping a strand of soaked hair back, Luna made her way to the conference room.

Just outside the open door she heard voices.

"She elbowed me, her coffee took flight, and she had the audacity to act like it was my fault."

Luna froze in the doorway.

Dark roast venti guy had his back to her.

Marcus stood to his left, shaking his head. "It feels like most people are walking around in a daze. Heads in their phones, earbuds blasting music. No one pays attention anymore."

"Tell me about it."

The fake smile she'd painted on only moments ago slid from her face. Seriously? This guy blamed her?

The nerve.

"There she is. My secret weapon for numbers," Marcus boasted once he caught sight of Luna standing there.

Slowly, Mr. Venti turned.

A sinister feeling of joy bloomed in Luna's chest as recognition hit his eyes.

Unaware of the silent communication between her and Venti, Marcus made the introductions. "Nate Warren, this is Luna Canning."

She placed her purse on the conference table and reached out to shake his hand. "Hello, Mr. Warren. You look familiar. Have we met before?"

His hand was warm, despite the fact that they'd both just come in from the cold.

"If we did, I, ah . . . certainly didn't catch your name." Nate gave her hand a little extra squeeze before letting her go. "Marcus has told me a lot about you."

"All good I hope."

To Nate's credit, he didn't break eye contact, even when her smirk of a smile said ten times more than her words did.

"Singing your praises, Luna. If I could sing," Marcus said as he patted her shoulder in a warmer welcome than a handshake.

"You're too kind."

That made him laugh. "Since when are you humble?"

It was then that Luna purposely looked away from Nate. "I have to try once in a while."

"Sit, sit."

Luna moved to a seat opposite Nate.

Marcus sat at the head of the table.

"I'm sorry for being late. It's a little . . ." She glanced at Nate. "Hectic out there."

Amusement swam in Nate's hazel eyes without the least bit of shame.

"So I've heard," Marcus said.

Melinda walked into the room, a cup of coffee in her hand. She sat it in front of Luna with a small caddy filled with cream and various types of sugar.

"Thank you."

"Can I get anything for you, Mr. Warren?"

Nate cleared his throat. "Ah, no. I'm good."

Luna glanced at Nate's Starbucks cup before doctoring her coffee to her liking.

Melinda closed the door behind her when she left.

"I've already told Nate about your prowess with numbers. You won't find a better forensic accountant in the state."

This time, Luna accepted the praise without humility.

"Nate is our new consultant. He worked as a criminal fraud investigator for the federal government. Now he works independently as a private investigator using those same skills."

Luna lifted the coffee to her lips and talked over the rim of the cup. "You're a little young to be retired from the Feds."

"I was more interested in the private sector with more room to do my job than bureaucratic red tape allowed."

Luna sipped her coffee, then put the cup down.

"And more lucrative," she said.

He raised an eyebrow. "No one likes to wait for Congress to approve their paycheck."

"Their loss, our gain," Marcus said. "And I have a feeling that with the two of you, we'll be an unbeatable team."

Luna placed her fingers on the charm she had hanging from her neck and slowly slid it along the chain.

Marcus handed them each a folder. "Our client is Joel Mercier . . ."

CHAPTER TWO

What could have been an hour meeting and an email turned into two hours.

On any other day the time wouldn't matter. But with the sky dumping like some kind of dystopian megastorm created by the earth's polarity shifting, and the very real leak in her roof, two hours was too long.

When Marcus finally wrapped up their meeting, Luna was quick to jump to her feet.

"Let me walk you out," Nate said.

Luna slid the papers into her oversize purse and pushed her chair in. "That won't be necessary, Mr. Warren."

"If we're going to be working together, I have to insist you call me Nate."

She smiled. "I hate to rush, Nate, but I have a date with a roofing contractor."

"That doesn't sound fun," Marcus said.

"As long as I don't get home to an unwanted swimming pool in my living room, I'll be fine." She hiked her purse on her shoulder and stood tall. "You have my number," she told Nate. "I respond to text messages quicker than emails. Anything urgent, text me please."

"Will do." Nate smiled.

With a nod to Marcus, she said, "I'll be in touch."

Luna stopped at the reception desk long enough to retrieve her coat but still made it off the floor before Nate left the conference room.

The rain made the trip home a little longer. You'd think with as much rain as Washington state received, the locals would all have driving in it down pat.

But there was always someone who pushed their bald tires a little too far, or ignored that brake light flashing, and ended up on the side of the freeway.

Still, Luna had twenty minutes to spare before her appointment time.

She entered the house shaking off the rain she'd accumulated from the short walk from the detached garage.

Luna hung her coat in the mudroom and dropped her purse and keys on the kitchen table on her way to the attic.

Her four-legged welcoming committee met her at the top of the first flight of stairs.

She bent down, picked up her cat, and kept walking. "Did you miss me?"

Midnight, aptly named for her completely black coat and dark eyes, head butted her chest.

"I'll take that as a yes."

She rounded the corner and took the second flight of stairs; at the top there was a door that led to the attic.

Luna set Midnight down and pushed the door open. The cold from the attic made her shiver.

She propped it open to hear the contractor if he arrived early and went to check on the damage.

Old homes had huge attics, and this Victorian built at the turn of the twentieth century was no different. Some of Luna's earliest memories were visiting her grandmother and escaping to the attic with her siblings on days that were simply too miserable to go outside. A couple of round windows let in natural light. The raw lumber floors were stacked with dusty boxes holding everything from Christmas decorations to childhood memories. There was an old crib that every Canning child had used . . . and furniture that really should have gone to Goodwill but was put up there "just in case."

And a half a dozen modern day pots and pans to catch the drips from the leaking roof.

Under the largest puddle maker, Luna had placed a plastic tub used to put ice and drinks in for backyard parties.

A good two inches of water sat in the bottom. The drip she'd left when she went to her meeting was more of a trickle now.

She walked around the vast space to see if there were any new leaks and luckily found none.

Back at the stairs, she glanced around for her cat. "C'mon, Midnight. It's too cold to leave this door open."

Her cat looked at her with what could only be described as disagreement. An attic was a great place to keep her busy.

Luna tapped a fingernail on the door and acted like she was going to close it.

Midnight got the message and walked over . . . slowly, and hesitated before walking into the hall.

"You can play up here later. I promise."

Her tail went up before leading the way down the stairs.

"Luna? You home?" Miley called from somewhere on the first floor.

"Yeah."

"I rushed back in case you got caught in your meeting."

Luna met Miley in the foyer.

"Thanks. The meeting went long."

Miley looked at the ceiling. "How bad is it?"

"Worse than this morning, not as bad as it could be considering the rain coming down."

"At least the wind isn't blowing."

They walked together into the kitchen. "I need to get this patched up before the next real storm."

Miley pulled her phone from her back pocket before sitting on a stool at the small kitchen island. "How was your meeting?"

"Interesting."

Miley looked up from the screen. "Interesting how?"

Luna opened the fridge to see if anything looked like a good option for a quick lunch. "Marcus is contracting with a PI he wants me to work with on this case."

"You've done that kind of thing before, right?"

"Some. But mainly with his in-house people. This guy is an ex-Fed with an extensive fraud investigative background. The case is going to require a lot from him."

"And you?"

"We'll see. Numbers don't lie."

"People do."

"Good thing or I wouldn't have a job," Luna said, laughing.

Luna closed the fridge and turned to her friend. "I wonder how good this guy is at spotting the liars," she mused.

"Not as good as you, I bet."

"I credit Nana. She had a pretty good bullshit barometer."

The Victorian home had been hers. The woman had been as eccentric as she was independent. She'd married seven or eight times; Luna had lost count. She was fairly certain she'd married and divorced Luna's biological grandfather twice. Did that count as two? It didn't matter. If it wasn't for the fact that the Victorian home had been in a trust given to her from Luna's great-grandmother, the house would have been gone in one of the divorce settlements.

"When is this roof guy supposed to get here?" Miley asked.

Luna glanced at the clock on the wall. "Between noon and three." It was twelve ten.

"Let's hope he doesn't flake and use the rain as an excuse."

"If rain was an excuse, he'd be out of business."

Miley slid off the stool. "I'll be in my room. I have to finish that online class for my CEs."

"You're not done with that yet?"

Miley smiled. "Why do now what I can put off until tomorrow?"

Miley was a nurse. She worked twelve-hour shifts in the emergency room three days a week. And despite what she said about procrastination, she was the most dependable person Luna knew. She simply didn't worry about shit that didn't matter. And when you spent your days in real life and death situations, not a lot mattered.

Luna's phone pinged in her purse.

"Maybe it's the roof guy."

Miley hesitated on her way out of the room.

Luna opened her messages.

The number was unknown, but the message made sense.

I owe you a coffee.

It had to be Nate.

Mr. Venti.

A slow smile accompanied a shake of her head.

"Well, well . . . that's a new look for you," Miley said.

"Nothing like that. It's the Fed guy."

Miley stepped closer and looked at the screen. "Coffee?"

"Yeah . . ." Luna started to text back. "He knocked mine out of my hand."

"He did what?"

Yes, you do, she replied.

"He wasn't watching where he was walking and bumped into me," Luna said while staring at her phone.

"Oh. Was this before or after the meeting?" Miley asked.

"Before. And when I walked into the conference room, he was talking shit about 'the distracted woman who dropped her coffee.' You should have seen his face when he realized who I was and what I'd heard."

Miley coughed on a laugh. "Bruh . . . did you call him out?"

"No. I let him squirm."

"Look at you being all sass."

Luna dropped her phone on the table and renewed her search for something to eat. "It's always better to have someone owing you something than the other way around."

"You're ruthless." Miley sighed as she started to leave the room again. "You know where I am if roof guy is creepy."

"Okay."

The phone pinged again.

And an apology.

Saying she deserved one and giving one were not the same.

That, too.

Luna leaned against the kitchen table, staring at her phone.

It took a few seconds for his reply.

You're enjoying this.

Damn right she was. Did the Feds teach you these investigative skills? Or were you born with them?

It took even longer for his comeback.

I'll tell you over coffee.

Fine, just try and let me drink mine this time, she told him.

Touché. I'll be in touch.

~

"Was I born with them?" Nate found himself laughing for the first time in what felt like forever.

He plugged his phone in to charge and sat it on one of the many U-Haul boxes littering the floor of his apartment.

Seattle had been his first choice after walking away from DC. Even with the endless rain, he loved the Pacific Northwest. Maybe because of the rain. It fit, the gray skies and dreary, drawn-out days. It made the sunshine and warmth even sweeter when it finally happened.

He picked his butt up off the lone couch and went into his kitchen.

On the counter sat a half-empty box labeled "Utensils."

He'd been in the apartment exactly two weeks. The moving boxes had only just arrived.

This was the second time he'd moved his life from one coast to the other. Those cross-country moves had a way of making you get rid of a lot of crap. The only belongings he'd shoved into his SUV for the drive were clothes, his computer, and a sleeping bag.

Outside of an air mattress he bought on arrival, he'd lived with next to nothing.

Even now, the two-bedroom apartment housed only a bed, couch, TV, and small dining table.

And everything for a kitchen.

Nate removed the butcher block set of knives and took each piece out to ensure they made the trip without damage.

His phone rang, halting his efforts to get settled in.

A picture of his mom lit the screen.

He answered on speaker. "Hey."

"Hey back. How did the meeting go?"

Taking his phone with him, he returned to the knives. "Good. I like the team I'll be working with. The attorney seems personable. Efficient."

"Those attributes sound contradicting."

Nate thought about that for a moment. "In most cases I agree. Marcus knows how to delegate, hence the efficiency. Personable because he asked all the 'how has the move been . . . did I need anything or recommendations on where to go and what to do.'"

"Well good. I hope he realizes your worth."

Nate paused. "Ahh, gee thanks, Mom."

"Can't a mother acknowledge how good her son is at his job?"

"I'm teasing."

"I know," she said. "What about your stuff?"

"It came yesterday."

"Anything broken?"

"I'm unpacking now. So far, so good."

"You sure you don't want me to fly up and help?"

They'd been through this. She wanted to help him unpack, which he absolutely didn't want her to do. And if she showed up now and saw how little he'd taken with him, she'd be back and forth to furniture stores and Costco to clutter his space.

"I'll be ready for you in spring."

"You don't have to be ready."

"I'm a grown-ass man, Mom." A statement he used often. She wasn't a helicopter parent, not even overbearing . . . just an empty nesting semi-retired woman who needed more hobbies.

"Okay, okay. I'll drop it. But if something changes . . ."

"You'll be the first to know," he told her.

"I'll let you get back to it."

"I'll call you over the weekend," he said, hoping that his commitment to the call would keep her from doing a daily check in.

He'd signed a one-year lease. Initially he only wanted six months. Which he felt was plenty of time to find a house in a neighborhood that met his needs.

Sadly, landlords didn't like the six-month thing. And the ones that were okay with shorter leases were in less desirable areas.

A year it was. And if he found a place he wanted to buy before that year was up, he'd deal with his landlord then.

It took the remainder of the afternoon to unpack and wash everything before finding it a place in the kitchen to live.

He'd tackle a grocery store tomorrow, tonight was leftover Chinese food and his laptop.

The files Marcus had sent over were the beginning of a very extensive case. His first one in the private sector. The kind that would set the tone for this new adventure. Yet when Nate logged in to his computer, it wasn't Joel Mercier's name, or any of the man's companies, that he looked up.

It was Luna Canning.

Was she really as good as Marcus boasted?

His first hit was her LinkedIn page. Her professional photographs were exactly that. Stiff back, fake smile, and likely taken shortly after college graduation. His conclusion came from the wisdom lacking in her eyes in the picture, which he knew was there now.

And from the long list of clients praising her abilities, that wisdom had been earned. She graduated college summa cum laude and interned with a prominent CPA group in Seattle during her senior year. Then worked with the same CPA firm for five years before breaking away and working for herself.

Bold move that young.

Nate looked forward to learning why she took that leap.

A question that would happen over coffee.

When he searched for the more personal area of Miss Canning's life, he was surprised to see that her social media persona was limited. Her Facebook page was at best a memoir of college and late high school. The usual suspects of school drama and selfies with her friends.

She'd been tagged in more pictures than she posted herself.

Same with her Instagram account.

Neither of which had been updated in a few years.

And both of which were public.

If not for those tagged photographs, it would seem that Luna walked away from any kind of online life.

Smart.

Nate had accounts on both platforms that he used primarily to find others, not to tell the world his life story. Working for the government always came with risk.

Criminal fraud investigations had a way of pissing people off.

Especially the guilty.

The less they could find out about the people working to send them to jail, the better.

Even though Luna seemed to have taken that same path, Nate still found a trail of friends that could easily help him find her exact location if he wanted to dig deep enough.

When he found himself writing names of the people who posted pictures of her, he stopped.

She wasn't the client. Looking up her professional contacts and recommendations was one thing, finding out where she lived and where she hung out for fun when she wasn't working was another.

Nate closed the windows involving Luna Canning and started his work clock when he opened the first file for the case.

CHAPTER THREE

The roofer showed up right on time, Luna mused sarcastically.

Thirty minutes past three.

"I'm sorry to keep you waiting," he said the minute Luna opened the door.

"How many times a week do you find yourself saying that?" she asked, opening the front door far enough for the man to step inside.

He was close to her age, tall with a build that suggested he worked in a labor force and not behind a desk. There was a kindness that sat behind his eyes that lit up when she asked her question.

"A lot this time of year, I'm sorry to say. You must be Luna." He stuck out his hand.

She clasped it in a firm handshake. "I am. You're Brian?" They'd spoken on the phone the day before when she'd noticed the leak.

"I am."

Brian had asked if she needed his immediate service, she'd told him no and said she thought the leak could wait until the next day to be assessed. Emergency service in the roofing industry had a steep price tag.

"Has the leak gotten worse?" Brian asked, his eyes cast toward the ceiling.

"The pots and pans seemed to be holding up."

He nodded as if he'd heard that before. "Show me what we're working with," he said.

Luna led him to the stairs. "We haven't noticed anything new other than the holes in the attic."

"Does the attic span the width of the house?"

"Yes."

They rounded the first flight of stairs.

"Is he finally here?" Miley called from the open door to her room.

Luna caught the roofer's gaze. Brian had the good sense to appear guilty for being late.

Luna had no sooner told her yes when Miley emerged in the doorway.

Brian lifted his hands in the air. "Honest to God there was traffic."

"He already apologized," Luna told her.

Miley rolled her eyes and turned back to her room.

Like earlier, cold air rushed forward when Luna opened the door leading to the attic.

The moment the door opened, Midnight rushed out with a disapproving cry.

"What are you doing in here?"

The cat scattered away without looking back.

"She must have snuck in earlier," Luna said.

"How many cats do you have?"

"Just the one."

They made their way up the flight of stairs. Luna flipped on the lights.

Brian poked around, looked at the pots and pans. "When did you last empty these?"

Luna stood by the door, her arms crossed over her body to ward off the chill. "This morning before I left for my meeting."

Brian kept looking up, seeing things she didn't. Every once in a while, he'd wipe a finger along one of the objects or boxes in the room and then move on.

"I've seen what I need to here. I need to get on your roof. While I'm up there I'll cover the area with a tarp."

Luna followed him down the way they'd come.

"Do you need me to hold a ladder or something?"

He shook his head and grinned. "I got it."

It was a three-story house with a long drop if he mis-stepped. "Better you than me."

Brian zipped his coat as he exited the house.

Luna watched from the window as he walked to his truck and removed an expandable ladder.

The sound of Miley's footsteps preceded her arrival at Luna's side. "He's going up there?"

"I'm guessing he's used to it." Luna sighed, turned around. "At least he's covering the holes."

Miley continued to stare out the window. "He's kinda cute."

"You think?" Luna brought her attention back to the man.

Miley nodded. "Does he have a ring?"

"I didn't look."

They were both watching him now.

Miley tilted her head to the side as if that angle would show her something else to admire.

Luna followed her lead. He was tall and fit enough to swing a huge ladder around without effort. She'd already noticed his eyes, and first impressions suggested she could trust him. But cute?

Both of them stood there silently watching with their necks crooked to one side.

Brian spotted them.

In unison, they stood tall, their chins held high.

Luna couldn't tell if Brian's smile was simply polite, or more of a smirk at catching them gawking at him.

Closing her eyes and shaking her head, Luna stepped away from the window. "Okay, we are officially the creeps."

Miley giggled.

They waited for him to finish his assessment in the kitchen.

Now and then they'd see Brian walking by a window as he moved the ladder around to get to various parts of the roof.

The longer he took, the more Luna thought the diagnosis would be costly.

She and Miley put together a chicken and rice casserole to pop in the oven a little later.

They'd alternate who cooked, but nothing was written on a calendar, and nothing was expected. On Miley's days off, they cooked together and often froze the leftovers. If it wasn't for the other one, they'd both be on the quick foods diet. Takeout, microwave boxed cuisine, if you could call a flash-frozen, preservative-rich meal *cuisine*, and bagged salads would be the extent of their nutrition.

"You don't have anything going on Friday night, right?" Miley asked while they washed the dishes they'd dirtied while prepping their meal.

"No, why?"

"I looked into that full moon, women only get-together thing at that new crystal shop on Main."

The two of them had stopped and looked at a poster that talked about a full moon circle. They'd tossed the idea around but neither of them took it any further.

"What's it about?"

"I don't know, manifesting, letting go . . . the owner reads tarot. It'll be fun."

And something to do that didn't involve a club and alcohol. Which as they got older, Luna and Miley were less and less attracted to.

"Your name is Luna for Christ's sake. This is right up your alley."

Her name often raised eyebrows. Most people thought it was a nickname. At most a middle name. It wasn't. "Why not," she said.

Miley beamed. "I'll sign us up."

A soft knock on the front door indicated Brian's completion of his inspection.

The three of them stood over the kitchen island as Brian pulled up an image on his tablet of the house's roof.

"I have some bad news, and potentially good news," he started.

Luna and Miley exchanged silent glances.

"Pull the Band-Aid off first," Luna told him.

Brian pointed to the parts of the roof that they knew were a problem. He talked about missing shingles and the immediate need to get those sections fixed. He went on to identify three other places where shingles were missing and his surprise that the house didn't have more points of water entry.

"You could get away with a temporary fix. I went ahead and tarped all of these spots. But a nasty storm and your neighbors will have the plastic, and you'll have more water intrusion."

Brian paused.

"And the good news?" Luna asked.

"I'm not done with the bad."

"Oh."

"The roof is literally missing flashing around the vents. I'm shocked you're not finding problems in those areas. The roof is twenty years old?" he asked with doubt.

"Give or take."

"Was there an inspection when you took possession?"

"No. It's a family home. I inherited it. There weren't any inspections for anything when I took possession." Luna looked at Miley.

Brian sighed. "It's a big roof and a big job. I can bring my guys over to patch things up. Rip out the areas surrounding the trouble spots. Lift the places the vents come through and do the same. You might get another five years out of it. I can only guarantee the sections we patch."

"We need a new roof," Miley concluded aloud.

Luna was seeing nothing but dollar signs.

"Yeah, you do."

Luna met Brian's eyes. "What's the good news?"

He smiled. "You said you noticed the leaks after that last storm."

"Yes."

"And you have homeowner's insurance, right?"

"Of course." Luna started to see the light.

"Your insurance company might be able to help out. Sometimes they even pay for the whole job. Your roof is old, but not ancient. There are several solid areas that are completely intact. Which suggests storm damage over age damage."

"Seriously? I didn't even think of that."

"That's great," Miley added.

"Most new homeowners don't. This is what I'm going to do. I'm going to write up two bids. One for repairs, essential repairs, that if not addressed could end up costing your insurance company even more money. Interior walls, floors . . . carpet. You know, that kind of water damage. And a second bid for the cost of a new roof. I need to disclose that I don't do bottom of the line roofs. I use the best material on the market and won't touch anything that I wouldn't put on my home. You might find material that's cheaper, but if I can't guarantee the product, I won't do the job. If the roof fails, it's me that ends up on the hook. It's my company and my name. I don't want you as a repeat customer. I want you to tell your neighbors about your experience and recommend me."

There wasn't one twitch, one break in eye contact. But most of all, Brian was passing the vibe check.

"Besides, the real cost of a new roof is all about labor. Unless you wanted to upgrade to tile."

"No. I can't afford that." Her wallet didn't want that.

"Call your insurance carrier. I'll fill out the paperwork on my end to help your case. I'll email you my estimates. Your insurance may say no, but it would be a shame not to try." Brian was smiling now.

His smile alone put Luna at ease. "This sounds good. I mean, as good as it can."

He turned off his tablet and tucked it under his arm. "I seldom have the opportunity to deliver good news. Nobody with an older home calls a roofer without a problem."

Miley smirked, a sly grin lifting the corners of her mouth. "Oh, I don't know about that."

It took a second, but Brian caught on and his eyes lit up.

Luna cleared her throat and scowled at Miley. At the same time, she glanced at Brian's left hand to find his ring finger bare. "What do I owe you for today?"

Brian looked away from Miley. "Ah, nothing."

"Seriously?"

"Yeah."

"And if I went with another roofer?" Luna asked.

"Still nothing. Just let me know when I can swing by to pick up my tarps."

That was surprising. "Okay, then."

They walked him to the door with the promise of talking to him later.

Through the stained glass windows surrounding the front door, they watched him walk to his truck.

"He didn't have a ring," Miley pointed out.

"I noticed."

Miley nudged Luna's shoulder.

CHAPTER FOUR

At any given time, Luna juggled four to eight clients. Or better said, four to eight cases from various clients. The more extensive the cases, the fewer she accepted.

Marcus and his firm always seemed to pull in the time suckers.

It took three days just to skim the digital files.

In those three days Luna knew she'd need to shed some of her current clients as soon as possible.

She had an expert witness case that was due to go to trial the following week, three divorce cases, one of which was pro bono, and another business owner who suspected, and was right about, his business partner skimming money off the top and attempting to launder it.

Luna had a whiteboard on the wall of her office, which was a bedroom she'd called hers when her grandmother was alive. Victorian homes had such large bedrooms, at least compared to new construction, something Luna loved about the house.

She'd upgraded her old high school desk, computer, and bookshelves. Gone were the posters of pop stars and high school mementos. Those were all boxed up in the leaking attic.

Luna drummed her fingers on her desk while staring at her computer screens.

The monitor on her left held her conclusions, the one on the right displayed the company files.

The whiteboard flagged the sticky spots.

And there were several of those.

She picked up her phone, dialed Nate's number, and put the phone on speaker.

"Hello," he answered.

"Good afternoon," she said before jumping straight into her questions. "How far have you gotten on the case files?"

"I'm great, thanks for asking. I haven't spilled coffee on anyone in thirty-six hours."

Luna pulled her tunnel vision away from the screens and sat back in her chair. "Sorry. When I'm dialed in, I assume everyone else is, too. Who wore your coffee this time?"

Nate chuckled. "Myself. I stubbed my toe on a moving box."

"That's never fun. Who's moving?"

"I did. I'm not completely unpacked," he said.

"Oh. Okay . . . well, if you haven't gotten far—"

"No, no. I've read through the CliffsNotes and started diving into the parent company."

"And your initial thoughts?" she asked.

"This case is going to take a while. Especially with only the two of us working it."

Luna glanced at her whiteboard. "I agree."

"What have you found?"

"There are several names signing off on the books. Looks like there was either a management purge, or exodus of employees three years ago."

"I saw that. Are the numbers saying anything?"

"They're telling me to start digging in the year before and after. And since we're working together on this, I'd like to coordinate our efforts. Make sure we're not overlapping."

"Agreed."

"I have to be in Denver for a trial on Tuesday. Can you focus your attention four years back and have something for me on Wednesday?" It was already late Friday afternoon. Luna assumed everyone worked the weekdays during daytime hours. But when you freelanced, there was no telling if weekends and nights were on the table.

For Luna, they were. Every hour of every day could be a workday.

"I can do that. Where do you want to meet?"

"We can Zoom."

"I can't repay you for the coffee over Zoom," he said.

"True," she said. "I'm up on Queen Anne Hill, where are you?"

He told her before they settled on a coffee shop in between both of them. "Let's avoid traffic, say ten?" Luna asked.

"Perfect."

"Great."

She was about to say her goodbyes when he asked, "How's the roof?"

Luna hadn't expected his question. "Still holey. But the contractor thinks I might be able to get some financial help to fix it from my insurance company."

"That's good news."

"We're optimistic," she said.

For a moment, the line went quiet.

"Nate?"

"Sorry," he said quickly. "I hope it works out."

His tone had changed, and his words felt rushed.

"Have a good weekend," she said.

"I'll try. Good luck at the trial."

"I'm testifying as an expert witness. It's not my case."

"Even better," Nate said.

"I'll see you Wednesday."

"Ten o'clock."

Luna ended the call.

Why had his tone changed? The bounce in his voice had flattened, almost as if she'd said something wrong . . . but what?

Luna recapped their conversation and couldn't find any fault.

With that behind her, she put her computer to sleep and ended her official workday.

Crystal and Clover was nestled in a patch of boutique shops and old homes that had been turned into retail space.

The outside of the store was framed with plants of all shapes and sizes. A park-style bench sat below one of the multipaned windows. On one side of the door was a water dish that offered a drink for the dogs that walked their owners.

It was dusk and damp.

Luna and Miley opened the glass door of the shop with the sound of chimes announcing their arrival.

The place smelled like incense and burning candles. Exactly like you'd assume walking into a store that sold what women had been burned at the stake for owning in centuries past.

An excited chill ran through Luna's body as they let the door behind them close.

The petite brunette at the register glanced up with a smile. "Welcome in." She paused, peered closer. "Miley, right?"

Miley glanced at Luna, then back to the woman talking. "Yeah."

"I'm glad you both came."

"Have we met before?" Miley asked.

"I'm Jorden, we spoke on the phone," she said as she rounded the counter housing the register.

"It wasn't a video call."

Luna kept looking back and forth between the two of them.

"Uhm . . . you're the only person who called that I don't know. I assumed." Jorden glanced at Luna. "And you're the friend."

"Luna," she said, extending her hand to shake Jorden's.

"That's appropriate."

Jorden shook Miley's hand as well. "Have you been in before?"

"I always seem to walk by when you're closed," Miley said.

"Didn't you just open?" Luna asked.

"Six months ago."

"That long? I thought for sure you were brand new."

Jorden sighed, "I get that a lot."

A young woman with bright red curly long hair walked from the back of the store juggling a huge box.

"Where do you want these?"

"In the window for tonight, tomorrow we'll shelve them," Jorden said.

She turned to Luna and Miley. "This is Brianna. My number one employee."

Brianna smirked. "I'm her only employee."

The door behind them opened and another woman walked in.

"Hi, Shayna," Jorden said.

Luna and Miley stepped aside when two more women followed.

By the time Jorden placed the "Closed" sign on the door, there were seven of them, including Jorden and her employee Brianna.

Jorden encouraged everyone to follow her into the back of the store where a room had been set up with cushions on the floor.

Crystals of all shapes, colors, and sizes were positioned around in a circle. At two of the cushions sat a notebook, a pen, and paper that reminded Luna of ancient scrolls with rough and burned edges.

"I set that up for you both," Jorden said.

The other women seemed to already have a notebook, but each space had the same scroll-like paper and a pen.

"Make yourselves comfortable," Jorden encouraged everyone. "If the floor is uncomfortable and you need a chair, I can get one for you."

Luna glanced at Miley.

She shook her head.

"We're good."

Setting their coats and purses aside, Luna and Miley settled in, sitting cross-legged on the cushions.

Soft music you'd expect during a yoga session or a spa session hummed in the background.

"It's cool, right?" Miley asked Luna quietly as they settled.

Luna nodded, unsure what to say.

The women were pleasant and varied in age. Jorden herself couldn't be much younger than Luna and Miley. Brianna might have been closer to forty. Two of the women in the circle had to be over fifty, and the woman that went by Shayna could have been anywhere from thirty to sixty. Her hair was gray, but her skin was taut. At least around her face. Her eyes were wise, her wrists full of bracelets, her fingers sported several rings. The only thing she was missing was a long bohemian-style dress to round out what Luna expected to see when walking into the shop.

Once Jorden took her place, she started the introductions.

"I'd like to welcome Miley and Luna. This is their first ever full moon circle."

That brought murmurs of approval and each woman individually saying hello in her own way.

"Before we get started, would you like to tell us what brings you here?"

Luna pointed to Miley. "She did."

A couple of the women chuckled.

"We've been threatening to do this for a while," Miley told them. "I work in an ER and completely buy into the power of a full moon. It has a way of bringing out the crazy and unpredictable in people."

Luna nodded. "It's kind of hard to debunk when I hear Miley's stories."

Jorden smiled. "Hopefully you'll get something out of this, and if nothing else have the opportunity to expand your understanding of what we do here. We're not a religion. There's no right or wrong. We believe in the power of manifesting, letting go, forging your own path. Awakening to your purpose, whatever that means to you. Sometimes we meditate . . . and with good weather we take this outside in the fresh air and moonlight."

The image of a witch's circle from the movies flooded Luna's head.

Jorden looked straight at Luna. "Any questions?"

With a shake of their heads, Jorden started.

First, she tapped the side of a singing bowl and let the sound vibrate through the room.

The hum instantly calmed Luna's nerves. Nerves she didn't realize she was holding on to.

Jorden's voice lowered. "We'll start with a few deep, calming breaths. Close your eyes if that feels good or soften your gaze."

She tapped the bowl again and Luna felt her eyes drift shut.

There were waves to Jorden's voice . . . calm and tranquil. Nurturing.

She spoke of the earth's relationship with the moon. The polarity that drove the ocean tides. The amount of water in the human body and how some believe that, too, is energized by the moon.

"Our minds are so very powerful and often untapped. Clutter pulls at us every day. I invite you to let go of whatever clutter does not serve you. Whatever just came up in your mind now . . . and now . . . Is it a person? A worry? A situation beyond your control? An obstacle? A memory or past haunt that keeps you from living your best life? When you're ready, take the paper in front of you and write down the things that you want to release this full moon."

The roof, Luna thought. She had yet to hear from the insurance company and worried that the expense to cover its repair would force her to take her sister's offer to help. And to include Ash to help.

Ash wouldn't want to, but he would do what he could if asked.

Luna never wanted to ask.

Luna picked up her pen and started to write.

Let go of worry and fear about the roof.

That thought brought her to the next.

The roof was only the beginning. The heater in the house was old. By the grace of God only knew what, it hadn't died.

Chipped and peeling paint had been patched over the years.

Maybe the reason Nana married all those times was so the men in her life could help keep the place up.

Luna had no intention of inviting a man in her life. Least of all to help with the house. She never wanted to feel obligated to a man again.

Luna paused, that thought rolled around.

Obligated to a man.

Where had that come from?

Dependent on a man . . . that felt right.

Like her mother and grandmother before her. Two women whose lives circled around men.

One whose still did.

Where was her mother? Was she still in Indiana where she'd followed the latest in hopes of being loved? One of the many men she placed in a position above her children and responsibilities.

Luna shook the thoughts of her mother from her head.

It didn't matter.

Luna's pen tapped into all of her whirling thoughts.

Let go of the pointless memories of Mom.

Let go of the worry of paint and plumbing . . . and heaters.

Luna stared at her paper.

I'll work harder, she mused. *Take on more to make up for the rising cost of the house repairs.*

She would not ask her brother and would continue to deny her sister's offer. Hell, Harper's husband always seemed to be out of work, or on probation with a company that ultimately downsized with him on the chopping block. They couldn't afford taking care of two houses.

I'm going to let go of the worry and focus on action.

I'm not going to run away from my responsibilities. Which is what her mother would do.

And just to prove a point, Luna wrote one final line on her paper.

Let go of my mother.

When everyone was done writing down their releases for the month, Jorden brought a lit candle next to a small firepot in the center of the circle.

"When you're ready, give the moon what you want to release by burning the paper."

Luna glanced at the ceiling, wondering if the smoke alarms would go off.

Shayna leaned in first. She gripped her paper with a pair of forceps and hovered it over the flame.

The paper caught quickly and burned clean as she dropped her intentions into the pot.

The forceps were passed from woman to woman.

Luna watched as the fire ate up her concerns and dissipated in an instant.

Jorden chimed the singing bowl again. "For a moment, imagine all the things you wrote down were gone. Like a magic wand made it all blow away. How do you feel? Lighter? Open for better things to come?"

The other women were opening their journals.

Jorden glanced at Luna and Miley.

"Write down what it looks and feels like tomorrow when you wake up and everything you burned in the fire is behind you. Focus on what comes after. See what comes up."

Luna pushed her cushion back against the wall and pulled her knees to her chest.

And her words flowed.

Thirty minutes later, Jorden offered tea while some of the women shared what they'd let go. Others talked about their wins from the last full moon. When it was Luna's turn, she shared about the home repair concerns but left out all the crap about her mother.

"Have you tried sage?" Shayna asked.

"Sage?" Luna asked.

"Yeah. Sage the house. Get rid of the bad energy."

The other women nodded as if they understood.

Miley shrugged.

"Does it work?"

"Cultures have burned sage and palo santo to cleanse spaces and rid bad energy for centuries," Jorden said. "Indonesian cultures make daily offerings with flowers with incense and set it by their front doors, at temples, at the entry to their business, all with different intentions. Prosperity, happiness, friendship, health . . . anything you can think of as a way to invite these things into their lives."

It was fascinating how Jorden didn't answer any of the questions asked with definite answers, more of an explanation as to why something would work.

"When I was married, I'd sage the room my mother-in-law used. She never stayed more than three days," Shayna told them.

Miley laughed. "Maybe she was allergic."

Shayna shrugged. "It worked."

On their way out through the retail space of the store, Jorden gave Luna a thatched bundle of sage mixed with lavender.

"What do I owe you?" Luna asked.

Jorden waved her off. "On the house. Consider this a tool, only you have to tell the tool what to do. If you intend this to clean your space, tell it to clean your space."

"Thank you," Luna said.

"Let me know how it works."

"I will."

CHAPTER FIVE

With an open suitcase in front of her, and a matching dress coat and slacks to wear on the stand, Luna packed what she needed for the overnight trip to Denver.

Her cell phone rang with a number she didn't recognize. Even without the words *Potential Spam* on the screen, she considered blowing off the call.

On the fourth ring she changed her mind.

"Hello?" she started, fully expecting a pause and then either a bot telling her about how she'd won something, or the voice of a complete stranger acting as if they knew her and then trying to sell her beachfront property in Kansas.

"May I speak with Luna Canning."

"This is her."

"I'm Greg Filmore with Alliance. Your insurance company."

Luna stopped tossing clothes in her suitcase and stood tall. "Oh, hello."

"I understand you have some roof damage that we need to take a look at."

"Yeah, I do. I wasn't expecting you to get back to me so soon," she admitted.

"I had a cancellation and can get there tomorrow."

Luna cringed. "I won't be here tomorrow." And Miley was working.

"Is there any way someone else can meet me? Otherwise, I can't get there until late next week. Your roofer said the damage is likely to get worse with next weekend's storm."

The last thing Luna wanted to do was push this guy off. "Can you guarantee a time? I might be able to get my sister here, but she works and can't wait around all day."

"You'll be my first appointment. Is eight okay?" he asked.

"Let me call my sister and I'll get right back to you."

Greg agreed and Luna called Harper.

"I need a big favor," Luna said without saying hello.

"What is it?"

"I have to be in Denver tomorrow. The insurance guy says he can check out the roof at eight in the morning, and Miley has to work. Can you be here? I really need my insurance company to help pay for these repairs."

"Hold on."

Luna waited while Harper put her on hold.

Ever since the pandemic, employers were a lot more lenient about working remotely. At least that was what Luna was banking on.

It wasn't long before Harper got back on the call to affirm her ability to help. "I don't have to hang out in the attic with this guy, do I? I hate it up there."

Luna grinned. Harper and Ash swore the attic was haunted.

When they were kids and staying at their grandmother's house in between the times their mother was married, they'd dare each other to go into the attic alone.

They never lasted long.

Whether their overactive child imaginations got the best of them, or there was something to their claims, neither Harper nor Ash volunteered to go into the attic even as adults. When they were kids, they swore they heard footsteps on the stairs only to open the door and find the room empty.

Other than the drafty space giving her a chill, even on warm days, Luna didn't hold any issues with the attic. If there had been anything running around up there, they were gone now.

"Nope. Just show him where it is."

"Good. Who's taking you to the airport?"

"I'm parking in the overnight garage. It's cheaper than an Uber."

"Okay. I'll be there before eight."

"Thanks, sis. I owe you."

Luna confirmed the appointment time with Greg and finished packing.

She sat on the edge of her bed and looked around the room. As the primary bedroom, this had been Nana's. When Luna moved in, she changed out all the furniture, especially the bed. Most of that furniture lived in the attic along with all those dusty boxes, some of it had been repurposed in other places in the house.

When Luna was home alone, the space felt quiet.

Too quiet.

It wasn't the first time Luna wondered how her grandmother had lived in the house all alone.

Well, that wasn't fair. With all the husbands she'd managed to acquire and subsequently get rid of, Nana had shared the house for many years.

And then there were the times that Luna and her siblings had moved in. A few times as a complete family, her mother and the three kids . . . but then each of them, Ash, Harper, and Luna, had lived with Nana separately. Harper more than Ash, Ash more than Luna.

Karen Canning, their mother, was proficient at finding the wrong men.

A trait Luna followed once, and never again.

Karen jumped into relationships with little to no regard for their possibility of longevity.

Karen's first marriage happened before she graduated from high school. Before she was old enough to drink in a bar, that marriage was over, and Karen had moved back in with Nana.

Harper was just a baby.

Baby daddy number two came along, and Karen followed this guy to Fresno, California. According to Nana, Ash's father had been in the military and had zero desire to get married. Karen stayed the course, had Ash, and things got ugly. "That man didn't want one kid, let alone take care of two," Nana had said once.

When that fell apart, Karen ran home, this time with two kids.

Ash doesn't remember his father, and all Harper recalled of him was bits and pieces.

Then came Luna's dad.

He married Karen the second the double blue lines appeared on the test. When Luna was born, Harper was four and Ash was two. Karen's marriage to Luna's father stuck until after Luna's second birthday.

Someone cheated on someone, and Karen Canning and her three young children were back at Nana's.

Harper's real father lived in Idaho. She'd gotten ahold of the man when she was in her midtwenties. The encounter put her in therapy for two years.

Ash's father was MIA. Either literally or by design.

And Luna's dad . . . he was in New York with his other family. The family he provided and cared for.

None of these men paid child support, and none of them wanted anything to do with Karen Canning and the baggage she came with.

Harper, Ash, and Luna were the baggage.

Then came husband number three. He lasted the longest and was by far the worst. Since Karen was obviously more fertile than the neighborhood rabbits, husband number three must have had an issue, since Karen stopped procreating.

Karen made a point of breaking all ties with her various baby daddies, so none of the Canning children grew up knowing their biological fathers.

Harper, Ash, and Luna all called Karen's third husband Dad, but he wasn't related to any of them.

The memory of Paul, husband number three, always made Luna cringe. And like looking away from the TV when something awful is happening on-screen, Luna turned her thoughts on something . . . anything else, other than him.

And then there were the multitude of men once Paul walked away.

Karen had stopped getting married to them, but that didn't stop them from moving in with her.

Luna stood drumming her fingers on the bed as memories of how she and her half siblings came to be floated in her mind.

She hadn't thought about this stuff in years.

And she likely wouldn't be thinking about it now if not for her sister reminding her of how much she hated the attic.

By Luna's hand sat the bag with the lavender laced sage from Jorden over at Crystal and Clover.

Removes bad energy.

Luna picked up the sage, found a lighter used for candles, and headed to the attic.

She found Midnight at the base of the stairs. "Are you protecting me?" Luna asked in the high-pitched voice that always came when people were talking to animals and children.

Midnight looked up, bored, and slowly unfurled from where she'd been napping.

Not exactly knowing what she was doing, Luna lit the sage until it started to smolder and entered the attic.

At the top of the stairs, she paused. "I should probably be saying something," she said aloud.

Midnight offered nothing but a yawn before walking off to explore the space.

"You're no help."

Luna glanced at the smoke circling toward the ceiling. "Okay, bad juju . . . it's time for you to go." It felt silly walking around the drafty space waving a bundle of burning sage. The scent was something close to a damp forest void of pine trees. The tiny hint of floral from the lavender wasn't enough to make the sage pleasant. "Let Greg find whatever he needs so my insurance company pays up."

She kept walking deeper into the attic. "Don't let anything freak Harper out. And, Nana, if you're listening, help Greg check the right boxes."

Luna repeated herself twice while waving the sage.

When she was done, she shooed Midnight out of the attic and closed the door behind her.

"There goes nothing," she said to the empty room.

At Luna's feet, Midnight sat staring at the door she'd just closed.

Then she pawed at it as if asking it to open.

"Sorry, kitty. I know I promised you more time in there, but Mama's gotta go."

Midnight meowed and pawed at the door again.

"Wednesday, okay?"

If cats could roll their eyes, Midnight would be an expert.

Nate strode up the steps to an old college friend's home with a six pack of beer in his hands. He rapped on the door with his free hand and sat back on his heels.

The two-story house was in the suburbs south of Seattle in a town called Sumner. The homes looked as if they sat on half-acre lots minimum with pine trees dotting the properties. The front lawns were perfectly manicured with shrubs and fountains and zero fences. Nate imagined there had to be some rather strict HOAs to keep any neighborhood looking this polished. Not one junk car or abandoned sofa could be seen.

It was nice.

The kind of nice one dreamed up when they wanted to settle down with a wife and kids in a good school district.

At least that's what Nate imagined his life would be.

Who knew, maybe that day would come.

The door swung open and revealed Clarissa, her blonde hair pulled back, her smile just as happy as the last time Nate had seen her.

"Nate! We're so glad you came."

She opened her arms.

Nate stepped into her hug with one arm to avoid smacking her with the beer. "It's been too long," he said.

"It was the wedding, right?" she asked.

Nate removed himself from her embrace and stepped inside. "Sadly."

"Is that Nate?" Tony yelled from deeper in the house.

"Nawh, it's Clarissa's boyfriend," Nate yelled back.

Clarissa playfully pushed Nate's shoulder and relieved the beer from his grasp.

Tony came around the corner and the two of them did the hug with an overzealous pound on the back.

"Damn, look at you," Tony said. "You still have your hair."

The same couldn't be said for Tony. "I don't have a wife and kids to help me pull it out."

"Don't blame me. His dad hasn't had hair for fifty years," Clarissa chided.

Tony motioned Nate into the house. "I was surprised to hear you moved back. I thought we lost you to DC forever."

"Not even the president stays in DC forever."

In the back of the home stood a great room. The kitchen ran into a formal dining room, which ran into a living room. A large sectional squared up with a television that took up nearly the entire wall.

Playing on it was the preamble to the game.

Primary color plastic toys were scattered about, played with and forgotten before being left behind for the next shiny object. Somewhere in the house was the three-year-old responsible for the Fisher-Price chaos.

"I thought all government fraud investigators had to work in DC," Clarissa said from where she stood in the kitchen.

"A lot do, but since I'm no longer working for the government, I can be anywhere."

Tony and Clarissa both looked surprised.

"Did the girlfriend get you fired?" Tony asked.

Nate placed a hand on his heart as if he'd been wounded. "No one in their right mind would fire me."

Tony didn't look convinced.

"There's more money in the private sector," Nate went on to say. "I could have stayed with the government job, caught a decent salary with a nice pension . . . and then hope it lasted when I'm old. But after the shutdown and working from home, going back to the office every day sucked."

"You can't work from home when you're making parts for Boeing," Tony said.

"Nate?" Clarissa waved one of the beers he'd brought in her hand.

"That would be great," he said. "My job is flexible, and fraud is everywhere."

"And Monique?" Tony asked.

"Intra-office relationships are always a recipe for disaster."

"You knew that going in."

Clarissa handed him the beer and said, "Her loss."

Nate shifted the subject. "This place looks great. Nice neighborhood."

"Thanks. We love it. The HOA police are stricter than nuns in a Catholic school, but no one is painting their house orange and purple."

Nate moved toward the back sliding-glass door that was half open. "What are you on, an acre?"

"Yup." Tony pushed the door open wider and stepped out.

A freestanding hot tub sat under a built-in gazebo. A small outdoor kitchen framed a set of table and chairs.

"This is ideal in the summer," Nate said.

"We got the hot tub last year. Clarissa wants a pool."

"You have the room for it."

"She wants TJ to start taking swim lessons now so when it goes in, he's ready."

Nate looked around, saw more toddler toys. "Where is TJ?"

"Napping. This is the best part of the day, trust me," Tony said, smiling.

"He's a handful?"

"Just like me, according to my mom. When people tell you kids are exhausting, listen to them."

"Good thing you only have one, then." Nate tilted his beer back, took a drink.

"That's about to change."

Nate's gaze shot to his friend. "Clarissa's pregnant?"

"She just passed three months." For all of Tony's bravado about exhaustion, he was beaming.

"Congratulations."

"Thanks, man."

Clarissa stepped out the back door and handed Tony a glass filled with what Nate assumed was a mixed drink.

"And you." Nate looked Clarissa up and down. "Tony just told me."

Clarissa placed a hand over her flat stomach. "What can I say."

"Are you ready to do it again?"

"Ready or not. I blame Tony's mom," Clarissa said.

Nate's brow furrowed. "I hope she wasn't in the room."

Tony laughed. "That's a nightmare thought."

"No, she offered to babysit for the weekend, this one decided we should rent an Airbnb on the coast. It rained nonstop the entire time we were there."

Nate laughed. "And there was nothing else to do but . . ." He left off the obvious activity they'd chosen to fill their time.

"Exactly."

Tony circled a hand around Clarissa's waist and pulled her to his side. "You enjoyed every moment of it."

"Good thing or you'd never hear the end of it."

While Tony teased his wife and kissed the side of her face, Nate couldn't help but wonder if he'd ever been in their situation.

For a while he thought that might be Monique.

He should have realized it was never going to happen when she refused to move in with him. She liked her independence and her condo. "Why ruin a good thing," she'd always say whenever Nate suggested moving to the next step.

Something closer to what Tony and Clarissa had. Nate wanted someone to build a life with, depend on . . . grow old with.

"Mama . . ." the sleep-filled voice of a child called from inside the house.

Nate looked around Tony to find a pint-size version of his friend standing in the doorway rubbing his eyes.

"Look who's up."

Tony set his glass down and reached for his son. "TJ, this is Nate."

"Hey, little guy." Nate wasn't versed in what to say to a three-year-old.

TJ plopped his head on Tony's shoulder and eyed Nate wearily.

"Don't let this quiet moment fool you," Clarissa said. "He'll be running circles around you before the game starts."

"You obviously love it, or you wouldn't be doing it again," Nate said.

Clarissa touched TJ's bare foot and gave it a tickle. "I wouldn't change it for the world." She reached for her son to take him from Tony's arms. "You might want to fire up the grill if we're going to eat."

They all moved back into the house.

Nate stood by and watched the interplay between husband and wife . . . and the slowly waking up toddler who was already scrambling out of his mother's arms.

He wasn't naive enough to think this was always rainbows and roses, but it was pretty damn nice.

CHAPTER SIX

Testifying as an expert witness had to be the most lucrative way to make money in her field.

One of Luna's college professors had pushed her to take extra classes in how to appear in court proceedings, write depositions and quick case studies to determine if the clients had a chance of winning in front of a judge. At first, Luna didn't see the payoff. After all, expert witnesses were often measured by the years they'd put into the profession.

No attorney wanted to call someone who graduated two years ago an expert in their field. Most would think she was completely wet behind the ears, as Luna's grandmother once said.

But Luna's professor kept pointing out that Luna's knack for the job, and the speed with which numbers came to her, would give her the title of *expert* faster than most. "Keep your fees low in the beginning. Even lawyers like to save money now and then." Truth was, if there was money to be made, lawyers wanted to keep most of that for themselves. Luna couldn't blame them for that.

That's what Luna did. She undercut the going rate for expert forensic accountants and overdelivered on the stand. When she was working for an accounting firm, she'd take her PTO days when she was needed to testify.

Taking a vacation in those first five years after she graduated wasn't a thing. Weekends and holidays were the extent of time for herself.

This did two fantastic things for her.

She was able to pay off her student loan debt, which wasn't exactly cheap. And it prompted her to break away from working for someone else and go out alone.

That had been a hard leap.

Stability in her life was the number one need she had after being jostled around so much as a kid.

Now she managed a hearty retainer for any case she took on. Her hourly rate rivaled that of the lawyers', and all travel expenses were paid for by the client.

Writing her own schedule made trial testimony much easier. And in times when she needed to stay available to be brought back on the stand, Luna could do her day job while waiting around in a courthouse or hotel room until she was free to go.

Luna didn't feel that the Denver trial would take any more than one day, and she'd been right.

She'd gone into Denver thinking the income from her testimony was going right into the roof of the house.

That was until Harper sent her a text message filled with good news.

The insurance guy is filing a claim. They're going to pay for a new roof.

Luna did a happy dance all the way to the airport as she made her way home.

Even though the flight from Denver to Seattle was relatively short, Luna used the time to work on the Mercier case.

Joel Mercier was what the wealthy called a *silent billionaire.*

His name didn't come out in the headlines, nor was it flashed around as the "owner of this, or the owner of that." That didn't mean he didn't own anything.

The man had acquired a lot in his sixty-five years.

He owned several private domestic companies that in turn owned international businesses. He'd actively invested in start-ups in Silicon

Valley, a couple of which paid off to the tune of hundreds of millions. When those companies went public, Mercier bounced. From what Luna could see by way of the numbers, the man spent money to make money like the average family shark does playing Monopoly.

But like many men with as much diversity in the portfolio as Mercier, there were so many spinning wheels that things were missed.

Luna opened up the file on one of Mercier's shell companies. One of which looked like it had been set up to help facilitate the acquisition of a business that made and sold shoes, of all things. Only after the acquisition was complete, the shell company wasn't dissolved. There was a continued influx and outflux of money. Some of that money going out was to a charity. Something in Africa that clothed children . . . and put shoes on their feet.

Shell companies were a hotbed for fraud and abuse. Add a charity, where money was given with nothing more than a tax break expected on the other end . . .

Luna grabbed her phone and shot Nate a text.

Have you spent any time looking at BOHO INC.?

She set her phone down, not really expecting a fast reply.

The pilot came on over the intercom. Or more accurately, the chimes overhead suggested an announcement was coming, but in reality, the mumbling of the pilot was completely unrecognizable.

The woman sitting in the middle seat beside Luna chuckled. "Why do they even bother," she asked.

Luna closed her laptop and prepared to store it for landing. "It's probably on the pilot checklist."

Luna had been on enough airplanes to know the routine. She flipped up her tray table and returned her computer to her bag that lived under the seat in front of her. After glancing at her phone and not seeing a reply from Nate, she tucked that in her bag as well.

Twenty minutes later Luna was off the plane and making her way out of the airport.

Her watch notified her of a text message.

It was Nate.

Hello to you, too.

Instead of trying to respond on her watch, Luna pulled out her phone.

I did it again, didn't I?

You did, and not really. Did you find something?

Luna stepped off the tram and headed toward the exit.

She attempted to text while rolling her suitcase and gave up after being bumped into twice.

Gone were the days of staying six feet apart.

Nate answered the phone before Luna even heard it ring.

"Texting wasn't working," she said instead of "Hello."

"Phones work, too."

She crossed the bridge leading to the parking lot and waited by the elevator to take her to the right level.

"I'm multi-tasking, so . . ."

"Where are you?"

"Airport. I'm on my way home. This place is a mess with all the construction." And it was. Main corridors were sectioned off, construction workers were hauling supplies among all the travelers, congesting the already squeezed space.

"I wouldn't know. I drove here from DC."

"Then take my word for it."

Luna stepped into the elevator. She was thankful no one was trying to get in with her. The last thing she wanted to be was "that woman" talking on her cell phone in a small space.

"In answer to your question, no. I haven't spent any time on BOHO. It's a shell company, right?" Nate asked.

"Yeah. A shell company that donates to a charity in Africa."

"Ewh."

The sound of Nate's voice suggested he understood where she was going. "My thoughts exactly."

Luna stepped off the elevator and headed toward the very back of the garage where she'd left her car.

"What else did you find?"

"The company was used to facilitate the acquisition of something in textile. Those numbers don't look off, but why . . ." Luna stopped short of where she thought she'd parked her car.

"Why what?" Nate asked.

Maybe it was the next aisle over. She knew for sure she was on the fourth level.

"Why would they keep BOHO, or more importantly why . . ." She didn't see her car.

Luna turned full circle and headed back to where she remembered parking. Did she walk by it?

"Why?" Nate asked.

"I'm sorry. I'm looking for my car. I thought for sure I . . ." Nope, it wasn't there. A small flutter of panic started to take root in her gut.

"Those parking garages all look the same. Are you on the correct floor?"

Luna stopped moving and reached into her purse for her key fob. "Considering what I do for a living, remembering the number four isn't that tough."

"You have a point," Nate said with a soft laugh.

With her key fob in hand, she pressed the horn button.

Nothing.

A chill ran up her back and the hair on the nape of her neck stood up.

She pressed it again.

Nothing.

Okay, now every nerve in her body was on alert.

"I'm sure it's there some—"

She started clicking the fob and waving it above her head. "The car isn't responding to my key fob."

Luna ran a hand through her hair. "Fuck."

"Okay, take a breath."

She did so, even though she felt the command was condescending. "It's not here, Nate. My car is not where I left it."

"What do you drive?"

Luna started to scramble . . . moving through the parking lot waving and pressing the key fob as she went. "It's a Hyundai and it's old."

"And you're positive you're on the fourth floor?"

The pillar with the number four was right in front of her. "Someone stole my car." Saying it out loud made it real. "Son of a . . . fuck, damn, hell. Why would someone want my eleven-year-old car?"

"Look around, are there cameras?" Nate asked.

She saw one at the end of the aisle. "Yeah. How am I going to get home?" And why had that thought even crossed her mind? Miley would be off work in a couple of hours and there was always Uber or a taxi. "I have to find the airport police."

"Can you call your boyfriend . . . husband?" Nate asked.

That question would have made her laugh on any other day. "I don't have one of those. I can't believe my car is gone." Luna walked twice as fast back to the elevator than when she'd left it. "How does someone rip off a car from an airport parking garage?"

"I'll come get you," Nate said.

"That's not . . . I can Uber."

"I'm an investigator, maybe I can help?"

"This isn't fraud, it's flat-out theft." Luna pressed the button on the elevator repeatedly as if that would make the lift come faster.

"I've investigated more than fraud. I can be there in forty minutes. It will take longer than that for the police to search the garage and take your statement. I'm sure they have a lot of false reporting because people forget where they parked."

"I did not forget—"

"Not you. Other people," he interrupted. "I'm headed out the door, I'll be there in forty."

The elevator finally arrived. "Okay, fine . . . thank you."

"Okay," he said and then hung up.

Luna watched the doors slowly close.

"Son of a bitch!"

CHAPTER SEVEN

Nate rolled into the airport garage forty-five minutes later. Considering why he was there, he found the closest parking spot next to the elevators that he could, with more foot traffic, making his car less desirable to steal. Parking in the back of the lot might help with door dings, but those don't matter much if the car is stolen.

After a brief stop at the information desk, he found his way to the airport police office.

He found Luna perched on the edge of a chair watching what looked like surveillance footage on a computer.

"Hey," he said, announcing himself.

Luna glanced up, gave a weary smile. "Hi."

One look at her face and he knew she hadn't mistaken where she'd parked. "They didn't find your car, did they?"

She shook her head and released a defeated sigh. "We're going over the surveillance videos from yesterday."

"Have you found anything?"

"The camera at the entrance caught me coming in, and again when I was looking for a spot."

Nate moved to her side and took off his jacket. "What about where you parked?"

"There's not a great angle."

"What do you mean?"

The officer at the keyboard pointed to the monitor. "We think that's her here. The cameras rotate and didn't catch Ms. Canning pulling into the spot. But this spot was empty when she entered and was filled at the next camera mark ten minutes later."

Nate removed a card from his pocket and handed it to the officer. "Nate Warren. I'm a PI. Formerly a federal investigator in DC."

The officer lifted an eyebrow. "A Fed?"

"Yeah."

The officer nodded, reached out a hand. "Officer Kempski."

"Pleasure," Nate said, shaking the man's hand.

He pulled a chair next to Luna and offered her a weak smile. "Are you holding up?"

"The initial shock has almost worn off."

He placed a hand on her back in what he hoped was a gesture of support. "I'm sorry."

"Me too. Thanks for coming," Luna said.

"Not a problem."

They both turned back to the footage that Officer Kempski was speeding through.

"How often are cars being stolen from here?" Nate asked.

"No more or less than usual. Most of the thefts are in the long-term lots."

Luna huffed. "I was going to park there but was running late. One night in the main lot wasn't going to break the bank. That backfired."

Her attempt at a joke was a good sign.

Kempski pointed to the monitor. "There's a lot of people coming and going. In order to determine when your car went missing, we're going to have to watch the exit footage, then return to this and determine if we can see who did it. And that's going to take a while. You don't have to sit here for this."

Hollywood made police work look exciting, but what Kempski was talking about was the ass in chair, fingers on keyboard police work that Nate knew was boring as all hell.

Kempski leaned back in his chair and swiveled to face the two of them.

Luna's shoulders fell. "What now?"

"I'll call the local police, get your car registered as stolen. They'll put it in a national database."

"Why do I get the feeling that 'putting it in a database' is a moot exercise?" Luna asked.

Kempski exchanged glances with Nate. Their unspoken conversation was loud in Nate's ears. Fifty percent of cars were never recovered.

Kempski shrugged. "Sometimes we get lucky."

Luna shook her head. "My car is eleven years old. And it's a cheap Hyundai. A luxury car I get, but a Hyundai?"

"Parts," Kempski blurted out. "The make, model, and year of your car is actually sought after for chop shops."

"Really?" Luna asked.

"Yeah. The year your car was manufactured Hyundai wasn't putting in immobilizers."

"What's that?" Luna asked.

"They make your car harder to steal because the engine won't turn on without key fob communication. It's pretty standard in all new cars. Then there's antitheft systems that track where your car is at all times."

"Mine didn't have that."

Nate moaned on the inside. Her car was gone. Probably already stripped and in unrecognizable pieces.

"Like I said, we might get lucky. But that isn't going to happen if I don't call Seattle PD and let them know what's going on." Kempski handed Luna a tablet. "Fill out everything, especially your insurance information so we can send the report to your insurance company. I can assure you we'll do everything we can to find the person, or people behind this. I'm here tomorrow. I'll call you and let you know where we're at, even if there's no progress. Sooner if there is."

"I have friends that can pull some strings if it can help," Nate told Kempski. "It goes without saying . . . if there's something I can do."

He nodded.

"I'll call Ash," Luna said as she stared absently at the tablet.

"Who's Ash?" Nate asked.

"My brother. He's a cop in Portland."

"It sounds like you have a good support system," Kempski said as he pushed away from his desk and stood. "You can finish that in here while I make the call. If you're done before I am, there's no reason for you to wait around for me. Take it to the front desk, they'll print out a copy for you. I'll call you tomorrow."

Nate stood, shook the other man's hand. "Thank you."

Luna looked up but didn't stand. "Yeah, thanks for your help."

Kempski nodded once and left the room.

Luna began tapping prompts on the tablet. "This sucks."

"Yeah, it does."

"I was having a great day. The trial was perfect. The cross examination was laughable. My sister called and told me that the insurance company is going to pay for a new roof."

"That's great news."

"Exactly . . . a great day. Blah!" She went back to the work in front of her. "I need a car."

Nate opened his mouth to say something.

Luna kept talking. "And I won't make our meeting tomorrow. I have to *rent* a car . . . and deal with my insurance company. The same company that is paying for my roof." She paused, looked up. "What if . . . shit. What if they think I'm responsible for this?"

"That's ridiculous," Nate said.

"Two claims in one week? That would look suspicious to me."

"You were in Denver when your car was jacked."

"You're right. You're right! I'm just . . . damn this sucks."

She was jumping all over the place. A trauma response if Nate had ever seen one. "Have you eaten?"

"What?"

"Food . . . when was the last time you ate?"

She looked up, then looked back down. "I'm not hungry."

"Breakfast?"

When she didn't reply, Nate had his answer.

She was in fight-or-flight mode. And the best way to deal with that was feed and breed.

Nate shook the word *breed* from his thoughts.

She needed food. That would bring her back down to earth.

He stayed silent while Luna finished the report.

Ten minutes later the officer at the desk obtained Luna's signature and gave her a copy of the report just as Kempski said they would.

Nate relieved her of her suitcase and led her out of the airport police headquarters.

"Your brother is a cop?"

"Yeah, surprisingly."

"Why is that?"

"He had his share of problems growing up," she said without elaborating.

"Criminal problems?"

"Nothing major" was her reply.

Nate wondered what Luna's definition of "major" was.

When they made their way to his car, Nate popped the trunk and tossed the suitcase inside.

"I bet this car has an immobilizer in it."

The way she said that made him laugh. "And a monitored security system."

Nate drove a Jeep Grand Cherokee. And it was less than a year old. Giving up the government job meant giving up his G-ride. A downside to be sure. After years of driving a government issued SUV, Nate couldn't see driving a sedan.

Nate slid into the driver's seat and glanced over his shoulder and watched as Luna fiddled with her seat belt.

She had that empty gaze as she stared straight ahead.

"Do you think they'll find my car?" she asked.

Nate started to respond.

Luna didn't let him.

"I don't think they'll find my car."

He didn't bother answering since he had to agree with her.

If the thieves wanted her car to resell it or paint it a different color and put on new plates to call it their own . . . then maybe.

But an eleven-year-old car that was worth more in parts?

Nate pulled out of the space and the lot.

There were plenty of cameras that should have picked up on something and someone.

Time would tell.

Nate headed toward the freeway and back to Seattle.

"Do you mind if I call my brother?" she asked.

"Of course not."

She fished her phone out of her purse and dialed.

With the phone to her ear, the first thing she said was, "Someone stole my car."

No hello . . . no preamble of "Hey, it's me." Just straight to the point of the call.

Nate chuckled.

Even though the call wasn't on speaker, he could hear a voice on the line talking.

"At the airport. I was in Denver overnight. Parked at Sea-Tac and poof, it's gone."

She paused.

"No. No clue . . . Yeah, I have that."

Nate crawled through late afternoon traffic as Luna once again reached for her purse.

"Hold up. I'm putting you on speaker."

She did just that and sat her phone on the console between them. "Are you there?"

"Yeah. What did the police say?" Ash's voice was low, his tone filled with concern.

"That my car was an easy target because it didn't have a tracker in it." Luna pulled the report out of her purse and unfolded it.

"They're right. But the airport, that's ballsy. There're cameras everywhere."

"Cameras that weren't pointed at my car."

"Thieves don't drop from thin air. There has to be footage of them coming and going."

Luna moaned. "I have the number."

"Okay, go ahead."

Luna recited the report number and Kempski's name.

Ash repeated it back.

"My car is toast, isn't it?" she asked.

Nate stopped himself from nodding.

"You're not going to want to hear this but yeah. Best case scenario, the thieves were in your car in seconds, out of the lot in minutes . . . and within an hour . . . maybe two, the frame of that car is sitting on the inside of a camper truck completely scrapped."

"How is that a 'best case scenario'?" Luna asked.

Ash paused.

Luna tilted her head to the side.

Nate found himself tuning in to the silence.

"Are you still there?" Luna asked.

"Don't freak out," Ash said.

"I don't like how this is starting," she replied.

"Best case, these guys are professionals that only want the car."

The word *only* stuck out in Nate's mind.

Of course . . . best case, the car was the target.

Worst case, it was a catalyst for something else.

Fuck.

"Statistically, that's all they were after," Nate said out loud.

"Who's that?" Ash asked.

"It's Nate. What statistics?" she asked, directing the question to him.

"Who is Nate?"

"A guy . . . What statistics?"

"What guy?" Ash demanded.

"I work with your sister," Nate said quickly before Luna could say the word *statistics* again. "I'm also a retired Fed and I know where you're going."

"What do you mean you know where he's going? Where is he going?" She took a breath. "Where are you going, Ash?"

"She needs to take precautions. I'd be there but I'm on shift until midnight. I can ask for time off to get up there, but that—"

"Will you two stop talking to each other in code and tell me what statistics and precautions I need to take? And why would you need to come to Seattle?" Luna had turned in her seat and was glaring between the phone and Nate.

"Because you and Miley live in that big house all alone. And your cat isn't a guard dog. Yes, statistically there is nothing to be worried about. But you're my sister."

Nate couldn't argue with that.

"All your personal information was in that car, right?" Nate asked. "Name, insurance company?"

"And the navigation system probably has a pre-programmed button that says 'Home,' am I right?"

Luna had stopped talking.

Nate didn't like the look that crossed over her face.

"Professional car thief . . . whatever, they won't look twice at your information. Too risky for them to do anything with it and be found out. So yeah, that's the best case, Lu. If these guys saw you leave your car . . . maybe they liked what they saw. You're cute, I mean I'm your brother, but you know . . ."

Nate wouldn't use the word *cute* . . .

Then again, he wasn't Luna's brother.

"You think they would come to the house?" she asked.

"They could. There are two kinds of people that leave cars in airport parking lots when they leave on a trip. The kind that live alone and don't have someone to drop them off . . . or someone who flies all the time, leaving their home unattended. They case your house, wait for you to leave, and now you're missing a car and half your shit. And then there's the part where you're cute. And men suck."

"Oh." Luna grew quiet.

"Yeah, sorry."

"Does your house have an alarm system?" Nate asked.

She shook her head and all but whispered, "No."

Traffic started to spread out, giving Nate the ability to pick up speed.

All the while no one was talking while Luna processed what she'd been told.

"Nate," Ash started. "I can get there tomorrow. I'll let my captain know what's going on. Can you stay there until I—"

"What? You don't even know Nate. Why would you ask him to stay at the house?"

"You know him well enough to let him pick you up from the airport police station. And he's a Fed."

"Ex-Fed," Nate corrected.

"You have a gun, though, right?"

Nate instinctively glanced at his glove compartment.

Luna saw him, her eyes widened. Then she pulled open said compartment.

Inside was his Glock.

"What the . . ." She reached out to touch it.

Nate placed his hand on her arm. "It's loaded. Don't."

Her hand recoiled.

"Yes, and yes," Nate said. "I can stick around until you get here."

Luna's side-eye and suspended breath suggested she wanted to argue. "But—"

"Lu, please don't. I know you're Ms. Independent and can handle everything, but humor me, okay?"

Luna slapped her lips shut. "Fine," she bit out.

"I love you," Ash told her.

The sentiment made Nate smile.

"Love you, too."

"Great, see you tomorrow."

With the call ended, Luna closed the glove compartment and stared out the window in silence.

"You don't have to do this," she finally said.

"I know."

CHAPTER EIGHT

Dusk was all but a memory when Nate pulled into the driveway and parked under the carport.

"Wow," he said, looking around the windshield to take in the house.

"Yeah. It is."

"You can afford this with your business?"

She regarded him from the corner of her eye. "Only when you skim off the top and hide it from the Feds."

Nate did a double take.

She met his gaze.

It took a moment, but Nate finally broke and started to laugh.

"It was my grandmother's," she explained.

"Ah," he said before he reached for the glove compartment and retrieved his gun.

"Do you always have that on you?" Luna asked.

"More often than not."

"Have you ever used it?"

He hesitated. "Yes. And no, I haven't killed anyone."

She felt a chill run down her spine, and not the good kind. "Let's hope you never have to."

"Couldn't agree more."

By the time Luna crossed through the back door of her house, she felt as if she'd aged five years. All the adrenaline of the past three hours had dumped into her system, leaving her exhausted and numb. One wall in the mudroom had hooks for coats and cubbies for muddy shoes. Luna shed her coat and hung it haphazardly on a hook.

Nate walked in behind her, her suitcase in his hand.

In the kitchen she dropped her purse on the island.

"Nice," Nate said, looking around the room.

Luna offered a noncommittal noise.

"Is that a greenhouse?" He looked through the glass door into what was exactly that.

"Yup. I'd love to say I use it to its full extent, but I'd be lying."

"Wow."

The house was quiet with only the hum of the refrigerator and the ambient noise of electricity filling the space. Some might say you can't hear electricity, but Luna always argued that point. If you really want quiet, wait for a power outage. Proof enough for her that electricity had sound.

"Miley should be walking in the door any minute. Don't shoot her."

Nate smirked. "I'll try not to."

Midnight announced her presence before strolling into the room.

"You have a cat?"

"Her name is Midnight. She doesn't take to men. Don't take it personally."

Midnight looked at Luna, then Nate.

Before she could hiss, Luna reached down and picked her up.

"Make yourself at home. I'll take this to my room and then show you around."

"Has the house been empty all day?"

"Yeah. Miley works twelve-hour shifts."

"Then how about I follow you upstairs and make sure there aren't any surprises," Nate suggested.

Luna stared at him, blinked, and kept staring. *Surprises?* "What . . . You think someone could be in the house."

Nate shook his head. "Probably not. But there is a reason your brother suggested I stay over."

There went that chill again.

Luna looked Midnight in the eye. "Is anyone here?"

Midnight's answer was a headbutt to Luna's chest and a purr.

"Fine. Follow me."

Victorian homes were made up of several rooms and expansive hallways. The Canning home wasn't any different.

The only real exception was when Nana removed one wall from what was an office and a sitting room and made it a family room.

Luna pointed and offered her dime store home tour. "There is the obligatory formal living room that no one ever goes into. And no, I didn't decorate it, and it hasn't been touched, other than cleaning, since Nana passed. The dining room," she said, pointing to the obvious. "The den . . . or family room. A bathroom." She stopped at the stairs and indicated farther down the hall. "There's a laundry room, storage room converted from a tiny bedroom, half bath, and stairs to the basement."

Nate nodded. "Is there a door?"

"Yeah. To the backyard."

They started up the stairs.

"Are these original floors?" Nate asked.

Luna glanced at her feet. "I would imagine."

"Amazing."

She'd taken them for granted, but looking at them through Nate's eyes, she had to agree. "They are, aren't they?"

The second level was all bedrooms.

Luna pointed. "Miley's room, Ash's room, another bathroom, guest room, my office . . ." She kept walking. "My room."

Nana had expanded the primary bedroom by removing a hall closet. There was a fireplace and an en suite bathroom. Along with a reading nook that looked out over the backyard. "You can set that down anywhere," she said, pointing at the suitcase Nate still carried.

"I'm impressed," Nate said.

Sound drifted up from the first floor.

"Luna?" Miley called from downstairs.

"Up here," Luna replied.

"The roommate?" Nate asked.

"Yeah."

Nate stepped around Luna and peeked into the bathroom.

"All clear?" she teased.

Midnight scrambled to get out of her arms and jumped to the floor.

"Looks like your guard cat did his job." Nate pushed aside the curtain and glanced outside.

It felt good to laugh considering her shit day.

"Whose car is in the driveway?" Miley asked before ducking around the corner and into Luna's room.

She stopped short, her eyes focused on Nate.

"Who are you?"

Luna waved a hand between the both of them.

"Miley, this is Nate, Nate, this is Miley."

"Nate? *Mr. Venti*, Nate?"

Luna moaned.

"Mr. Venti?" Nate asked with a grin.

"The coffee fiasco? It earned you a nickname."

"Fair."

"What is Mr. Venti doing here . . . and in your bedroom?"

The shit-eating grin on Miley's face was ill placed. She of all people knew that Luna wasn't one to entertain men at her home. Or at all for that matter.

Luna tore off the information Band-Aid and explained her crap day. "My car was stolen at the airport. I was on the phone with Nate when I realized it wasn't in the parking lot, and he volunteered to pick me up and drive me home. I called Ash to see if he could help in getting my car back, and between these two"—Luna pointed at Nate—"it was determined that the piece of shit that jacked my car would also have our address, which sufficiently freaked me out, so Nate is staying with us until Ash gets here sometime tomorrow."

Miley stood stone cold still. "Your car?"

"Yes."

"Gone?"

"Yes."

"And Ash thinks someone might come here . . . and what?"

"I don't know. Wait for us to leave, rip us off. Or not wait for us to leave." Luna let the truly ugly image go unsaid.

"Fuuuuck," Miley sighed out.

"My thoughts exactly."

"Oh my God, Luna." Miley moved to her side and placed a hand on her shoulder. "Are you okay?"

"I'll let you ladies talk," Nate said, excusing himself.

"Thanks," Luna said.

When he reached the hall, he turned back. "What is up the next flight of stairs?"

"The attic."

"Mind if I look around?" he asked. "I want to poke into all the places someone might hide."

"You're the one with the gun." She shrugged.

Miley's head pivoted. "You have a gun?"

"I'll let Luna explain," he said before walking away.

Miley turned back around. "He has a gun?"

"He worked for the Feds . . . he carries a gun." Luna backed up until she reached her bed and then flopped her butt on it. "My f-ing car, Miley."

"Jesus." Miley sat beside her.

"It just wasn't there. I thought the worst thing that could happen at an airport was my luggage not making it. Never in a million years did I think my car would be stolen."

Miley placed a hand over Luna's shoulder. "Do they think they'll get it back?"

"The cops didn't really say. Ash hopes it's in a chop shop."

"That's rude."

"No . . . no he's right. If they bothered to look at the registration, they might see the address and aim for something worth more than my old car. Hence Nate spending the night and Ash coming tomorrow."

"What are you going to do?"

Luna released a long-suffering sigh. "Call my insurance company . . . again. Give them the police report, then rent a car."

"That sucks," Miley offered.

Luna dropped her head on her best friend's shoulder.

Nate poked his head in. "If it's okay, I'll see what you have in the kitchen. You need to get some food in you."

"You cook?" Miley asked.

"Doesn't everyone?"

Miley shook her head.

"We can order something. Pizza, whatever." Luna's words sounded as defeated as she felt.

"I can do better than pizza," Nate said.

"You cook *and* carry a gun?" Miley was stuck in a loop. Luna could see it on her face.

"I'll figure out dinner."

And he was gone.

"And he's hot," Miley whispered.

Luna nudged her friend. "He might hear you."

"I'm sure he knows he's hot. Hot guys always know. I mean, look at Ash."

"He's my brother, I try not to." Luna dragged her ass off her bed.

"Arrogant and hot," Miley muttered.

"I don't think Nate is arrogant."

"Not Nate. Ash."

Luna couldn't argue that. "Maybe, but he's loyal. He's coming to deter any criminals from ransacking the house." She started toward her bathroom. "I'm taking a shower. Try not to drool on Mr. Venti, I need to work with him after this night is over."

"I'm on my best behavior." Miley sat up straight with way too big of a smile on her face.

Luna rolled her eyes and turned away.

Luna Canning's kitchen was the kind of space chefs dream of. The island had plenty of room for prep. A drop-in sink, the porcelain kind that gave off the Victorian charm of the house. The stovetop and oven weren't over the top, and certainly not state of the art, but they looked like they could take on any job Nate demanded of them. There was a mix of open shelves with floral teacups and decorative plates and serving dishes. Ones that were likely used that one day of the year that the formal living room was occupied.

But it was more than Grandma's antiques and keepsakes. There was an espresso maker beside the refrigerator and an emulsion blender beside that.

Nate stepped into the walk-in pantry to assess what Luna and Miley considered food. Canned soups, tomatoes, and several types of beans. Dried pasta and jars of tomato-based sauces. There were several boxes of protein bars and containers of protein powders. In the refrigerator was a package of chicken breasts, which Nate considered pay dirt. Several different varieties of greens, from rainbow chard to spinach. All of which he assumed made it into the blender with the powder and ended up being someone's meal. Onions, tomatoes, lemon juice . . . yeah, he was set.

Nate removed his jacket and rolled up his sleeves.

When Miley walked into the kitchen Nate already had the chicken seasoned and set aside, and he was attempting to cut up the vegetables he needed.

Luna needed new knives. At first, he thought maybe they just needed a good sharpening. With further inspection he noticed the chips and wear on the cheap knives and determined that they were better off in the trash.

"Wow," Miley said, looking at the countertop.

"I hope you two don't mind."

She slid onto a chair next to the island. "Anyone who minds when someone is cooking for them needs to have a brain scan."

Nate smiled and kept chopping. "What do you do in the medical field?"

"ER nurse."

"That must be intense."

"It has its moments."

Nate looked up. "Do you like it?"

Miley nodded. "I like how it changes every day. Every hour at times. I could do without the hospital bureaucracy."

"Nobody likes bureaucracy. Especially if the rules that are being made are done by people who don't do the job."

"Is that why you left your federal job?" Miley asked.

"Partly."

Luna stepped into the kitchen fresh from the shower.

The edges of her hair were wet, her face void of makeup. But most of all, she appeared less stressed.

"Feel better?" Nate asked.

She nodded. "I do."

"Good." He turned back to the refrigerator and removed the tiny jar of minced garlic.

"When you said you'd make dinner, I didn't think it would look like this," Luna said.

Nate kept moving as they talked. "How do you make dinner?"

"We have a four-ingredient cookbook," Miley offered.

"Please tell me that doesn't include spices."

Luna and Miley looked at each other, giving Nate his answer.

"Did your mother teach you to cook?" Miley asked.

Nate nodded and kept moving. "She laid the foundation. I worked my way through college in a kitchen."

"As a chef?" Luna asked.

"Dishwasher."

The women laughed.

"Eventually I was promoted to salads. And when there was no one else, the chef barked orders at me."

"Are we talking Chef Ramsay barking?"

Nate paused long enough to put the chicken in the oven. "I didn't get paid enough to put up with that. I did learn a lot, though. In my senior year, my grandfather had a stroke from what the doctor said was decades filled with a diet of microwave meals and energy bars. I decided I was better off embracing the kitchen to avoid a nursing home when I'm old."

"If it wasn't for energy bars on the days I work, I wouldn't eat," Miley admitted.

"My grandmother lived on martinis and sin."

Nate glanced at Luna. "The grandmother that owned this house?"

"Yeah."

"Speaking of alcohol. Anyone want some wine?" Miley was already out of her chair.

"God yes," Luna said.

"Nate?"

"Sure." Though he'd keep it to one. Not that he expected any trouble. But overdrinking defeated the purpose of him staying over.

"Your grandmother sounded like a character."

"You have no idea."

"Luna's grandmother was a riot," Miley said. "Did you ever figure out how many husbands she went through?"

"I don't even think my mother knows the answer to that. I counted six of them."

Nate stopped moving, his eyes snagged Luna's. "Six?"

She nodded. "Harper thinks it's seven, eight if you count the fact that Nana married her baby daddy twice."

Nate thought those kinds of statistics only happened in the movies. "How long did her marriages last?"

"I don't know, most of them happened when I was a kid. Every time we ended up in this house there was a new one."

Miley sat a glass of red in front of Luna, and another for Nate.

"Thank you." Red with chicken wasn't ideal, but he always believed that you should drink what you liked.

Nate turned back to Luna. "What do you mean 'ended up in this house'?"

Miley snorted. "How much time do you have?"

"All night."

Luna sighed. "My mom took a page out of Nana's playbook. Except Mom couldn't keep her own roof over her head when her marriages or relationships fell apart. And they always fell apart."

Nate couldn't tell if that was sadness he heard in her voice, or complacency.

"How many times was she married?" he asked.

"Three . . . well, maybe four. Harper's dad, my dad, and . . . Paul. I don't know if she's married anyone since." Luna stared into her wine.

"Wait . . . she's still alive?"

"Yeah."

Miley watched her friend and stayed quiet.

There was a hell of a lot more to this story. "I assumed since you're living in this house that she'd passed."

"No." Luna sipped her wine. "Nana left the house to us. Harper, Ash, and me. She knew that Mom would lose it. And while Nana had her faults, this house was always a safe haven for us. She wanted to assure that after her death."

It took everything in him to not pry about Luna's mother. But there was a darkness in talking about her that Nate wanted to dispel. Luna had had a hard enough day.

"Now I understand why your brother has a room here."

A small smile lifted the corners of Luna's mouth. "He doesn't come around very often. The occasional weekend. Holidays. Harper's room is now the guest room. She's married, has her own place."

The smell of the chicken told him he needed to finish the sides.

"Tell me more about Nana."

Luna and Miley both smiled and launched into one of many stories.

CHAPTER NINE

Luna ate more than she thought she would. And it was fabulous. How Nate could make homemade hummus and tzatziki from the paltry offerings in the kitchen, Luna would never know. He whipped together a Mediterranean dinner fit for a fine dining restaurant.

With her plate clean, and a second glass of wine half empty, Miley was telling a story about Nana and husband number five. "I'm telling you; he was a driver for the mob."

"He drove a cab."

"Which was a cover," Miley insisted.

"It was suspicious," Luna told Nate. "His name was Joe Chaney. Anytime we came over, he'd have gifts for us. Didn't matter if it was our birthdays or not."

"He's the one that Nana was with when she remodeled the kitchen and her bedroom," Miley said. "How can a taxi driver afford that?"

"I see your case for a side hustle. But what made you think it was the mob?" Nate asked.

"Nana told us after they split that all of Joe's friends were Italian. His late-night cab runs were more consistent than Uber drivers at Sea-Tac Airport, only they ran down by the pier. Late at night," Luna said. "Back when no one was at the pier at night except the homeless."

Nate leaned in. "Did you ever meet any of Joe's friends?"

"No. Ash did. On accident."

Nate's brow narrowed so Luna explained. "Nana had an open-door policy. We could show up anytime for any reason. But we were living in Auburn so it wasn't like we could just walk down the street to get here. Most of the time we'd give Nana a heads-up. Only that wasn't the case this time. Ash and our stepdad were fighting so he hitchhiked his way here."

"Hitchhiked?" Nate asked. "How old was he?"

"A teenager. I don't remember exactly. Anyway, Nana was at work. Joe wasn't home, Ash let himself in. At some point Joe came home with a big Italian guy dressed in a suit. Ash heard them talking and came down from his room. Before they saw him, Ash noticed Joe taking a 'fat envelope' from suit guy. When they realized they had an audience, suit guy got up in Joe's face. According to Ash, he acted like he hadn't seen anything and introduced himself to Joe's friend. Joe asked why he was there. Ash said there was trouble at home. Then suit guy was all . . . 'What kind of trouble?' 'Could he help?' Joe shut it down and they both left. Shortly after that, Nana and Joe split. Joe gave her a pretty good chunk of change when he bailed." The image of Joe, albeit faded in her mind, made her smile. He gave the best hugs.

Nate's sharp gaze found hers. "Did Nana ever say what happened that split them up?"

"Irreconcilable differences." Luna laughed. "That's what she said about all of them."

"She bored easily," Miley chimed in. "It was the hippie in her."

Luna agreed.

"Did you ever see Joe again?"

"Once. He told me that if I ever needed him, he'd be there. Not that he gave me a phone number or anything." If he had, so many things might have been different.

"Mafia help comes with strings," Nate pointed out.

"I'm thinking Nana caught on to that. She was rather fierce about protecting us kids. Since Ash ended up living with Nana for a while, Joe and his friends had to go."

Nate sat back after taking in the whole story. "You do know I'm going to look up these names, right?"

"What kind of PI would you be if you didn't?" Luna asked. "I'm sure Joe is gone by now. He'd have to be in his midnineties if he was still alive."

"We'll find out," Nate said. "People with Mafia connections tend to have short lives."

Miley let out a huge yawn.

"Are we keeping you up?" Luna asked.

"Sorry. Two twelves in a row wipe me out."

Luna grabbed her plate and started clearing the table. "Dinner was amazing, Nate. Thank you."

"Yeah," Miley said. "Anytime you need to practice your culinary skills, we're here as your test subjects."

Nate followed them from the kitchen table to the sink. "I'll keep that in mind."

Miley excused herself after the dishes were done, leaving Luna and Nate alone.

"I can't believe how late it is. I don't remember the last time I sat for a two-hour dinner," Luna admitted.

"But did you forget about your car?" Nate asked.

"Yeah, actually. I can thank you for that."

He shook his head. "I'm just the new guy you get to share old stories with."

"You've been a good sport about it."

"Are you kidding? Your grandmother was what made-for-TV series look for. I can't wait to hear more."

Luna ran a hand over the back of her neck. "That will have to wait for another time. I'm shot."

"I look forward to it."

She started for the stairs. "Ash has clothes here. Sweatpants and a T-shirt will be okay?"

"Perfect."

Nate followed her.

"The guest room has clean sheets. I'll make sure there's a clean towel in the hall bathroom."

"How about a pillow and a blanket and I'll crash on the sofa downstairs."

Luna paused and turned. "What's wrong with the bed?"

"Nothing. I'd likely hear someone outside that shouldn't be here if I'm closer to the front door."

For a minute, Luna forgot why Nate was staying over. "Do you really think someone is out there watching?"

"Did you really think your car would be stolen when you left for Denver?"

She glanced over her shoulder. "Good point."

In Ash's room Luna turned on the light and stood away from the door. "Find whatever you think will work, I'll grab the pillow and blanket."

Nate moved to the closet. "Any chance you have an extra toothbrush hanging around?"

"I'll grab one."

"Do you mind if I shower?"

"Of course not."

Luna set Nate up in the bathroom before finding what she needed to make a bed out of her couch.

The old pipes in the house rattled when Nate turned the water on in the spare bathroom.

Midnight, who had been hiding all evening, now followed Luna around like a puppy.

"Be nice to our guest," Luna told her cat.

Midnight lifted her nose and walked in between Luna's feet.

With a clean sheet over the cushions, two pillows, and a blanket, the sofa was as ready as it would ever be.

Lights from a car passing by illuminated the room, drawing Luna to the window.

It was pitch black as rain clouds filled the northwestern sky, blocking out the passing full moon. The thought of the moon made her think of the sage she'd burned in the attic.

That seemed to work for the insurance guy.

Too bad she hadn't burned some in her car.

The thought made her laugh.

Her car.

Her former car.

She tried to recall any and everything she had in it.

An unopened roadside emergency kit. A blanket and water. Chains. An umbrella, reusable grocery bags . . . maybe a few dollars in change she had on hand for parking meters. Nothing of real value.

Other than the car itself.

"Is anything out there?" Nate asked, catching her staring out the window.

"Rain."

"Let's hope that's all we see tonight."

It was difficult to not look at what Nate had changed into. Gray sweatpants and a black T-shirt on many men wouldn't look all that great.

But Nate did seem to have that "hot" factor Miley had talked about. The sweatpants hung on his hips, showing off the curve of his . . .

Luna diverted her eyes.

"It looks like Ash's clothes worked out."

If Nate noticed her gawking, he didn't comment.

"They're a little big, but yes."

"My brother spends more time in the gym than the average person," she told him.

Nate set his pile of clothes along with his gun on the coffee table that Luna had pulled away from the couch to give him more room.

"Is there anything else you need?" she asked.

Nate tilted his head to the side. "A phone charger?"

"Of course, yes." Luna went into the kitchen and returned with a spare cable.

When she handed it over, Nate's fingers grazed hers.

An unexpected static snap made both of them flinch.

"I haven't felt that in a while," she said.

Nate shook his hand before taking the charger.

"Thank you again."

"It's really no problem, Luna. I'm still living out of boxes. This house is a nice change."

Still, the man hardly knew her, and he certainly wasn't under any obligation to put his life on hold for the night to babysit her and Miley.

"You already know where everything is in the kitchen. If you need anything . . ."

"I know which room is yours," he said.

"Right." She turned away. "Good night, then."

"Good night."

"Right," she said again.

Why were her hands shaking? And why the sudden flutter of nerves?

There's a stranger sleeping in my house. Shaking and nerves should be expected.

Before heading up the stairs, Luna made sure the front door, mudroom door, and the back door were locked. At the same time, she turned off the lights, leaving only the few night lights plugged in at ankle level.

The sound of Nate settling in offered a bit of solace. If he hadn't stayed over, Luna would have left lights on and would probably be sleeping on the couch herself.

And do what? she mused. *Throw a candlestick at an intruder if one came?*

Ash had told her more than once that a shotgun wasn't a bad thing to have in a home.

For the first time in her adult life, she considered her brother's suggestion.

~

How did he get here?

Nate rested against the arm of Luna's sofa, a pillow under his head and images of the day taking up space in his brain.

There was a lot more to Luna Canning than her accounting skills.

Her life had been anything but boring. And after an evening in the Canning home, Nate understood why Ash would be concerned that a thief might see Luna's address and come around looking for more.

The house was packed with antiques. Nate was clueless of the value, but that wouldn't mean a thief didn't know. Thieves believed big houses meant expensive stuff inside. So even if Nana's old belongings weren't worth crap, thieves would turn the place upside down looking for gold.

He was glad he made the choice to stay. It was obvious that Luna and Miley were capable of taking care of themselves. But there was a certain amount of safety in numbers. And even as sexist as it sounded, a man's presence deterred other men.

Nate felt his eyelids getting heavy. A steady clap of rain against the window was a perfect sleep meditation. The house creaked as old houses did. Even from the living room he heard the hum of the refrigerator. And footsteps.

He pulled the comforter up to his chin and shifted his hips to the side. The house was a little drafty and smelled faintly of gardenia.

Sleep started taking hold with one last thought for the night.

Mr. Venti.

Nate fell asleep with a smile.

Bright rays of sunshine pulled Nate out of his restless dreams.

That and the wiggling and purring of a cat attempting to get comfortable on his chest.

One eye opened and found two green eyes staring at him.

"Hello."

Midnight looked directly into Nate's soul.

"I thought you didn't like guys," Nate said.

In answer, Midnight rested her head on her paws and sighed.

Did cats sigh?

Crazy how an eight-pound domestic animal had the power to keep you from moving.

Even the slightest twitch felt like a disrespect to the feline that had just settled in with the full intention of falling asleep.

Only Nate had to pee.

He shifted his hips.

Midnight wrapped her tail around her body and nudged one of her ears onto a leg.

"I'm going to have to get up," Nate whispered.

Midnight closed her eyes.

Nate lifted his torso a couple of inches.

Without opening an eye, Midnight struck one paw out as if saying, "Not right now you're not."

"Oh, boy."

Nate didn't know what would be crueler: letting the cat fall asleep and then moving her, or disturbing the peace now.

With careful precision, he slowly lifted Midnight up, using the blanket the cat lay on, and tried to slip out from under it.

The cat lifted its head but didn't move.

"I have to do it, sweetie."

The cat didn't budge. She simply let Nate pick her up and set her back down once Nate moved away.

Sometime during the sleepless night, Nate had removed the T-shirt he'd gone to sleep in. Wearing any clothing at all wasn't his bedtime choice. And since retrieving the shirt would have meant disturbing the cat again, he decided against it and moved through the house bare-chested.

After making use of the downstairs bathroom, Nate made his way to the kitchen.

Coffee.

He knew there had to be some somewhere considering coffee was what had acquainted him to Luna in the first place.

Nate considered himself a chef, not a barista. He'd leave that talent to someone else.

It didn't take him long to find what he needed, and soon a pot was brewing next to the espresso machine.

He retrieved his phone from the charger that sat on the table beside his bed for the night.

Midnight was fast asleep exactly where Nate had left her.

Leaning against the kitchen counter, he scrolled through his news app to catch up on whatever had happened the previous day.

Halfway through his first cup of coffee, he heard one of the women in the house approach.

Luna walked into the kitchen already dressed in a pair of leggings and an oversize sweatshirt.

The second she caught sight of him, she stopped. Her eyes drifted down his chest.

"Oh," she said.

He set his cup down. "Good morning."

Luna kept staring. "Good . . . ah, you're not wearing a shirt."

Nate picked himself up off the stool he was perched on. "Your cat hijacked my . . ."

Luna brought her eyes up to meet his.

"Right. I'll go put something on."

She nodded. "That would be a good idea."

He should probably feel embarrassed, but there was a rosy color that flushed Luna's cheeks that made him smile after he walked past.

Then he heard her sigh once he was out of sight. And that made him smile even more.

Back in the living room, Midnight had vacated her spot and was nowhere to be seen.

Donning the loaner shirt, Nate returned to the kitchen.

"Better?" he asked.

Luna didn't say yes or no. Instead, she asked, "How did you sleep?"

"Not bad," he lied. "You?"

"Not at all. Once the rain let up an owl must have perched on the chimney from my bedroom fireplace. He didn't stop hooting until the dawn. I think I managed three hours tops." Luna held her coffee cup with two hands and spoke over the rim.

"Look on the bright side. Nobody tried to break in."

She half laughed. Then moaned. "My car."

"Sorry."

She forced a smile. "It's okay. Kempski is going to call, say they found the car and everything is fine."

Nate narrowed his gaze.

"It's my delusion, let me keep it for a while."

"I didn't say anything," Nate pointed out.

Luna sipped her coffee. "What do you have planned for today?"

"I'm meeting my co-worker for . . ." He stopped and smiled when Luna caught on.

"I'm screwing up two of your days," she said sheepishly.

"No worries."

"The least I can do is send you off after a good breakfast," she said as she pushed away from the counter.

"You don't have to—"

"Yes, I do. I hope pancakes and eggs are okay." She set her cup down and moved to the pantry.

"That would be great."

CHAPTER TEN

Nate was easy to talk to.

And way too easy to look at.

The morning bare chest completely short-circuited her brain.

She expected to walk into the kitchen and find a slightly disheveled man behind a cup of coffee. Instead, she found what some men made a killing on TikTok recording and posting while doing nothing more than cutting logs with an axe or spinning around in a desk chair.

Sure, Nate's hair was a little out of sorts, and his face showed a day's worth of stubble. But that only added to the snap she felt when she realized he was in her kitchen half naked.

"Sin and bad decisions" were the words that kept rolling through Luna's brain. Something her grandmother had said once Luna was old enough to understand the context.

The "walk of shame" wore smeared mascara and smelled faintly of wine and stale cigarettes. But "sin and bad decisions" looked exactly like Nate. Like someone you wanted to jump right back in bed with, damn the consequences.

Only Nate's bed had been the couch and there was zero romantic involvement between the two of them.

As it should be.

Luna moved between frying the bacon she'd forgotten was in the refrigerator and mixing the pancake batter.

"So, what's the real reason you left DC?" she asked.

"What do you mean 'real reason'? I wanted to branch out on my own."

"Without any clients standing in line?" Who did that? When Luna had taken the risk, she already had a half a dozen lawyers wanting her service.

She saw Nate struggle to answer her question.

"Who was she? A wife?" Luna asked.

"I didn't say anything about a woman."

"That's exactly what someone would say if it *was* a woman. You don't have to tell me. It's not really my business. But since you're barefoot and were half naked in my kitchen, I figured we're past the 'none of my business' part of this friendship." And it was a friendship. Any person willing to spend the night and play temporary bodyguard was friend material.

Nate let go of a breath with a laugh and a shake of his head. "How did you know it was a woman?"

"My mother was an expert at fleeing one state for another when things ended. I see the subtle signs others might miss."

"Like what?" he asked.

"For starters, you said you were still living out of boxes and at the same time suggested that a 'home' was a nice change. Which means you don't feel at home here . . . yet. When you move to a place you're meant to be, it feels comfortable. Like your favorite pair of jeans."

"Huh," he uttered.

"And last night when you were making dinner, you were clearly in your element. Now, I don't doubt you enjoy cooking, but doing it in front of an audience . . . that was your crack. You like community and probably don't have a lot here."

"I still have college friends in the area."

"But you had more in DC."

"True."

"So, moving wasn't so much of going where you truly wanted to be, but to get away from something that needed distance. Hence . . . a woman." Luna turned back to the stove and gave Nate the time he needed.

Eventually he said, "She wasn't my wife."

"Fiancée?"

"No," he said quickly.

"Oh." That changed things. She had more questions, but Nate started asking his own questions.

"What about you? Have you ever been married?"

"Sadly. Once."

"This I've got to hear."

From the corner of Luna's eye, she saw Nate lean on his elbows with rapt attention.

"I was young and stupid. He came from a stable family, and the sex was . . . it worked." *Kinda.*

Nate laughed. "That's all it took? A family and mediocre sex?"

She pointed a spatula in his direction. "Earth-shattering sex is for romance novels, and considering how I grew up, a stable family was my nirvana."

"What happened to this match made in heaven?"

"I was a sophomore in college. He was in his last year. His parents were paying for our apartment. 'We'll help you kids get started.' You know, all that. What I didn't know was that he was failing. When he dropped out, my in-laws were not happy, and they stopped paying our rent. And then Landon started driving for Uber."

"His name was *Landon*?"

"I thought it sounded aristocratic. The name of a man in an epic romance novel." What a fool she'd been. Romantasizing a name and not digging deeper before falling in.

Nate laughed. "If you say so."

"Anyway. He drove a car that his parents had paid for, that was still insured by his parents, and had their credit card that paid for the gas."

"This guy sounds like a real catch."

The bar had been low. Find a man who said he loved her with even the slightest bit of ambition . . . "I was killing myself at school and tutoring high schoolers for money. Landon started drinking, eventually couldn't drive for Uber . . . not that it was a career path, but it did help."

"You left because he was a loser." This was less of a question and more of a statement.

She shook her head, flipped the bacon, and stared off, recalling the final straw play out like a film projected on the wall. "No. That would have been too easy. That would have been a reason my mother would have walked away. I didn't want to be anything like my mother. Still don't."

"What happened?" Nate's voice softened.

Luna touched the side of her jaw. "He hit me. He got drunk one night, said I was the reason his parents had cut him off, and when I put the blame on him, he responded with his fist."

"Fuck."

Luna glanced at Nate and snapped away from the memory. "I put everything I owned that could fit into the back of my car and came here. Nana took one look at me and said she was going to kill him. Ash nearly did."

"Damn, Luna, I'm sorry."

"It's okay. Well, not okay, but I learned a very valuable lesson super early in life. From more than just Landon if I'm honest. Depend only on yourself and no one else can take that away. My marriage was a one and done."

Luna oiled up the griddle and poured out the first pancake.

"So that's it. You gave up on romance?"

"I don't have to be hit twice," she said. At least not as an adult.

"Landon isn't an example of all men."

"Based upon my upbringing, statistics are very clear on the kind of man I'll attract. Which I've already proven true with my first choice." Luna started removing the bacon from the pan and turned off the burner. "Numbers don't lie, Nate. It's why I like them."

"A life of celibacy sounds like hell."

She laughed. "I didn't say I didn't have sex. I just don't invite them in." She tapped her chest.

"All right, then." Nate sounded resigned and a little sad.

Something Luna would overanalyze if old painful memories weren't finding their way to the surface in her brain.

"It's not all doom and gloom," she told him. "I'm happy. I have a great job, my own home . . . great friends, a brother and sister that care about me. The obligatory cat for a single woman." She laughed.

"You don't want more?"

"Like what?" she asked, looking over her shoulder. "The fairy-tale ending? Do you need me to quote divorce statistics? Think about it, between Nana and my mother there were at least ten marriages and divorces. The men my mother invited into her life were mean, and before you ask, yes . . . violent. I married my abuser. Statistically, I'd do that again. That or become them. Something Harper, Ash, and I have all managed to avoid. And if I have one mantra to live by in my life, it's that I don't want to be like my mother."

They were both quiet for a moment.

Luna flipped the pancake and added another one to the griddle.

"Shit," Luna said quickly. "The eggs."

Nate pushed back from the counter. "Let me."

"But—"

"It's my crack, remember?"

Their eyes met and Luna retreated. "Fine."

A half an hour later, Luna and Nate had cleaned their plates and were on a second cup of coffee before Miley stumbled into the kitchen in a bathrobe and fuzzy slippers.

"Someone slept in," Luna teased.

"Someone paced in their room all night," Miley said accusingly.

"I did not. And even if I did, I'm all the way down the hall."

Miley glanced at Nate.

"Don't blame me. I slept great."

"Liar," Luna said.

"Bullshit," said Miley.

"Hey!" Nate protested . . . but he was smiling.

"No one sleeps great on a couch in someone else's house unless they're pass-out drunk," Luna said.

"Another statistic?" Nate asked.

"Math," she said as if it was the answer to everything.

The sound of a motorcycle penetrated the peace outside.

Miley moaned and Luna smiled.

"Ash."

"I haven't even had my coffee yet," Miley protested.

Luna ignored her friend and went outside to greet her brother.

Ash drove his police issued motorcycle. Not something he did very often, and almost never when out of uniform.

He'd already hopped off his bike and was in the process of removing his helmet when Luna spotted him.

An overwhelming sense of warmth and peace filled her every fiber. For a brief moment, vulnerability pooled behind her eyes. He was there for her. To make sure she was looked after. Luna was convinced that if it wasn't for Ash, she might have craved a man's loyalty enough to fall prey to a second lousy marriage.

Ash looked up, saw her, and opened his arms.

Luna fell into them. "I'm glad you're here."

"Are you okay?" he asked softly.

"I am."

He hugged her like he needed to.

Ash pulled away, looked her in the eyes. He was searching for the truth through the unspoken words of siblings. "Good," he said.

Luna drew back and glanced at the bike. "You didn't have to bring that."

Ash removed a pack and the shotgun strapped to the side. "Nothing deters criminals more than the sight of the po-po," he teased.

"I suppose that's true."

He nodded toward Nate's car. "Is that your friend's?"

"Yeah. We were just finishing breakfast."

Ash swung the pack over his shoulder. "Who is this guy?"

"I told you. A colleague."

"That's it?" Ash gave her the side-eye.

"That's it. I barely know him." *Barely* was subjective after a night and morning of oversharing family and personal secrets.

They both turned in the direction of the back door and walked toward it.

"How many days are you staying?" Luna asked.

"Trying to get rid of me already?"

Luna nudged her shoulder against his. "That's not what I'm saying."

"A few days. More if something goes down."

They walked into the house together.

Miley huddled over her first cup of coffee, and Nate was in the process of putting dishes in the dishwasher.

Ash started laughing the second he saw Miley. "Suzie Sunshine just rolled out of bed?" he teased.

Miley flipped him the bird and a half smile. "Good to see you, too," she said.

Skipping Miley, Ash moved straight to Nate, setting his pack and shotgun down in the process. "You must be Nate." Ash stuck out his hand.

Nate wiped his hand on a kitchen towel and the two of them shook. "A pleasure."

"I appreciate you sticking around last night."

"It wouldn't have felt right to leave," Nate said.

They stopped shaking hands, Ash took a step back. "I take it nothing happened."

"Not a thing," Luna replied.

"Good. I'm going to try and keep it that way," Ash said.

"What does that mean?" Miley asked.

"First, I'm leaving this here." Ash set his hand on the shotgun. "And I'm taking you both to the range, so you know what it feels like to shoot it."

"Ash!" Luna started to protest.

"It's not up for debate. I should have insisted on this years ago."

"Leaving it here doesn't mean it will get used," she told him.

"Hopefully you'll never have a need to pull it out. But if you do, you'll be happy it's here. And if something happened and I didn't insist, I'd never be able to live with myself."

"So, this is for you." Miley wasn't asking a question.

"Sure," Ash said.

Luna narrowed her brow. "What's the second thing?"

Her brother smirked and said nothing.

"You said, first was the gun . . . What's the second thing?"

It was never good when Ash paused before answering a direct question.

"I'm putting in an alarm system."

"Good idea," Nate said from the side.

"Thanks," Ash said.

"An alarm system?" Luna asked.

"Yup."

"You mean, door alarms, windows . . . motion detectors?"

"All the above. We can hit the hardware stores and get all the things we need."

"We?" Luna asked. "I have to deal with this stolen car thing."

"Fine, me." Ash wasn't fazed. "It's a wireless system so it's just a matter of getting everything mounted and programmed in."

"It's a big house. That's going to cost a fortune."

"You're worth it," Ash said with a grin.

"Are there cameras in this system you're suggesting?" Miley asked.

"Yup. One for the doorbell, two more for the side and back doors."

"A motion one for someone coming up the drive," Nate suggested.

"Good point. With automatic lights when they're tripped at night," Ash said.

"Glass breakage detectors."

Luna looked at Miley while Nate and Ash went on about securing the fort.

"Voice controlled. We need to set up some lights that the system can access inside the house," Ash said. "I should write all this down."

As he moved around Luna to dig into the junk drawer, she protested. "Who sees what's on the cameras?"

"Those of us who have access to the system."

"So, you?" Miley asked.

"Yeah. And both of you. It's probably a good idea to give Harper access."

Luna shook her head. "Why? So she can be annoyed every time the wind blows and the trees set off the alarms?"

"She can put it on silent."

"But that means you can see anyone who is coming and going from the house," Luna said.

"Essentially."

Miley tisked. "Have you heard of privacy?"

"This isn't about spying on *you*," Ash directed his statement to Miley. "It's about being aware when something shitty goes down. It's about knowing if someone broke into your house before you walk into a crime in progress."

"No cameras inside," Luna said.

"There should be—"

"None. Outside cameras, front doorbell . . . that makes sense. But no spying on the inside."

"It's not spying," Ash protested.

"And if I walk down here in my underwear, do you want to accidentally see that?"

Ash cringed. "Fine. Outside cameras only."

Luna knew her brother. This was a protective bone she wasn't going to shake loose. She knew she needed to compromise on a few things. "This all sounds really expensive. Need I remind you that I'm out a car and if it's not found and I have to buy a new one—"

"I'm not asking for you to pay for anything," Ash said.

"But—"

"I got this, Luna. You take care of everything else around here. It's the least I can do."

That wasn't how she saw it.

"Need a hand setting it all up?" Nate asked.

All eyes turned to him.

"That would be great," Ash said.

"You've already done too much," Luna said. "I'm sure you have better things to do."

Nate waved a couple of fingers in her direction. "I did have a meeting I was going to today, but that was canceled."

"Smart-ass."

"I take it that meeting was with you," Ash said, catching on.

Nate nodded. "I just need to go home, shower, change my clothes. It's probably a lot easier to transport all of this in a car instead of a police motorcycle."

Ash looked Nate up and down. "Are those my clothes?"

"Yeah, hope it's okay."

"No problem."

"Ah . . . hello?" Luna waved a hand in front of both men. "I hate to break up this 'bro' moment, but we can't ask Nate to do any more than he already has," she said to her brother.

Ash lifted a hand, palm up, in Nate's direction. "We didn't ask, he volunteered."

"I set up sting operations before we brought down the perps. I might know a thing or two about camera placement," Nate told her.

"See. How do you put a price tag on that kind of experience?" Ash asked.

"Price tag? We're not paying him." Luna turned to Nate. "I'm not paying you."

Nate pointed at Ash. "He said something about pay. I'll work for pizza and a beer."

She wasn't buying it. "This from the gourmet cook."

"You're a gourmet cook?" Ash turned to Nate and asked.

Nate lifted a hand, gave it a tilt back and forth. "Maybe a little."

"They aren't listening to you, Luna," Miley pointed out. "Not that your brother ever listens once he sets his mind on something."

"That's not true," Ash defended himself.

"High school prom," Miley challenged.

Ash conceded if ever so slightly. "That guy was a dick."

"I haven't heard the 'dick from high school' story," Nate teased.

Ash opened his mouth.

Luna shushed him with a hand in his face. "No." She turned to Nate. "You don't have to do this."

"The sooner things around here normalize, the sooner you get back to work . . . the sooner I can get back to work. Think of this as a selfish act."

She kept staring. What could Nate possibly be getting out of this?

"Give it up, Luna." Miley dragged herself out of the chair. "I'm gonna shower. I'll be ready to take you to the rental place after that."

Luna hated to depend on anyone, yet here she was looking at all the people she needed to get though the next twenty-four hours. She lifted both hands in the air. "Fine. I'll call my insurance company and Officer Kempski. You guys do whatever"—she waved between them—"you need to do."

Ash acted as if he were going to pat her on the back.

She stopped him with one dirty look. "Don't even think about it."

Ash stifled a smile and stopped his hand midair.

CHAPTER ELEVEN

A shower and change of clothes . . . his clothes, had Nate feeling alive after a restless night.

When he returned to Luna's house to pick up Ash and proceed to the hardware store, Luna and Miley were already gone.

As Nate pushed the bright orange cart around the massive store, Ash tossed in box after box filled with everything one would need to alarm a small village.

"I've been looking for an excuse to do this ever since Nana died," Ash said as he added two more boxes of window breaking sensors to the five he already had in the cart.

"Is the neighborhood that bad?" What Nate had seen of it, it seemed upscale and pretty void of criminal activity.

"No. The neighborhood is fine. Twenty years ago, there were some sketchy parts. It was great when I wanted to find trouble as a teenager. But eventually that element was priced out and the people who bought up the area turned it around."

"Did you?" Nate asked. "Find trouble?"

Ash shrugged. "More than I care to admit."

Nate had questions, but he kept them to himself. Stories of a misspent youth required beer. "If the neighborhood is decent, why have you wanted to alarm the place for years?"

"Luna and Miley. They can call me sexist, I don't care. I see the aftermath of home invasions. What people go through when they come home to a house that's been ransacked. Alarms and dogs deter criminals. Not black cats."

"Looking out for your sister is admirable."

Ash pulled an outdoor camera with a sensor light off the shelf and read the back of the box. "She fights me most of the time."

Nate laughed. "She does seem strong-willed."

Ash laughed. "How long have you known my sister?"

"We met last week."

Ash stopped reading and looked up. "You're kidding."

"Nope."

"Then why?"

Nate picked up another camera, this one had brighter lights than the one Ash held.

"What do you mean?"

"Why are you doing all this? Why stay last night, why pick her up from the airport?" Ash asked.

"I was on the phone with her when she realized her car wasn't there. I'd have felt like a real piece of shit if I'd just said, 'That sucks, talk to you later.'" Nate handed the box in his hands to Ash. "More lumens."

Ash still stared. "No ulterior motives?"

Nate hesitated for a nanosecond. "No." He shook his head. "No. I don't get romantically involved with people I work with, if that's what you're asking."

"Huh."

"I have a sister," Nate told him. "Your concerns last night aligned with mine. Which is why I stayed. And this." He indicated the cart filled with supplies. "I like doing this kind of stuff. Your sister and Miley seem like good people. Why not help out?"

Ash nodded a few times and went back to reading boxes. "You don't work with Miley," he said.

True, but Nate didn't have the slightest tingle when he looked at Miley . . . Luna on the other hand.

Right as that thought popped in his head, Nate pushed it back.

"I think Miley would be a full-time job."

Ash busted out laughing. "You nailed that. That woman never lets you live anything down."

"Like the shitty prom date?"

Ash tossed the box into the basket and grabbed three more. "If you know the guy is a player, you don't let your sister learn the hard way."

"Sometimes that's the only way we learn," Nate said.

"Not Luna. She can be stubborn, but she's hella observant and figures out the consequences long before she does something to reap them. Most of the time anyway."

Nate considered the conversation about Landon and understood what Ash alluded to.

"But not Mr. Prom?" Nate asked.

"That's the problem with attraction. It short-circuits your brain into seeing things that aren't there," Ash muttered.

"I thought that was whiskey."

"That, too." He laughed. "But Luna's much better now. She spots the bullshitters and doesn't even bother with a first date. And she overanalyzes everything."

"That," Nate said, "I already know about your sister."

"I'd rather her overanalyze men to be safe than think we're all great."

"You sound like a skeptical father," Nate said.

Ash pulled the cart down the aisle. "Someone has to do the job."

~

Kempski had nothing.

The local police had nothing.

And Luna was screwed.

She'd called her insurance representative and told him what had happened. He was currently in the process of obtaining the police record and making sure Luna was clear to move forward with renting a car.

Luna and Miley decided a trip to Crystal and Clover was in order.

“The sage worked for the holey roof,” Miley reminded Luna.

Luna couldn’t argue that. The insurance guy confirmed what Harper had relayed and added that Luna was clear to move forward with the repairs.

The door to the shop chimed when they passed through.

Brianna was behind the counter talking with a customer. She glanced up and waved.

“Hi,” Luna said, smiling.

The scent of incense and candles instantly brought Luna’s hyper nerves to a simmer.

“Do we even know what we’re looking for?” Miley asked while she picked up a round pink crystal.

“Something to bring my car back would be nice.”

“If it were only that simple.” Miley put the crystal down and picked up another one, this time yellow.

Luna waited while Brianna finished with the woman at the register.

“Back so soon?” Brianna said.

Luna rolled her eyes. “My car was stolen,” she said, jumping right to the point.

“Damn.”

“I used other four-letter words. I wonder if there is anything in here that can call it back. Or at least stop my current bad luck streak.”

Brianna pointed to where Miley stood looking at the multitude of crystals. “Are you looking for crystal energy?”

“I’m looking for whatever will work. I saged my attic space like Jorden suggested and surprise, surprise . . . the insurance company is going to cover the cost of my new roof.”

“That doesn’t sound like bad luck to me.”

Luna couldn’t argue with that.

“I don’t like the weekly surprises.”

“What you need is a reading. That way you can anticipate and be ready for stuff when it comes.”

Luna liked the sound of that. “Do you do readings?”

"Kinda, but it's Jorden you want. She's in the back, let me go get her."

Luna joined Miley when Brianna left. "A reading?" Miley said, her voice low.

"It can't hurt."

"Not unless Jorden tells you to put the rent money on the fifth horse in the sixth race."

They both laughed.

"Hi, ladies." Jorden walked up with a smile. "Brianna said your car was stolen."

"Yup. At the airport," Luna reported.

"Ouch." Jorden narrowed her eyes. "Something else is going on."

"What do you mean?"

"Step into my parlor," Jorden teased and turned to Brianna. "Show Miley some personal protection crystal options."

"Do I need protection?" Miley laughed.

"It won't hurt," Jorden said.

Luna glanced over her shoulder and caught Miley's *what the fuck* face.

A small room, not much bigger than an oversize closet, was dimly lit with a desk in the center. The walls were covered in images showing the seven chakras and all their colors and symbols. There was a lotus flower tapestry, and a multitude of symbols Luna was completely clueless about.

A radio softly played music she'd expect in a spa. Soothing and soft . . . relaxing.

Once Jorden closed the door behind her, the room felt like a cocoon of silence. No windows, no ambient noise.

"Have a seat."

Luna kept looking around the room. "I've never had a reading," she admitted.

"That's surprising. You seem intuitive. Like reading someone else's character comes easy to you."

Luna turned her focus to Jorden. "It does."

"Turning that lens inward is difficult."

Luna nodded.

Jorden lit a candle and removed three decks of what Luna assumed were tarot.

"How long have you been doing this?"

"Since I was eleven. My aunt taught me. Or more accurately, showed me how to harness my sensitivity."

Luna had questions.

She always had questions.

Jorden smiled. "We'll talk about me later. Let's talk about you."

Now she had more questions. The most pressing was, Did Jorden read minds? But Luna stayed silent and leaned back in the chair.

Jorden was a small woman. Her slight frame matched her five feet four inches at most. Her porcelain skin didn't appear to have been touched by the sun her entire life. Not an uncommon occurrence for people who'd lived in the Pacific Northwest most of their lives. Her rich brown hair fell past her shoulders, even with the thickness gathered in a band at her neck and draped over one shoulder.

Jorden tapped the decks in front of her, each one different in colors and imagery. "Pick a deck."

Luna immediately picked the one to her right. Dark wisps of contrasting color that felt like the time between autumn and winter. The deck in the middle looked more like spring, all soft greens and flowers. And the one on the left felt as nondescript as the back of a deck of cards in Vegas.

Jorden pushed the other decks aside. "Before we begin you need to know a couple of things. If we pull the death card, it doesn't mean death as in someone is going to die. Don't let that scare you if it comes up. The devil card is another one that has a bad reputation, but both of these can have very positive meanings depending on what is around them."

"Okay."

She picked up a lighter and lit a stick of incense. After a long-winded sigh she asked, "What do you want to know?"

"If my lousy luck is going to change anytime soon. Is my car coming back? Is my insurance company going to give me enough money to replace my car?" So many questions fell out of Luna's mouth. "Can the cards tell me all that?"

Jorden picked up the deck, tapped on the cards twice, and took a deep breath. "Tarot is based on timeless human experiences. Love, conflict, growth, and transformation. These patterns repeat throughout our lives. Tomorrow, like today, is a dance of choices, energy, and possibilities. When we shuffle and draw a card, we're tapping into this moment's vibration. Can it tell the future?" She shrugged. "That's not how I put it. I'm helping someone like you uncover what your deeper self already knows."

"Someone like me?"

"Someone who is already highly intuitive, your subconscious knows things long before your conscious mind catches up. Like sensing a storm. You're not 'predicting rain,' you're seeing the signs that it's coming unless something shifts."

"Which is why the death card doesn't mean death," Luna concluded.

"Exactly. If it did, you'd shift the outcome by avoiding that skydiving trip you planned or see that doctor your subconscious mind has been telling you to see because you know, deep in here"—Jorden placed her hand over her chest—"that something is wrong."

Luna blew out a breath. "Let's do this."

Jorden shuffled the cards several times, tapped on them again, and then set them down. "Cut the deck."

"How many times?"

"However many you want."

Luna cut the deck once, hesitated, and then did it a second time with the stack on her right.

Jorden picked them up and started to rapidly shuffle the cards from one hand to the other. One card popped out of her hands followed by a second. Jorden sat them next to each other and paused. Then she shuffled again until a third card jumped out.

"Seven of swords and nine of swords," Jorden said.

Luna studied the images.

"See how the crow is flying away with several swords?"

"Yeah."

"Someone has done you dirty. Took something that wasn't theirs."

Luna laughed. "My car."

"Probably," Jorden confirmed. "And the nine . . . see how the woman on the bed of swords is dreaming of the crow?"

"Her eyes are open," Luna pointed out. "She's not asleep."

"Did you sleep last night?"

"No."

"In this I see the theft of your car, and here I see that you're anxious about it. All of this is easily interpreted knowing what you've told me and the questions you asked. But then this guy shows up. The knight of pentacles. Someone was or is going to be quick to help."

"My brother drove in this morning and is putting an alarm system in at the house," Luna said.

"Could be." Jorden started shuffling again.

This time when a card jumped out of the deck, Luna read the number and name at the bottom before looking at the picture. "Two of cups?"

"That's interesting." Jorden was smiling.

"What?"

"The twos are about making choices. And the cups are about connection, love . . . could be family."

"Then the knight *is* my brother."

"Not necessarily. The two of cups is about a new choice, something that has or will enter your life. A new partnership." Jorden picked up the knight card and the cup card and studied them.

The image of Nate walking around her kitchen that morning in nothing but a pair of gray sweatpants and a crooked smile circled above Luna's head, much like the crow in the nine card. "It could be—"

Jorden lifted a hand. "Don't tell me."

The next two cards were the moon and the five of cups.

Luna smiled at the moon until she saw Jorden's face.

"There is a period of calm and in that you're going to be reminded of old pain, regret. Someone you lost is going to resurface, either in your memories or in person."

None of this was feeling good.

"Whatever is going to happen, the only way out of it is through."

And then the card Luna least wanted to see came immediately followed by another.

"The death card," she muttered.

Only Jorden was smiling. "This is the death of the old pain. And this . . ." She tapped the ace of cups. "This is a new beginning. You can put whatever all this old shit is aside. But the old pain has to be addressed first."

Jorden sat back and met Luna's gaze. "You're worried," she said.

"None of this sounds easy."

"Transformation is seldom easy. A caterpillar turning into a butterfly is bound to feel pain. But imagine being a bug that is easy to step on suddenly being liberated to fly. The pain is worth it."

Luna moaned. "So right now, I'm the caterpillar."

Jorden winced. "Do you feel like one?"

"I don't know."

"Your questions were about your lousy luck, will you get your car back, will the insurance company pay. If there was a simple yes or no to that, what do you think the cards suggested?"

Luna hated that she knew the answer. "I'm not getting shit back."

"And did you think that was the case before you walked in today?"

Luna leaned her head on the back of the chair in defeat. "Yes. Statistically the car is already toast. Insurance companies are notorious for not paying for what the car is worth to replace."

"The subconscious mind knew these answers. The cards just shed light on them." She paused. "Now . . . who is he?"

"Who is who?"

"The person who wasn't your brother that you thought of."

Luna lifted her head. "Nate."

Those damn gray sweatpants.

"A lover?"

"What? No! He's just . . . We just started working together."

"Just work?"

Luna didn't know Jorden enough to read her, but the smirk definitely gave off the *I don't believe you* vibe.

"It's not what you think. I was talking to him on the phone, about work, when I discovered my car had been jacked. He came to the airport and picked me up."

"That's it?"

"Well . . . no, he—" Dammit, Luna couldn't say what had happened the night before without looking at the knight card face up on the desk. "My brother suggested that the car thieves might come by the house. The car has my address in the GPS, phone numbers. Nate stayed the night. On the couch," she said quickly. "He's a private investigator. Armed, PI."

"Is Nate single?"

"Yes."

"Attractive?"

Gray sweatpants!

"Yes. But no. I'm not . . . we're not. There's no way anything can evolve."

"You sure about that?"

Luna narrowed her eyes. "Are you a psychic or therapist?"

"I'd make more money as a therapist," Jorden said. "Listen, I'm not saying Nate is your knight. You're the one that thought of him. All of this turmoil . . ." She patted the first few cards. "And then this calm followed by even more is going to be worth it. My advice to you would be to be patient with yourself. Trust your intuition but don't be afraid of a shift in your reality." She lifted the death card. "Something has to die before it's reborn. Like flowers in the winter. Right now is your winter. Spring will be here before you know it."

Miley was huddled over a book talking to Brianna when Luna and Jorden walked out of the room.

Miley smiled. "You're getting your car back?"

"No."

"Then why are you smiling?"

"Because I'm turning into a butterfly."

Luna glanced at Jorden and they both started to laugh.

CHAPTER TWELVE

It was a little after one when Luna and Miley returned to the house. This time in separate cars.

What was left of a take-out pizza sat in a cardboard box on the kitchen table. In addition to the pizza box there was a stack of unopened boxes that held all the equipment Ash had threatened to buy. But it was the opened boxes that took up most of the room. It was as if the men had ripped through them, pulled out all the packaging to grab what they needed, and then tossed the trash to the floor.

"Damn," Miley said when she saw the mess.

"My brother was never great at keeping his room clean."

"You should see what a trauma bay looks like after we've taken the patient to surgery," Miley said. "At least here there isn't any blood."

"Yuck."

"I'll grab a trash bag from the garage."

Luna found Ash and Nate in the back of the house. Nate was on a ladder, and Ash stood below with his phone in his hand, looking at the screen.

"You sure we don't want this to cover the entire backyard?" Ash asked Nate.

"If you do that it will go off with every gust of wind and be ignored. At this angle only a person or an animal will trip the sensor and turn on the light."

Luna stepped out, careful not to bump into the ladder. "How's it going?"

Ash glanced at her, then back to his phone. "Slow, but we're getting there."

Nate had changed out of the sweatpants and into a pair of jeans. Something she shouldn't have noticed.

"Any news about your car?" Nate asked.

"Kempski hasn't called."

"Sorry."

Luna shrugged and moved to stand by her brother.

On the screen of his phone, she saw the both of them through the eye of the lens.

"Right there," Ash said.

Nate stepped off the ladder and joined them. "That's good."

Ash looked around them. "I don't know. I still think we need another one with a wider angle looking down at the house. Maybe on the fence?"

"We can, but I'm telling you it will go off so often it would rival the spam robocalls we all ignore. Some of that's going to happen anyway. You'll be adjusting the settings for a while to reduce the false alarms," Nate insisted.

"This is connected to an alarm?" Luna asked.

"The outdoor cameras will alert you when there is movement. If a door opens or a window is breached when the alarm is set, an alarm will go off."

Luna had seen enough movies to understand the basics of home security systems.

"What did you use with the Feds to obtain better coverage?"

"Nothing you're going to find at Home Depot," Nate said.

"How about some James Bond laser beam action?" Luna teased.

"I like that idea," Ash said quickly.

With a roll of her eyes, Luna turned to walk back into the house to let the man-bonding continue. "Have fun."

Back in the kitchen she helped Miley break down boxes and get rid of the trash.

"Your brother is out of control. There must be enough stuff here to protect the *Mona Lisa* at the Louvre."

"Ash takes sheltering his own very seriously." And it was easy to guess why.

"But all this?" Miley lifted the garbage bag that was quickly filling up.

"Do you want to lay a bet that he goes back for more?" Luna asked.

Miley shook her head. "I'd lose."

After the last empty box was broken down and shoved in a bag, Ash walked in and grabbed two more boxes. "I would have cleaned that up."

"We got it."

Ash smiled and left.

"I should call Harper, let her know Ash is here."

"I'll make a list and get to the grocery store. We can't live on pizza," Miley said.

Luna headed up to her room while everyone else stayed busy.

She liked this. The way everyone in the house took part in keeping things moving. And not because they had to but because they wanted to.

Luna couldn't help but wonder if this was the calm Jorden hinted at.

And if it was, when should she expect the storm?

~

Nate believed in protecting his family, but Ash took it to a whole new level.

They were currently modifying a door sensor to work on a bug screen. That way Luna and Miley could set the alarm when they were home even with a window opened. There weren't many summer nights in Seattle that were hot enough to leave a window open all night, but when they happened, everyone liked taking advantage of it.

"Ash?" Luna yelled from downstairs.

"Yeah?"

"Harper is here."

"Go on ahead, I'll finish these up," Nate offered.

Ash took him up on his offer, leaving Nate alone in Luna's bedroom.

He put in the final screw on the screen he'd been working on before moving to the last one. Upstairs windows were less likely to be breached by an intruder, but apparently Ash had responded to a call where a woman was assaulted by someone who had climbed up a tree, onto the roof, and into the bedroom. Then he waited for his victim. The alarm never went off. Ash had gone on to spell out the details, facts that churned Nate's stomach. After that he was completely on board with the second-story window sensors.

Nate did enjoy the work, but it was nice to see the end of the project.

He collected the tools but didn't have enough hands to take the trash with him in one trip. Taking a final look at Luna's personal space gave him a sense of calm. No one was getting in that house without alerting the people inside.

In the hall, sitting on top of the stairs, Midnight regarded him with a side-eye and a meow. "Where have you been all day?" he asked the cat.

With a whip of the tail, the cat led the way downstairs and into the kitchen, where all the voices were coming from.

"All done," he announced.

"You have to be tired," Luna said.

He was more hungry than tired. And the smell coming from the oven had his stomach rumbling.

"I'm good," he said.

"Who are you?" Harper asked.

"Oh, sorry. Harper, this is Nate."

She hesitated. "*Mr. Venti*, Nate?"

He fixed his gaze on Luna, who tried not to smile.

"Did you tell everyone about the coffee?" Nate asked Luna.

"She was the one I was picking up coffee for. Harper works with an attorney in the building," Luna told him.

"What's the coffee all about?" Ash asked.

"It was nothing," Luna said before quickly changing the subject. "Where is Jerry?"

"He has a new job and is putting in long hours trying to make a good impression."

"What happened to his old job?" Ash asked.

"It was a start-up that didn't start," Miley reported dryly.

"He's done that a couple of times now, hasn't he?" Ash opened the fridge and removed a longneck beer. He looked at Nate and offered it with a nod.

"Sure." He needed to counter the energy drinks with something or he'd be up all night. "Who is Jerry?"

"My husband," Harper said.

"Jerry is allergic to manual labor," Ash told Nate. "He probably heard there was a project going on and chose to work late because of it."

"Oh, shush," Harper said.

Luna glanced at Nate. "Every family has their drama."

"So, Nate . . . how is it you've known Luna for what, a week now? And you got roped into a full day of labor?"

"Day and night. He slept over to ward off any bad guys that might have come by," Miley said.

"You stayed the night?" Harper sounded shocked.

"It wasn't a big deal," Nate said.

Luna moved past her siblings and toward the oven. "Can we take this in the dining room? I want to eat while it's hot."

With Luna's request everyone grabbed something from the kitchen island and hauled it to the other room.

"Nate, can you grab the wine?" Luna asked.

"Sure."

Luna and Miley had made a baked ziti, and it smelled delicious.

Food was passed around the table, and the conversation never stopped.

Across from Nate, Harper kept the questions coming. "Luna said you worked with the FBI."

"It sounds more glamorous than it was."

"Investigating fraud is long and tedious work," Luna said.

"Still . . . the FBI, that had to have some perks."

"Sure . . ." Nate passed the garlic bread to Ash, who sat at the head of the table. "Delays in pay when Congress shut down. Long hours on salary without compensation. Understaffing. It had a ton of perks."

"You didn't like it?" Ash asked.

"It taught me a lot. Ultimately it was a stepping stone. Like being a beat cop."

While Ash and Nate had worked, Nate learned a little bit about Luna's brother's ambitions. And working the streets wasn't his ultimate goal.

"Any movement toward a detective position?" Luna asked her brother.

"I'm going to take the test in the spring."

Harper, Luna, and Miley all spoke at once.

"That's great."

"You'll pass."

"About time."

The last one was from Miley, but it was said with a smirk and a smile.

"Love your vote of confidence, Miles."

"Miles?" Nate asked.

"Miles of trouble!"

"And don't you forget it," she said, shaking a finger in his general direction.

"What's up with this?" Ash pointed to the beaded bracelets on Miley's wrist.

Luna lifted her arm and revealed similar bracelets on her wrist. "Protection."

"Excuse me?"

"Crystal energy."

Nate tried not to laugh and failed. "I guess with a name like Luna I should have guessed that would be something you're into."

Luna picked up her glass of wine. "First of all, I didn't pick my name, that was Nana. And second, you can laugh all you want but before the insurance adjuster came to look at the roof, I saged the entire attic, and my insurance is going to cover the cost."

"That's completely coincidental," Ash said.

"I don't know, Jorden is pretty convincing."

"Who is Jorden?" Harper asked.

"The lady who owns the crystal shop," Miley said. "She did a tarot reading on Luna today."

Ash laughed.

"What did this woman tell you?" Nate asked, doing his best to act like he was genuinely interested. In reality he wanted to see just how into the cosmos his new business colleague was.

Luna opened her mouth and then stopped whatever she was going to say. Her eyes traveled up and down his torso and settled on his eyes. "Nothing that would make sense to you."

"I don't know. I'm open minded." And if he was reading Luna right, she was hiding something.

"Did she tell you that for two hundred dollars she'd pick the winning lottery numbers?"

Luna pulled her eyes away from Nate's and scolded her brother. "Don't be an ass."

"I'm serious," Ash laughed.

"She told me to expect some turmoil and that my past was coming back to haunt me. But that it would all be worth it in the end," Luna told him in a rush.

Ash stopped laughing.

"In this house, there's always something around haunting you," Harper said in a sobering voice.

Nate watched as something unspoken passed between Luna and Ash.

"She also said that Luna wasn't getting her car back," Miley said.

"I could have told you that." Ash picked up his beer.

Tension that wasn't there a moment before started to thicken.

"Do you really think this house is haunted?" Nate asked Harper in an effort to remove the stiffness that fell on Luna's face.

"I don't think it, I know it."

Luna picked up her fork and looked away from her brother. "It's an old house, it makes noises," Luna said, dismissing the subject.

"Wood settling and windows letting in tiny squeaks of air when the wind blows is one thing. Pots and pans pulling themselves out of the kitchen drawers and banging on the floor was another."

Nate turned his attention to Luna's sister. "What are you talking about?"

Harper rested her fork filled with food on her plate. "We were living here after Luna's dad bailed. It was late at night when noise from the kitchen woke Mom up. She thought one of us was down there playing drums on the pots and pans, only when she came down to yell at us, none of us were there. We were all upstairs sleeping. Every pot and pan sat in the middle of the kitchen floor."

"You can't take Mom's word for anything," Luna protested. "She drank . . . a lot," she told Nate.

"Nana said it happened several times."

Nate felt a slight chill down his spine. "Was it always when you guys were here?" he asked.

"Not always. But when it did happen, Nana said it was guaranteed that one or all of us would show up at her door. Tell him, Ash. It happened when you were living here. You heard it."

Nate looked at Ash.

"If you're in this house long enough, you'll see things you can't explain," he said.

"Whatever might have been here has left with Nana. I haven't seen anything I can't explain away," Luna said.

Nate turned to Miley. "You live here . . . what have you noticed?"

"Nothing like pots and pans flying around."

Nate leaned forward. "But you have seen something."

"More like feel," Miley said. "Like when someone is watching you, but no one is there."

The hair on Nate's neck stood up.

The fact that everyone, with the exception of Luna, had expressions of complete sobriety and conviction said they believed what they had seen.

"Now that the place is wired up like Fort Knox, we're bound to capture something on a camera if there's anything to see," Luna said.

For a moment, everyone ate silently.

Then Harper said, "Maybe sage in the attic isn't a bad idea. It will stop the old woman from walking around up there."

From that point Ash and Harper talked about their attempts at catching the woman in the attic when they were kids. Some of it sounded a lot like what kids imagined once they got their hands on a Ouija board. As they went on, Luna sat back and shook her head.

And Nate watched Luna as she silently played with the beads on her wrist.

Dinner finished with laughter and friendly banter. The tension of flying pots and pans seemingly forgotten.

After what felt like a week, Nate needed to say his goodbyes.

Ash thanked him once again for all his help and hoped he'd see him again the next time he was in town.

"I might see you in the office," Harper said.

Both thanked him for being there before Luna walked him out.

"I know I've said this a dozen times, but thank you."

"Your family is very entertaining."

"That's putting it mildly. You would have loved Nana. She was the true storyteller."

"It sounds like she had a lot of stories to tell," Nate said.

"She did."

Nate stopped at his car. "Do you think you'll have time to put some work in before Friday to go over a few things?"

"Yes. I have a honey-do list for my brother that will keep him busy so I can work while he's here."

"Good call."

He opened the car door, the light from inside illuminated the night. "Something you said earlier I meant to ask you about."

"Yeah?"

"You said your grandmother named you. How did that happen?"

"The short version?" Luna asked.

"I do need to get home tonight," he chuckled.

"Nana was at the hospital when I was born. My dad didn't make it, and according to Nana, Mom was so pissed that she let Nana name me to get even with my dad. Dad and Nana didn't get along."

"You were named out of spite? That sounds petty with some lifelong consequences."

"That's the way things rolled in my life."

Nate couldn't tell if she was resigned to that turmoil or trying to hide any residual pain from it. "Why 'Luna'?"

She looked at the sky. "I was born on a full moon. The nurses were so busy they barely caught me coming out. Nana decided on Luna. She told me later that she really thought my mom would veto the name. She didn't."

"How do you feel about it?"

"My name?" she asked.

"Yeah."

"I was teased as a kid. Moonbeam, moon child . . . all the unoriginal things kids cast shade on. No one bats an eye at it now. Or if they do, they don't tell me."

Nate moved around the door and tossed his jacket inside. "For what it's worth, I like it." Not that his opinion mattered one way or another.

"Thanks . . . I think."

Their eyes held for a brief moment before Luna broke it off. "I'll see you Friday."

"If you need anything beforehand, you have my number."

With that Nate slid behind the wheel and closed the car door.

Luna moved to stand by the back door where the solar powered light and camera clicked on with her movement.

On his drive home, the clouds parted enough to show the star filled sky and the moon that wasn't quite full. Nate knew he'd never look at the moon the same again.

CHAPTER THIRTEEN

Everything seemed to be in a holding pattern.

The roofer was working the house into his schedule, so that hadn't started. And with winter completely set in, there was no telling if Luna would have plastic whipping around on the roof until spring.

There was zero movement on the car, something Luna had given up on. Ash was right, the car was long gone, or unrecognizable if it was ever recovered.

Luna had started a search on the least stolen cars out there. The ones with decent gas mileage or a hybrid that wasn't going to cost her an arm and a leg. A car payment wasn't on her bingo card for the year, but neither was having her car jacked.

"You don't have kids to support, take advantage while you can," Miley had said when they debated buying something new or used.

By the time Friday rolled around, Luna had managed several hours on the Mercier files but still felt less prepared for her meeting with Nate than she'd have liked.

They met at a quiet coffee shop that had a library vibe complete with books and people spread out reading.

Luna set up with her laptop in the far corner with a clear view of the door while she waited for Nate.

He pushed through the door two minutes early and immediately snagged her gaze. His smile was quick, familiar.

She gave a little wave.

He shrugged out of his coat on his way to her table. "I forgot how much it rains here," he told her as he set his bag on one of the empty chairs at the table.

"You'll remember how much it's worth it in the spring." There was nothing quite like looking out over the lakes and bays that surrounded Seattle with the lush green landscape framing the scene. And then there was Mount Rainier. Her beauty unmatched as far as Luna saw it.

He looked at the table and pointed toward the baristas. "What are you drinking?"

"Large cappuccino with milk from a cow."

Nate turned and made his way to the counter.

He was wearing jeans. The kind that hugged his backside and made it look . . . "Stop it," Luna scolded herself out loud.

Realizing the man had a nice ass wasn't a crime.

Pining over it, at least in her world, was.

Good thing he isn't wearing gray sweatpants, she mused.

Luna grinned at the memory and pulled up the BOHO files.

Nate returned with their coffee and took a seat at her side. "Any word on your car?" he asked.

"What do you think?" she asked.

"Sorry."

"It's okay. I'm trying to talk myself into something new and not used to replace it."

"Are you opposed to something new?"

"There's the depreciation the minute you take it off the lot," she said. "But then you have the full warranty and know exactly what the car has been through if you've had it since mile one. Not to mention all the new bells and whistles that keep the car from being stolen." She paused. "I should have put an AirTag in my old car. Why do we only think of these things after there's a problem?"

Nate stared at her after a short pause. "Does your mind run like this all the time?"

"It's a lot to think about. I'm going to have a car payment either way, but for how much and for how long?"

"If there's anyone that can answer that, it would be the forensic accountant."

Luna moved the cursor around on her computer to bring up the files she wanted to go over. "I hate making these decisions. I don't want to screw it up."

"Screw up with the kind of car to buy?"

"Less about the type of car, and more about the finance of it. You'd think I'd be used to it by now but I second guess myself all the time. I think Ash inherited all the 'make a decision and move on' genes in the family."

Nate picked up his case and removed his laptop. "Can I ask you something personal?"

Oh shit.

When she didn't answer, Nate asked anyway.

"I've seen your portfolio. I've heard about your reputation and seen your list of clients, at least those who've gone public with it."

"Okay." Everything he spoke of was easily found on the internet.

"People in your area of expertise make decent money. More than decent money."

"Yeah . . ."

He paused, looked at her. "Do you gamble?"

"What? No!"

"Have a habit that costs a lot of money?"

"What are you getting at?" she asked.

Nate regarded her with a tilt of his head. "You're single, in your early thirties, without kids. You live in a house you don't have a mortgage on with a roommate. Buy the car. Buy the newest, the greatest, the one that makes you smile every time you get behind the wheel. You have money. What are you saving it all for?"

She blinked.

Twice.

"Did you investigate me?"

"Deductive conclusion. Am I wrong?"

She didn't want to answer that. "I have to think about retirement."

Nate laughed.

"People that don't plan for their future end up on the street after one emergency," she argued with his laugh.

"Do you have an emergency fund?" he asked.

"Yes."

"A 401(k) with a cap on what you can put into it every year?"

"Yes."

"Stocks and bonds accruing compound interest?"

She let her silence be her answer.

"You're not going to screw up your future by buying a car you can afford. I do suggest you avoid a Ferrari."

The thought of a Ferrari brought Luna back to earth. "I'm making too much out of this."

"I'm sure you have your reasons, but yes. From where I'm sitting, you're spinning without need."

He was right.

Luna was so worried she'd make the wrong decision that she'd avoid making it. A pattern in her life that she repeated constantly.

"Thanks," she said under her breath.

Nate sat his hand over hers for the briefest of moments. "Let's chat about our client's mismanagement of money. I looked at BOHO INC. Something isn't adding up."

Luna slid her hand into her lap and launched into what she'd learned.

Luna had been with Alliance Insurance company ever since she'd moved into the house on Queen Anne Hill. Other than sending the company a check every year and every six months for her car, Luna didn't have a need to know the man that represented the company.

She'd met Greg Filmore once, shortly after she moved in.

He was a round man, thinning hair, somewhere between fifty and sixty. He stared at her from across his desk. The office couldn't be more than sixty-five degrees, yet he was dabbing a handkerchief against his face to mop up the sweat beading on his forehead.

Luna wouldn't need Jorden and her tarot cards to suggest the man wasn't in good health. He reminded her of many of the CPAs she met in her career right around April fifteenth. Stressed, overworked, and one fried meal away from a heart attack.

"I spoke with Officer Kempski with the airport police earlier this week," Greg started. "As far as they're concerned, the theft of your car is already filed as a cold case."

It had only been two weeks. "My brother said it was cold after forty-eight hours."

"We still have to wait the entire thirty days before Alliance will consider a payout."

"Consider?"

"It's a formality. I'll make sure the company has everything they need on day thirty. The police report, the follow up report from Seattle PD and the airport PD. Sometimes they drag their feet verifying everything, but once they have all that I should have a check for you rather quickly."

"The car was eleven years old, with a depreciation rate of fifteen percent per year—"

"Twenty," Greg interrupted.

"Fifteen to twenty, but the miles on the car were well below average and it had never been in an accident. I would expect Alliance to take that into consideration." Luna came in armed with the industry standards and was ready to instruct Greg to fight for as much money as he could.

"If it were up to me, I'd give you the lower depreciation number. It isn't up to me," he told her. "You also have a two-thousand-dollar deductible, which will be taken out before they send a check."

"Is the rental car coverage included in that?"

"Yes."

It wasn't much, but it was something.

"If I were you, I'd replace your car sooner than later. If your car turns up, you'd likely be able to sell it for more than what Alliance will give you for it."

She'd already concluded that.

"Have the repairs on the roof started yet?" he asked.

She shook her head. "Brian's backed up with his other projects because of weather delays. He has it penciled in to start in a couple of weeks, but according to the weather report, we won't get a break other than a day or two until next month."

"Not surprising."

"How long do we have to get this done?" she asked.

He waved her off. "You're good for up to a year. Just make sure you're doing everything in your power to prevent any internal damage."

"He has tarps covering half of the roof."

Greg patted his brow with the cloth in his hand. "Good. Keep them up there. Your contractor knows the insurance drill better than anyone."

Luna leaned forward and asked the question she really wanted an answer to. "What is all this going to do to my rates next year?"

He hesitated.

Shit. Hesitation was always a bad sign.

"You should be fine."

"Should or will?"

"It depends on what you buy. New cars cost more to insure."

"That I understand. But will I get dinged as if I'd been in an accident?"

Another dab of his forehead.

"If Alliance can't find any fault with you, it won't go up."

"*If*? I left it in a secure lot at the airport, not running with the keys in it in downtown Seattle."

"It's not up to me, Luna. I'll do everything I can to get you as much money as we can from them. I don't want to lose you as a customer."

Now *that* was why he was sweating.

He knew she was going to get shafted one way or another, but he wasn't about to admit it.

She didn't press him more and stood to leave.

"Be sure and call me as soon as you buy something. If you're worried about what the rate is, call me before you purchase and I'll give you a quote."

She shook his hand. "Thank you, Greg."

As soon as she was out of his office, she patted her palm on the wet side of her jacket. She preferred rainwater over sweat on her hands.

Luna pulled out of the parking lot in her rental car and set out to see if Harper was free for lunch.

~

The building where Marcus Peterson's law practice resided was home to several attorneys. Many of which Nate solicited in the weeks before he arrived in Seattle and followed up with after he'd started the Mercier case. Finding clients was easier when you could drop a familiar name that you were currently working with.

Wearing a power suit, one that cost him close to two grand, Nate sat across from Ms. Elenore Prescott, having lunch a couple of blocks from her office. Elenore specialized in corporate mergers. Unlike Marcus, Elenore exclusively used external help when investigating the companies she worked with.

The perfect fit for the business Nate was building.

Several booths were filled with women and men in suits, with very few appearing like they'd wandered in off the street for a quick bite.

"I hope this is okay," Elenore said as they took their seats. "It's literally the only decent business lunch place within walking distance."

"That's surprising, there seemed to be several restaurants in the area."

"Ones that are only open for dinner. So many shut down altogether with the pandemic and have yet to be replaced."

"That sounds like a business opportunity to me," Nate said.

Elenore paused and offered a coy smile. "I like the way you think. If you hear of any investment opportunities, please let me know."

"I will."

Elenore Prescott was the kind of woman who didn't show her age. From her portfolio, Nate knew she was one year shy of sixty, but to look at her, she didn't look a day over forty-five. Her face was absent of age lines either from Botox or simply good genes. From the look of her, Nate assumed she coveted her time with her Pilates instructor, and occasionally her private trainer. He envisioned the car that she drove as a 7 series BMW or something equivalent. A large house in a gated community and maybe even a second home in Florida. She'd been married twice but was now single with two adult children of her own. She was as competent as she was beautiful. She did everything she could to keep her clients from going to trial, but when they did, she kicked ass.

The "kicked ass" came from an article buried in the back of a newspaper Nate had found in a simple Google search.

The waiter arrived before Nate had a chance to pick up the menu.

"Good afternoon, Ms. Prescott."

"Hello, Charles. How are you?"

"I'm well. Can I get you some sparkling water?" he asked.

"Of course."

"And you, sir? Still or sparkling?" Charles asked Nate.

"Still is fine."

Charles left them alone with the promise of returning soon.

"Clearly you come here often," Nate said.

"My offices have been in the same place for fifteen years. My relationship with Charles has lasted longer than my last marriage."

That made Nate laugh. "I hope that's a good thing."

"Have you ever been married?" she asked.

"No."

"Don't. Trust me, it's overrated." She didn't sound bitter so much as resigned to her convictions.

Nate wanted to tell her that some people got it right. Although arguing that fact with a lawyer he wanted to hire him was probably a bad idea.

Elenore made small talk until they ordered and then leaned back and started the interview.

"I work with very high-profile clients. When they decide to merge or break up, I'm involved. There is nothing I loathe more than discovering a company's dirty secrets once contracts are drawn up."

"Do you investigate everyone you work with?" he asked.

"Not all," she told him. "When you've worked in this field as long as I have, you develop a sixth sense. I can count on one hand how many investigations I've worked that didn't find a skeleton or two. Being on top of what my clients are hiding is what keeps me out of court."

"Why hide anything from your attorney?"

"Everyone lies. Most people think they're good at it. If they didn't lie, I wouldn't have a job, and neither would you. I demand honesty with the people I work with, not for. I have to trust you. If you work with me, I'd expect written updates on an agreed upon schedule, and phone calls if you find something that we don't want found in discovery. Attorney client privilege has its perks," she said.

"I worked for the government, I'm familiar with discretion."

"Yes. I've been told that. I called your superior in DC."

Nate felt the muscles in his back tighten. "You spoke with Monique?"

"Yes. Ms. Fields spoke highly of you."

"We worked together for several years." And slept together for two.

"She asked how you're doing. When I told her that I hadn't interviewed you yet, she told me I'd be losing out if I didn't hire you. That you were one of her top investigators and were sorely missed."

"That's kind of her."

Elenore reached for her water. "I asked why you left. She told me personal reasons. But that if you ever chose to return, she'd hire you back."

"I left on good terms, if that's what you're looking for," Nate explained.

"I was looking for dirt."

That didn't surprise him. "Did you find any?"

"No," she said slowly.

Nate smiled but didn't reply.

"How are you enjoying working for yourself and not the government?" she asked.

"Freeing. Billing by the hour and not being glued to a time clock is more efficient and ultimately cost-effective," he said.

"I couldn't agree more. It's one of the reasons I outsource my investigators. You cost me less in the end."

"What are the other reasons?" he asked.

Elenore looked him dead in the eye. "I find that intra-office relationships not only interfere with work, they ultimately have me refilling positions left behind by good employees."

To Nate's credit, he didn't so much as blink.

Was it something Monique said, or how she said it?

Telling Elenore she had nothing to fear would be right up there with a complete confession.

Instead, Nate kept her gaze until she broke it with a knowing smile.

"Is your hourly rate negotiable?" she asked him.

"Is yours?" he countered.

Respect swam in her eyes. "I think you and I will get along very well."

CHAPTER FOURTEEN

"Thanks for meeting me here. I'm tired of the deli and bored with anything I bring from home," Harper said.

"I'm glad I caught you."

"You sound stressed. Is everything okay?"

Harper was always good at reading Luna, and even better at talking her off any ledge she might be teetering on.

"Nothing new. The roof isn't fixed. My car is still missing. The insurance company will pay out the car in the next month, give or take. And by *pay out*, I mean five grand if I'm lucky. Greg pretty much said I should expect my rates to go up even though none of this was my fault. And I need to buy a car. Which should be a fun thing. Right?"

"Right."

"Then why am I stressing out about it?"

"It's a big purchase," Harper said.

"But it's not a house. These things paralyze me. Why?" Luna needed her big sister's advice. The tossing and turning every night since her car was stolen was taking a toll.

"I call it the single tax."

"What's that?" Luna asked.

"When you're married or living with someone who is co-mingling with your finances, there's someone else invested in helping you make the decisions. If you screw up, you both screw up and it's easier to swallow. When it's just you and things go bad, you kick yourself and second guess yourself forever. I see it with the divorced women I deal with every day. It's exhausting."

"I've been divorced for a long time," Luna reminded her.

"I know. You should be better at this by now." Harper laughed.

Luna ran a hand behind her neck, found a sore spot, and lingered to massage it out. "Exactly."

"How did it feel when Ash came up and put in the alarm system without hesitation?"

"What do you mean?" Luna asked.

"If he'd asked you. Or wanted your approval or input, how would that have felt?"

"Like one more thing I don't want to deal with," Luna said.

"And when he didn't do that? When he just did the thing?"

Luna dropped her hand in her lap. "Relieved, I think. The alarm system makes sense. I probably wouldn't have spent the money on it. I offered to help him pay for it, but you know Ash."

"Ash likes to be needed. He'd make someone a good husband one day if he'd let his guard down long enough to go on three dates with the same person."

The waiter arrived with their twenty-dollar salads and left.

Luna placed her napkin in her lap and picked up her fork. "Do you say the same thing about me?"

"No. You'd make a terrible husband."

Luna rolled her eyes. "Ha. Ha."

"It's different for women. Especially us Cannings. Even Nana, for all her independence and bravado, she always had a man around."

"But she didn't depend on them. Not like Mom," Luna said.

"Nana was in love with the idea of being in love, I think she wanted to depend on the men in her life. Someone to lean on. Probably for the same reasons you struggle with making a decision about a car. Mom is not only dependent on a man in her life to validate her, she's co-dependent to a fault. She always finds the guy she thinks she can fix, even if it destroys her."

"Or us," Luna reminded Harper.

They both sat in their own thoughts for a moment.

"Mom makes all the wrong decisions. Nana made 'some' wrong decisions. It's up to us to make the right ones and break the cycle." Harper took a bite of her salad.

"Maybe that's the problem. I'm trying to be perfect, which is an unachievable goal."

Harper finished her bite. "Okay. You don't want to be Mom, so ask yourself 'What would she do?'"

"She'd never be in my—"

"Humor me."

Luna paused. "She'd wait for someone to tell her what to do. Or say fuck it and blow every dollar she had on something she couldn't afford."

"You're too frugal for that. Do you want someone to tell you what to do?" Harper asked.

"No. Not really."

"Okay then. If you want someone to bounce ideas off of, that's what I'm for. Ash . . . Miley. We're not going to let you do something stupid without telling you. Buy the car. You got this. As for the roof . . . it's better than a mortgage. And if it feels like too much, get another roommate."

"You sound like Nate."

"You told Nate about this?" Harper sounded surprised.

"I brought up the stress about the car. He thinks like Ash. Something needs to be done, do it. Within your means . . . but do it." Luna pulled apart a piece of bread.

Harper paused. "I liked him."

"Yeah, he's a decent guy."

When Harper didn't say more, Luna looked up.

"What?"

"He's good-looking," Harper pointed out.

"Oh my God . . . you and Miley. I work with him. No. That's not gonna happen." Her back stiffened and heat rushed to her neck.

"When was the last time you went out on a date?" Harper asked.

"The last time someone asked me who didn't give off the ick factor before the date."

"You didn't answer the question, Luna," Harper argued.

Luna put the bread down. "I get it. I'm glad you and Jerry have found each other. That you have that person to bounce ideas off of, so you don't have to pay the single tax. I find the whole process of dating repulsive. Just when you think you've found someone remotely compatible; they're likely married or in a relationship. By my age they have kids and psycho exes and when they start talking about their kids and exes you know exactly why they're single. If a man pays for a meal on a date, it's a transaction. The more expensive the meal, the more likely they'll ask to come in for a 'nightcap.' Who even uses the term 'nightcap'? And none of them have their financial shit together. *None.* When you ask them about that, they blame it on an ex. You lower your guard, put the dress on, and go through all this effort and for what?" Luna lowered her voice, looked around. "Even if you take them up on the nightcap, they can't find the spot if you drew it on a map. I'm better off with my membership to Adam and Eve with a monthly box subscription with satisfaction guaranteed."

Luna stabbed her salad like it had talked back to her and shoveled it in her mouth.

Her sister stared, jaw slackened.

Luna talked around her food. "Women are the only species on earth that are expected to mate with their number one predator. Did you know that?"

Harper's gaze softened. "Not everyone is Landon."

"No. But the last guy that got past all those things was Landon. And yes, Nate's a good-looking guy, you should see him in gray sweatpants. It's like one of those music pumping thirst traps on TikTok. But all of those things I said before." Luna waved a finger in the air. "One or more of them will play out. So even if . . . *if* I lost my head enough to ignore the fact that we work together and went out with him, that's when the ex, or the kid, or the crushing debt or excessive drinking or abuse starts in, and then it's game over and that working relationship is now gone. There is one thing I do have one hundred percent confidence and control of in my life and it's my work. My reputation. It's what assures me that I'll never be dependent or co-dependent on a man. I will never be our mother."

Harper had stopped eating; all humor had left her eyes.

"I'm sorry," she whispered.

With the tsunami of words out of her system, Luna felt like she'd been punched in the gut. "Me too. I didn't mean to go off on you like that."

Harper shook her head. "It's okay. That's why I'm here. To support you in whatever is best for you. Go buy the car. And if it's the wrong decision, you can blame me."

Luna reached across the table and squeezed Harper's hand. "I love you."

Harper cleared her throat and went back to eating her lunch. "Do you really have a subscription to Adam and Eve?"

Luna thought for sure someone close by laughed. Only nobody was looking their way.

Nate sat in his car, hands on the steering wheel, eyes focused on absolutely nothing in front of him.

Elenore had gotten up to use the restroom when a familiar voice came into focus from the tall booth behind his.

Luna.

Before Nate could look around the partition and say hello, he heard his name and froze.

He heard everything.

While Luna mapped out what dating was like in your thirties, Nate found himself nodding and agreeing. It wasn't common to get to your thirties without children, or a crazy ex, or both. He had to admit that men his age that were single did in fact blame their financial demise on someone else. Cheating in relationships went both ways, but men tended to lie about it where women were up front. And the men they hooked up with didn't care. It was at that point in Luna's monologue that Nate heard the tone in her voice shift.

Pain seeped in and pulled Nate's heart right out of his chest.

Man is the number one predator to a woman. And yet women were expected to ignore that and take a chance. No wonder Luna had pitched in the dating towel. Not only did she understand the facts, but she'd also lived them. From the sounds of it, she'd lived it her entire life. What kind of men did Luna's mother bring into the home? He wanted to ask but didn't think he'd like the answer.

Then when Luna poked holes in the moments she did let her guard down, if even to notice him in sweatpants . . . which he didn't think much of at the time but would certainly use in the future . . . she immediately rushed to the possibility of red flags. That there had to be something wrong with him that would cut him out of being in her life romantically.

Luna was right. They worked together. That was reason enough to avoid anything emotional.

Hadn't Nate told himself exactly that a few times since they'd met?

Yes, yes, he had.

Then why, when he sat there listening and agreeing with so much that she said, did he want to prove her wrong?

Luna wouldn't have to draw him a map. He'd make damn sure he found her spot and others she didn't know she had.

Nate closed his eyes and gripped the wheel.

"What the fuck is wrong with me?" He turned over the engine and shoved the car in reverse with quick, stiff movements. "I need a God damn twelve-step program to stop fantasizing about the women I work with."

~

The entire surface of the dining room table was filled with every car option in her price range.

Luna had looked up what cars were most likely to get stolen, and which ones were off the car thieves' radar.

Several of the top non-stolen cars were things she would never drive. Not on purpose. Gas guzzling sedans. Cars made by manufacturers that hadn't changed the frame in nearly a decade. Then there were the stupid expensive models that were eliminated by price alone.

She decided on an SUV. Not the huge ones that would house a family of six, but something compact. She didn't need to off road the thing, but getting around the Pacific Northwest in the winter sometimes required driving in the snow.

A chime on the alarm system alerted her to a car coming up the drive. Luna didn't bother looking to see who it was since Miley normally came home at this hour.

Lights from a car bled through the windows and within minutes Miley was walking in the mudroom door.

The sound of rain followed her in.

"Hey," Luna greeted her while she repositioned the images of the cars in order of hybrid efficiency.

"What a shit day," Miley replied.

"That bad?"

Luna peeked over her shoulder to see Miley hanging up her raincoat.

"You'd think that the drivers in this state would be better at driving in the rain, but no. One trauma after another . . . all damn day."

Luna looked at the photos and decided crash safety trumps miles per gallon.

"Is this a wine night?" Luna asked.

"You know it."

When Miley didn't walk into the kitchen, Luna glanced at her again.

Miley was stripping her scrubs off and was down to her bra and panties.

"Ohhh, that bad?" Luna had seen her friend do this on several occasions. When too much of the ER came home with her, she did her best to leave it at the door.

"Arterial bleeds are projectile. Even with an extra layer of PPE, it still found its way in."

Luna had known Miley long enough to understand most of the lingo. Personal protective equipment was more than a mask. There was eye protection, covers for your shoes, and surgical gowns that covered your clothing.

Miley shivered as she walked into the kitchen holding her bundle of clothes. She stopped at the table. "What's this?"

"I'm deciding on my new car."

Miley laughed. "Most people just go drive them."

"There's no point in test driving something that doesn't fit in all my boxes."

"Huh . . ."

Luna looked down at her half-naked friend. "Go shower and come back and help me decide."

Miley scurried away as Midnight waltzed in. "Where have you been hiding?"

The cat yawned, as if she'd just woken up, and jumped on a chair.

Luna reached over and gave her a little love and then began moving the photos around for the umpteenth time.

By the time Miley returned from her shower, Luna had a glass of wine poured for her.

"Bless you."

Luna lifted her glass, and they sipped together.

They'd long since made a rule that they didn't drink alone. Luna was cognizant of the slippery slope of that habit, and Miley knew the statistics of substance abuse among health care workers.

"There are leftovers," Luna told her.

"I'm not hungry."

That wasn't a good sign. "Do you want to talk about it?" Luna asked.

Miley shook her head. "Some days hit home more than others."

Luna didn't press. Miley would open up when she was ready. If she opened up at all.

"Tell me about the cars."

Neutral subject, nothing life ending.

"SUVs, mostly hybrids. I thought about a complete EV, but I'm worried that if I got stuck in the snow somewhere it would run out of battery and I'd freeze to death."

"That's very specific. When was the last time you got stuck in the snow?"

"It could happen."

Miley laughed.

"All of these cars are on the list of least likely to get stolen. All of them have superior theft protection and tracking. And the thieves know it."

Miley picked up a picture. "A Buick?" She wrinkled her nose. "Really?"

"It's on the list."

"It's ugly."

"It's safe."

Miley wadded up the piece of paper and tossed it over her shoulder.

"Hey!"

"I'm not letting you buy something my own grandmother wouldn't drive."

As pushy as that sounded, Luna felt her heart swell. This was how a single woman got past the single tax.

There were still eight cars to pick from.

"What is this?" Miley pointed to the number Luna put on the bottom right of the page.

"Miles per gallon."

"You work from home."

"Gas is still expensive," Luna said.

Miley pointed to another number.

"Crash rating."

"Base price?" Miley asked, pointing to the biggest number.

"Yeah."

"With what features?"

"Keyless entry, antitheft, built-in emergency calling."

"Heated seats?" Miley asked.

"And steering wheel. I mean, why not?" It was strange justifying such a luxury. But if she was likely going with a hybrid and on the off chance she was stuck in the snow, she might as well have heated and cooled seats.

"What is this?"

"Customer satisfaction star rating, and below that is customer service at the dealership rating." Luna kept going. "This is the average cost of oil change and service. Tire replacement. This is the approximate cost to insure. It goes up if I hit a luxury package, but not by much. Greg said that since I'm looking at the least likely to be stolen cars, the insurance company gives you a break. Oh . . ." Luna turned to Miley. "And guess what?"

Miley sipped her wine.

"The alarm in the house . . . that will bring my home insurance rate down. Or at least keep it from going up too much after this claim."

"That's great. Did you tell Ash?"

Luna nodded. "Yeah, I texted him earlier. He told me to keep the fact that there is a gun in the house to ourselves. Insurance companies only think of guns as a liability."

"There are plenty of accidental shootings."

"I guess. It feels dishonest," Luna admitted.

Miley looked at her as if she were crazy. "And do you stop by the police department and confess every time you speed so they can fine you?"

Luna paused. "Good point."

"Are you going to test drive all of these?"

"If I have to."

Miley set her wine down and picked up the last three photos of the cars. "Of these three, which one would you least likely want?"

Luna's choice was instant. "This one has the worst crash score."

Miley put the paper aside and picked up another one. "Eliminate one of these."

Luna pointed.

Again, Miley offered three cars. One by one Luna's choices narrowed until there were only three left.

"Start here. But leave your favorite choice for last."

"Why last?"

"Because you don't want to have gone through all this work to only test drive one car. If you start with the one you think you'll love and you do and you buy it, you miss out on this one." She picked up a random photo. "And this one might blow your favorite out of the water."

"What if I don't like any of these?"

"Then you have all these, starting with the top, to consider. My money is on you buying one of these." Miley pointed at the last remaining cars. "Now . . . the most important question."

Luna looked up.

"The color."

~

It had been four days since Nate overheard Luna's conversation, and two weeks since he saw her face to face.

They met in the same coffee shop, at the same table.

Nate arrived early, set up his computer, and waited.

Every day that week, when his thoughts moved to Luna, he recalled the things she'd said to her sister. When he pushed back the painful parts, he was left with words like *thirst trap* and *music pumping*. And when the word *pumping* ran like a ticker tape at the bottom of the breaking news feed, he envisioned a road map of a woman's body—Luna's body—with an *X* marking the right spot.

When Luna passed through the door Nate knew he was seeing her through a different lens.

The first time he'd seen her, she was scowling at him. The day he earned the name Mr. Venti. Then she smirked through the first meeting with Marcus. The corners of her small mouth up ever so slightly, her stare piercing and at the same time challenging. A look he'd seen several times since.

She had soft brown hair, thick with a small amount of curl. Not the kind that came from a styling tool, a fact he knew since he'd seen her hair wet from rain more than he'd seen it dry. She didn't wear a lot of makeup, and her lips were always a rosy shade of pink. She wore heels when she wanted to make an impression, rain boots when she was running errands, and canvas tennis shoes for everything else.

Why her shoes stuck out, Nate had no idea.

He was a full head taller than her, but she wasn't unusually short.

And curves.

Nate liked curves.

All those attributes walked toward him now.

Her shoes clicked as they met the floor with each step.

Nate forced himself to stop staring, and damn near sat on his hands to not offer to help her with her coat.

Colleagues didn't help each other out with their coats.

They didn't spend the night in the other's house the first week they met either, but he ignored that fact now.

"You're early," she said instead of hello.

"So are you. Hello."

Luna put her jacket on the back of a spare chair at their table. "Hi. Twenty-ounce dark roast?" she asked, pointing to the barista.

"I can get it."

"No, no. It's my turn."

"If a man pays for a meal . . . It's a transaction." Her words floated in his head.

"Dark roast is fine."

She smiled and turned away.

She was wearing a pantsuit. Her hair was pulled back, exposing her neck.

Stop! he scolded himself. *Her neck. I'm thinking about her neck!*

Nate shook out of his obsession with what she was wearing, and how she appeared, and focused on the progress report they were delivering to Marcus.

Luna returned to the table and set her purse to the side. "They'll bring our coffee over," she reported.

He smelled lavender.

Luna smelled of lavender.

If Nate could kick himself without being obvious, he would.

"Do you have a meeting today?" he asked.

She looked surprised. "Yes. A pro bono divorce case. How did you know?"

"The shoes give you away."

Luna glanced at the floor, turned an ankle to the side, and shrugged. "That's fair."

"Why pro bono?"

"To keep my finger on the pulse of the regular guy. Most of the people I work with have so much money they haven't gone to the grocery store for themselves since college. Pro bono keeps me grounded."

"That's . . . nice."

She furrowed her brow. "You sound surprised."

"No . . . yeah. I never considered pro bono work."

"Not too many people do. Most just donate to a charity instead of offering free labor," Luna said.

"You can write off charity donations against your taxes. Working for free . . . not so much," he said.

"Which is exactly why the rich write a check. Chances are they don't even do that; their secretaries do."

Nate stared. "I'll have to consider that once my PI business is established."

"Say the word. Harper will have a case on your desk within twenty-four hours. Until then, let's focus on what we're paid to do." Luna reached into her bag and removed her computer.

Mom would like you.

Nate shook his head and cleared his throat.

He needed to shut this down.

Fast.

Long after the coffee was consumed, and the lavender scent of Luna's skin had faded away, Nate sat back in his chair and rested his chin on his hand.

As if they were mirror images, Luna did the same.

"We need to go to Texas," he concluded.

She stared beyond him, lost in her own thoughts. "I need to see the original files. I need direct access. This isn't adding up. It's too easy to doctor what they send in a Dropbox."

"I need to interview the main players. That should help us narrow down what files you should spend your time on," Nate said.

Luna leaned in and brought up her calendar. "This week is out. I have a divorce trial that's been postponed twice that I can't get out of."

"What about flying in a week from Sunday?"

Luna shook her head. "Miley's gone over the weekend on a ski trip, then works Monday and Tuesday. My roofer seems to think the weather will break enough for him to get in and out. Someone needs to be at the house during construction."

Nate waved his hand. "I wouldn't be comfortable leaving either."

"Best I can do is leave on Wednesday. I'd say Tuesday night but there is no guarantee Miley will be home on time. The hospital is notoriously short-staffed and sometimes she's stuck."

"I'll look for early flights on Wednesday, back late Friday or Saturday morning. Unless you think you'll need more time."

"I won't know until I get my hands on the files."

"Refundable tickets it is."

Luna closed her laptop. "I'll send you my information to book. Direct flight, please. I'll book the hotel."

Nate smiled and shut down his computer as well. "Direct flights are the only way to go. Will Marcus have any issues covering this?"

"Nope. We'll get confirmation during Monday's meeting. This won't be the first time I've had to go to the files when the doctored ones were the ones that came to me."

"I find it best that we come in without warning," Nate said.

"I agree."

Luna glanced at her watch. "I've got to go."

"Go. I'll take care of the flight. If you get delayed let me know and I'll take care of the hotel as well." He stood.

Luna tucked her computer away and pushed her chair back. "I'm glad we're on the same page."

Nate could do one better. "I'm glad we're on the same team."

She paused and smiled at him.

"I'll pick you up. Drive us to the airport."

"That's not—"

"Aren't you buying a new car this week?" Nate asked.

"That's the plan."

"Do you really want to park it at the airport?"

Luna literally shivered. "Point taken."

"I'll call Kempski, tell him we have to leave a car there."

"You think that's going to make a difference?" she asked.

"If I was running security, it would."

Luna pushed one arm into her trench coat and fished for the other arm with her free hand.

Nate reached over without a thought and held her coat open for her to put it on.

Once it was, she cleared her throat. "Thanks."

He dropped his hand. He hadn't meant to do that.

They walked out together; the mist that never seemed to lift this time of year hovered around them.

Nate saw her rental car parked on the opposite side of the street.

"I'll see you on Monday, then."

She wanted to say something, Nate saw it on her face.

When she didn't say more, he replied, "Monday."

For the second time in a week, Nate sat behind the wheel of his car kicking himself.

CHAPTER FIFTEEN

With a huge bowl of popcorn in her hands, Miley curled her feet up under her on the couch at the same time Luna grabbed the remote.

Midnight lounged on the carpet in front of the fireplace, basking in the glow of the flames.

"What are you in the mood for?" Luna asked.

"Anything that doesn't include hospitals."

Luna clicked through the thousands of shows the various streaming stations had on offer. "When was the last time we did this?"

"Right before Christmas. We burned through everything Hallmark filmed in the last two years."

She laughed. "Maybe next year we should do a bingo card before we start watching."

"I'm not sure I know what you mean."

Luna paused on an action movie.

Miley shook her head.

Luna kept clicking. "You know, by trope. Hometown hero returns. Heroine returns to take care of sick grandma. The family business needs the elusive daughter to rescue it."

"North Pole needs to find Santa and save Christmas."

"In love with the boss's daughter," Luna added.

"Single mom fired before the holiday." Miley tossed more popcorn in her mouth.

"Stranded in the snow with your ex from high school."

"The gardener is really a prince."

"Did we see that one?" Luna asked.

Miley shook her head. "No, but I like the idea."

Luna reached for the popcorn and kept scrolling. "This one?"

"We saw it."

"I don't remember," Luna said.

"That's because it was dumb and we both fell asleep."

"Maybe we should pick a subject and look from there. Action?"

Miley shook her head. "All this rom-com talk has me craving a Disney ending."

"Why do we do this to ourselves?" Luna asked and at the same time clicked on the romance heading.

"We're hopeless. We want what isn't out there."

"You're not kidding. This divorce case I'm working with Harper on . . . holy cow. This guy was such a scum ball. He had a two-year-old with the wife, and an eighteen-month-old by the mistress. Both boys."

Miley wrinkled her nose. "How did he keep the names straight?"

"That's easy, Russell Junior. Both of them."

"No."

"I can't make that shit up. He has an office here and another in the Bay Area. Two houses but claimed the one with the mistress isn't his."

"That should have been easy to find," Miley said.

"That's public record, but the money that went into the mistress's bank account came from a company she was a 'consultant' for." Luna made air quotes with her fingers.

"His company?"

"It was hard to find, but yeah. It was buried in a shadow company."

"What does that mean for your client?" Miley asked.

"It's a fifty-fifty state, the wife is entitled to half of the San Francisco house," Luna explained.

"Why would she want it?"

"She doesn't. It's leverage for her to get one hundred percent of their home here, plus alimony, child support, and she's asking that he pay for her to go back to college." Luna smiled. "Judges don't like it when you hide assets and lie in court. This guy has money. He's going to have to part with some of it."

"Is this the case you did for free?" Miley asked.

"Yup. When Harper's boss didn't find anything on their initial investigation, he advised the client to settle and deal with moving and living on less. Baby daddy owned his company before they got married and convinced the wife she wouldn't get shit. Harper smelled a rat and called me."

"Does that mean you're going to get paid?"

Luna shrugged. "It should mean that Harper gets a raise."

"Considering Jerry can't keep a job, she needs it," Miley pointed out.

Luna had to agree. "It's a good thing they decided not to have kids. That would be a lot of stress on my sister."

"The term is DINK. Dual income no kids. Emphasis on *dual.* He needs to stop dreaming of making it big with a start-up and get a secure job like everyone else."

By now Luna had stopped scrolling through their movie options. "It sounds like you and Ash have been talking." Ash had been wary of Jerry from the beginning, and through the years Ash became less tolerant. He didn't like the fact that Harper supported a grown-ass man capable of doing his part.

"It's one of the rare things I agree with your brother on."

"I know. But Harper loves him."

"Charm and good looks only go so far," Miley argued.

Luna went back to looking through their movie options.

"Speaking of charm and good looks. How is Nate? You had coffee with him today, right?"

Luna dropped the remote to glare at her roommate.

Miley just laughed.

"This will get you going, so get it out of your system now."

Miley stopped laughing and leaned forward. "He made a pass at you."

"No. No!"

"What then?"

Luna took a deep-cleansing breath. "We have to go to Texas a week from Wednesday for this case we're on."

Miley slowly started to nod. "Niiice . . . forced proximity. That's always a good Christmas movie."

"It's not Christmas. And the hotel has plenty of rooms. I need to look at the books and he needs to interview people. We probably won't see each other outside of driving and dinner."

"Do you need more than that?"

"We work together."

"Barely. Besides, where else are we supposed to meet men? Bars attract the wrong guys, and dating apps are dead. That leaves work or friends that set you up."

"Or construction workers and roofers," Luna suggested. Putting the spotlight onto Miley.

"True."

"I deliberately suggested next week for Texas so one of us is here when Brian comes in for the roof. You should have plenty of time to flirt with him."

Miley placed a hand to her chest. "I'll take one for the team."

Luna tossed a kernel of popcorn at her.

"Try and distract him *after* the roof is on, please." Luna squared herself back to the TV.

"You ruin all my fun."

Luna settled on a movie and pressed play.

And for an hour and a half watched two fictious neighbors fall for each other while co-parenting a stray dog they both thought was theirs.

~

Luna unearthed Miley's snowboard from the garage and set it out onto the driveway for her friend.

The sky had turned a special shade of gray and threatened to release a decent amount of rain before the day was done.

So much for starting the roof before the weekend.

According to Brian, the next window of opportunity was when Luna and Nate were in Texas.

Luna ran from the garage to the house in an attempt to avoid getting soaked but failed.

Miley had rolled her suitcase into the mudroom and set her ski boots to the side of that.

"It's getting cold."

Miley was all smiles. "It's snowing at the pass. Fresh powder."

The alarm chimed and both Luna and Miley turned to the back door.

It was crazy how quickly they became accustomed to a house alarm alerting them to a car coming up the drive.

Miley's friend Reese drove a double cab long bed truck that she backed up the driveway.

Reese left the engine on and jumped out of the cab.

"I'm glad you're ready. It's dumping at the pass; we need to get up there before they close it." Reese glanced at Luna. "Why aren't you coming?"

"My roof has holes in it. Next time."

Luna didn't dwell on what couldn't be helped.

Miley shoved everything that needed to stay dry in the back of the cab while Luna and Reese secured the snowboard in the bed of the truck.

"Text when you get up there," Luna said as Miley jumped into the passenger seat.

"I will."

Luna ducked out of the rain as soon as Reese put the truck in drive.

Midnight met Luna at the back door with a loud cry.

"What's the matter?" Luna asked her cat.

Midnight meowed again.

The sound of the wind pushing against the house made the tarp on the roof slap around.

Luna shrugged out of her raincoat and rain boots before scooping up the cat and walking through the house, up the stairs, and into the attic.

The house was chilly, but the attic was freezing.

Midnight struggled to get free and bounced away as soon as her paws hit the floor.

The sound of the tarp was louder, but so far it seemed to be doing its job.

Luna checked out the areas that were problematic and didn't see anything dripping through.

A gust of wind outside howled through the vents in the attic, and at the same time the lights flickered.

"No, nope, no." The last place Luna wanted to be in the house if the power went out was in the attic. She headed to the door, calling for her cat. "Midnight. C'mon."

The cat ducked behind a stack of boxes.

"I'm going to leave you up here," she warned.

Still nothing.

Luna flicked the light off, then back on. "C'mon."

It wouldn't be the first time Midnight wanted to hang out up there.

"Last warning. I'm closing the door. It's too cold to leave it open."

Midnight didn't so much as meow in response.

The power flickered again.

She gave up, turned off the light, and closed the door.

Eventually Midnight would cry when she wanted to be let out.

Luna headed straight to her office and logged off her computer and closed it down. Even with a battery backup, the last thing she needed was for a power surge to screw up her desktop.

Her phone on her desk buzzed.

The back and side yard cameras were constantly suggesting someone was walking around the house. Even though Ash and Nate had taken into consideration the occasional blowing trees, they didn't have them set for storms.

Luna snoozed the alarms on the cameras for the next hour. If they didn't stop going off after that, she'd disarm them until after the storm passed.

No sooner than she set the phone down, it rang.

It was the Lexus dealership.

The one accomplishment the week had finalized was her new car. She'd test driven a Toyota, a Volvo, and the Lexus NX 350 hybrid, and the Lexus won.

"Hello," she answered.

"Can I speak with Luna Canning?"

"This is her."

"Hi, Luna, it's Misha from Lexus. I have some bad news."

Luna lost her smile. "Oh?"

"We're not going to be able to get your car here until after this storm. It's too risky for semis on the pass."

Her car was coming from a dealership in Spokane, and Luna was supposed to take possession the following day.

As much as she was bummed, she understood. "That makes sense."

"We're looking at Tuesday, possibly Wednesday."

Luna had turned in the rental the day before, knowing she could use Miley's car over the weekend.

"I have a work trip planned. Why don't we aim for next Saturday," she told him.

"Thank you so much for your understanding," Misha said.

"You can thank me by giving me a full tank of gas upon delivery."

The salesman laughed. "I'll see what I can do."

"I have faith in you," she teased.

Considering Luna dwindled the car from forty-nine thousand to forty-four, with zero percent financing for the first twelve months and five percent APR after that for four more years, Luna knew she was asking a lot.

"Have a good weekend, Ms. Canning. And safe trip."

"Thank you, Misha."

Luna set her phone down and heard Midnight crying from the attic door.

"That didn't last long."

CHAPTER SIXTEEN

Nate looked out the window of his apartment toward the light across the street.

Right before the sun had set, the temperature dropped, and snow started to mix into the rain. He wouldn't be surprised if he woke up in the morning to a few inches or more. It was a good thing it was the weekend and he didn't have anywhere to be.

His phone buzzed where he had it plugged in next to his sofa.

Ash's name came up on the screen.

Why would Ash be calling?

Luna.

"Hey," Nate answered right away.

"Hey, Nate, it's Ash Canning."

"What's up? Is everything okay?" Nate didn't like the alarm he heard in his own voice. But he didn't know Ash well enough for a random social call, so something had to be wrong.

"That's what I need to figure out. I can't get ahold of Luna. I've been trying for a few hours."

"What about Miley?" Nate asked.

"She's on a skiing trip. Said the last time she heard from Luna was right before noon. I logged in to the house cameras, but they were turned off before the entire system went offline."

"Sounds like a power outage." Some of the tension left Nate's shoulders.

"That's what I think."

"I hear a *but* . . ."

"But I don't like it. I called Harper to see if she could go by and check on her, but she's in Bend with her husband and in-laws. Harper also suggested it's just the power, but then we started talking. Luna's pretty good about keeping her phone charged. And I'm sure she has a portable charger somewhere."

Nate smiled and looked around for his shoes. "Do you want me to go and check on her?"

"Wow, yeah . . . that would be great. Wish I had thought of it."

Nate laughed.

"Seriously. I know I'm overthinking this but, ah . . . ever since I was there, I've had this feeling like something is coming."

That made Nate pause. "Probably all the ghost stories you guys kept telling."

"Right. I'd drive up myself, but we're all on mandatory overtime. We're expecting several inches of snow and the roads are already layered in ice."

Nate put the phone on speaker and slipped on his shoes and started to tie them. "I got ya, Ash. I'll call you when I get there."

"You're a good man, Nate. I owe you."

"No problem."

It was a problem.

Not only were the side roads covered in snow, but there was also plenty of black ice under that white layer.

What should have taken Nate fifteen minutes to do, took him forty.

Luna's neighborhood was dark.

No streetlights, no house lights, no nothing.

Nate took one look at the slope of Luna's driveway and decided he was better off parking his car on the flat street outside or risk sliding right off the road. He was lucky he made it this far without finding a ditch to park his car in, he didn't want to press his luck.

A dark night with silent snowfall held a certain power that no other weather created. It was Mother Nature's way of telling everyone and everything to slow down and enjoy the quiet. Giant flakes hit his face when he got out of his car, flashlight in hand.

One step on her driveway, and Nate was fighting for balance. Tennis shoes were not the best choice.

The air was filled with the scent of fresh snow and wood burning from a fireplace.

One careful step at a time, Nate made his way to the side door of the house. "Luna?" he called out as he knocked. "It's Nate."

There wasn't an answer. And the kitchen was dark.

"Luna?"

He knocked again.

It was still quiet.

He angled his flashlight to look through the kitchen window.

He saw the silhouette of a person holding a shotgun and immediately dropped into a squat.

Nate reached for his gun; his heart shoved firmly in his throat. "Fuck."

Slowly, he inched away from the back door toward a shrub on the side of the house for shelter.

That's when he heard her.

"I have a gun. I already called the police."

Nate stopped moving and nearly collapsed onto the ground.

"Luna," he yelled. "It's Nate. Don't shoot."

She didn't respond.

"Luna?"

The back door slowly creeped open.

Nate quickly dropped his gun. "It's me."

"Nate?"

Luna stepped from the door; the barrel of the gun swung toward him.

"Don't shoot!" he yelled. He shot his hands in the air.

Without any light, Nate couldn't tell if she understood him or not. And the gun was pointed directly at him.

"What are you doing here?"

"Can you point that somewhere else, please."

She lowered the weapon.

"Shit."

"Nate?"

"Give me a second." He needed the adrenaline in his veins to catch up and his heart rate to slow down. He grabbed the flashlight with one hand, his gun with the other.

"You scared the hell out of me," Luna scolded him.

"That makes two of us." He stood and pointed the flashlight toward her.

She shielded her eyes.

Nate lowered it once again. "Ash called me. Asked me to come over and check on you."

"What?"

Nate stood and brushed the snow off his knees. "You weren't answering your phone."

"For crying out loud. I turned it off. It's almost out of charge. The power's been out all day."

Luna stood there in a bathrobe and slippers, holding a shotgun. It would have been comical if Nate's life hadn't just flashed in front of his eyes. He tucked his gun back into his waistband holster, the cold metal gave him a jolt.

"Come in," Luna said as she headed back inside.

He set the flashlight on the kitchen island and pointed it up toward the ceiling.

"I can't believe Ash called you." Luna set the shotgun next to the flashlight.

"I forgot you had that," Nate said.

Luna stood close enough that he saw that her face had turned white. "I could have shot you."

"I'm aware."

"I'm going to kill my brother."

"He said the cameras went out before the alarm system went offline. He called Miley and your sister. I was his last resort."

Luna started to laugh. Slowly at first but then the laughter grew.

Nate felt a smile hit his face and then he joined her.

"It's not funny." But she kept laughing.

"I'm pretty sure I shit myself."

That made her laugh harder. Luna placed a hand on his arm. "The look on your face."

"I couldn't see yours." He kept laughing. "Thanks for not shooting me."

Luna dropped her forehead to his chest as she gained control of her laughter.

Nate felt the moment Luna's adrenaline dropped.

Her knees buckled and Nate caught her before she could crumple to the floor. "Oh, God."

"It's okay."

She was shaking now, the laughter forgotten. "I could have killed you."

His arms tightened around her. "But you didn't."

Nate felt her fist grab at his jacket and her face flatten against his chest.

He closed his eyes and held her close. "It's okay."

Slowly, one breath at a time, Luna came back to herself.

He'd had that moment more than once in his career. Pulling his gun, finger on the trigger. One split second and it all could have ended tragically.

Nate waited for her to draw away before loosening his grip.

Luna looked up at him. He saw moisture in her eyes.

He placed a hand to the side of her cheek. "I'm okay."

Her gaze drifted over his face, hesitated on his lips.

Without thought, his eyes fell on hers. Soft, pink . . . slightly parted. What would she taste like, he wondered. Sweet like honey, or spicy like the rim of a glass of a jalapeño margarita?

The meow of Luna's cat snapped them both out of the moment.

Nate dropped his hand and Luna leaned back.

She glanced at the gun lying on the counter. "I want that thing out of my house."

"If I were an intruder, that could have saved your life."

"I don't care. I'll take my chances," she said.

He'd argue the point another day. Now was not the time. "Wait, did you call the police?" Nate asked.

"No. My phone is upstairs."

Smart, he mused. "Here." He removed his phone from his back pocket and handed it over. "Call your brother."

She took the phone from his hand and walked away.

Nate grabbed the flashlight and took a step.

Midnight stood under his feet, meowed, and peered up at him. "Great timing," he whispered.

The cat put a paw on his leg.

He reached down and picked her up and followed Luna.

"Really, Ash? The power has been out for hours . . . Yes, I'm all right."

Luna walked into a dark hall, and Nate moved toward the soft glow of the fireplace in the family room.

He put the cat down and peeled off his coat.

Luna's side of the conversation was impossible to miss.

And she wasn't happy. "I could have shot him. No. That's not the point."

Nate leaned down and put another log on the fire and used the poker to set it right.

He looked over at the sofa, the one he'd slept on, to see that Luna had set herself up to sleep there for the night.

"Then you can call them and let them know that you're a paranoid psychopath and that I'm fine."

Poor Ash, Nate thought. The man was more protective than the father of a teenage daughter on her first date.

Nate took a seat on the smaller sofa. His gun reminded him that it was there, so he pulled it out and set it on the side table.

Luna's voice had softened. "I know. None of that was your fault."

Nate stopped moving when he heard what she said.

"Well, I'm fine, so you can stop thinking like that."

Midnight jumped up next to him and nudged his hand with her face.

Nate responded by rubbing his fingers to the side of Midnight's neck and under her chin.

Luna had either moved farther away or she'd lowered her voice enough that Nate couldn't hear.

It wasn't long before the soft shuffle of her slippered feet walked his way.

"Is everything worked out?" he asked.

By now the fire was roaring enough that he could see all but the dark edges of the room.

Luna curled her feet under her on her makeshift bed.

"I know he means well, but he needs more distractions in his life so he can stop stressing about me." Luna set Nate's phone beside her and pulled a blanket onto her lap.

"Being a motorcycle cop isn't enough I suppose."

"It's only made him worse," Luna told him. "Seeing the aftermath of violent crimes has increased his 'wellness' checks on me tenfold. He feels guilty and he has no reason to."

"Guilty? Because of your ex?"

She nodded. "And other things. He used to extend this paranoia onto Harper, until he realized that Jerry wasn't even the primary spider killer in the house."

Nate looked down in his lap, where Midnight had curled up and was nodding off to sleep. "Isn't that your job?" Nate asked the cat.

"Since when do you flirt with guys?" Luna directed her question to her pet.

Midnight sighed in response.

"Animals are pretty good judges of character."

"Boosting your own ego?" Luna asked, smiling.

"You're the one that said she doesn't like boys."

Luna laughed. "True."

He nodded toward the sofa. "Wouldn't it be more comfortable in a bed?"

"It's pretty cold up there already and it's supposed to snow all night. I'll deal with a stiff sofa for the heat of the fireplace."

Nate found himself getting lost in the images of the flames lapping onto each other. "That's the nice thing about these old houses. They still have wood-burning fireplaces." Nate paused. "Wait, don't you have a fireplace in your bedroom?"

Luna winced. "There's something wrong with the ventilation and it blows back smoke. It's on my list of home repairs. Maybe this summer."

"That's too bad."

Luna stared into the flames. "I tried getting ahold of the power company to see how long this was going to last. I never got through. Did you see any down lines on your way over?"

"No. It's pretty quiet out there. Not a lot of people on the road," he told her.

"Where did you park your car?"

"Bottom of your driveway. It's covered in black ice. I had a hard time walking up."

Luna's jaw dropped. "Not only could I have shot you, you could have gotten into an accident on the way over."

"And a meteor could have fallen from the sky and hit me on the head. I see where Ash gets his overactive imagination."

"Point taken," she muttered.

"I should probably get going before it gets too much worse out there." Nate nudged the cat in an attempt to move her without making her upset.

Midnight ignored him.

"Are you sure that's wise? They don't call it Queen Anne *Hill* for nothing."

"I'll be fine." Besides, staying would be tempting.

She would be tempting.

Much to Midnight's disappointment, Nate picked her up and moved her to the side.

Luna stood with him, handed him back his phone.

Together they walked through the kitchen and to the back door.

Wind rattled the windows, and the cool air of a drafty house put a chill down his spine. "Do you have enough firewood?" he asked.

"Absolutely. There's a small shed to the side of the garage that keeps it dry. Ish. Dry-ish."

"Do you want me to bring some in before I leave?" he asked.

"I brought in plenty before it got dark."

Nate slipped into his jacket and opened the door.

Wind pushed against him, and snow started blowing in. Something outside had shifted, and the casual snowfall had decided to look and feel like a blizzard.

Seattle didn't have blizzards.

Seattle barely had snow.

He swung the flashlight to see what he was in for.

The footprints from where they'd both been standing barely thirty minutes before were completely covered.

Snow that had been difficult to see through coming over had doubled in amount and the size of flakes.

"Oh," he uttered.

Luna moved to his side to take in his view. "I'm not okay with this," she said.

"I'll be f—"

Luna stepped in front of him, pushed him back, and reached for the doorknob. "You'll be fine because you're not going anywhere," she said.

"Are you channeling your brother?"

"A little. But I know that's a problem." She pointed outside. "Ash only *thinks* there's a problem and acts on it. It's bad enough I almost shot you. If you died on the way home, I'd never be able to live with myself. If you left, I wouldn't get an ounce of sleep. It's not like you can call me and let me know you made it safely. Sure, I could turn my phone on and check my messages, but if you didn't call, then I'd use Miley's car and try and find you, and then—"

"I get it," he said, stopping her. Luna was right. The drive over had been sketchy as fuck. "I'll stay."

"Good. Glad that's settled." She marched past him.

Bulky bathrobes weren't normally a turn-on . . . however.

CHAPTER SEVENTEEN

For the second time since moving back to Seattle, Nate woke up on Luna's couch.

The smoldering embers inside the fireplace did very little to warm up the room at this point. But sometime during the night he'd kicked off the covers to cool down the heat that had built inside of him.

He blamed the woman on the floor in front of him.

Luna lay flat on her stomach, her arms splayed out, taking up the entirety of the queen mattress Nate had wrestled down the stairs the night before.

Her face was angled toward him, her lips slightly parted and her face completely lax as she slept.

They'd stayed up playing cards and talking for what felt like hours. Card games Nate had completely forgotten existed.

Games of speed were Luna's strong point.

Poker . . . not so much.

Something Nate would have exploited in his college years.

When they bored of games, they talked about different cases they'd taken on in their careers.

Luna had a soft spot for women trying to get out of awful relationships and went in looking for ways for these women to financially survive once their divorces were final.

She insisted she was "giving back" by taking on cases without pay.

Nate still wasn't sure what she felt she needed to "give back" for.

At some point they'd both found their heads on their respective pillows and the conversation drifted off.

Eventually Nate had asked a question and Luna didn't reply.

He watched her then.

If they weren't somewhat trapped in the same room in an effort to stay warm all night, he would have felt guilty for his voyeurism.

She looked younger when she slept. Not that she looked old, but the stress lines that seemed to live behind her eyes softened and all that worry melted away.

Nate had fallen asleep looking at her only to find her awake in his dreams.

Very awake.

And very interested in exploring what he had under the gray sweatpants he'd commandeered once again from Ash's closet.

The choice had been intentional.

Even if it was torturous to watch Luna try and hide her gaze from time to time.

He should feel bad.

He didn't.

But he really should.

The sound of a tree tapping against a window brought his attention to the bright day starting outside.

Nate pushed himself up, keeping as quiet as he could, and took in the stillness behind the panes of glass.

There had to be a good six to eight inches of snow blanketing everything.

He could tell by the sound of silence in the house that the power hadn't been restored.

The time on his cell phone said seven twenty.

Nate couldn't remember when he'd slept past six, with or without an alarm.

The bite in the air brought his gaze to the ashes in the hearth.

The odds of him waking Luna while attempting to re-energize the fire were too great.

The gas in the house was still on when they'd gone to sleep, which meant he'd be able to at least boil water for tea in an effort to get his morning dose of caffeine. He feared even that would wake up the sleeping woman in front of him.

Nate pushed himself up on the arm of the sofa and reached for his phone. He'd placed it on airplane mode to extend the battery life, which had worked. Fifty percent charge would get him through most of his day unless he started streaming videos.

According to the online news, Seattle was virtually shut down. Residents were encouraged to stay home until the main roads had a chance of being cleared for safe travel. Even then, getting to those main roads would prove difficult for the average driver without cars that were meant for these conditions.

The weather report said that the snowfall was past, and what they had would likely stick around throughout the day and even into the night. But rain was expected to return by Monday morning's commute.

As for the twenty thousand residents without power . . . the power company was "working on it."

The sound of Luna sighing was followed by her shifting positions.

There was something intimate about watching someone else wake up. The moments between awareness and dreams were vulnerable and not something you shared with many people in a lifetime. And certainly not colleagues.

Except maybe for him.

Luna rolled onto her back and her eyes fluttered open.

He knew he shouldn't be staring, but his thoughts and actions weren't in sync, making it hard to look away.

Luna propped herself up on an elbow and looked over her shoulder at him.

"Did I wake you?" he asked.

She shook her head and ran a hand over her face. "What time is it?"

"Almost seven thirty. How did you sleep?"

"Pretty good, considering. How was the couch?" she asked.

"Better than the last time."

She laughed. "What is it saying that you have more than one night on my couch to compare against each other?"

"If you were a girlfriend, I think it would be normal." The words came without filter.

Narrowed eyes looked back at him. "Any boyfriend that needs to be reduced to the sofa wouldn't be a boyfriend for long."

A slow smile reached his lips. "That's a good rule."

Luna pulled her eyes away from his and peered outside. "Holy cow." She pushed herself up and walked to the window. "That's a lot of snow."

With her awake, Nate unfolded from the sofa and moved to the fireplace to rekindle the fire. "The neighborhood kids will be happy."

"Ha. They'd be happier if this was a school day."

"True."

Nate noticed the second Luna saw him bent over the fireplace. He ignored the fact that her gaze lingered on the lower half of his body and pretended not to notice.

She cleared her throat and grasped her bathrobe with jerky movements. "I think I have instant coffee."

Nate moaned. "What about black tea?"

"That's a better idea."

Luna left while Nate placed a few scraps of old newspaper under the new logs he wanted to catch flame.

One spark split into two, then three, until the edges of the bark on the wood started to emit heat.

In the kitchen he found Luna staring wide-eyed and the shotgun she'd left there the night before.

Even though he knew she saw him walk in, she didn't tear her gaze away from the weapon.

"When I was a kid, I always thought I'd have a gun. I thought that was the answer to being safe." Her voice was steady, almost monotone.

"When my marriage failed, I realize if I'd had one, things might have ended differently."

Nate didn't need to be a rocket scientist to understand what she meant.

He stepped closer and covered her hand that was resting on the counter with his.

She blinked twice and slowly raised her eyes to his.

"Your marriage didn't fail. Your husband failed you."

She smiled and her face softened.

Luna stacked her other hand on top of his, squared her shoulders, and then pulled away.

Nate didn't like to sit still.

That was the conclusion Luna came to over the course of the day.

After a workable breakfast of cereal and fruit, Nate raided Ash's clothing and discarded shoes and put himself to work.

First order of business was tightening the cameras that were going off before the power cut out. Even in the snow he dragged a ladder around the house and cut away at the tree limbs that set the sensors off.

Then he brought in enough firewood to last for a week if the electricity didn't return.

While he fussed with wood, Luna made use of a snow shovel on the path between the shed and the back door.

Nate stacked the firewood in the greenhouse, which wasn't something Luna had thought of.

They let Miley's car idle long enough to put a charge on both their phones.

Luna was starting to think Nate would be staying another night, when he walked in the back door and announced that the road in front of her house had seen enough traffic to melt the snow.

"You're welcome to stay," she told him. And he was, although she was starting to worry that they were becoming way too comfortable with this co-habitating thing.

"If you need me to, I'm happy to stay. It won't be a choice if I stay after sundown and everything starts freezing over."

Part of her wanted to say, "Stay," another part said that would be crossing some kind of line. "You know I'm not usually in need of rescue. Stolen cars and snowstorms aside."

"And I'm not usually a hero on call. But the next time I am, I'm bringing an overnight bag."

"Tired of wearing Ash's clothing?" she asked.

"Your brother has an abnormal amount of gray sweatpants."

And just like that, her gaze lowered, even though she knew Nate had changed back into the jeans he'd arrived in the night before.

She cleared her throat and found a knowing smile on Nate's lips.

The ambient noises that you didn't hear until they were gone sang back into life, and the sweatpants were forgotten.

The hum of the refrigerator.

The buzz of the lights that had been on when the power went out, now blipped back on.

"That's a relief," she said.

Nate pointed toward the living room. "I'll haul that mattress back upstairs and get out of your hair," he concluded.

"You're not in my hair."

He looked at the top of her head as if seeing her hair for the first time.

For the briefest of moments, she thought he was going to reach out and touch the ends of it.

Nate's gaze snapped away.

"The mattress," he said before leaving the kitchen.

Luna released a breath she'd been holding before they both returned to the living room.

After they put her bed back together upstairs, Luna followed Nate as he prepared to leave.

He zipped up his coat and turned to her by the back door.

"This is starting to become a habit," she told him.

"What's that?"

"Me thanking you for doing things no one would ever expect of you."

He regarded her with a tilt of his head. "I try my best to do the right things, whether it's expected or not," he said.

"That's rare. In my experience, so few men do."

His voice lowered. "Then you need to meet better men and set the bar higher."

Nate opened the back door.

Luna stepped forward to follow.

He stopped abruptly and turned into her.

Luna kept herself from falling into him, but only by a couple of inches.

Nate reached out and grappled with her arm.

Her eyes caught in his as a snap of energy pulsated around them.

"Y-you really need to stop doing that," she said softly, the hair on her arms prickled with nerves.

"Doing what?" He looked at her lips.

Luna cleared her throat and still managed to stutter. "M-Making me run into you, Mr. Venti."

"I don't know . . . I'm starting to like it." His voice was low and hummed in the very center of her body.

Oh, damn.

She should say something witty. A retort.

Nothing came.

Words didn't surface.

Nate moved his hand from her arm to her face.

His grin dropped; his eyes searched hers. God help her, she leaned into the warmth of his palm.

"I'm going to leave now before I do something I can't take back," he whispered. Yet he ran his thumb under her bottom lip in one languishing stroke.

Her hands trembled and every internal muscle in her body cried out for his touch. "That's a . . . probably a good idea."

One final look at her lips, and Nate eased back, letting his hand fall away.

She missed it immediately.

This time she kept her distance as gravity, or more accurately *reality*, fell back in.

A few steps away he turned around again. "Set the alarm tonight."

"Is that a request or an order?" Finally, she found her words.

Nate smirked. "This kind of weather brings out opportunistic criminals."

"Don't worry, I'll shoot first and ask questions later."

He was smiling now and slowly walking backward. All while he let his eyes travel up and down her frame. "We should probably have a safe word."

"Oh?"

Nate was flirting.

Damn if she wasn't flirting right back.

"What do you suggest?" she asked.

"Broccoli."

She burst out a short laugh. "If you're going to pick a vegetable, why not a cucumber?"

Nate slipped and righted himself before he fell onto his butt.

The warmth that came with her laughter lit something inside of her. Something she hadn't felt in a long time.

Nate shook a finger her way and she heard him moan.

"Text me when you get home, so I know you made it."

"Is that an order, or a request?" he shot back.

She didn't answer.

Luna crossed her arms over her chest and watched as Nate walked out of her orbit.

He sent her one last look and smile before he disappeared out of sight.

CHAPTER EIGHTEEN

It was Tuesday night.

The snow and everything it brought, mainly Nate, had all melted, leaving a muddy mess where it had once been pristine and white.

Innocent.

There was nothing innocent about the dreams that Luna remembered every morning.

Nate holding her.

Nate smiling down at her.

Nate bending close and just when she thinks he's going to kiss her in her dreams, she wakes up. Always at the good part.

With her bags packed and waiting by the back door for his o-dark-hundred arrival time to get them to the airport, Luna was a mass of bundled nerves.

And Miley was laughing . . . at Luna's expense.

"It's because I haven't been laid in forever," Luna explained away the hormonal dreams and anxiety about the thought of spending a significant amount of alone time with Nate over the next few days.

"That can be a problem."

They were currently standing over Luna's bed, where they'd hauled their laundry to fold and stack into piles.

"And those damn sweatpants. I swear I'm going to burn every last pair of them when I get home."

Miley scoffed. "Don't you dare. I kinda like checking out your brother's ass in those things."

Luna tossed a sock aside and searched for its match.

"What do I do if he makes a pass at me? He was so close. I was so close."

"What do you want to do?" Miley asked.

"Want and should. What I want I shouldn't do. Why does he have to be so . . . *nice*?" She spit out the word as if it left a bad taste in her mouth.

"Nate is right, your bar is too damn low."

"You're not helping, Miley."

Miley took up the edge of the bed and stopped folding the shirt in her hands. "You're thinking too hard on this. This isn't a workplace romance. You don't work in the same office."

"But we do work for the same person," Luna reminded her friend.

"Subcontractors. It's not the same."

Luna had said that to herself a dozen times since Nate had driven away.

"It's never pretty when things end," Luna moaned. "And they always end."

This point Miley didn't try to argue. "But it's fun while it happens. You have to admit that. And when was the last time a decent man showed up at the door that offered a little romance?"

"You're supposed to be talking me out of this." Luna gave up on the sock search and shook out a pair of jeans.

"Luna . . . Lu!"

She stopped folding the jeans and gave Miley her full attention.

"After your divorce you made me promise you that I'd never sit back and watch you make a mistake like Landon again. I don't think giving Nate a little bit of your . . . time, is a bad thing."

"But—"

"What has you so worried? And don't tell me the 'you work together' line. I'm not buying that," Miley asked.

Luna rolled her shoulders and shook her head. "I don't know. He's . . . different."

"By 'different' do you mean a decent guy? I've seen the ones you've chosen to hook up with over the years. Let's just say they were perfectly safe from you falling for them."

Luna rolled her eyes. "That's not fair."

"Isn't it? I'm not judging. I get it. Sometimes you just need to be held. You have to admit the few that have been around since Landon were intellectually or emotionally unavailable."

"That's by design." Luna was the poster child for emotionally unavailable, and she was highly cognizant of it.

Miley pointed to her chest. "I think that's the crux of the problem. I think you like Nate. I think he makes you feel something you're afraid of feeling."

"When did you become a psychiatrist?"

"I'm serious, Luna. Nate goes beyond the 'nice guy' category. You barely knew the man, and he showed up when your car got jacked. Then stayed with us in case something sinister went down. Then he hung with Ash all day. And you know Ash. If he thought there was an ounce of ugly in Nate, there was no way in hell he'd have suggested he drive over in the middle of a snowstorm to see if you were okay."

"True."

"There isn't a more overprotective brother than yours. He knows your triggers, even if he can't identify his own. He'd just as soon jump in front of a train than let anything happen to you again."

Luna sighed. "I know. He creates monsters that aren't there sometimes."

Miley scrunched up her face. "I don't know about that. He goes with his gut and isn't often wrong when he does."

"No one showed up at the house the night my car went missing," Luna argued.

"We don't know if someone drove by . . . saw Nate, and decided it wasn't worth it."

Luna hadn't considered that.

"You said yourself you felt like something is off. Something was coming," Miley said.

"I think a lot of that was Jorden's tarot card reading," Luna excused away.

"No." Miley shook her head. "You said that before Jorden's reading."

"I'm not sure what all this has to do with Nate."

Miley picked up another shirt. "Do you want to hear my final thought about why this thing with Nate is bothering you so much?"

Probably not.

When Luna stayed silent, Miley told her anyway. "You never go into anything with a man without knowing exactly why it won't work. When it ends, you get to say, 'I knew it.' You can't do that with Nate. And that scares you."

Luna felt her shoulders relax. "That's where you're wrong. It won't work with Nate because we work closely together. If we start something, it will end because of that."

"Workplace geography? I'm not buying it. Geography issues evolve when the guy you're with is in San Francisco when you're in Seattle. Like that lawyer . . . what was his name?"

"Reuben."

"Right, Reuben. You worked with him, and you didn't use this excuse."

"He was too far away for anything serious," Luna said.

"Bingo!" Miley lifted her voice. "And Nate isn't. And he doesn't have a wife, or crazy ex, or a place in the unemployment line, or an alcohol problem, or kids, or a bookie on speed dial . . . Did I miss anything? Oh, yeah . . . and his dates aren't transactional. The man has literally spent the night here twice and the closest he came to anything remotely sexually suggestive was an 'almost' kiss that you haven't stopped thinking about."

Midnight jumped up on the bed and planted herself right in the middle of the clean clothes.

Miley placed a hand over Luna's. "Sometimes we're so busy looking for the red flags we ignore the green ones. Right now, Nate is kinda perfect. I'm sure he's not. I'm sure he snores or has bad morning breath."

Luna wanted to cry. "He doesn't snore."

Miley laughed. "Maybe he has a small—"

Luna stopped her with a stare. "Gray sweatpants!" Which didn't exactly hide everything.

"Then he might not know how to use it."

Luna felt laughter bubbling.

"Give the guy a chance. He might be Don Juan in bed. If he is, I'll be the one telling your brother to do a background check on the dude," Miley said. "Nobody is that perfect."

"Exactly."

They both laughed, the tension and worry inside Luna started to ease.

Midnight jumped up and growled. A guttural sound Luna only heard when she saw an animal on the other side of the window threatening her existence. The hair on her back stood on end, eyes sharp on the bedroom door.

Luna and Miley abruptly stopped laughing and looked toward the empty hall.

A loud noise coming from downstairs brought every cell in Luna's body alive. A metal sound, like something banging on a pipe.

Were they having an earthquake? Luna looked around the room to see if anything was shaking. Everything was still.

Luna grasped Miley's hand.

The noise stopped.

"What the fuck was that?" Miley whispered.

Midnight jumped from the bed and inched to the door.

"Where's the gun?"

"Downstairs in the hall closet," Luna whispered.

"Lotta good it is there," Miley whispered back.

Making as little noise as possible, Luna stepped to the door. Like the night Nate had been outside lurking, every hair on her body stood on end, and her heart was beating out of control in her chest.

Everything was quiet.

Midnight swished her tail, and some of the rigidity in her stance eased.

"Do you hear anything?" Luna asked.

Miley shook her head.

"Did you leave something on the kitchen counter? Maybe we had a tremor." California wasn't the only state that had earthquakes.

Luna peeked beyond the door.

Miley stood directly behind her.

"Anyone there?" Luna yelled. Her voice sounded like nails on a chalkboard in the quiet house.

Silence.

Then she remembered what she'd yelled at Nate when she thought he was a criminal sneaking around the house during the winter storm. "I called the police. They're on their way."

There was nothing.

Midnight had sat back and was now licking her paw.

"Something must have just fell," Luna said.

Still, they moved slowly to the stairs, eyes and ears alert.

Miley ducked into Ash's bedroom and came back with a baseball bat.

By the time they made it to the ground floor some of the tension had left.

Midnight walked in front of them.

"No one's here." Luna stood tall and used a normal voice. "Look at the cat."

Tail wagging, disinterested in life.

Even the night Nate showed up, Midnight had been on full alert until Nate followed Luna into the house.

"What was that?"

And then Luna saw it.

On the floor in front of an open cupboard door sat a saucepan and a frying pan.

Miley grabbed Luna's arm.

Luna stared, mouth wide open.

She shivered.

"Maybe Harper and Ash know something I don't," Luna choked out.

"If you're in this house long enough, you'll see things you can't explain."

Luna squeezed Miley's hand. "We're going to need more sage."

Luna hadn't been in the car five minutes before Nate heard the words.

"The house is haunted."

"What?"

"It happened last night. Just like the stories I'd heard. Miley and I were upstairs. We heard noise in the kitchen. We went down to investigate and there were two pans on the floor in front of an open cupboard."

Nate gripped the wheel and kept looking at Luna in the passenger seat.

"Maybe the cat—"

"Midnight was with us," Luna said.

Nate looked out the windshield, then back at her. "Are you sure it wasn't . . ."

"What? The wind? An earthquake? On the floor several inches from the open cupboard, Nate. Right before we heard the noise, my cat howled. By the time we got to the kitchen, Midnight was scratching her butt." Luna stared out the window.

"What did you do?"

"Freaked out. Miley slept in my room, with the door closed and the cat with us," Luna told him.

"I don't think I would have slept." Just hearing about it would give him nightmares.

"We didn't."

As if to prove that, Luna yawned.

"And Miley's okay with being there alone?"

Luna shrugged. "She's asking a friend from work to come over. I doubt she'll explore the attic or basement."

He didn't believe in ghosts, or anything paranormal. Those were the things of science fiction and movies. "There has to be an explanation."

"Nana insisted there was a ghost. I thought it was the ramblings of an overimaginative, eccentric old woman." Luna looked up. "Sorry I didn't believe you, Nana," she said to the ceiling of the car.

Nate glanced up. "Do you think she heard you?"

"Go ahead and laugh. You wouldn't be if this had happened when you spent the night."

Nate changed lanes on the freeway, somewhat surprised with the number of people on the road at four thirty in the morning. "Okay, assuming this is a ghost, why now? Why has it been quiet all this time?"

Luna looked his way. "Maybe it hasn't. Maybe I just wasn't paying attention."

"What do you mean? Dishes on the floor of the kitchen isn't something you can miss. Unless you have a three-year-old in a house filled with plastic toys and a toddler with a severe case of ADHD."

"There have been plenty of times I wondered if Miley was home because the floor is creaking upstairs. Then she walks in the back door."

"Old houses," Nate explained away.

"That's what I tell myself." Luna shifted in her seat. "I'm not sure I'm going to be able to do that from now on. After Nana passed, when the deed was transferred over to us, there was a section in the property disclosure about the possibility of it being haunted. Right beside that was a statement of 'No known recorded deaths on the property.' Apparently, answering these questions is a normal thing when you buy a house. Did you know that?" Luna asked.

"I did. I never gave it a lot of thought." Now he would.

Luna was quiet for a minute. "There're boxes of Nana's personal things up in the attic. I'm pretty sure there were a few diaries or journals. I think maybe it's time to read them."

Nate saw her shiver and placed his hand over hers that rested on the console. "From what you've told me about your grandmother, it doesn't sound like she would have left you the place if she thought it was dangerous."

Luna offered him half of a smile. "I wish I'd paid more attention to what she said about the house before she passed."

"And you think her journals might shed light on your ghost?"

"It's worth reading to find out. It scared the crap out of us."

He blinked and stared absently at the traffic on the freeway. "You can't shoot a ghost."

Luna shook before reaching over and turning up the heat on her side of the car.

When they arrived at the airport, Nate followed the instructions he received from Officer Kempski. Not only was the requested parking space better lit, but there were also cameras in several directions and it was close to a monitored entrance. The "Reserved" space was waiting for them.

They both exited the car, and Nate moved to the back to retrieve their suitcases.

"I feel like we were just here," Luna said.

Nate set the car alarm and took a long look at his vehicle. "Why don't you ask your nana to look over my car. I don't need a new one."

Luna nudged her shoulder against his. "Poke all the fun you want. She said she'd be around after her death, and I'm starting to think she is."

It was Nate's turn to look up. "We don't want to walk home, Nana. Make sure it's here when we get back."

Luna rolled her eyes. "C'mon. I need a decent cup of coffee. Try not to spill it on me."

There was the smile that he'd been thinking about ever since he'd left her side the day after the snowstorm.

The flight to Houston was bumpy, but rather uneventful.

Nate had assumed they'd get a little work done on the way. Instead, Luna leaned her head back as soon as they were seated and kept nodding off. When she shook herself awake, she looked to the man sitting beside her, next to the window, and struggled to stay awake.

Clearly the night before hadn't lent itself to enough sleep to make it through their busy day.

Nate took the sweater she'd set in the seat beside her, rolled it up, and placed it on his shoulder between them. "Here," he said. "Get some sleep."

She didn't argue. And within five minutes her breathing had slowed, and her head was heavy on his shoulder.

He leaned in and caught the scent of her hair.

Lavender.

He'd have a hard time seeing those flowers in the future without thinking of her.

Nate leaned his head back and looked at the woman sleeping on his shoulder.

It was going to be a long three days.

Directly from the rental car company, Luna and Nate headed to Joel Mercier's offices in Houston.

The solid hour and a half of sleep Luna had managed on the plane did wonders for clearing her mind.

She should probably be embarrassed for drooling on Nate's shoulder.

She wasn't. And she wasn't exactly sure why.

Those thoughts and that of pots and pans . . . and kitchen floors were for another time.

The two of them had a lot of work to do if they were going to get back on a plane early Saturday morning.

The only person who knew they were coming was Joel Mercier himself. Marcus had vetoed the two of them showing up completely unannounced.

Though according to Marcus, Mercier agreed to keep their arrival unannounced and only explain their purpose at a morning meeting.

Luna felt her spine growing taller and her shoulders squaring off as the two of them walked into the building.

She and Nate stopped at the reception desk.

"Good morning," Nate started. "We have an appointment with Joel Mercier."

The man behind the desk lifted his chin and clicked into the monitor in front of him.

"Your names, please."

"Luna Canning and Nate Warren."

The receptionist clicked a few buttons. "I don't see your names on the list."

"That's a good sign," Luna said under her breath.

"Please call his office, I assure you we're here at his request," Nate said.

Luna stepped away from the desk and took in the lobby around her.

The ceiling had to reach forty feet with walls made of glass. The lobby had exactly three colors. White, silver, and gray.

The Scandinavian-style furniture and sleek lighting hanging from cylinder pendants were the exact opposite of what you'd think of as an office in Houston, Texas.

"Someone will be right down to escort you up," the receptionist informed them.

Luna smiled and Nate thanked the man.

"Not one cowboy hat to be seen," Luna muttered when Nate turned back to her.

"From what I've read, all his offices look like this. No matter where in the world they are," Nate said.

"That's boring," she said.

"Steve Jobs wore the same thing every day to avoid decision fatigue," Nate told her.

She'd heard that before. "That makes a little bit of sense, but this? I mean, it makes sense for a hospital." The sterility of it.

"Mercier does have pharmaceutical holdings. Maybe he was inspired."

Luna chuckled.

"Mr. Warren, Ms. Canning?"

They turned when their names were called to find a slim, tall woman wearing a perfectly pressed skirt and suit jacket, her hair slicked back in a tight bun, and a polished smile.

"If you'll follow me."

Nate indicated for Luna to walk in front of him as they made their way to the office elevators.

The ride up was silent, and stepping out onto the executive floor was a mirror of what they'd seen downstairs.

They were led directly to Joel Mercier's office, where the man stood behind his desk in anticipation of their arrival.

"Welcome," he invited them in. "That will be all, Cynthia."

With a nod, the woman who had escorted them in left in silence.

"Marcus's dynamic duo," Joel said as he circled the desk to shake their hands. "He speaks highly of you."

"We appreciate his support. Luna Canning," Luna introduced herself.

"Your reputation precedes you, Ms. Canning." His handshake was firm and quick.

"Nate Warren."

"I understand the FBI is missing out on one of their top investigators."

Joel was quick to compliment.

"Thank you," Nate said.

"Please, sit. Cynthia is informing my staff of an emergency meeting and directing their secretaries to reschedule their days. While she does that, I'd love to know why the cloak and dagger."

Joel Mercier wasn't a tall man and surprisingly didn't have an ounce of a French accent as his name might imply.

Luna set her bag to the side and folded her hands in her lap.

"That's easily answered for me," Nate started. "Interviews with people who aren't expecting them are less likely to be scripted or collaborated. Body language tells me a lot."

Joel leaned against his desk. "Then you've found something?"

"As you suspected or you wouldn't have hired Marcus," Luna said.

Joel looked between the two of them, his head bobbing with a nod. "What do you need from me?"

"Access," Luna said quickly. She pulled a packet of papers from her bag and handed them over. "I need these physical files placed in a room, and two of your newest accountants on staff. Preferably interns or new hires."

"Why such inexperienced staff?"

"They don't have loyalties to individuals yet. You're the one they need to impress. I find that new graduates skim less and pay attention to details more."

"I'll have Cynthia make a call to HR to make the recommendations."

"Thank you," Luna said.

"And you, Mr. Warren?"

Nate had his own list. "I will need to speak to each of these individuals. After the introductions, I'll announce who the first one is. It's important that no one thinks this external audit is for anything other than good stewardship for your shareholders."

"This is a lot of names," Joel said.

"You have a very large company, Mr. Mercier. Several companies. There are many places that numbers can be misaligned," Luna told him.

Joel laughed. "That's very politically correct for *doctored*."

"Everything is an unintentional mistake until patterns are found and coincidence can't be explained away," she told him.

The phone on Joel's desk rang. He answered on speaker.

"Everyone is waiting, Mr. Mercier."

He thanked his secretary and they all stood.

"Let's get this started."

~

Mercier's human resource department delivered Lewis and Gina. Both of whom were in their infancy as accountants and still in their probational period with the company.

When they'd first arrived in the room, wide-eyed and confused as to why they were summoned, Luna put them completely at ease.

After introducing herself, Luna gave them her expectations and a promise.

"Everything we are going to do over the next few days is completely confidential. The only people that should be asking you about our findings are myself, Mr. Warren, and Mr. Mercier. Not your immediate boss, supervisor, HR rep . . . no one. If someone asks you what you were asked to do, the answer is . . . I asked you to double-check my numbers and find the files I need to save me time. Which is what you'll be doing."

Gina, who couldn't be older than twenty-three, looked at the slightly older Lewis. "Is that all we'll be doing?" she asked.

"That depends on what I find."

"You're a forensic accountant?" Lewis asked.

"Yes."

"That's a little beyond our pay grade," he said.

"Your probationary pay barely covers your rent, car, and groceries, let alone those student loan bills that start coming way too fast. What we potentially find here will prompt Mr. Mercier to assure your success in his company, and I will personally advocate for compensation for your work with me."

That had both of them smiling.

The door to the conference room opened and several people walked in with their arms filled with boxes. Luna directed the files to be placed in order of business and year. Then waited for the room to empty out.

BOHO was the first box she opened in the year she'd found the first discrepancy. Using the information Nate had given her, she directed her helpers to locate everything in the file pertaining to a certain individual's involvement.

Within an hour, the files stacked to her side were a foot tall and both Lewis and Gina were locating files, checking numbers she requested, and barely keeping up.

Two hours in, Luna found the first thread to follow.

The satisfaction of digging for gold and knowing you were going to find it was what she lived for.

Set in a direction, she shifted her focus and searched for a pattern.

Five o'clock came around way too fast. Gina and Lewis left for the day, giving Luna the privacy she needed when Nate made his way to her side.

He came into the conference room for the first time and stopped short. "Holy shit."

Luna looked around at the organized chaos surrounding her. "It always seems so much smaller when it's on a digital file."

"Find anything?" he asked.

She let her smile say everything. "You?" she asked.

Nate took a seat opposite her. "Mercier is respected, not loved, not feared."

"Which makes loyalty limited," she muttered.

"My thoughts exactly. Most of his executive staff have been with him for a decade or longer."

Luna handed him her notepad with names and dates. "Anyone here on your list today?"

Nate lifted an eyebrow. "Couple of them."

She handed him a stack of files. "Let's compare notes."

Nate draped his jacket over a chair and scooted it back.

~

They left the office at seven, got to the hotel at seven thirty, and were eating dinner at the hotel restaurant by eight fifteen.

They'd both taken a quick shower and were changed into more casual clothing.

Luna had put on a sweater; her hair was pulled back in a ponytail.

She'd scrubbed her face clean of the makeup she'd had on at the office and had ordered enough food for two people.

She was brilliant, Nate mused. The enormity of work and files she'd gone through in one afternoon was astounding.

"How are the kids you're working with?" Nate asked.

"Eager. They were a little scared at first, but they came around."

"Why do I get the feeling they're not checking your numbers?" he asked as he cut into the steak in front of him.

"Documenting, not checking. Most of it I do in my head, write the sum down, and have them run a tape and tack it on. Saves me time down the line."

Nate smiled. "By morning they'll have googled you."

"They won't find much," she insisted.

"You'd be surprised."

She stopped midbite. "Is there something you need to confess?"

He didn't answer right away.

"Nate?"

He shrugged. "I needed to know who I was working with." And flirting with . . .

Luna huffed. "Is this before or after you spent the night on my couch?"

The first time? "Before. Your LinkedIn photo doesn't do you justice."

"What are you talking about? That was a good picture." Luna took a bite.

"Yeah, from the college résumé assignment. You have a lot more wisdom behind those eyes now."

"Are you saying I'm old?" She was teasing.

Nate lowered his eyes. "I'm saying you looked too young for a safe word."

It was Luna's turn to look away. "Wow, talk about changing the subject."

Nate stuck a fork in the broccoli on his plate and looked at it.

Luna shifted her gaze from the vegetable to his eyes and back again. Her face flushed and she wiggled in her seat.

Her silence spoke volumes.

Safe word volumes.

Luna pointed at his food. "That . . . is a bad idea."

"I've had worse ideas."

"Nate."

"You're right," he said, his tone resigned.

"Of course I am."

Luna didn't sound convinced. And the steak she was cutting into would be crying by the way she stabbed at it.

"We work together," he said for both of their benefits.

"Exactly what I thought. The workplace and broccoli should not hold the same space."

Nate put the food in his mouth and slowly chewed. Once he swallowed, he cleared his throat. "But to be clear, you have thought about it . . . right?"

Luna looked away. "It crossed my mind."

He liked that she didn't try to lie.

Luna looked up.

Nate looked down. "So have I. A couple of times." A couple *dozen* times.

He heard her sigh. "It's good that we discussed this and put it to rest."

That was where she was wrong.

Admitting there was an attraction only fueled his desire to see what it would take to hear her whisper a safe word in his ear.

"Wouldn't you agree?" she asked.

No . . . he wouldn't. Because he was a fucking idiot who didn't learn from his past mistakes.

Their eyes met and held.

"We have an early morning," he said. "We should probably wrap this up."

~

For the second night in a row, Luna and the sandman did not become acquainted.

When she did manage to fall asleep, she had dreams of Nate handing her a heart shaped box. When she opened it, instead of chocolate covered cherries or strawberries . . . it was broccoli. Even in her dreams she knew that wasn't right. But Nate stood there in all seriousness as if he were gifting her with a diamond necklace.

Luna didn't even like diamonds. She thought the whole industry was a scam to make one family incredibly rich and everyone else jonesing to get a tiny chip to make them feel complete.

As those thoughts floated in her dreams, memories of Landon and the ring he'd given her . . . and how little it meant in the end, had her waking up.

The ride to Mercier's office the next morning gave zero hints of the previous night's conversation.

Which Luna thought was for the best.

She needed to focus.

They both needed to move through this case with a little fire while they had access to the players and files.

Nate finished with his interviews after noon and joined her and the young accountants.

The flow changed from there.

While Nate wasn't an accountant, he was highly trained in following the money used in fraudulent ways.

Sitting in the same room, moving information back and forth between them, was as smooth as slicing into butter that had been sitting on the counter in summer.

Alone during a coffee break, Luna turned to Nate and kept her voice low.

"Check this out." She shoved three ledgers in front of him and pointed to a line item.

He shrugged. "Consultant fees?"

"Right, not a big deal . . ." Luna brought another ledger for the first one. "Look what the consultant fee is for."

"Office design," he said slowly.

"Why would you need a consultant when all of your offices look the same?"

Nate's slow smile matched hers.

"Who was the consultant?" he asked.

"That's for us to find out." She shoved the ledgers at him. "But I would bet money that it's one of the LLCs that were run through the shell company. There are two manufacturing plants in Africa that were part of the merger, one sends their goods here to Houston, the other Vietnam."

"What do they produce? Coffee?"

"We would have caught coffee or cocoa early on if that were the case." Anytime fraud or money laundering was suspected, and the company was involved with coffee or cocoa beans, that was the first place she looked. "No. One produces soap . . . bath bombs, the kind that is marketed as organic and costs ten dollars apiece at a mall store. The other is textiles. Where the shoes are made and then sent back to Africa."

"I'm guessing Vietnam makes the shoes."

"Yes." Luna tapped a finger on one of the ledgers. "I have a hard time believing there's an office building that looks like this one outside of Hanoi."

"They sent us files on these companies."

"Tax returns, not all the worksheets from the junior accountants that are only looking at their calculators, not what they were adding up. Do you think Lewis or Gina have any clue that 'all' of Mercier's offices look the same?"

"No." Nate smiled. "That's my job."

"Mercier seems the OCD type. I bet that décor isn't the only place that is run exactly the same."

"This is good . . ." Nate said, nodding.

"I wouldn't have noticed this if we hadn't come. And wouldn't have looked at the line items for chandeliers and office furniture." Luna sat back in her chair and swiveled from side to side.

Nate put his fist out.

Luna bumped hers with his.

Now that they knew what they were looking for, it was full steam ahead.

They knew how the money in the company was going out . . . now they needed to find where it was coming back in.

They brought in takeout on Thursday night, arriving back at the hotel only to drop and do it all again on Friday. Luna put Lewis and Gina in charge of copying the junior accounting worksheets that hadn't been part of the package they'd been given originally, while she identified the files that needed to be audited.

Nate organized Zoom interviews with a handful of offshore players. From management to manufacturing.

When it was time to say goodbye to Mercier's Houston office, they were both riding pretty high on everything they'd found. Luna was looking forward to locking herself in her office and using an entire wall to map out the flowchart to where the money was going and coming. This was what she lived for.

"There's a steak house a few blocks from the hotel that was recommended," Nate told her on their way back to the hotel Friday night.

"We had steak Wednesday," Luna said.

"It's Texas," Nate said as if that was all the explanation he needed.

Luna laughed. "Fine."

Luna expected a restaurant but was met with a club. Complete with a live country band, dancing . . . and barbeque.

Just because the establishment was in the city, didn't mean there weren't a lot of cowboy hats and boots.

And Luna and Nate were celebrating.

"Are we drinking?" Nate asked.

"I think so."

Luna ordered a lemon drop, and Nate ordered some kind of whiskey drink Luna had never heard of.

"To a successful trip," Nate said, lifting his glass.

Luna took a sip and set her glass down. "This is going to wrap up much faster than I first thought."

"Marcus will be happy."

"And have us on another case within a week if we let him."

Nate set his glass down. "I can use the work."

"Have you acquired any other cases?" she asked.

"More like firms. Elenore Prescott."

"Oh. She's a shark. Smart," Luna told him.

"You've worked with her?" he asked.

"Couple of times. You'll like her. She did try to talk me down on my rates."

Nate laughed. "Me too. I didn't budge."

"Good. She can afford you."

The band started, and Nate moved his chair a little closer to hers, making it easier to hear him.

Or maybe he just wanted to get closer.

There hadn't been so much as a raised eyebrow or heated look since the night they talked about vegetable safe words. Because of that, Luna had managed a decent night's sleep the night before.

"Have you heard from Miley?" Nate asked. "Any more ghost sightings?"

"We talked this morning. It's been quiet."

"Are you anxious about going home?"

"Not really. The family has insisted for years the house has . . . energy." Using words like *ghost* or *spirit* gave the entire situation a label Luna didn't want to use. "It's never harmed anyone."

Nate shook his head. "Maybe you need to give this *energy* a name. Like Ethel."

"What makes you think it's a woman?" Luna took another sip of her drink.

"She likes the kitchen."

"That's sexist," Luna chided.

Nate smiled and leaned forward on his elbows. "If she's been there since before your memaw, and she was familiar with the kitchen, it has to be a woman."

"I see why they pay you the big bucks, Mr. Private Eye."

Nate's gaze bored into her. "You have beautiful eyes. They see a lot."

Instant heat rose in her chest. "Why do you keep doing that?"

"Doing what?" His gaze moved to her lips.

"You know exactly what."

With his hand sitting on the table close to hers, Nate used one finger to run alongside her hand.

There wasn't anything overtly sexual, or suggestive.

Just a simple touch of a finger against a completely unsuggestive part of her body.

Yet every sexual fiber of her being sprung to life.

Did he expect her to run away? Move her hand in retreat?

Instead, Luna looked at their hands, then met his eyes.

"I like watching you blush."

"I am not," she denied.

"Would you like me to prove it?"

Her back teeth clamped down on each other so hard to keep from smiling that her jaw ached.

The waiter arrived and broke the tension.

Pulling her hand away was less obvious when someone was placing a plate of food in front of her.

They dug into their meal, the first few bites without conversation.

The band entered another song much louder than the one before.

Nate scooted a little closer, leaned in. "Do you like country music?"

"It has its place," she said.

"Any chance I can get you on that dance floor?"

Luna turned to look at the dancers. "The closest I've come to line dancing is doing the Macarena at weddings."

"What about the two-step?"

She'd blacken his toes. And maybe if she did, he'd stop bringing up her blushing and the beauty of her eyes. "Do *you* know how to dance the two-step?" she asked.

He shrugged. "It's two steps . . . how hard can it be?"

Once their plates were empty and a second drink was ordered . . . they both learned just how hard two steps were.

But the steps weren't the point.

It was Nate's hand on her waist, and the other holding her hand.

It was the way his body kept pressing against hers while they tried to stay away from the other dancers.

It was the two of them blowing off some much-needed steam after a week that started with a snowstorm and a ghost and ended on a dance floor in Texas.

And Nate talking into her ear. "We suck at this."

"Fast, fast . . . slow, slow. Just count."

They may have been doing the fast, fast, slow, slow . . . except at unequal times.

All they ended up doing was laughing at their efforts.

Luna noticed a few couples around them laughing at them, too.

Back at their table, Luna took the last sip of her drink and looked at Nate over the rim.

"Want another?" he asked.

She shook her head. "Tipsy is fine, drunk is not. And we have an early flight."

Nate looked around them and signaled for the waiter.

Luna reached for her purse.

Nate placed a hand over hers. "My turn."

She shook her head. "You paid for lunch."

"If I let a woman pay for my meal and drinks in a place like this, they'll revoke my man card."

That made her want to pull out her credit card even faster.

Only Nate kept hold of her hand so she couldn't dig for a wallet.

She wasn't about to wrestle him for it.

Then she thought . . . maybe that was his goal.

The wrestling.

The cool winter air in Houston slapped them both as they exited the restaurant.

And the pounding beat of the music retreated as soon as the door closed behind them.

Luna gathered her coat around her to ward off the chill for their brief walk back to the hotel.

Nate moved around her, so he was walking on the street side of the sidewalk.

It wasn't lost on her what that meant, but she couldn't recall a time when a man had actually gone out of his way to be closer to traffic.

"Thank you . . . for dinner," she said.

"Thank you for letting me keep my ego."

She laughed. "Saving face amongst people you'll never see again in this lifetime."

"My mother would know."

"How?"

"She'd ask. 'Nate . . . you didn't let that woman pay, did you? I taught you better than that.'" His voice rose an octave to mimic a female.

"It's 2024. We've evolved. And we're here on business," Luna insisted.

Nate moved closer, placed a hand on her back, and gave way to another couple walking past.

His touch wasn't expected, but not a surprise.

The man had made physical contact with her more in the last three days than all of them since they met.

"You can get the next meal," he said.

"I will."

He smiled at her.

And she realized he hadn't taken his hand off the small of her back.

Their brisk walk back to the hotel had them shivering by the time they made it through the door.

In the elevator his hand slipped away, only to return as they were walking down the hall on the way to their rooms.

"You do know I noticed that, right?" she asked.

Nate looked at her from the side of his eyes. "You would have told me to stop if you didn't like it."

He was right.

Luna stopped at her door and removed the keycard from her purse.

Nate stood in front of her instead of moving one door down to his room.

She swallowed. "I . . . I'm not going to invite you in."

He lifted an eyebrow. "I wouldn't accept, even if you did."

She peered closer, looking for the lie that had to be there. He wanted to . . . the way he looked at her said he'd already been there in his head.

Or was that her projecting?

"Really?"

"Hmmm," was his answer.

Nate took a step closer and slowly brought a hand to the side of her face.

She caught her breath.

Her lips parted.

A first kiss was seconds away . . . a couple of inches from wondering to knowing.

He leaned closer.

Luna's heart thumped hard in her chest.

"Good night, Luna."

Nate let her go, turned, and walked to his room.

It took her brain a minute to process what had just happened.

Nate smiled at her before disappearing into his room.

Luna slapped her keycard against the lock and pushed the hotel door open.

"What was that?" she whispered to the quiet room.

She tossed her purse on her bed. Her coat followed, and she kicked her shoes off before attempting to sit.

She stood the second her ass hit her bed.

He smelled like whiskey and really good bad decisions.

He had nice lips. The kind that would swallow her whole as she melted into him.

The images flowing in her head had her body responding.

Luna paced the room.

The view from the window looking out over the Houston skyline was filled with flickering lights. The perfect kind of light to get naked in.

And . . . what the fuck?

She wanted to get naked.

She wanted Nate to make her that way.

That was rude.

Thoughts flew as she paced the room wondering exactly what Nate was doing on the other side of the wall.

Luna grabbed the keycard to her room and stormed out.

The knock on Nate's door was so loud, it hurt her own ears.

He opened the door, she stepped in. "That was r—"

CHAPTER NINETEEN

Nate didn't let Luna finish her sentence.

He pulled her into his room, captured the back of her head with one hand, and enveloped her in his arms.

And the kiss he'd been wanting since they met was on his lips . . . on hers.

Luna was fire, her eyes wide until they rolled back and Nate molded every inch of her body in contact with his.

His mouth coaxed hers open with a moan. Long, indecent kisses had him questioning how any kiss before this compared.

Nate felt Luna's hand in his hair, her nails digging in as her hips pushed into his.

He saw stars.

He'd been hard standing in front of her in the hall. Wanting so desperately to kiss her then. But he remembered her belief that meals out were a transaction, and he'd be damned if he fell into any of her "red flag" categories.

He pressed her back against the door and tilted his hips against her.

"Do that again," she demanded.

The sweet torture of his cock pressing against the fabric of her jeans was exactly what he needed.

Luna gasped either from pleasure or in need of air, but Nate used that moment to move his lips to the side of her neck, the lobe of her ear. Her skin was sweet, scented by the night air.

"I needed this more than my next breath," he whispered.

Luna ran a hand down his side and around to his ass and squeezed. "You left me in the hall."

His cock strained against his jeans. He was gone, already lost in her touch. Nate whispered in her ear, "We're crossing all the lines, Luna."

"I don't care," she told him.

"And tomorrow?" he asked as he pulled back far enough to look deep into her soul.

Luna pressed one hand to the side of his face. "We do this again . . ."

Yes! He found her lips again, and the weight of her breast in his palm.

The touch of her fingers sliding into the waistline of his jeans drove home the fact that they had way too many clothes on.

Nate pulled her away from the door and deeper into the room.

Luna lifted his shirt over his head and tossed it on the floor; Nate did the same to hers.

Her bra was pink and soft against the swell of her breasts. He cupped them both through the thin material and kissed them one at a time.

Nate didn't know if Luna pulled him down, or she simply fell and he was on top of her, but either way this beautiful woman he'd been craving was responding to every touch, every kiss in a bed that he called his.

Her leg slid up his and wrapped around his waist.

Nate freed his hands, kept his lips on hers, and reached for the zipper of her jeans. "Too many clothes."

She adjusted her hips so he could slide them free of her body.

He left her pink panties on and took his time looking at her.

Luna opened her eyes and smiled. "Don't stop now."

"Yes, ma'am," he cooed.

With both hands, he lifted her farther up on the bed before trailing his lips down the tight planes of her stomach. His teeth grazed and nibbled all the way to the V of her legs.

He sucked in her scent as if it was the nectar of the gods.

He let his breath and the touch of his fingers coax her open. So warm . . . so inviting.

Nate brushed her panties aside to have his first taste.

I'll find your spots, he mused. *All of them.*

He teased one side of her sex, moved the tiny cloth covering her to the side, and tasted the other.

He hadn't touched what she wanted . . . not yet.

It was there, swelling, asking for his attention.

Luna dropped one hand from his head to her hip and pushed the panties down. "Off. Get these off."

He smiled over her sex. "Demanding."

"Nate."

His name was a warning.

And that made him laugh as he nearly ripped the material from her body.

Pushing his own needs aside, Nate settled in for however long it took.

There was nothing shy about the beautiful woman in his arms, or the raw need of his touch.

He teased her again, one side, then the other.

Her hips shifted, and he ran the tip of his tongue exactly where she wanted it. She buckled, retreated, and returned for more.

He found the X, now he needed to find what made that X sing.

Where his mouth wasn't, his fingers were.

Up and down . . . no, that wasn't it.

Side to side . . . mmm, closer.

Fast? No, slow. He pulled that tiny seed between his teeth and Luna gasped, and her thighs tightened around his head.

He felt the heel of one of her feet dig into his back.

Nate smiled. "Hold on," he whispered.

Luna started to say something, but it was lost on the gasp she made when he went in with purpose.

He found the spot and the rhythm and put it to memory.

Slowly her climax started to build. He felt it from the tension in her legs, the way her hands grasped between his shoulders and the back of his head. It was as if she didn't want to force him to stay, but she couldn't help herself. God, he loved that. Loved the way she responded, the surprise in the gasps that escaped her lips.

It was when those tiny noises stopped and all he heard was her breath suspended, hardly a breath at all, that he knew she was close.

His neck was starting to throb; his lips numb from the desire he was milking from her.

And fuck his cock was throbbing.

He didn't change a thing.

Not.

One.

Thing.

The sweet sound of his name, a tidal wave from her throat, cried out. Her sex clenched the fingers he'd slid inside of her.

He just kept pulling at her, taking every single drop until she pushed him away. "Too much, oh, God."

He relaxed the side of his head on her thigh and took a full breath.

Her body had gone limp, the smile on her face said it all.

Luna looked at him now, her smile matching his, and she crooked a finger, asking him to come to her.

He wiped some of the evidence of her orgasm away with the side of his hand and crawled up her body. Her bra had disappeared, but he didn't remember taking it off.

"You still have your pants on," she said.

"I didn't want to assume," he teased.

She rolled her eyes and pushed at his shoulders until she was staring down on him.

As Luna pulled his jeans from his body, Nate reached for his wallet and removed the protection he'd put in the day he learned she liked him in sweatpants.

Luna took the condom from his hands before he opened it and looked at his erection as if it were her last meal.

I'm in trouble, he mused as she lowered her mouth onto him.

It was his turn to call her name at the first touch.

So much trouble.

~

The cold sound of an alarm ripped Luna from the best sleep she'd had in days.

The unfamiliar weight of a person in her bed brought the memories of the night before flooding in.

Nate tightened one arm around her and reached for his phone with the other to turn off the alarm.

"Let's stay here," he said on a sigh.

"Okay," she said, settling back in his arms.

"Really?" His voice was more awake.

She chuckled. "No. Get up, lazy. We have a plane to catch."

Nate tilted her chin to look at him and kissed her as if that was the way she needed to wake up. "Good morning."

"Mmmm."

"I love that I put that smile on your face."

She tried to frown. "Who said that was you? I was dreaming of Jason Momoa."

He dropped his smile. "Jason who?"

"You know, Aquaman?"

Nate stayed silent.

"The Great Khal of the Dothraki?"

Nate pinched his eyebrows together. "You want a Great Khal?"

He flipped her on her back and was on top of her before she could blink.

"I'll give you the Great Khal."

She started laughing.

Nate pinned her hands to the bed and kissed her.

"We don't have time for this," she said, still laughing.

Nate lowered his forehead against hers.

She ran her thigh up along his.

"You don't play fair," he moaned.

"You knew that going in," she said.

Luna pushed him away and crawled out of bed.

She wore one of his T-shirts and her panties, everything else was scattered all over his room.

Luna picked up her clothes but didn't bother putting anything on. "I'll be ready in twenty minutes." She paused. "Thirty. I need to pack."

"Really? How is that possible for a woman?"

"You've seen me without makeup more than with it on." She found her key and headed for the door.

"You're going out there like that?"

Luna looked down at herself. "Do you want your shirt back?"

Nate stumbled out of bed and peeked out into the hall. "You're crazy."

Luna ducked under his arm, looked up and down the hall, and then stepped out of his room. "Thirty minutes."

She felt the palm of Nate's hand smack the back of her ass before she moved out of his reach.

There was something fun about being in a hotel hall half naked.

Luna took a long enough shower to wash away the aerobic activity of the night before.

She was lax . . . so damn comfortable and at ease it was as if she'd taken a weekend at a spa and not a week at work.

It had been a long-ass time since she'd had sex that good.

Or had she?

Had sex ever been that good?

She wanted to call Miley and settle into a sofa and give her all the details . . . but that would have to wait until she got home. Besides, it was too early to call anyone.

And what would Luna say? "I caved. I have the willpower of a child loose in a candy store with a hundred-dollar bill. I knocked on his door and practically demanded sex."

When she'd drifted off to sleep once the two of them were too tired to go on, Luna had waited for regret to sink in.

It didn't.

The vision of his ass outside of the gray sweatpants was even sweeter, and Luna wasn't about to wish that image away.

The fierce need of pushing them both to climax contrasted the soft way he held her and kissed her when it was all over. The sweet things he said.

Luna shoved everything into her suitcase, double-checked the room to ensure she didn't leave anything behind, and was standing outside Nate's door when he emerged.

"Wow," he said. "You really meant thirty minutes."

"Punctuality is important."

He gave her that look, the one that said whatever was going to come out of his mouth next would make her blush.

Nate looked her up and down. "So is timing."

Luna cleared her throat and walked toward the elevators, pushing her suitcase by her side. "I haven't screamed out *broccoli* yet, Mr. Venti."

"No, but you did push me off and tap out after I made you co—"

The elevator doors opened, inside was a family with two school aged children.

"Good morning," she said innocently to the strangers.

Inside the elevator, Nate took her hand in his by her side and ran his thumb over her palm.

Damn if she didn't feel her body clench as it had right after she'd pushed him away.

Their flight was uneventful, but instead of sleeping on his shoulder, she felt his now familiar hand on her thigh, her arm, his fingers intertwined with hers.

Why had she kept herself from this feeling?

The one that only came with a man's touch.

A good man's touch.

Nate's car was exactly where they'd parked it. A privilege Luna would never again take for granted.

It was on the drive to her house that Luna felt the need to set some ground rules.

"I think we should keep things professional when we're at the office, so to speak."

Nate looked at his watch. "That took longer than I thought it would."

"What are you talking about?" she asked.

"Boundaries. The ones I knew you were going to set the second you screamed my name."

She couldn't stop smiling. "You're really full of yourself."

"I am *really* happy you charged into my room."

"You teased me. Kept that first kiss to yourself."

"I did not kiss myself," he argued.

"And I didn't charge. I'm not a bull." Technically that was wrong. She was a Taurus.

"Okay, then, what do you call it? Pounding on my door, wagging a finger in my face?"

"Confronting."

Nate reached a hand across the console and placed it on her knee. "You can confront me anytime you want."

Luna covered his hand with hers, felt the joy in such a simple act. "Boundaries . . ." she directed them back to the subject at hand.

"I agree," he said. "No public displays of affection in front of Marcus . . . or anyone we're working with professionally. So long as that doesn't apply to our home offices when we're alone."

"That might make getting our work done harder."

Nate shrugged. "I don't know. I kinda feel like I could take on the world today."

That feeling was mutual.

"And no games," she said. "That would piss me off and ruin any post-relationship working arrangement."

There was a beat of silence. "You already thinking of the endgame?" Nate said, much of the humor in his voice was gone.

"I'm being realistic. Things end. People change; stuff happens. You know it's true or neither one of us would be single."

Nate turned his palm up and grasped her fingers. "I have a boundary," he said.

"Let's hear it," she said.

"I don't juggle women. I've never understood men that do. If the person you're with doesn't check all the boxes, then they should find someone else."

"Monogamy," she muttered.

Nate nodded. "If you want someone else, you need to tell me. Not have me find out another way."

The way he swallowed and didn't make a point of looking at her suggested he'd been through this before. "Someone cheated on you."

He looked at her then and gave a single nod.

"Agreeing to monogamy is easy. I don't juggle either. If I find myself being attracted to someone else, you'll be the first to know." Luna noticed his shoulders relax.

Nate grasped her hand and brought it to his lips. It was as if that kiss was the signature on a contract.

Which was good enough for her.

"One more thing," she said.

"Name it."

This was hard. The part of her she didn't like to face but knew it would come out sooner or later. "It's not so much of a boundary as it is a heads-up."

Nate looked over, then back to the road. "Okay."

"I get triggered, sometimes . . . over the strangest things."

She saw her words processing over Nate's features. "Because of your ex?"

"Yes. And . . ." She stopped. "I don't want you to think that it's you. If it is, I'll tell you." She offered a half smile. "I'm good at keeping things honest. Like last night. I'm a little surprised that I was able to sleep . . . after . . . with you. Even if everything is great, that doesn't always work."

Nate smiled. "I saw how you sprawled out over the mattress in the living room."

"Yeah."

"But we can try, right? Like last night? And if it doesn't work, I'll find the couch. It's not like I haven't been there before." Nate glanced at her before looking over his shoulder to merge into the exit lane from the freeway.

"We can try."

"I'll never hurt you." He paused. "I will never put a hand on you with the intention of causing you pain. And so long as I'm in your life, no other man will either."

The way he spoke his promise put a weight in her throat that made it hard to talk.

Thankfully, Nate didn't ask her to.

He let her hand loose to maneuver his car through traffic. "Now that we've covered the rules and expectations . . . when can I see you again?"

Nate had a wonderful way of switching the subject at just the right time.

"Well . . . I have to have the obligatory girls' night with a bottle of wine to talk about you. Miley's going to ask *all* the questions."

His shoulders moved with his chuckle. "Is anything off limits in that talk?"

"Nope." Luna lifted a finger, wagged it at him. "If you wanted that in the rules, you should have said that before."

"Would you have agreed to it?"

"No." Her answer was quick.

His laugh was quicker.

They drove the rest of the way to her house in comfortable conversation.

This felt good, Luna had to admit. It almost felt like she'd started sleeping with a friend. Luna already knew she could count on him. And he cared enough about her to make sure her needs were met.

Boy had those needs been met.

Miley was going to eat this up.

Nate pulled up into the driveway and parked beside Miley.

"When do you pick up your new car?"

"I almost forgot about that." She hadn't considered the car since she left.

He turned off the engine. "A good man will do that to you. Make you forget life's little issues."

Luna rolled her eyes and pushed herself out of the passenger seat. "I should be able to pick it up today."

"Want me to take you?" he asked.

"Girls' night starts the second you leave," she told him.

They both moved to the trunk of the car.

Nate pulled her suitcase out, set it on the ground, and lifted the handle to make it easier to roll.

Luna moved to take it from him.

Nate kept it out of her reach and closed the trunk. "I can take it up to your room."

"I sense an ulterior motive." Not that she was complaining.

He stepped into her personal space and with his free hand, tilted her chin up ever so slightly. "I can behave. It's you we need to worry about."

Nate kissed her before she could reply.

Her response proved she was the problem.

The sound of the back door closing and Miley saying, "What do we have here?" broke them apart.

"I'll let you explain," Nate whispered before they turned to Luna's friend.

Two steps closer to the house, Luna saw the stiffness of Miley's body and the lack of a smile on her face . . .

"What happened?" Luna asked.

Miley looked over her shoulder and walked to them. "I tried calling. It went to voice mail."

"I had the phone on airplane mode, forgot to take it off. What's up?"

Miley looked at her, then Nate, then back. "Your mom's here."

Luna stopped all forward movement. The air in her lungs was kicked out.

"When?"

"First thing this morning. You were already on the plane."

Luna looked up at the house. "Is she alone?"

Miley nodded.

That was a relief.

"One bag, no car. Said she took the bus."

Fuck.

Nate put a hand on Luna's shoulder. "Is everything okay?"

No. This was the opposite of okay.

"It will be," she said.

Nate looked between the both of them. "Do you want me to come in?"

Luna quickly shook her head no and turned to Miley. "Can you give us a minute?"

Miley gave Nate a quick smile and returned to the house.

"What's going on?"

"It's long and complicated," she told him. "There's not a CliffsNotes version I can give you before I walk in the house."

Nate placed both of his hands on her face and searched her eyes. "I don't like the look on your face."

Luna tried to change it, then gave up. "She's . . . stressful. Doesn't normally stay long."

"Triggering," he concluded.

"Yeah," she admitted. "I'll call you later."

"You sure you don't want me to come in?"

"I'm sure."

Nate pulled her into his arms and placed his lips on hers briefly. A kiss that said he was worried, that he cared . . . and that he was there for her.

Luna let him hug her for a very long time before forcing herself out of his arms.

She turned to the door, straightened her shoulders, and walked in . . . dragging her suitcase behind her.

CHAPTER TWENTY

"Is that my baby girl?"

Karen Canning held on to the banister of the staircase as she made her way to Luna's level.

It had been five plus years since she last saw her mother.

So many memories flooded Luna's system at the same time, she knew better than to linger on any one for fear that they would paralyze her.

"Mom. What are you doing here?" Luna kept her voice lifted, as if surprised instead of judgmental for her mother's lack of announcing her visit ahead of time.

Karen opened her arms. "Do I need a reason to visit my little girl?"

Luna moved into her mother's arms to accept her embrace.

Her mother was soft, for many reasons. Poor eating habits and an allergy to exercise had always been a big reason for the numbers on the scale. It also didn't help that Karen was five four on a good day. In her youth, Karen had dyed her hair every color: black, blonde, brown, and red. Luna wasn't really sure what the normal color had been. Now half of her head was filled with gray, the lower half dirty blonde from a bad dye job. At Nana's funeral Karen had insisted on seeing Luna's hairstylist for a professional color and cut, but then conveniently didn't have the "cash" on her when it came time to pay.

And Karen never had access to a credit card.

The memory of paying the hairdresser flashed in Luna's head.

Why that memory of all of them surfaced, Luna would question later.

Miley stood on the landing of the stairs, turned, and watched from above.

"Not a reason, but I would have been here had I known you were coming."

Karen held on to Luna's arms when she pulled away and looked her up and down. "Look at you. All put together and jet setting all over the place. Miley said you were in Texas?"

"Yes. Houston. For work."

"I knew a man that lived in Texas. He said it was hotter than hell in the summertime, and the roads went on for days."

"It's not hot in winter."

Karen dropped her hands. "Why don't you get situated and come down so we can visit."

"Okay."

Her mother walked toward the living room as Luna took her suitcase upstairs.

Miley trailed behind.

When they walked past the spare room, Luna noticed the one bag her mother had brought with her. It was open . . . and empty.

"She's settled in already?" Luna whispered.

"Her clothes were dirty. They're in the wash."

That was not a good sign.

In Luna's room, they shut the door but still whispered. "How did she look when she got here?"

"Like she'd been sleeping on a bus for a week. First thing she did was take a half hour shower before talking my ear off."

"Did she tell you anything useful?"

Miley sat on the edge of the bed. "Said she was living in Alabama but didn't say much more than that. She asked about you, Ash . . . Harper. Asked if you had a man yet."

Luna turned and headed to her bathroom. "I'm glad I told Nate to leave before she could see him."

Miley followed her. "What happened there?"

Luna let a smile slip.

"I'll tell you all about it later. But nothing in front of Mom, okay? With any luck she'll be gone before they have a chance to meet."

"Just tell me this . . . was it good? Was he—"

Luna looked at her friend through the reflection in the bathroom mirror. "A-maze-ing," Luna sounded out the word and let her expression say the rest.

"Yes! About time."

Luna rested her palms on the cold tile and lowered her head. "Why does she have to be here now?"

"When has your mother's timing ever been optimal?"

"Do you work tomorrow?"

Miley nodded. "Sorry."

"I need backup," Luna whined.

"Call Harper."

"I'm not sure if she's back from her in-laws'."

"Ash, then."

"Ash will avoid this place like the plague. He's worse than I am."

"I'm off Monday."

"Nate and I planned to work here on Monday." That was going to change.

Miley placed a hand on Luna's arm. "It'll be okay. Maybe she's changed."

Luna flat out laughed. "You think pushing sixty has made her grow up?"

They both knew that was a fantasy.

"Go on, get back downstairs or she'll accuse us of talking about her."

Miley left and Luna stared at herself in the mirror.

Where did the smile go that Nate had put on her face?

Where was the happy that lived in her eyes only a few hours before?

"You can do this. A few days and she'll be gone."

~

Nate had zero doubt that Luna would have a few daddy issues. From what he'd been told, all of the Canning siblings probably had some trauma they had to deal with because of their fathers. But Nate wasn't familiar with mom drama. Sure, he knew it was out there, but the way Luna reacted when Miley said her mother had shown up . . . He'd bet that there had been more color on her face after walking into the kitchen and seeing evidence of a ghost haunting the house.

After dumping the contents of his suitcase in the wash, and the pile for the dry cleaners, Nate gave Ash a call.

It went to voice mail, where he asked that Ash call him back when he had a second.

It took a very long hour for Nate's phone to ring.

"I got your call. What's up?"

"Thanks for calling me back." Nate took a breath. "Luna and I flew back from Texas this morning."

"Yeah, Miley said you guys were there on work. Is everything okay?" Ash asked.

"I was hoping you could tell me. When I dropped Luna off, Miley met us in the driveway to tell us your mom had shown up . . . unexpectedly."

For a moment there was silence over the line.

"Ash?"

"I'm here. I ah . . . I'm surprised."

"So was your sister. But it was more than surprise. Her reaction made me wonder if your mom is dangerous."

Ash coughed. "No . . . well, not really. Not anymore."

Nate did not like that answer. "Once dangerous, always dangerous. You're a cop, you know that."

"What I mean is, she can't inflict harm now. Not the way she could when we were growing up," Ash explained.

"You're not making me feel any better about leaving Luna there."

"Was my mom alone? Did she come with anyone? A man?" Ash asked.

"Luna asked Miley the same thing. And no. Apparently, she came in on a bus. Where was she living?"

"I'm not really sure. Alabama . . . Tennessee. She moves around a lot. As long as she didn't bring any garbage with her, Luna will be all right. Stressed and ready for a week on a beach somewhere after Mom leaves, but . . . wait." Ash stopped himself. "Why are you asking?"

"What do you mean?"

"This is a sensitive subject. I'm not sure Luna would want me to talk to someone she works with about this."

Nate leaned against the counter in his kitchen and moved his phone to his other ear. "That's laughable considering the late-night distress call and handyman efforts I've put in since we've met."

"Huh. You're asking as a friend?"

Nate cleared his throat. "Your sister and I might be a thing."

"Might?"

The image of her sleeping on the pillow beside him put a smile on his face. "Are. *Are* a thing. Obviously, it's new. I don't want to overstep, but I don't want her to think I don't care. I'm asking you if there's anything to worry about," Nate said.

Ash laughed. "That wasn't hard to predict. I saw the way you looked at her."

"Does that mean you approve?"

"It's not my approval you need, but yes. You're a decent guy and your background check was a boring read."

It was nice to know that Ash was as thorough as he was protective.

"Back to your mom," Nate redirected the conversation to what he needed to know.

"I'm not giving you details. That's Luna's place to share. I will tell you that our mother is a really bad judge of character with the men she's picked in her life. We were all subject to it but Luna . . . Luna had to deal with it longer." Ash's voice trailed off. "Karen plays the victim . . . always. That's her default. She takes zero responsibility for her life choices, regardless of who they hurt. But like I said, we're all adults now. And as long as she hasn't brought a lowlife piece of shit with her, Luna will be fine. My advice to her new *boyfriend* is to check on her. Often. Distract her if you can. The fact that Nana left the house to us and not her . . . that's an issue. Mom will go out of her way to make Luna feel guilty for having a better life." Ash's voice trailed off and silence followed.

"Ash?"

"Anyway, she doesn't stick around for long. She'll probably ask for money. I'll call Luna, make sure she abides by the limit we've all set."

"You have a pre-determined loan limit on your mom?" Nate couldn't imagine having the need for that.

"Damn right. And it's not a loan. That's why we figured out the limit early on."

The sound of a police scanner describing an incident stopped their conversation. "I gotta go," Ash said.

"Thanks for the information."

Nate ended the call and tossed his phone on the counter.

He would check on Luna before going to bed, he decided.

The sound of a clock ticking made him look at the time.

Of course, a couple of text messages between now and then weren't a crime.

Luna emerged from her bedroom to find Miley and her mother sitting at the kitchen table drinking coffee.

"There you are," Karen said. "I was just telling Miley about how I ended up in Alabama."

"I thought you were in Tennessee."

"I was. But you know how it is. My job was fine when it started, then management changed and suddenly I wasn't young enough or pretty enough and my hours kept getting cut."

Luna took an empty cup from the cupboard and poured herself some coffee.

"Where were you working?"

"Bartending at the truck stop. Tips were good. Until they put me on days."

Luna sat in a chair opposite her mother to hear the details of the last five years of Karen's life. The times they'd talked on the phone were few and far between and usually took place on a holiday.

"Truck drivers work twenty-four seven if I remember correctly," Luna said.

"Well of course, dear, but the drivers don't do a lot of drinking during the day. I know you find that hard to believe." Her mother's voice went from softly explaining what she took as fact, to a hint of condescending.

"Right." Luna didn't bother arguing. Besides, if memory serves, the drivers her mother had brought home drank on their days off and were loaded on speed or cocaine during the day.

"Once they cut my hours, I had a hard time paying rent."

"You had a roommate, right?" Luna asked.

Karen rolled her eyes. "Maureen. Useless. I was floating her for months. As soon as I moved in, she started having all these issues. A sprained ankle that she couldn't work on. Then she thought she had carpal tunnel from stacking plates at the restaurant. As long as I was paying her share, everything was fine. Then when I started having trouble, she was in my face threatening to kick me out."

Luna felt her jaw tightening.

Same old story.

Different players.

"That sounds terrible," Luna said, believing almost none of what she'd just heard. The negativity that always accompanied the time spent with her mother was so quick to arrive, Luna hardly recognized it. Yet as she started to map out what her mother would say next, Luna felt the familiar walls of her past self closing in. The child born into toxicity, lies, and the illusion of safety and love that had always been and will always be conditional.

As those defensive walls surrounded her, Luna pulled out the only weapons she had against them.

Smile, nod, and remind herself that the time spent with her mother would only be temporary. Stay quiet, agree . . . and tiptoe around her mother's exposed nerves.

"Is that why you moved to Alabama?" Miley asked.

"That and Cody. I've always been a sucker for blue eyes."

Luna sat back and listened to her mother ramble on about the latest. Cody was a long-haul truck driver. Mostly a north, south route, but on occasion he'd go from the East Coast to the West. Two times divorced, with kids that lived with their mother on the panhandle of Florida. "He's a good dad," Karen told them. "Drives to Florida twice a month to see his children."

Kids that were still in school.

Cody was younger.

When Luna asked how much younger, her mother refused to answer.

Much like the story about the roommate, Luna instantly doubted the truth her mother preached. Cody was the earth and the stars.

"What happened with Cody?" Luna asked.

The expression on her mother's face twisted. "He started drinking a little too much."

Luna looked directly in her mother's eyes and said nothing.

"I know what you're thinking," Karen said.

"I'm not thinking anything," Luna lied.

Karen leaned forward and lowered her voice. "I'm nobody's punching bag. I learned my lesson with Paul."

When was that? The first time? The second time? The time he beat the shit out of Ash, and you still went back? Or the time when Paul . . .

Luna's heart pounded in her chest with a force that felt as if it was going to jump out of her body.

"When did this happen?" Miley asked.

"Couple weeks ago," Karen said on a sigh. "I thought it was best to come back here and reset."

Luna's brain glitched on her mother's words. Karen didn't have an end date to when she was leaving. And that fact felt like claws digging deep into Luna's throat.

Karen picked up her oversize purse and plopped it on the table and started digging through it.

She pulled a pack of cigarettes and a lighter from the depths of her bag and started to tap a cigarette free of the box.

The second she put the thing in her mouth, Luna placed a hand over her mother's. "We don't smoke, Mom. I'd appreciate it if you'd do that outside."

A flash of irritation was quickly replaced with a fake smile. "Oh, of course, honey. Habit. I used to smoke in this house all the time. I keep trying to quit. I've actually cut down a lot. Only about a half a pack a day. Sometimes less than that."

Luna nodded like one of those bobblehead dolls fashioned after baseball players.

"Thanks," Luna said without so much as a "good job" to anything else her mother had said.

Karen scooted her chair back and squinted her eyes with a tiny laugh. "I'll take my dirty habit outside."

"Thanks, Karen," Miley said, too.

As soon as Karen was out the back door, Miley grabbed Luna's hand with both of hers.

"I'll try and push my schedule around so I can be here."

"Don't be ridiculous. Besides, it doesn't sound like she has anything to go back to."

Miley glanced over her shoulder toward the door Karen had just slipped out of. "Do you think she'll try and move in?"

"I can't think about that right now. You know how she'll act if I ask her."

Miley unfolded from her chair. "I'm going to let your brother and sister know she's here and give them a heads-up on what she's said. There's no reason for you to shoulder the burden of your mother by yourself."

Luna didn't argue. "Thank you."

Alone in the kitchen, Luna looked at her watch. It had been less than two hours since Nate had dropped her off.

This was not how this day was supposed to go.

CHAPTER TWENTY-ONE

Karen finally ran out of words after ten in the evening.

Miley had tapped out at eight thirty, insisting that she needed a good night's sleep to get through her shift the next day.

Which was complete and utter bullshit, but Luna didn't try and stop her friend. Dealing with Karen was exhausting. A constant dodge and weave of not saying something that would put her on the defensive.

Luna took a few minutes to sit in complete silence once she retired to her empty room.

She slowly moved through her evening routine and then checked the hallway to see if the door to where her mother was sleeping was closed.

Once she was certain her mother couldn't hear her, Luna isolated herself and dialed Nate's number.

"Hey," he said, answering the phone.

"Hi." She knew her exhausted hello would be riddled with questions.

"You sound tired."

"You have no idea." Luna pulled back the covers on her bed and stacked pillows up so she could get comfortable.

"I called Ash."

"I know. Miley talked to him."

"I hope you don't mind. You didn't look happy when I left," he said.

Luna snuggled into bed, pulled the blankets up to her waist. "It's okay. I'm sure Ash gave you an earful about our mom."

"Not as much as I would have liked. Do you want to talk about it?"

"Yes . . . no." Luna pinched the bridge of her nose. "My head feels like it's in a vise. She's exhausting, Nate. My guard goes up the second she walks in the room. As much as I try and shut it down, she's right there to remind me why it's up." Luna paused.

Nate was quiet for a second. "I'm listening."

Luna winced. "Are you sure you want to hear this? Family drama doesn't come into relationships until at least month six. Three if that family lived next door."

Hearing Nate's soft laugh reminded her that he was turning out to be one of the good ones. And outside of her brother, Luna didn't know many "good ones."

"I've slept in your house twice, and that's before I had the privilege of kissing you. I think we're past the six-month mark in terms of quality time together."

The warmth of his words lifted her spirits, if only a fraction.

"Okay, Mr. Therapist, don't say I didn't warn you." *And if this freaks you out, I'm better off knowing now.*

"My mom wasn't a mom," Luna started. "Yeah, she gave birth to all of us. And occasionally we had some good times. But for as long as I can remember, I felt like *the* mother. You hear about kids that grew up in the '80s that came home from school with a house key and knowledge that at some point in the day a parent would be home. That was us, only at a time when every other parent knew where their kids were. My mom's career path is bartending and waiting tables. Fine, except you can't feed your kids on that. Forget having your own home. Not without another income. This was something I was cognizant of from the time I was in second grade. I was one hundred percent aware of the fact that my mother was staying in shitty marriages and relationships because she believed that was the only way to support us."

"Was it?" Nate asked.

Luna thought on that for a second. "Probably. At times. Except for brief glimpses of my mom living on her own. Or with the help of Nana, things felt good. We didn't have the temper of her latest husband or boyfriend threatening . . . us. I've tried so many times to put myself in her shoes. Raising three kids without so much as a high school diploma. No support from our fathers."

"Why was that? Why didn't any of your fathers step up?" Nate asked.

"She didn't make them. Bottom line. She got out of her marriages as quickly as she went into them. There was a court judgment for my father to pay child support, she didn't make him. 'I don't need his money.' It was all personal to her. Like her ego mattered more than our hunger. Our safety."

Luna lost herself in the memory of the fast-food joint she worked at in high school. "Do you know what I did with my first paycheck once I had a real job?"

"I'm afraid to ask." Nate's voice was soft.

"A dentist." Luna laughed . . . a sad, pathetic laugh at the memory. "I was sixteen and had an abscess on a molar. And while my friends were spending their weekend burger-flipping money on designer jeans that their parents thought were excessive, I was giving my paycheck to a dentist."

"You're serious."

"I wish I wasn't."

"I'm sure she qualified for government assistance," Nate concluded aloud.

"She did. And occasionally we were on it. But instead of using that along with whatever she was making in her job to better our lives, she was buying cigarettes and liquor. I can forgive all of that . . . I can. It had to be hard. But as I grew up and became more aware of her life choices, I realized how much they screwed us up. Bars close at two a.m. When she was in between husbands she'd bring random men home. I'd wake up and find some creep staring at me while my mom went out to buy bacon to make *him* breakfast." Luna was on autopilot now. The memories flooded in with an acute level of detachment. The kind that kept her safe and emotionally distant from her history.

"Damn. Did they . . ."

Nate didn't finish his question, and Luna didn't need to hear it to know what it was. "Some just looked. Some were decent enough to feel awkward that they were left in a house with a teenage girl that didn't think she needed to leave her bedroom clothed as if she was walking out into the snow. Others were inappropriate. There was a lock on the bathroom door. I used it . . . a lot."

Nate was silent on the other end of the line, but Luna was too far in to not mention the deepest hurt.

"And then there was Paul. He was with her the longest." As emotionally detached as Luna wanted to be, tears threatened. "He was a mean man. But he had a steady job, and with him, Mom didn't drink as much. There was food on the table and the tiniest sense of normal. But then the peace in the house would shatter at midnight and us kids would be dragged out of bed to find out who ate the last of the ice cream and left the empty container in the freezer. Our punishment was never a scolding. It was naked backsides and belts. Fists if we so much as looked at him wrong." Luna felt herself shaking. The way Paul had peered at her with her nightgown pulled up and her floral panties down at her ankles. It didn't matter how many lashes she took. The shame of his stare was a punishment that would never go away.

"Fuck . . . fuck."

"He made the guys from the bars look tame. So yeah . . . when my mother comes to town it's really hard to be in the same room with her." Luna stopped talking. Tiny details of more and more stories picked away at the edges of her brain.

"I can be at your door in ten minutes. Say the word and I will."

Emotion clogged the back of her throat. Luna looked at the ceiling and held in her cry. "I appreciate that," she whispered. "I'm okay."

"You don't sound okay."

She wasn't.

"I got out of it. We all did."

"The odds of that, statistically . . ."

"I know," Luna said. "I'm about the math, remember?"

She heard Nate fake a laugh. Even over the phone, she knew the sound was forced and not meant.

"Harper beat the odds because she moved in with Nana early on. She didn't live with Paul for long. Then Ash and I dealt with the brunt of Mom's choices. Paul was quick to punch on Ash. Ash ran away and came back several times. Mom would leave Paul; Ash would move home. She'd get back together with Paul, Ash would leave. But I couldn't leave." The guilt her mother put on her for even suggesting it at the time still sat in the far reaches of Luna's memories. *"If you leave, too, I'll have nothing to live for."* The implication of her mother taking her own life kept Luna exactly where she was.

"It was all a vicious cycle. It's why Nana left the house to us and not her. No matter what was going on in our lives, this place has always been the safe home we were led to."

"I understand that now," Nate said on a sigh.

Luna felt emotionally purged. As difficult as it was to tell all of that to Nate, hearing her own reasoning for the feelings she had toward her mother felt justified.

"I wish I was there with you," Nate said.

"Because this sounds like a party?" Luna attempted to lighten the conversation.

"No. Because I can't do a damn thing about your past, but I can be here for you now."

Luna didn't know what to do with that. Landon had brushed over Luna's past before she even had a chance to tell him everything. He didn't want to know about her "baggage" because she was with him now.

Part of her wanted to lean into Nate. The other, louder part said she needed to deal with this on her own.

"Is it safe to assume you didn't pick up your car today?" Nate asked.

She chuckled. "Sure, between reminding my mother that we don't smoke in the house and navigating the minefield of emotions that come with her visits, I broke away and bought a car." She closed her eyes. "I'm sorry that sounded bitchy and directed at you."

"You don't have to apologize."

"I do if I take something out on you when it's not your fault. I'll pick it up tomorrow." Something that should be filled with joy suddenly felt like a chore.

"Miley works tomorrow, right?" Nate asked.

"Yeah."

"How are you getting to the dealership?"

"Uber."

"Let me be your Uber," he suggested.

"You don't have to—"

"I want to," he said. "I want to see you, hug you, and let you know I'm here."

Depending on a man for this kind of emotional support was a slippery slope Luna didn't want to fall prey to. She shouldn't have unloaded all of this on him.

She should have gone to bed with only a good night text.

Forcing a smile on her face in the hope that Nate would hear a lift in her spirits, Luna said, "That would be great. We can go over a new plan for where we're going to work." Work was a safe subject. Diving into it would be the perfect distraction.

"What time do you want me there?" he asked.

"How about ten?"

"I'll see you then."

"Okay." Luna closed her eyes for a moment and had a hard time opening them back up. "I need to get some sleep." She rubbed the space between her eyes.

"Sounds like it. Call me if you need anything," he told her.

"Thank you," she said.

"Good night."

Luna ended the call and dropped the phone on the bed.

She could do this. Dealing with her mother when she was a kid felt impossible. Now she had choices. Smile and pretend that everything is fine, until it is.

Midnight meowed from outside of the bedroom door.

Luna tossed back the covers and went to let her in. After the cat waltzed into the room, Luna closed the door behind her.

Then paused a few steps away.

She turned, looked at the doorknob. Completely unaware of what she'd just done.

She'd locked the door.

~

Just like Uber . . . Luna met Nate in the driveway the next morning. Not giving him a chance to knock on her door.

He was dedicated to respecting Luna's boundaries when it came to her mother, but damn it hurt to do so.

Nate wanted to meet the woman to put a face and personality to Luna's history. How did she put up with it? Why did Luna continue a relationship with someone who obviously didn't have the capacity to care for others?

Why did Ash?

Because she's family only goes so far.

Easy for him to say. The woman wasn't his mother.

Luna slid into the passenger seat before Nate had a chance to cut the engine.

"Thanks for doing this," she said after a quick hello.

He wanted to kiss her and nearly leaned in to do just that when Luna looked up at the house.

Instead of giving in to his desire, he put the car in drive and started his GPS to direct them to the dealership where Luna had purchased her car. "How did you sleep?" he asked.

Luna huffed a laugh, looked at him, then away.

"That good, huh?" he asked.

"Thanks for listening last night."

Clearly, she didn't sleep. Though the way she looked, he wouldn't have known. Her makeup was a little heavier than she normally wore it, but when he looked closer, he could see the tired behind her eyes.

"How did the morning go?"

"Fine. My mother was never a morning person. A by-product of working late shifts. Now that she's older, it's even worse. She'd only been up for about an hour," Luna said.

"Not enough time to do any damage?" he asked.

Luna laughed. "Exactly."

Nate opened his mouth to ask more questions.

Luna cut him off before he could. "We need to figure out our schedule. Do you have any commitments this week?"

The emotion and passion of the previous night's conversation was gone and replaced with calm efficiency.

"I have a meeting with Elenore on Thursday. Otherwise, I'm open."

Luna nodded. "The delivery of the roofing materials is coming tomorrow, in addition to a giant dumpster."

"You need to be home for that."

"I know. Tuesday, then."

"There's too much information to go over in a coffee shop," he reminded her.

"Right. How about your place? Between my mom and the pounding—"

"No problem." Nate smiled her way.

An hour later the two of them were sitting at the desk of the car salesman as Luna finished signing everything needed for her to take possession.

From there, Nate stood by while Luna was shown some of the bells and whistles of her new ride.

He stood back and watched.

Luna smiled and asked all the questions Nate expected, but there was something missing in her interactions. Less fire . . . less spark. He'd never seen one person have such a profoundly negative effect on someone else in such a short amount of time.

Once the salesman was finished, and he'd shaken their hands for the last time, Nate slipped into the passenger seat. "There's nothing like a new car smell," he said as he ran his hand along the leather seat.

"Formaldehyde," Luna said.

"What?"

"That's what you're smelling. The formaldehyde used in the leather seats. There are other components. Plastics, oils . . . but yeah. The same chemicals used to keep that frog from decaying in high school science lab is part of that 'new car' smell."

Nate winced. "That just ruined it for me."

Luna laughed. A genuine smile this time. "Sometimes random facts stick in my head. That is one of them."

Nate reached for his seat belt. "Let's take this out for a spin. You owe me lunch," he teased.

She smiled again. "You're not eating in my new car."

"Good thing I don't like fast food."

Leaving his vehicle behind, Luna drove off the lot and slowly adjusted to the feel of her car. The brakes were quick to catch, and the gas was quick to accelerate.

Nate kept quiet and noticed all the minor adjustments Luna made as they drove down the street.

Her seat a little forward, the mirrors tweaked . . . the seat a smidge back. When she was satisfied both her hands sat on the wheel and a grin spread over her face. "I like it," she said.

"It's a sweet ride," he said. "I can't believe how far navigation systems have come."

"It's one giant moving computer," Luna pointed out. "That's harder to steal."

They looked at each other and laughed.

"Do you like Thai food?" Luna asked.

"Love it. The spicier the better."

Luna switched lanes. "You like your food like you like your women?"

"Now that you mention it. Pulling a gun on someone is definitely spicy."

Lunch put her in a better mood.

They sat beside each other in a booth and looked over the owner's manual of the Lexus while they waited for their food.

"This is my first brand-new car," she admitted.

"Really? I'm surprised."

"Considering it's worth ten percent less than it was an hour ago, you shouldn't be," she said.

"That's depressing."

They talked about their first cars, their dream cars, the cars they thought they'd buy when they grew up, and the ones they never wanted to own.

They talked about food and work and the weather.

And when they finished with their meal, Nate reached for his wallet only to be scolded for doing so.

The drive back to the dealership so he could retrieve his car was a lot lighter than the one earlier. Luna had shifted back to a less guarded version of herself.

She parked beside his car and turned to him. "Thanks for the ride . . . again."

"You get to be the chauffeur for a while."

"Fine by me," she said.

Nate reached over and guided her head to his.

Their lips met, in a not so quick kiss . . . the kind he'd wanted to greet her with but didn't have the chance.

He pulled back and waited for her to open her eyes, then kissed her again.

Luna covered his hand with hers and lingered as long as he did.

"I like that," he whispered.

"I do, too."

Nate peeled himself away. "I'll see you Tuesday. I may or may not be able to control myself the whole time."

"We have work to do," Luna said with a laugh.

"Don't worry. We'll work."

She narrowed her brows. "First. We work *first*."

Nate winked and put two fingers to his forehead for a salute. "Yes, ma'am."

CHAPTER TWENTY-TWO

Once Luna's car was safely parked in the garage, she made her way into the house and found it surprisingly quiet.

"Mom?" she called out from the bottom of the stairs.

There wasn't an answer.

She called again on the level of the bedrooms, still nothing.

The guest room still had her mother's belongings tucked in one corner, and a messed-up bed with clothes tossed on top.

"Mom?" she yelled again.

"Up here."

The door to the attic was open a few inches, letting the cold seep into the house.

Luna heard Midnight before seeing her mother.

Karen sat among a pile of boxes, several opened and the contents spread around her. "What are you looking for?" Luna asked as she reached down to pick up her cat.

"I'm just finding old pictures." Karen lifted one and waved it in the air.

"This must have been right after we moved back from California."

The picture was taken in front of the house with Nana, Luna, and her siblings.

"Did you take the picture?"

"I don't remember. I'm not in any of these."

Luna looked at the photograph. There was a huge maple tree in the front yard that wasn't there now. "I don't remember that tree."

"You wouldn't. You were probably three when a big chunk of it fell off in a storm and what was left threatened to fall on the house. Mom complained for weeks about what it cost to have it removed."

Karen kept sifting through pictures.

Midnight squirmed out of Luna's arms.

Another stack of pictures, taken maybe a year or so later, included her mother, Nana, and a man Luna didn't know. "Who was that?"

"Uhmmm. That was Larry. He was the husband before Joe."

Luna sat on the edge of a plastic box and walked down memory lane. "What happened with him?"

"Who knows. Mom always thought the men in her life were cheaters."

Another photograph was passed, much like the one before with Christmas in full swing. "Were we still living here?" she asked.

"Yeah. We didn't move out until you were almost four."

Luna smiled. It was moments like this that made her feel like her mom was like any other. Sharing old memories and stories of a time before Luna had any real memory of what was happening in her life.

"Remember Levi?" Karen asked.

"The Lab?"

Karen handed Luna a picture of the dog they had back in her elementary school days. "Best dog ever."

Luna smiled at the image of Levi lying across both her and Ash at a very young age. "Whatever happened to him?"

"He got old. He came to us old, though. He had the smelliest farts."

That made Luna laugh.

Karen stopped shuffling through the images and sighed as she studied one. From the smile in her face, it held a piece of her heart.

"What are you looking at?" Luna asked.

Karen shrugged and turned the picture around.

It was her and Paul.

Luna lost her smile. All humor and warmth fled in an instant.

"I really thought he loved me," Karen said.

A knot developed in Luna's stomach.

Karen looked at the image again.

"He was an asshole," Luna reminded her, her voice flat.

Her mother didn't agree . . . didn't disagree. "You have to admit, I did pick good-looking men."

So much for quiet, wistful moments with Mom.

Luna set the pictures in her hand aside and stood. "I have some work to do."

Karen barely looked up as Luna walked away.

Midnight followed her down the stairs and into her bedroom.

"I pick good-looking men," Luna muttered to herself. "You're just as mental as he was."

~

Luna and Miley stood in the yard watching what amounted to a conveyor belt carry bundles of roofing materials to the highest peaks of the house.

Brian had two guys with him as they moved around on the steep pitches of the roofline as easily as Luna would walk up a flight of stairs.

"How do they not fall off?" Miley asked.

"I have no idea."

"That would be a total trauma code if they did. That's at least thirty feet."

Luna smirked. "Let's hope they drank their coffee this morning."

Karen joined them wearing an oversize bathrobe that belonged to Ash. "That's a fun sound to wake up to."

"They can come at three a.m. for all I care. This needs to get done," Luna told her.

"What is this costing you? It can't be cheap."

"It's not," Luna said.

They were all quiet for a moment.

Then Karen said, "A new car and a new roof in the same week. I should have been an accountant."

"You're never too old to go back to school," Miley said.

"I have three kids. I'm not going back to school now. You guys can take turns caring for me when I'm old."

Luna felt an invisible fist punch her stomach. "You're not old, Mom."

"I feel old." Karen opened her mouth wide with a yawn. "I need coffee," she said and walked away.

"Your mom thinks you're rich," Miley said quietly once Karen disappeared into the house.

"Compared to her, I am."

"Why didn't you tell her that the insurance company is paying for this? Maybe she wouldn't act so entitled."

Luna stepped back to get a better look at the men on the roof. "She used to brag about one day slipping and falling in a Walmart so she could sue them and get a boatload of money. If she thought my insurance company would pay her off in some way, there's no telling what she'd pull."

"You really think she'd do that?" Miley asked in disbelief.

"She was ogling a picture of Paul yesterday. Looked like she wanted to kiss it. Yes, I think she'd do that."

Miley started to walk away. "I need to call my mom and let her know I love her," she said.

At least Karen sparked others to be grateful for what they had in their lives.

~

Later that night Luna took her mom to the grocery store for a few things . . . mainly cigarettes. And since her mother came without transportation of her own, Luna could either drive her mother around or loan her the Lexus.

Being her mother's taxi it was.

They skimmed through the supermarket, grabbing snack food Luna and Miley never ate, but that would make Karen happy. And the ingredients for "family favorite" recipes Karen insisted on making.

At the checkout, Karen pulled out her wallet.

Which surprised the hell out of Luna.

Then she saw the card.

A government EBT card.

Luna looked around her to see if anyone she knew saw them. "I'll get this. You save that for yourself," Luna told her mother while she pulled out her credit card.

"Are you sure? I don't mind."

"You can buy your own cigarettes and the vodka," Luna said. She wasn't walking out of a grocery store using EBT money and loading the groceries in a brand-new Lexus. That was wrong on way too many levels.

"You can't buy cigarettes and alcohol with this."

Luna tried to smile at the teller.

The woman behind the register didn't seem to care.

Luna slid the vodka aside. "I've got this."

The woman removed the price of the vodka and totaled up the bill.

Karen was reduced to paying for her "dirty habit" with her own cash.

That was a line Luna had no intention of crossing.

Luna still wondered what her mother's endgame would be. A morbid thought for sure, but one she couldn't stop herself from thinking. Would it be cancer? Liver failure . . . an accident?

A man?

Luna highly doubted that her mother would pass from "natural causes."

As they walked out of the store, her mother said she needed to pass by an ATM for cigarette money.

Even though Luna agreed to stop at a bank, her expression must have given some of her thoughts away.

"I know you hate my smoking," Karen said.

"I didn't say anything." Luna backed her car out of the parking lot and took joy in the clarity of the car's backup camera.

"You don't have to say anything. You still give me that look whenever you see me smoke."

"I probably give everyone I see smoking the same *look*."

"No." Karen's voice had taken on a defensive tone. "You save that for me."

"Do you want me to pretend like I like it?" Luna asked.

"No. But you don't have to be so judgy. It's not like I haven't tried to quit. It's hard."

"I imagine it is. Anything worth doing takes effort," Luna said.

"See, there you go. I've tried."

"Can we not argue about this, please?" Luna asked.

"You used to come home from school and lecture me about what they taught you that day. Give me statistics on how long I'd live and the likelihood of me needing oxygen by the time I'm sixty."

"I was good at math back then, too." Luna attempted to laugh and make light of where her mother was headed. "Clearly you're beating the odds."

Karen sighed. "I didn't expect you to buy my cigarettes. I would *never* ask. You didn't have to point it out in front of the teller."

So that was what this was all about. "If I embarrassed you, I'm sorry. It was not my intention."

That was what her mother needed to hear.

The tension in Karen's body eased. "I really am doing better."

"I'm glad," Luna said aloud. *I really don't care.* The battle had long since been lost, and worrying about her mother's health was no longer a priority.

"I have to work tomorrow," Luna said, changing the subject. "I'll be leaving early and probably won't be home until the afternoon."

"I thought you worked from home."

"I do. But I'm working with a team on a case. I asked Brian not to bother you. If any questions about the roof come up, he'll call me."

"Is Miley going to be home?"

"She isn't working but that doesn't mean she doesn't have plans," Luna said.

"I don't need anyone to entertain me."

Yeah, but leaving her at the house without anyone else there itched a part of Luna's spine that made her squirm.

When she'd first moved into the house, she saw her nana everywhere. And Karen.

All of that eventually faded and the place felt like hers. Her responsibility.

Home.

Something she could depend on, that would be there for her. That no one could take away.

Somehow her mother being there without Luna threatened that security.

Or maybe she associated her mother with a lack of security and that caused her anxiety.

Luna pulled into her bank's parking lot, and her mother hopped out to use the ATM.

Luna's jaw hurt. She noticed because the second her mother was out of her orbit, she felt it relax.

"I need to see a therapist," she muttered to the empty car. "This can't be healthy."

~

Nate's modest apartment was furnished in dark gray and white tones. He had a TV that took up the space of one wall and a dining table for four that they'd set up as their office for the day.

The décor was modern, but not stuffy.

He had a couple of large plants that looked like they'd just come from the nursery. Luna had to look twice to see if they were real.

She liked it.

And it fit Nate's personality like a glove.

He met her at the door with a kiss and then promptly gave her a cup of coffee before they got started. For three hours it was nonstop deep dives into tax reports and company ledgers.

It wasn't until they were taking a break and eating lunch that Luna's unexpected company was brought up.

"You haven't said anything about your mom," Nate said.

"That's because I'm trying to forget that she's waiting for me when I get home."

"Still no idea how long she's staying?"

Luna shook her head. "I'm honestly afraid to bring the subject up. We went by an ATM, so I know she has a little bit of money. I assume she doesn't have a job to go back to in Alabama, and she hasn't said anything about her living situation there. Does she have a car? Her name on an apartment lease? Any belongings outside of what she brought with her? Ash and Harper are coming on Saturday. Ash will ask all the important questions and get away with them."

"Are you saying he is the 'favorite'?"

"I'm not sure it has anything to do with favorite. More like, he's able to say the same things Harper and I do but she doesn't get as offended. She accuses me of being judgmental of her, which is completely valid. Ash can be just as critical, but she never calls him out."

"Do you think it's a gender thing?" Nate asked.

"Oh, a hundred percent. She's a completely different person around men than women. Always has been. When you meet her, you'll have a hard time seeing the person I've described."

Nate grinned. "*When* I meet her?"

Luna rolled her eyes. "I can't imagine why you would want to, but yes . . . when. I can't put my life on hold while she's here. On Saturday we're going to have a midday family dinner. Kinda like what you do on a holiday. My sister and her husband will be there, Miley . . . Ash. Ash asked if you were coming."

Nate kept his lips sealed and lifted his eyebrows.

"Too much wine and it could be a complete shit show," Luna warned.

Nate leaned forward and placed his hand on her and asked, "What can I bring?"

"You've been warned."

"You're entirely too stressed." He looked at her lips.

Luna smiled, feeling the shift in his energy. "We're working."

"We've got a lot done. We deserve a break." His thumb massaged the inside of her wrist.

"This is highly unprofessional, Mr. Venti."

"Do you want me to stop?"

Luna leaned forward, licked her lips. "Where is the fun in setting your own hours if you don't make the most of your time?"

"My thoughts exactly."

Nate pulled her in and placed his lips on hers. Slow, coaxing, until her mouth opened and welcomed him in.

She needed this. The perfect distraction.

Nate's hands on her body, in her hair.

He tugged her to her feet and broke their kiss only to take her by the hand and guide her to his bedroom.

Luna fell into him, mind, body, and soul and let him take her to another plane. One where it was just the two of them and a strong desire to please the other.

Unlike their first time in Texas, Nate made love to her slowly. Just like the last time, he found every spot and others she didn't know she had.

After they were both spent and wrapped in each other's arms with only a sheet pulled over them, Nate ran his fingers over her hair and whispered beautiful things in her ear as her eyes drifted shut.

Luna woke up with a jolt.

Her head was on Nate's chest; her thigh nestled over one of his.

His chest rattled with a hum.

"I fell asleep."

"You did." He kissed the top of her head.

She looked up, found him smiling.

"How long?"

"About an hour."

She pushed herself up on an elbow. "Why didn't you wake me?" The dark sky beyond the window said the weather had shifted and rain was once again falling.

"I didn't want to. I'm selfish." He pushed a lock of her hair aside.

Even sleepy she managed a witty reply. "Selfish men don't do what you do with your tongue."

His grin was comical. "You like that, do you?"

She tried to act unaffected. "I mean . . . it works."

"It works?" Nate squeezed the top of her thigh where his hand was resting.

Luna moved her leg higher until she felt the most sensitive part of him touch her knee.

His eyes widened.

His cock twitched.

"Oh, what's that? Didn't you get enough?" She ran her hand down his hip, her thumb barely grazing his growing erection.

Nate moaned. "Feels like someone else wants more."

Luna climbed on top of him and straddled his hips, welcoming the length of him into her body. Her core clenched and her eyes rolled back.

She could get very, very used to this.

CHAPTER TWENTY-THREE

A week with her mother felt like a year.

The never-ending dance of side stepping her insecurities and risking an argument should be easier as an adult.

It wasn't.

Someone once said that when family is visiting, it's kinda like fish. Any more than three days and they started to stink.

This rule applied to Karen.

Her pleasant side started deteriorating the night Luna took her to get cigarettes. The more comfortable Karen became, the worse it was.

Noise from the roofers in the morning was "disturbing." And Karen didn't approve of how they sat around the patio when it was time for them to take their lunch. "They think they own the place," she bitched.

Luna attempted to stay up with her mother a couple of times but eventually gave up, leaving the den with her mother watching TV. With the volume so loud that even with the thick walls of the old home, Luna could hear it in her bedroom.

Karen would stay up late, and try and sleep in, ergo the complaints about the construction crew.

Then there was the constant push and pull of the cigarette drama.

Luna thought the smell in the kitchen from the cigarettes was from her mother tossing the butts in the kitchen trash. Then at dinner one night, Luna, Miley, and Karen were sitting at the kitchen table, and when the meal ended, like clockwork, her mother needed to smoke.

She walked to the back door, opened it, and lit the cancer stick up, letting it dangle from her fingertips just outside the open door.

As Miley and Luna cleared the table, Karen attempted to carry a conversation from the mudroom.

"I wouldn't call that smoking outside, Mom," Luna chided.

"I'm blowing the smoke outside the house."

"Where the wind blows it right back in."

Clearly aggravated, Karen closed the back door with a hateful sigh.

"She doesn't get it," Miley whispered.

"She does. She just doesn't care."

When she returned to the kitchen, she ran the cigarette butt under the faucet and tossed it into the trash.

"I'm going to find an ashtray with sand in it so you can leave all of that outside."

"Does this bother you, too?" she asked as she closed the door to where the garbage lived.

"It's starting to smell," Luna told her.

Karen opened the cabinet back up and yanked the trash can from inside. "I'll take the trash out, then."

That wasn't the solution, but Luna wasn't going to argue any more about it. She'd find an ashtray, set her mother up away from the back door so the smoke couldn't blow back in, and insist that she use it.

Karen once again stormed out of the house, this time with a half-full garbage bag in her fist.

"I'm sorry you have to put up with her," Luna said to Miley when they were alone again.

"Don't be. I know your mom. She feels alienated. That's obvious."

On the return trip to the kitchen, Miley smoothed things over. "I'm going to have another glass of wine. Karen, can I get you something?"

Miley was speaking her mother's language.

"Absolutely."

On the street, just above Luna's driveway, sat a roll-off container that was filled with discarded roofing material.

In all of the conversations Nate had with Luna over the past week, very little was said about the new roof that was being put on her house.

He pulled in behind Miley's car and saw two more cars and a motorcycle parked in and around the carport.

Apparently, he was the last to arrive.

Luna greeted him before he had a chance to knock on the door. "Were you watching for me?" he asked, teasing.

"The alarm on the driveway makes it impossible for anyone with a car to sneak in."

Nate had a side dish in one hand, and a bottle of wine in the other.

He leaned down and kissed her. "Hello."

"Hi." She took the wine and stared him in the eye. "This is your last chance to back out."

"I've been looking forward to this all week," he said. And he had. The more he learned about Karen, the more he needed a face to match the stories.

Luna opened the back door and led him into the house.

Everyone was gathered in the kitchen around the island.

Miley crossed to him and relieved him of the dish in his hand. "Hey."

Ash had his back to Nate.

Harper stood beside her brother.

The conversations quieted when Luna cleared her throat in an attention-grabbing way.

Ash turned, giving Nate a first glance at Luna's mother.

"Hello, Nate." Ash stepped forward and shook his hand. "I'm glad you could make it."

Nate smiled at Luna. "You couldn't keep me away."

Ash pointed two fingers in his direction. "Remember you said that."

"Oh, stop it." Harper stepped closer and offered Nate a hug. "Hello."

"Good to see you again," Nate told her.

"This is my husband, Jerry," Harper introduced the man standing to the side.

Jerry, the guy that couldn't keep a job.

The thought escaped Nate's conscious faster than he could slam it back in.

Another handshake and appropriate greeting from Jerry.

"And this is our mom, Karen," Luna made the introduction.

Karen looked him up and down with a smile that reminded Nate vaguely of Luna's. Mother and daughter had the same nose and color eyes.

"Mom, this is Nate."

Karen's handshake came from a woman who clearly didn't shake hands often. Soft hand, limp wrist.

"A pleasure to meet you." Nate wanted to say that he'd heard a lot about her but was fearful she'd ask what that was.

"The pleasure is mine." Karen looked at Luna. "He's much more handsome than that last one."

"Mom!" Harper scolded.

"What last one?" Ash asked.

"The husband," Karen explained.

"That was a thousand years ago, Karen," Miley said.

"Karen has zero filter," Jerry pointed out.

"When you're as old as I am, you don't have to hold anything back."

"What was your excuse twenty years ago?" Ash asked.

Karen pushed Ash's arm, a playful smile on her lips. "Oh, stop."

Nate glanced at Luna.

The smile she wore was fake, her expression neutral. He wasn't sure what part of the introductions had bothered her, but he could see that some of the sparkle behind her eyes that was there a moment ago was gone.

Nate placed a hand on her arm.

She looked up, smiled. "What can I get you to drink?"

"What are you having?" he asked.

She pointed to a glass of white wine that sat on the counter.

"I'll have that," he said.

Luna left his side and Karen moved closer. "My son told me that you used to work for the FBI."

"It sounds more glamorous than it was." Nate delivered the statement he always did when someone mentioned the FBI in such wistful tones.

"Looks like we have to be careful around here, with my son the cop and an FBI agent standing by."

"He's a private investigator now, Mom," Luna said.

"Even less glamorous," Nate said quickly.

"Do you spy on married couples having affairs?" she asked with a gleam in her eye.

"I specialize in fraud investigations."

"Is that how you two met?" Karen asked.

"Luna didn't tell you?" Ash asked.

"Luna doesn't tell me anything. I didn't know he existed until this morning."

"*Luna* . . . is standing right here."

Nate moved closer and accepted the glass of wine she handed to him.

"And I didn't want to invite twenty questions," Luna said.

Nate knew exactly why his existence had been kept a secret and wasn't the least bit offended. "Luna and I are working on a case together," he explained.

"You must be very smart."

Miley laughed. "Oh, I don't know. He nearly got himself shot a couple of weeks ago."

Nate slid his arm around Luna's waist as the story of Ash's call and Nate's late-night visit was retold by Miley and Ash.

The dynamics of the Canning family were layered in nuance.

Ash was absolutely the favorite. Karen was quick to smile at her son and make snide remarks to her daughters. Jerry said very little at first but warmed up within the first hour of Nate's arrival.

And Miley was the house referee.

She put Ash in his place. Made any questionable comment that came out of Karen's mouth a joke or quickly moved the conversation on. Then there was Harper, who didn't seem all that affected by any of it.

~

The never used formal dining room was filled with noise.

It took a prime rib dinner, all of her family, and Nate sitting beside her with one of his hands touching her every time he had a chance, to calm Luna's anxiety.

The dinner felt almost normal.

Not her normal, but "Christmas card perfect," normal.

For a couple of hours, they were a functioning family having typical conversations about everyday stuff.

Until Karen's eyes started to show the number of drinks she'd consumed.

"What have you been doing with your life, Mom?" Ash asked.

"Working."

"What kind of work?" he asked.

"Bartending. The money is better than waiting tables, even for an old broad like me."

Her mother was really good at calling herself names and waiting for someone to say she wasn't.

Jerry stepped up. "You're not old."

The expected smile passed her lips.

"When does your boss expect you back?" Harper asked.

That was the ten-thousand-dollar question Luna wanted the answer to.

Her mother tilted her glass back before launching into her answer. "There was a problem in the kitchen, something flooded. The health department closed us down until the owner actually spends some money on the place."

There were big chunks of that story Karen was omitting. Luna knew it in her bones.

"How long will that take? The owner can't expect their employees to wait around and not find other jobs," Jerry said.

"You'd be surprised. Jobs aren't that easy to find in Alabama. Especially serving alcohol. They still have dry counties, for God's sake."

"No offense, Mom, but that doesn't sound like the place for you," Ash said.

Luna shifted her eyes to her brother and waited for her mother's response. If she'd said that, her mother would take immediate offense.

Karen shifted in her chair, lifted her chin. "From the looks of this table, I don't think any of us belong there."

"Fair," Harper said.

It didn't escape Luna's attention that her mother didn't answer the question. The one about when Karen was returning.

"When was the last time you guys all got together?" Nate asked.

A chorus of "Nana's funeral" came from all ends of the table.

Luna smiled. "Almost five years."

"Feels like a lifetime ago," Harper said.

"It was," Miley added.

Karen leaned forward and tapped one finger on the table. "Do you know what is missing in this house?"

"Yeah . . . Nana," Harper said.

"That, too. But no." Karen looked between her children. "Babies. When am I going to get my grandbabies?"

Harper barked out a laugh. "Don't look at me," she said. "Jerry and I decided a long time ago that wasn't for us."

"I don't know how you can say that. You'd make beautiful babies."

"You're going to have to get that from someone else," Jerry said.

Everyone looked at Ash. He lifted his glass, talked over the rim. "I had a vasectomy."

"Excuse me?" Karen asked.

"Seriously?" Nate asked.

None of this was news to Luna. She and Ash had talked about it several years back, although he hadn't told her when he actually did it.

Luna and Harper exchanged glances.

"I'm not into surprises. No accidental kids on my watch," Ash insisted.

"What if one day you want one?" Nate asked.

"I'll have it reversed."

Even if it wasn't that easy, Luna respected her brother's decisive action. The Canning children had all been oopsies, something that had been pointed out to them often.

"I can't believe you did that," Karen said. "You never said anything about not having kids."

"That is probably the most responsible thing I've ever known you to do," Miley told him.

Ash smiled at Miley. "Becoming a cop was pretty responsible."

She shrugged. "And now you risk getting shot at for a living. I don't know if that qualifies as responsible."

"Nurses, especially ones that work in the emergency room, are assaulted more than cops ever are." Ash glared at Miley.

"Is that true?" Harper asked.

"Statistically, yes," Luna told her sister. "Dementia patients, crazy ones. Those on drugs. Families that can't control their grief. The list goes on."

"Have you ever been hurt?" Nate asked Miley.

Luna knew the answer but waited for Miley to say something.

"Nothing serious," she said.

"I rest my case," Ash said.

"I guess that leaves the two of you." Karen stared across the table at Luna and Nate.

"Jesus, Mom. They just started dating." Harper voiced her outrage for both of them.

Nate squeezed Luna's hand under the table.

Her heart rate rose. "I told you a long time ago that I'm never getting married again. And I'm certainly not going to have kids alone," Luna told her with a calm that was quickly going away.

"What's the point of you two dating if the endgame isn't marriage and kids?" Karen stared at her.

Luna glanced at Nate. "Are you trying to make me uncomfortable?" she asked, turning her glare onto her mother.

Karen lifted her nearly empty drink and waved it in the air. "I don't understand. I know you're a feminist but—"

"Mom!" Ash interrupted.

"What do you think?" Karen asked Nate.

"I think it's a little early for discussions about marriage and kids," Nate said.

"Knock it off, Mom," Ash told her.

Luna glanced up at Nate and hoped the apology in her eyes translated to him.

"Okay fine." Karen picked up her drink and focused her glossy eyes on Nate. "None of them want to have babies because they think I was a shitty mom. I wasn't perfect, but I always put a roof over their heads, and nobody starved."

"If it wasn't for Nana, you couldn't say that." The words were out of Luna's mouth before she could pull them back in.

Tension so thick you could slice it with a knife fell over the table.

"That's not fair," Karen said.

"What isn't fair is for you to put Nate on the spot two hours after you've met him. In my home, at my table."

"This was my home long before it was yours," Karen shouted.

Heat built and threatened to explode inside Luna's veins. She scooted her chair back and stood. "Can someone please remind our mother what Nana wrote in her will."

Without another word, she walked out of the room.

Halfway up the stairs, she realized Nate was following her.

She walked into her bedroom and waited until Nate was beside her before closing the door.

"I'm so sorry."

Nate pulled her into his arms. "Don't be. You warned me."

"She was a shitty mom," Luna said into his shoulder. "Still is. I'm a different person when she's around. I don't recognize myself."

Nate pulled her closer. "I noticed."

She half hoped he hadn't. Then she realized how like her mother that reaction was. Luna wasn't quite calling herself a name and waiting for validation, but it was too close to her mother's behavior for comfort. "Never stop doing that," she told Nate.

"What?"

"Being honest. Call me out on my own shit, okay?"

"I can do that," Nate said.

She sighed. "I don't like how I talk to her. I don't like how I judge her. I don't like how I complain about her. I don't like that I can tell when something crappy is going to come out of her mouth. I can't stand the fact that I know the second she starts lying."

"You're talking about her lost job story," Nate said.

"You caught that?"

"I think the only people at the table that bought it were your sister and Jerry. The dismissive laugh . . . the lack of eye contact with anyone . . . the way she didn't answer the question. It was classic."

"You see it, then. I'm not going nuts."

Nate smiled. "You're not crazy. Even when she was suggesting she was a crappy mom she was lying. At least to herself."

Luna leaned on his shoulder. "This wouldn't be so hard if I knew she was leaving in a week."

"Tell her she needs to go."

Wouldn't that be simple. "Easier said," was Luna's reply. "If she starts looking for a job here, I'll force the issue."

There was a soft knock on the door with Miley calling out from the other side. "Is it safe to come in?" she asked.

Luna glanced at Nate and whispered, "Sadly."

Nate winked. "Yes," he said.

Miley walked in and closed the door behind her.

"Things have calmed down. Ash pulled your mom outside and talked to her."

"Did he remind her that she has no claim on this house?"

Miley nodded. "In a way. She started crying about how she missed her mother." Miley held up her fingers for air quotes. "Grief was clouding her behavior."

"Five years. She stormed out of this house after the will was read and has barely talked to any of us in five years. She's blaming her behavior on grief."

"Narcissists can't blame themselves. They're incapable," Nate pointed out. "I'm not defending her." He tossed one hand in the air in surrender.

Luna squeezed his other hand that sat in her lap. "I know."

"I'm on the outside. It's easy to see her behavior for what it is. There's a lot of psychological training with the FBI."

"That'll come in handy if you stick around," Luna said.

Out of nowhere, the sound of a door slamming made all three of them flinch.

"What the . . ."

Miley opened the bedroom door.

Luna and Nate came up behind her.

The hallway was empty.

Voices from downstairs drifted up.

"Someone must have left a window open, caused a door to shut," Nate suggested.

A chill ran up Luna's spine. "All the bedroom doors are still open."

"The bathroom, too," Miley said.

Luna peeked into the room her mother was occupying.

The window was shut.

"Guys?" Nate called them.

Luna and Miley turned to look at what caught Nate's attention.

The door to the attic was open.

Midnight stood beside it, the hair on her back straight up, her eyes sharp on whatever she thought she saw.

Luna took a step closer. "Is anyone up there?" she called out.

No answer.

"That sounded like a door slamming, right?" Miley asked.

"That's what it sounded like to me," Nate said.

"Hey . . . what was that?" Harper yelled from the stairwell.

"Did anyone come upstairs?" Miley asked.

Harper came into view. "No."

"Then who opened the door to the attic?" Luna asked. She would have noticed if it was left that way earlier. If only from the cold that was permeating the otherwise warm hallway.

"Ethel," Nate said slowly.

"Who?" Miley asked.

Luna looked at Nate as she realized what he was saying.

She turned back to Midnight, who was now sitting and licking her paw.

"Nate named our ghost," Luna said quietly. "Ethel."

They all turned and looked at the attic door.

CHAPTER TWENTY-FOUR

"I met someone."

There was nothing like meeting someone's dysfunctional parent to make you appreciate the sanity of your own.

Nate made a point of calling his parents shortly after meeting Karen.

His mom picked up the phone.

"That's good news. Who is she?" his mother cooed.

"Her name is Luna. We met on a case we're working on."

"Oh . . . this isn't like Monique, is it?"

"She isn't my boss. She's an independent contractor. I'm an independent contractor. No one is out of a job if it doesn't work out."

"Oh, good." His mother's relief was felt over the phone. "Tell me about her . . . is it serious?"

He chuckled. "I wouldn't be telling you about her if she was a one-night stand."

"Oh, stop. You don't have those . . . do you? Wait, I don't want to know." Even though it wasn't a FaceTime call, he could see his mother's squished face in a pained expression.

"Of course not, Mom," he said sarcastically. "I've never done that. Not once. Not in college, or in Vegas at Tony's bachelor party. Or at—"

"Okay, I get it. You can stop now."

Nate liked teasing his mom. She fell for it every time. Or maybe she just acted that way. "Time will tell how serious it is. You'd like her. Completely down-to-earth. Smart."

"What does she do?"

For thirty minutes Nate painted a picture of Luna for his mother. He told her about the stolen car and accepted the praise for being a gentleman for helping Luna out. He even brought up Ethel and was surprised to learn that his mom believed in Ethels. Or ghosts . . . or whatever it was in Luna's house.

"I don't understand people who believe in God but not spirits. They go hand in hand."

Talking to his mother stood in sharp contrast to the interactions between Luna and Karen. And when his mom passed the phone off to his dad, Nate realized what a privilege it was to even have a dad to call.

Not one of the Canning children could say that.

Luna's conviction to avoid marriage . . . all three of them avoiding parenthood . . . it made sense.

What did that mean for him . . . if Luna did turn out to be more than a placeholder for someone else.

Just thinking that made him wince.

She wasn't a placeholder.

He thought about her entirely too much for her to be that.

Even in the short time they'd known each other, he knew she was different. And isn't that what everyone he knew said about their spouse. *"This one is different."*

Tony flat out said he was going to marry Clarissa a week after they met.

Nate didn't know what falling in love with a woman looked like. Especially one who didn't want what most people consider "normal" in terms of marriage. But he did know that he didn't want to miss out on the possibility of something great. Something right in front of him and real versus something imagined.

There was an iconic line from a movie Luna had never seen, something about needing a bigger boat. Between the quote and two notes being played on a piano at just the right time, *Jaws* was reimagined and laughed at.

That line danced in Luna's head as she and Miley stepped into Crystal and Clover looking for something more powerful than sage.

If someone led Luna into the store blindfolded, she'd be able to tell you what it was by scent alone. A mix of candles and incense . . . herbs and flowers made a unique perfume that instantly calmed her nerves.

A difficult task of late.

Brianna greeted them by name. "Luna, Miley, it's been a while. How are you two?"

Luna lifted an eyebrow.

Miley glanced at Luna.

"Ohhh."

"I want to know when the 'butterfly' stage is coming," Luna told her.

"The what?"

"Jorden's reading," Miley explained. "Is she here?"

"She's here," the woman in question said as she emerged from the back of the store with a box in her hands.

After placing it behind the register, she turned her attention on them, looked at Luna, and lost her smile. "Oh, boy."

"I'm starting to wonder if the butterfly you spoke of was really a moth born in a bug zapper."

This time both Luna and Miley stepped into the quiet space where Jorden did her readings.

Jorden calmly picked up a deck, tapped on it, and set it down.

"This is cool," Miley said, looking around the small room.

"I'm glad you like it." Jorden lit a candle and then interlaced her fingers and set her arms on the table separating them.

"I'm not even sure where to begin," Luna said.

Unlike the last time, Jorden pushed the deck in front of Luna.

Without being asked, Luna cut the deck, twice, and pushed them back to Jorden.

"Your energy has shifted," Jorden told her.

"The old pain you said was coming . . . came."

Jorden spread the cards in a line between them. "Who are they?"

"My mother."

"Pick a card and turn it over."

Jorden leaned forward. "Pick another."

Two cards stared back at her.

"Judgment reversed . . . queen of cups also reversed. Your mother doesn't take accountability, she doesn't think she's wrong. In addition to that she's manipulative and uses emotions to control others. You."

"Fuck," Miley whispered.

"Pick another one." Jorden had stopped smiling as extreme concentration marred her face.

Luna looked at the card in her hand. "Two of swords." A battle? A fight? Lord knew she was fighting with her mom daily.

"You're avoiding a choice that needs to be made." Jorden tapped the cards again.

Luna picked another one.

"The tower . . ." Jorden blew out a breath. "The death card and the devil get the bad rap, but the tower . . . There's a big *something* coming. Or more importantly, crashing and burning. Something is going to shake up your world. Even if you think you know what this is . . . there will be something unexpected."

Luna glanced at Miley.

"This is crazy," Miley whispered.

Jorden tapped the deck again.

Luna picked a card.

"Eight of cups."

Jorden smiled, tapped the deck again.

Luna kept pulling cards.

Jorden sat back, picked up the eight of cups. "Letting go of painful relationships is hard. When it's a parent, it's almost impossible. You want to see redemption, and maybe there is some, but you're not going to find it in the same patterns. Your mother is toxic . . . yes?" she asked.

"Yes."

"This . . . the six of swords. You'll find a way to create emotional distance so you can heal. You can't do this if you're in the fight . . . in the trauma." Jorden looked up. "But you already know this."

Luna nodded. "Dealing with my mother when she lives half the country away is much easier."

Jorden shook her head. "But you're not 'dealing with her' then. You're avoiding. You're not growing. You have to face what is left when the tower falls. The only way over this is through."

"No amount of sage is going to help," Luna said softly.

Jorden smiled.

"What about this card?" Miley asked.

Jorden picked up the card . . . studied it. "The three of swords here could mean heartbreak and betrayal, but coming at the end of the reading I think it means something else. The ripple effect. You have some deep-seated pain that shuts you down. You don't come off as insecure, but deep inside there is a real fear of letting someone in."

"Do you mean romantically?" Miley asked.

Jorden looked at the card. Then Luna.

"Could be . . . maybe. Living a life in fear isn't living. It's existing."

"That sounds like it came from a self-help book," Luna said.

"No. My therapist said that. She's not wrong."

"You see a therapist?" Miley asked.

Jorden nodded. "I do. I find that there are two predominate histories of people who find themselves on this side of a tarot reading. The ones who grew up with it. Parents or a family member that nurtures this practice. Or they grew up with family that strictly prohibited anything but their own beliefs. I found tarot as a rebellion to my upbringing through my aunt. But once the door opened and my intuitive nature spilled out . . . it wasn't going back in. I could either embrace it or try and fight it, which I'm still working on. That's where therapy has helped."

"What does 'embracing being an intuitive' look like if not sitting in a dark room flipping cards?" Luna asked.

Jorden was silent for a moment. "The cards help you see. I'm only a conduit that makes you analyze your life."

"You said something similar the last time we did this," Luna said.

Jorden smiled. "Yeah, I have a good ten different ways I can say that. Psychics use these tools. Cards, crystals. That's how they see. I see without them, and these just clarify."

Luna leaned forward. "Do you see or sense something that the cards didn't clarify?"

Jorden's answer was instant. "I do, and it's with both of you. Very intertwined. I sensed it the second I saw you today. But then you sat down and all I sensed was the chaos of your mother. There is definitely something else going on."

"What is it?" Miley sounded as awestruck as Luna felt.

"There's a woman. She has an old name, I want to say it's Beatrice, but that isn't right. Mable? It's a nickname. The name doesn't matter. She doesn't have the energy of your mother," Jorden said to Luna. "Your mother's energy is dark. This other energy is misunderstood. Whoever she is, she's trying to help. Maybe an aunt?" Jorden asked.

"We don't have an extended family. There was Nana, but she's gone."

"It's not her."

Miley grabbed Luna's arm. "Ethel?"

"Yes!" Jorden cried out with a huge grin. "That's the name. Who is she?"

Every hair on Luna's arm prickled. "We're pretty sure our house is haunted. We've nicknamed her Ethel."

Jorden slowly lost her smile. "A ghost?" she asked.

"Yeah. My brother and sister swore there was one in the house, but until recently, Miley and I never saw anything to support that."

"What happened?"

Miley's nervous laugh filled the room. "No big deal, late in the evening . . . Ethel pulled a couple of pots and pans from a cupboard and left them in the middle of the kitchen floor. Made sure we heard it."

"And yesterday she was slamming doors. Or one door," Luna said. "Why do you look so worried?"

"Because I don't want to see dead people. I'm not a medium. Borderline psychic, but not a medium," Jorden insisted.

"Are you sure?" Miley asked. "We actually came in today to see if there was anything we could do to move Ethel along."

"No. Don't do that," Jorden's voice rose in warning. Like a person yelling "stop" before you walk into oncoming traffic.

"Why not? She's freaking us out."

Jorden ran both hands over her face, then looked between her fingers. "I don't want to be a medium."

"I'm not even sure I believe in mediums . . . but okay, let's say you're not one. Why shouldn't we get rid of Ethel?" Luna asked again.

"She's helping," Jorden said.

"By scaring us?"

"Fight or flight . . . When you're scared, you're at the ready. She's loud to get your attention so you're ready . . . and I really hate that I know that."

"Ready for what?"

Jorden pointed at the tower card. "Whatever this is."

"Does Ethel know what this is?" Luna asked.

"I don't know. I'm not a medium."

That sounded more like a chant than a statement of fact. Like the little train going up the hill saying, "I think I can, I think I can . . ."

"Do all mediums see dead people?" Miley asked.

"No, but they do communicate with them."

Luna reached across the table and placed a hand on Jorden's arm. The distress in her face was palpable. "Can you fight being a medium? Is it a choice?"

Jorden shook her head. "That's a floodgate I don't want to open."

"I suppose asking you to come to our house to clarify or rule out this medium thing is out of the question," Miley said.

"Thank you for the opportunity, but I'm going to pass right now."

"I'm sorry," Luna said. "I didn't mean to cause you so much stress."

"You don't need to apologize for what isn't your fault."

That didn't make Luna feel any better.

"Watch for a pattern with Ethel. What's happening when she lets you know she's there. What immediately follows her presence."

Luna scooted back her chair, Miley and Jorden followed her lead.

"Thank you, my non-medium, semi-psychic friend."

Jorden hesitated at the door and then looked at them both. "Don't let fear paralyze you."

CHAPTER TWENTY-FIVE

Apologies with a *but* are not an admission of fault. Nor can they be classified as a desire for forgiveness. "I'm sorry *but* being here without my mother is hard. I'm sorry *but* I really thought one of you would have had a baby by now. I'm sorry *but* I'd had too much to drink and didn't mean to make anyone uncomfortable."

"I'm sorry *but* . . ." was the closest Karen was ever going to get to admitting guilt.

Once Ash returned home after the weekend, and Harper and Jerry retreated to their sanctuary, Luna and Miley were left to hear all the "I'm sorry buts."

One week turned into two, then morphed into three.

Miley started picking up overtime shifts, and Luna made excuses to work outside of the house.

The Mercier case was coming together much quicker than expected. It helped that the incentive for a day of hard work was an afternoon of pillow talk.

All the while Karen spent her days watching TV or scrolling through social media on her phone like a teenager. She'd treat every evening as if she was on vacation with an all-inclusive drink package. It wasn't like Luna's mother drank all day, but she never went to bed sober.

Luna felt like she'd taken a deep breath and couldn't let it out. Relaxing in her own home wasn't possible.

She'd stopped the occasional glass of wine at dinner because drinking one prompted her mother to drink more. If Luna so much as glanced at the glass in her mother's hand, an argument ensued.

It wasn't worth it.

When Nate suggested a weekend away, Luna jumped at it.

"I have some friends that live in the suburbs. They're going up to Leavenworth for the weekend and wanted us to come along."

"I haven't been up there in years." The town mimicked a Bavarian village in Germany, both in aesthetics and styles of food . . . and of course beer. It was in the mountains that were currently covered in snow. It sounded cozy and quiet . . . and perfect.

"Then you'll come?" Nate asked.

"You couldn't keep me away."

When Miley learned of the trip, she planned something of her own. Staying home with Karen alone wasn't something she wanted to do either.

The night before the trip, Karen drank a little more than the average and with that intoxication came a boldness that only alcohol inspired. "Leave me the keys to your car. I might need something."

"No," Luna said without apology. "We're taking my car."

"Why not take Nate's? Or don't you trust me?"

"If you need something, Harper isn't far away. Or call an Uber." And no, Luna wanted to add, she didn't trust her mother. Not with a car that didn't even have its permanent license plates yet.

"I don't have Uber money. I barely have enough for my smokes."

"Good thing there's food in the house. And you bought cigarettes two days ago," Luna told her.

"I know how to drive. I taught you how to drive."

No, that was Harper and sometimes Ash. And Luna had practiced with Nana. The only thing Karen did was drive her to the DMV on the day she took her test.

"We're driving my car. My brand-new car that I don't even want the guy at the car wash to drive. If someone is going to put a scratch on it, it's going to be me."

Karen's eyes were heavy with alcohol while they argued in the den watching the TV that neither of them was paying attention to. "Does it make you happy to talk to me like that? Am I not *good enough* for your fancy car?"

Here we go.

Luna released a defeated sigh. "I'm not talking to you like anything. I'm telling you no and you don't want to hear it."

"Telling me no like I'm a child," Karen bit out.

"If you wanted your own transportation, you should have driven here from Alabama instead of taking the bus. Or have the means to rent something while you're *visiting*." Luna slowed down that last word to remind her mother that she was a guest.

At this point a very unwelcome guest.

Who was Luna kidding, her mother hadn't been welcomed. A fact they both knew but didn't say out loud.

"You always thought you were better than me. I thought that after Landon, you'd realize we . . . we're not that different."

Her mother's insult hit exactly where she wanted it to.

"Most parents want their children to do better than them. They don't stand around with a measuring stick comparing notes and hoping they come out on top." This pissing match wasn't going to get them anywhere. Luna knew that but found it impossible not to engage.

Karen took a big pull of her more vodka than soda and looked away. "I'm sorry I wasn't good enough for you."

Luna removed the pillow that had been in her lap and set it aside. "You know what, Mom. That worked on me when I was twelve. When you said that if you weren't good enough, I could come here and live with Nana. Then you'd cry and tell me how lonely you'd be if I left. You'd start the fight, just like you're doing now, and I'd coddle your feelings, ignoring my own."

"You did leave me."

The absurdity of this conversation plucked at Luna's last nerve. "You moved to bum fuck nowhere to live with your latest boyfriend and said I was old enough to figure it out on my own. I'd just turned seventeen."

"That is not what I said. We were being evicted. I needed to move."

"Narcissists can't blame themselves, they're not capable."

Nate's words rang in Luna's head.

"You're right," Luna said. "You needed to move. I moved here and Nana let me drive her car back and forth to school that was forty minutes away so that I didn't have to endure yet one more crappy man you invited into your life." In a calm Luna knew would piss her mother off more than yelling, she added, "Isn't it funny how none of us lived with you when we turned eighteen. Yet somehow that was all our fault."

Karen was pouting now, huddled over her drink like it was her only friend. "I did my best. It wasn't easy."

If only Luna believed that were true.

She unfolded from her chair, not caring that she towered over her mother in the process. "I'll be gone before you get up in the morning. You have the house to yourself for the weekend. I think you should use that time figuring out what your next move is. Staying here indefinitely is not it." With that, Luna turned on her heel and left the room without looking back.

By the time she made it to the top of the stairs, she was exhausted.

Emotionally spent.

Something caught her attention out of the corner of her eye.

The door to the attic was open by only a couple of inches.

And with God as her witness, Luna heard footsteps running away.

Luna walked to the door, opened it farther, and stared into the void. "If you're going to eavesdrop on the conversation, at least close the door when you're done, Ethel. I can't afford to heat the attic."

Nate and Tony stood just inside the door of what Tony called a *chick store*.

Luna and Clarissa had hit it off the minute they met.

Tony Junior was living the good life with his grandparents, giving the four of them an adult weekend. Something Tony and Clarissa coveted.

While the women shopped for whatever it was they didn't think they could live without, Nate and Tony talked about them.

"I like her," Tony said. "Not that you need my approval."

Nate smiled. "She's something else. She's going through a lot right now and you'd never know it to look at her."

"The mom?" Tony asked.

Nate had already mentioned the stress Luna had been under with the unwanted family visiting. And how much she needed time away.

"They have a complicated relationship." Nate nodded toward the women. "This is the closest she's been to normal since her mother arrived."

"When is Mom leaving?"

"Hopefully soon. Luna took the first steps to moving her along her way."

Tony scoffed. "Did she think she was just going to move in?"

"I think so," Nate said.

"That's fucked up."

"Tell me about it. I'm kinda hoping this weekend relaxes her enough to push and demand her life back. Even in the times we do spend together, she's constantly checking her phone and the cameras at her house to see what her mother is doing."

"Cameras? Like a baby cam?" Tony asked.

"Not inside the house. Outside . . . you know, an alarm system."

"Oh."

"I don't know why she bothers. Her mother doesn't go anywhere. And ever since she got there, the alarm hasn't been set." They'd stopped setting it at night after the first time Karen had opened the back door to have a cigarette and set off the alarm, waking everyone up.

"You know what they say," Tony started. "You don't just marry the woman. You marry her family."

He sighed. "That's not something I have to worry about for a while," Nate said.

Tony looked over, lowered his voice. "She's not a keeper?" he asked. "I thought you really liked her."

"I do. But she's pretty determined to not get married again."

"She told you that?" Tony sounded surprised.

"She tells everyone that. Her ex was a real winner," he said sarcastically.

"Maybe she'll change her mind."

Nate watched Luna from across the store. She was holding up something and showing it to Clarissa and they were both laughing. "We're still new. We work together like we've been on the same team for years. We laugh. We talk about serious shit. The sex is . . . incredible. She isn't needy or possessive. She even asked me to call her out on her own shit. She's thirty-five and does pro bono work. I've never met anyone who literally works for free for people they don't know."

"That's a lot of green flags, my friend."

Those green flags turned to look his way.

Luna smiled and waved them over.

"Let me know if you see a red one, will ya?" Nate asked his friend.

"I will."

Later that night when Nate and Luna had retired to their room at the Airbnb, Nate opened the door of communication on a subject he knew was sticky. But Tony and Clarissa wouldn't be the last who asked the question of what was next, and he wanted to be united with Luna in his response.

"There's something I wanted to talk to you about," he started.

Nate sat against the back of the bed in a pair of gray sweatpants.

Luna poked her head out of the open door to the bathroom with a washcloth in her hand and surprise written on her face. "That sounds serious."

"No," he said. "Maybe . . . could be."

She tossed the washcloth on the bathroom counter and moved to sit at his feet on the bed.

She was wearing a spaghetti strap nightgown that teased more than it covered, and Nate forced his gaze away from the swell of her breasts.

"Which is it?" she asked.

"All three."

She cocked her head to the side, her eyes narrowed. "What's wrong?"

"Nothing. Absolutely nothing. Something that Tony said that got me thinking."

Luna crossed her legs on the bed and waited.

"What's up?"

"I'm not sure how to bring this up organically, so I'm just going to dive in."

"I don't think I'm going to like where this is going."

Nate smiled and pulled her hands into his. "You made it very clear that you don't want to get married again. And after meeting your mother, and hearing the stories about Landon, I can't blame you. We both know that the longer we date, the more people will ask where we're headed."

"That's inevitable."

"I'm inclined to tell anyone who asks that it's too soon to discuss long-term, regardless of how that looks."

"That sounds safe."

"How does it look? Have you thought about what happens when the love of your life . . . say, me . . ."—Nate placed a hand on his chest and added a coy smile—"comes along and sweeps you off your feet?"

Luna bit her lip and started laughing.

"I'm serious," he said.

"I think I just saw the face that you gave to your mom to get away with just about anything growing up."

Nate shrugged. "I'm not sure, you'll have to ask her."

"I will," Luna assured him.

"Seriously, though. When I told Tony that you were against marriage, the first thing he asked is if I think you'll change your mind."

Luna slowly tilted her head in a half no shake. "Nate . . ."

"We're going to get that question. I can easily respond with 'We don't need a piece of paper to be in a committed relationship.' But then the next question is going to be—"

"What about kids?"

She had thought about this.

Nate nodded.

"Do you want kids?" she asked.

"With the right person, yes." His answer was instant.

A shadow passed across Luna's face. "You're asking these questions to find out if you're wasting your time with this relationship."

Nate reached for her hand again. "No. I know I'm not wasting my time. You're fucking amazing. You check off so many boxes I'm starting to wonder if AI invented you out of the ether. And I know you feel the same."

Her eyebrows lifted and her lips turned up. "Somebody's cocky."

Nate winced. "Maybe."

"Completely."

"Somebody has a confession to make," Nate said with a fake grimace.

"Oh?"

He cleared his throat, sat taller. "Remember how I told you I am working with Elenore Prescott?"

"Yes?"

"We had a lunch meeting at Salt and Spoon. By the office building."

"I know the place."

"I know you know the place. I might have been sitting in the booth behind you when you and Harper were having lunch a while back. Before you and I became you and I."

Luna looked confused. "I didn't see you."

"I know."

"Why didn't you say hello?"

"I was going to," Nate began. "But then you started telling Harper all the reasons you don't bother with dating. The men are married, or they have kids . . . crazy exes, they live in their mom's basement . . ."

Luna's mouth started to open. "What else did I say in this conversation?"

Nate looked at his lap. "I know you like gray sweatpants."

Luna followed his gaze. "Oh my God."

"You also said men can't find the spot without a map—"

"Oh my God!" She was trying not to smile again.

Nate took that as a good sign.

"I considered that a challenge."

"Nathan!"

"Oh, boy." Only his mother used his full name.

Hearing it from Luna gave his heart a little kick.

"I don't . . ."

"I couldn't have turned around at that point and said 'Hi, ladies. How was your lunch?'"

"So instead, you made sure you wore these . . . every chance you got." Luna pinched the fabric of his sweats and let it loose.

He didn't feel the least bit guilty. "Of course. I was attracted. Believe me, I was just as wary of a relationship with someone I work with as you. My ex is a little crazy and we *did* work together."

"You haven't said much about her," Luna replied.

"Talking about an ex with someone new is taboo."

"I told you about Landon."

"That's different. I need to know about him so I can try and be sensitive to your needs. Monique was a chapter, not a book. And since she was technically my boss, when it ended—"

"She fired you?" Luna sounded outraged.

"I chose to leave. I could have just as easily made a lateral move to an office here if I wanted to. Instead, I took a leap. My plan was to move here, take the year to get my business going. Decide where I wanted to put down roots and buy my own place. I didn't see you coming."

"I can do one better," Luna said. "I didn't think men like you existed."

Nate sat taller. "Like I said . . . what will you do when you meet the 'end all be all'?"

Luna sighed and looked at her lap. "When I married Landon, I envisioned I'd do it all. Have the career, the husband, house . . . kids. But then he . . ." Her voice trailed off. "I'm not like Harper. I don't have an absolute conviction against children. The problem is, statistically, fifty percent of all marriages end in divorce. And that rate is even higher in second marriages. When you take into consideration how I was raised, it isn't a wonder that the marriage I had was abusive. It's almost guaranteed. When you remove marriage from the plate, kids seem impossible."

"Nothing is impossible," Nate said. "Not with the right person."

Luna placed a hand on his knee. "I can tell you this with complete honesty. I am one hundred percent open to a long-term relationship with the right person. I would consider co-habitation but can't see that outside of the house I'm in right now. Not at this time anyway. And children could be open for consideration once the relationship has been proven with the test of time. And I'm not going to rush anything because of age. Raising kids is twenty years of your life. Less if you're a shitty mom."

Nate started to smile and felt it spread over his entire body. There was nothing here he couldn't work with. "Okay, then . . . we'll figure out the next step in nine months? Ten months?"

"What's in nine months?" Luna asked.

"I can't move in with you until my lease is up. No matter how much you beg."

"Beg? You think I'm going to beg?" She was smiling again.

Nate unfolded his legs and swung them off the bed, then turned from her and patted his own ass. "It's hard to say no to your own personal thirst trap."

Luna reached out to push him away.

Nate captured her hand and pulled her half off the bed. "You love it," he whispered close to her lips.

"I'm never going to live that down, am I?" she asked.

Nate leaned in to kiss her.

She pulled away, smiling.

He cupped the back of her head and brought her so close only a hair could fit between their lips. "Never."

They fell onto the bed, into each other's arms, and took turns making the other one demand release.

CHAPTER TWENTY-SIX

The weekend without the company of her mother was exactly what Luna had needed.

At Nate's apartment, Luna picked up her car to drive home. Despite what she'd told Karen, they had taken Nate's car since he had chains and there was the possibility that they'd need them.

Luna held no shame for the white lie she'd fed her mother.

With promises of seeing Nate again on Tuesday when they were going over their final report for Marcus, Luna made her way back home.

Ten minutes to her front door and her phone rang.

"Hey, Miley."

"Are you on your way home?"

Something was wrong. "Yeah, about ten minutes. What's up?"

"Your mom has company."

"She what?" Luna demanded.

"She introduced him as Ben. They're in the kitchen making dinner."

Luna put a death-grip on the steering wheel. "What? Fuck no . . . She what? Do we know this guy?" Even as the words came out of her mouth, Luna realized how stupid they sounded. Of course they didn't know the guy. Her mother hadn't visited in five years, so unless this was one of her ex-husbands, Luna and Miley wouldn't know him.

"You did not just ask that. No, we don't know him," Miley half shouted.

"How long has he been there?"

"I didn't ask. I've been home for ten minutes."

Luna picked up the pace, pushing the speed limit as much as she could without gaining attention and getting a ticket. "Are they drunk? Is he belligerent?"

"Drinking, yes . . . drunk? I don't think they'd pass a Breathalyzer. He was polite, shook my hand."

"Fuck." This wasn't good.

"You've been warned. I'm gonna shower. I'll come downstairs once you're home."

"Dammit, Miley."

"I know. Deep breath. He seems nice, for what it's worth."

She disconnected the call.

Of course . . . of course her mother has a "friend" over. A male friend. The minute Luna stepped away.

Her mother was like an insubordinate child.

She'd told her not to burn the house down while she was gone but failed to say she couldn't have a sleepover.

Had the man been there all weekend?

Luna hadn't noticed any car in the driveway from the outside cameras. And after watching the few times her mother stepped outside to smoke, Luna had stopped pulling up the app to spy on the house.

Clearly that was a mistake.

Miley had gone straight to work from her friend's place that day, so there was no telling how long this *Ben* had been there.

Luna pulled up the driveway, her headlights only catching Miley's car where she always parked it.

Luna tucked the Lexus in the detached garage, gathered her suitcase, and rolled it to the side door.

A familiar sense of dread echoed with each heartbeat. Squaring her shoulders and stiffening her spine, Luna stepped inside to an unfamiliar voice.

"Is that you, honey?" Karen called out sugary sweet.

Textbook. When a man was around it was all "honey" and "sweetie." Like they had the best relationship in the world.

"It's me."

Luna hung her jacket on a hook and pushed the luggage off to the side. She'd deal with that later.

Stepping around the corner, Luna saw her mother first.

Standing behind the island, Karen had her hair pulled back and makeup on. And she was wearing a shirt Luna hadn't seen before. Considering her mother had come with one suitcase and Luna had seen every article of clothing her mother probably owned at least twice, the new shirt stuck out.

Karen was ear to ear smiles. "Did you have a fun trip?"

Small talk? Luna dug her fingernails into her palm to keep her composure.

A man that stood a good foot taller than her had his back to Luna, his hands on a pair of tongs as he flipped what smelled like steak in a pan, and her mother was uttering small talk.

"I did," Luna answered.

"We were just about to have dinner," Karen said.

"We have plenty if you haven't eaten." Ben finally turned around and spoke in a slight Southern accent.

He had a mustache and a beard, not completely out of control, but *GQ* wouldn't be calling him anytime soon for a photoshoot. He looked like a rinse and repeat of every man Luna had ever known her mother to be with. His smile displayed a back tooth that was missing, the teeth that were left were yellow, likely from the cigarette habit all of Karen's men seemed to share. Nobody wanted to kiss an ashtray unless you were an ashtray. The worn-out jeans covered his slim hips, and he had to be a good eight years younger than her mother.

"I'm sorry . . . do I know you?" Luna asked him directly.

"No, honey. This is Ben. Ben, this is my youngest baby girl, Luna."

Ben wiped his hands on a towel before taking a few steps in her direction.

Luna had no choice but to greet the man with a handshake.

"Your mother's told me a lot about you. She said you liked red wine. I brought you a bottle. There's a winery in Napa that I stop by every time I drive through." Ben let go of her hand and offered his tarnished smile.

Luna glanced at the counter where the wine sat.

"You didn't have to do that." Luna kept a forced smile on her face.

"It's the least I could do. I appreciate you letting me stay here tonight."

Ben nodded once and turned back to the stove.

"Right . . ." Luna blinked . . . twice. "Mom, can I talk to you for a minute?"

Luna didn't wait for an answer and started walking toward the hall.

"I'll be right back," Karen said to Ben.

Luna waited until they were deep in the house where voices didn't carry.

"Really, Mom?" Luna said in a tight whisper.

"It's not what you think," Karen started.

"It's exactly what I think."

"He's only driving through. I asked him over because I'm trying to get him to give me a ride back to Alabama. I know me being here isn't easy on you."

Every cussword swam in Luna's head. Her mother was saying what she wanted to hear . . . that she was going to leave. But Ben? In the house?

"It's only one night."

"Is he going back to Alabama tomorrow?" Luna asked.

"No," Karen said. "He has a job up and down the coast. He'll be back around later in the week to pick me up."

Luna looked up to see Miley standing a few feet away.

She'd heard Karen's explanation.

Miley lifted her shoulders and mouthed the words *one night* and nodded.

Luna hated this. "One night, Mom. If there's any indication of something shitty, he's out."

"You don't have to worry about that. Ben will be on his best behavior. I told him how much you like your privacy and don't care for strangers in your home."

Well at least her mother was remembering whose house it was.

Karen was smiling again and then extended hospitality as if she owned the place. "He makes a mean steak. You should join us."

"I'm good."

Karen made her way back to the kitchen.

Miley followed Luna until they were standing in the laundry room by the only downstairs bedroom.

"You sure you're okay with this?" Luna asked.

"If this means your mother is going to leave in a few days, I'm totally good with this."

And that was the bottom line.

They both needed their peace back.

Resigned to her mother's will, Luna said, "Lock the door to your room tonight."

Miley messed up her face. "Seriously?"

"My mother's judgment in men sucks. He came with a bribe, he knew damn well I didn't okay his stay and acted like it was a done deal. And you can see how she's acting."

"Women sometimes act different around the men they're sleeping with," Miley said.

"Only ones who are putting on a show," Luna countered. Unfortunately for her, she'd seen this act before and had memorized all the lines, knew how it ended. "The only reason I'm letting this happen is to get my mother to go without a massive blowup. I don't think our relationship can stand much more."

Miley placed a hand on Luna's arm. "Only a couple more days."

"From your lips to God's ears."

Luna dozed off sometime after three in the morning.

By six thirty, she was wide awake again.

Ben was gone.

She'd heard her mother giggling in her bedroom and the occasional deep voice of a man the night before. Then there was quiet . . . and then not so quiet.

Neither Luna nor Miley had had sex in that house in well over a year, and yet Karen . . .

Luna's morning coffee met the acid in her stomach and churned it.

Miley stumbled into the kitchen, looking just as sleep deprived as Luna felt. "Did you get any sleep?" she asked.

Luna pointed at her own face. "Does it look like I did?"

Holding herself up in front of the coffeepot as she poured a cup, Miley moaned. "My bedroom is closer to hers than yours."

"That's so disgusting." Luna could practically smell the stale perfume of sex, cigarettes, and alcohol.

"The second the imagined image of the two of them going at it hit my frontal cortex, I couldn't unsee it," Miley said.

"Thanks for that," Luna said sarcastically. That wasn't where her mind had gone, but now that Miley led it there, that's all Luna saw. A picture to go with the odor.

"I'm a giver."

"He's gone," Luna said.

"I know. I heard him leaving."

Luna felt guilty. "I'm sorry."

"Don't be. I agreed to him staying." Miley moved to the kitchen table and took a seat opposite Luna. "I get it now, though. All the things you've told me about your mom. In full color and sound . . . sadly. I only saw the fake side with the occasional eye roll. Not that I didn't believe you about how she was . . . is."

Luna lowered her voice. "She can only hide the bitter and ugly side for so long. Until you've lived with it, you can't possibly understand its depth. There's a reason why Harper, Ash, and I all lived in this house with Nana at one time or another."

Miley glanced over her shoulder. "I think once she's out of here, we need to set some clear boundaries about any future visits."

"I'm one step ahead of you. If I'd called Ash last night and told him about Ben, he would have been here by midnight, and hell would have broken loose. He'll tolerate Mom, but not a boyfriend. When he hears about this, he'll go off. Putting Mom in her place is already a done deal, she just doesn't know it yet."

"When are you going to tell him?" Miley asked.

"After she leaves. Unless there's some excuse as to why she doesn't. Or he notices something on the cameras and asks. I won't lie to him directly." By omission on the other hand . . .

"I take it you didn't tell Nate."

"No!" Luna exclaimed. "He would have called Ash. If Mom follows her normal pattern, she'll be on her best behavior between now and the time she leaves. That way when she gets home, she can rationalize any fault she carries about being here. Tell us that we overreacted about Ben, or smoking in the house, or showing up unannounced and uninvited. She'll conveniently forget anything ugly. She believes her own lies after she repeats them to herself time and time again."

They both turned to the sound of footsteps getting closer.

The subject of Karen was instantly dropped.

"How was Leavenworth?" Miley asked.

Luna lifted her voice to a normal volume. "Fabulous. Nate's friends were super nice."

Karen all but bounced into the kitchen. "Good morning."

"Good morning," Miley replied.

"Someone is up early," Luna added.

"A good man will do that to you."

Karen's answer to everything.

"Or an early morning job," Miley said.

"We all know that's not me," Karen said, some of that syrup in her disposition dripped with each word.

Stop it! Luna told herself. She really needed to take her mother's good mood without standing in judgment.

"Luna, hon, do you have any time today to maybe take me to Supercuts or something like it? I really need to do something with this." Karen pulled at the edges of her hair. "Ben gave me a little money to float me until I get back to work."

Of course he did.

Stop it!

"Sure, Mom. No problem."

"Great. And thank you both for making Ben feel so welcome last night. He thinks you're something, Luna. 'Beautiful and smart.' When I told him you were working with an FBI agent, he about shit himself."

Why? Does he have warrants?

Stop it!!!

There was so much wrong with what her mother had just said, but instead of calling it out or correcting her, Luna smiled and said, "That's great. Mom . . . you really did put Miley and I on the spot, though. We both agree well in advance before we invite a man to stay over." Luna's words were steady and as kind as they could be.

Karen nodded and smiled. "I know. And I am sorry to have done that to you, but . . ."

Luna bit her tongue to avoid rolling her eyes. *I'm sorry, but . . .*

"He surprised me. I figured if he didn't linger it would be okay. And when he drives back through, I'll give you girls your privacy back." Her mom's voice bounced on the word *privacy*.

"Did the bar open back up?" Miley asked.

"The what?"

"The bar. The one you work at that closed down because of the health department?" Miley clarified.

"Oh, uhm . . . yeah." Karen looked away and searched for a cup. "One of the girls I work with said it's all back up to speed. They really do need me there. These young kids make every excuse to avoid weekend shifts so they can hang out with their friends. It's us old farts that they can depend on."

Why did Luna have to spot a lie a mile away? Wouldn't it be great if she could just hear her mother mutter on and believe her? Not one thing she'd just said affected Luna, but the fabrication of the truth grated on her every nerve regardless.

"That's great, Karen," Miley said.

"They were even talking to me about management before I left. I already do some of the scheduling, and inventory."

"That would be good." *If it were true,* Luna mused. "What's the name of the place? Is it a chain?"

Karen shook her head. "Not a chain. It's called the Roadhouse."

Luna wondered if her mother knew that violations to health codes were publicly available.

Stop it!

CHAPTER TWENTY-SEVEN

Nate and Luna entered the offices of Allen and Associates together, even though they had driven separately. Nate wore a full suit, Luna looking similar but without a tie and better shoes.

Melinda shuffled them into the conference room to wait for Marcus.

Luna had already mentioned that her mother was destined to leave by the end of the week.

"We need to celebrate," she'd told him.

"Tell me what to bring and I'll be there."

"Bleach" was her reply. The ashtray that used to be a guest room needed some TNT to make it right.

Nate placed a hand to his heart and said, "I'm a great guy, but I draw the line on scrubbing the walls."

Luna had already decided to remove the curtains and the bedding, wash both, and then box them up for the next time her mom visited. She even considered a fresh coat of paint. "Getting rid of the bad energy," Miley quoted Jorden.

Sounded like a plan to Luna.

Marcus entered the conference room with bold steps and a lifted chin. "Hello, hello."

They shook hands and made the pleasantries. "How are my secret weapons?" he asked.

"We're great," Nate answered.

Luna nodded in agreement. "We think you're going to be happy with what we found."

They'd given him a status update, but the details . . . that's where the magic happened.

"Let's get into it." Marcus took a seat at the head of the table.

Nate and Luna sat opposite each other.

Nate slid a folder over to him. "These are the interviews."

Luna pushed her folder forward as well. "These are the numbers." Luna pushed a third folder. "This is the findings."

Marcus smiled, sat back. "Talk to me."

For an hour Nate and Luna bounced between each other as they spelled out the fraud they'd found in not only BOHO, but a mix of Mercier's other holdings. Millions of dollars had been laundered through bogus consultant fees and labor costs. Money was moved through shell companies in both Vietnam and Africa. Shell companies that needed the Mercier corporate touch with Scandinavian furniture and chandeliers . . . only it went much deeper than that.

Luna would direct Marcus to the numbers, and Nate painted the picture of who they believed were the responsible parties.

The bottom line, they'd found the leak, now it was up to Marcus to direct Mercier how to fix the hole and move on to prosecute the guilty parties involved.

And after today, the only thing Luna and Nate would have to do with the case was testify in court when the day came. And considering how slowly courts moved, it would probably be in a couple of years.

Marcus sat back shaking his head. "I can't believe how much you found in such a short amount of time. I thought for sure this would take a couple more months at least."

Nate smiled across the table at Luna. "We're a great team," he said.

"If the two of you ever decide to merge your businesses, I'll set the paperwork up for you. Pro bono."

"Are you feeling okay, Marcus?" Luna asked. "An attorney giving away his services for free . . . you're losing your touch."

He sat up quickly. "You're right. Forget I said that. Temporary insanity," he teased. "But seriously, good work. You've saved this firm hundreds of hours."

"Be sure and remember that when I send you my last invoice," Luna said.

Nate was surprised to hear Luna talk about an invoice. He was still working on the retainer he'd secured for the job.

Marcus rolled his chair back.

"One more thing." Luna stopped their exit.

"Name it," Marcus said.

"There were two probationary accountants that were instrumental in some of the early discovery at Mercier's offices in Houston."

Marcus slowly smiled and shook his head. "You did it again, didn't you?"

Luna shrugged. "What can I say. I remember those student loans."

Nate looked between the two of them. "What are you guys talking about?"

Marcus pointed at Luna. "Our bleeding heart over here has a clause in her contracts."

Nate lifted an eyebrow in question.

"Are you okay with me telling him?" Marcus asked Luna.

She nodded. "Nate's going to ask me, and I'll tell him, so go ahead. I want to hear how you spin this."

Marcus winked at her. "When Luna first started working for us and hadn't proven herself, her hourly rate felt a little steep. As you're aware, as a subcontractor you retain funds up front based on the estimated time it will take to do the job. Luna lured us in by keeping her hourly rate, yet only taking half the retainer with the promise that she'd get the job done before the original agreed upon amount was reached. And then she would bill for the remainder of her hours at the end."

"Damn," Nate said. "I knew you were smart, but that's one hell of an angle. What does that have to do with the interns?"

Marcus looked at Luna. "You can explain this better than I can."

"The hours and therefore dollars I save the firm by working quickly are added up and a percentage of that is my bonus. I mean, I could easily draw this out longer, take the whole paycheck."

"Only you don't take the bonus half the time, you give it away," Marcus argued.

"The interns," Nate concluded.

Luna shrugged like it was no big deal.

"Oh, it gets better," Marcus said. "Once I present this to Mercier and tell him that his interns will be receiving student loan relief from Ms. Canning here, nine times out of ten, the client matches her gift. Some pay them off completely."

Nate felt a section of his heart slip out and fall into her. "You're incredible."

Luna dismissed him, "Don't look at me with those puppy eyes. I get a tax write-off. It's not completely selfless."

Marcus snorted.

Which made Luna laugh.

All Nate could do was stare. Pro bono work, student loan relief for virtual strangers, and at the same time pinching pennies when it came to buying herself a new car.

Luna met his gaze, and her cheeks found the perfect shade of pink.

The room grew quiet until Marcus cleared his throat.

Nate pulled out of Luna's orbit, and they both turned to Marcus.

Marcus shifted his gaze between the two of them.

Luna sat a little taller.

"Well . . . that's an interesting development," Marcus said.

"What is?" Luna asked.

"Oh, please, Luna, I know you better than that." Marcus looked at Nate then back to Luna. "I can see it. Just keep it professional when you're here. I don't need any of my employees getting any ideas."

"I don't know what you're talking—"

"Hon," Nate stopped her. "You're not that good of a liar."

"That is *not* true," she denied.

"He's right. It goes with that bleeding heart." Marcus chuckled and lifted himself out of his chair.

Nate watched on when Marcus took Luna's hand and leaned in for a friendly hug. When he did, he whispered something in her ear.

Luna gave him a coy smile and uttered, "Thanks."

Nate shook the man's hand.

"We'll be in touch," Marcus said as he walked them out of the room.

In the elevator, Nate casually intertwined two of his fingers around two of hers while their hands dangled at their sides. "What did Marcus say?" Nate asked.

Luna slowly looked up at him, then directed her attention on the closed elevator door. "I'm not going to overinflate your ego."

She was blushing again.

Nate rocked back on his heels and couldn't stop smiling.

Karen's visit was less than twenty-four hours away from ending.

Luna already felt some of the stress her mother created leaving her system.

An added bonus was the fact that Harper had taken the afternoon off and was out with their mom doing lunch and shopping.

Harper felt guilty for not taking on more of the mom load, and Luna was happy to help her sister feel that guilt.

Ash, on the other hand, was not making an extra trip.

He'd given Luna an excuse and then owned the fact that it was just that, an excuse. "I suck, I know . . . I'll make it up to you another time," Ash had said.

Luna didn't press the issue.

If Ash came up and he learned of Ben's sleepover . . . yeah, Luna didn't want the drama.

It was almost over.

Luna was in her office, but instead of catching up on the other cases she'd put aside to work on the Mercier investigation, she was searching the internet for bedroom makeover images. There was currently a dull yellow on the walls with equally uninspiring bedcoverings made with quilted lace.

There hadn't been any significant family history with the décor, and if any of it had been handmade, Nana never mentioned it.

The large plastic bags that you could suck the air out of for storage were already on their way in the mail.

The only thing Luna planned on keeping in the room was the bed, well, the mattress and box spring. The bed frame and ancient dresser were going on Facebook Marketplace as soon as the taillights to her mother's goodbye were in sight.

Luna was looking forward to the project.

With her tablet in hand, Luna went to the room in question and pushed the door open.

The bed was unmade, and her mother had tossed clothes on a chair in the corner.

Luna had forgotten about the chair.

Clear the room, paint it, dress it up with fresh linen and then take her time finding the right furniture. The side table and lamp would go to the attic.

On second thought, they would be sold off as well.

Soft green on the walls . . . a white plush headboard, nothing too expensive, two nightstands and two lamps.

No dresser.

A dresser invited people to stay longer.

The closet was small by current day standards, but there was plenty of room in it to hang a few days' worth of clothes.

Key words being *few days*.

She needed measurements.

Luna left the room and tried to remember the last time she'd seen her tape measure.

She owned two . . . one lived in the garage, and the other in a small toolbox that was in a closet downstairs.

Except she was pretty sure she'd left it somewhere else.

The attic.

Luna exited her mother's room and only realized when she walked away from it how much it smelled up the house.

Cigarettes. She'd never understand the desire for such a nasty habit.

Luna left her laptop on the hallway table to go up in the attic.

She opened the door and flipped on the light switch.

The attic had lost the bitter cold with the new roof. A silver lining to her winter debacle.

Luna looked around in search of the tape measure.

Her eye caught on the space she'd found her mother sitting in when she'd first arrived, going over all the pictures. Most of which were still scattered about.

An attic wasn't a space that needed to be tidy, but it also didn't need to look like the bottom of a dumpster.

Luna scooped up the pictures without a lot of care and dropped them in the box from which they'd come.

When her hand landed on the image her mother had cooed over, Luna froze.

Paul had been a nightmare. A man they had all hated.

He'd taken such pleasure in punishing them. The familiar memories that were never far away when Luna thought of the man, surfaced. Ugly pages in a book Luna never wanted to read.

She thought of the belt he liked to use.

Felt the sting of it hitting her.

Sensed the shame in how Paul looked at her half naked with a belt in his hand.

Karen saying after the fact that they shouldn't have done whatever travesty they'd done to deserve it.

Luna stared at the picture as another memory swam in and out. Ash in an urgent care and Karen lying to the staff about him falling.

God, she'd forgotten about that. She couldn't have been more than six.

But when had Paul hit their mom?

Oh, they fought. Loud, angry fights but Luna could only remember one time her mother walked away with a bruise.

The last time.

They'd broken up and reconciled repeatedly but it wasn't until Karen was punished that she called it done.

The lights in the room flickered, dragging Luna away from the awful memories.

The creak of the door to the attic pulled Luna's gaze down the stairs.

She paused. "Is that you, Ethel?"

There wasn't an answer.

"If you start answering me, I'm going to have to check myself into a mental facility."

Still no answer.

Luna looked around the room and saw a wastebasket.

She grabbed it and tossed the picture of her mother and Paul in it.

When she found another one of him, she tossed it . . . then another and another, until all the photographs were back in the box, omitting the man.

If only she could rid herself of all the echoes.

Luna stood tall, her back hurting from bending over the box for a good hour.

There was entirely too much crap in the attic. Maybe a garage sale would be a better idea. Force her siblings to take what they wanted and get rid of the rest. Not a lot of it meant something to any of them. Why not clear out the space? Maybe Luna could find a hobby. Painting or something.

She started to warm to that idea.

The lights flickered again.

"What? Do you need your privacy?" Luna asked the room.

She made it halfway down the stairs before remembering why she'd gone up there in the first place.

Back up she went and poked around until she found the tape measure.

It sat on a box labeled "Journals."

Luna opened it.

It was small, and there were only three bound journals in it.

She recognized her nana's handwriting immediately and smiled as she made her way out of the attic with her nighttime reading material in hand.

~

"He was supposed to be here by six," Luna complained to Nate over the phone.

The sun was staying up longer as winter started to lose its grip to invite spring in.

Nate was looking forward to the Pacific Northwest in drier weather.

"What's the excuse?"

"Something about unloading the trailer and traffic, and a warehouse closing early."

"Do you think she's lying?"

"No," Luna said instantly. "I think she's repeating whatever Ben told her. Now she thinks he isn't going to pick her up until the morning."

Nate knew the situation wasn't funny. Yet hearing Luna moan about a few hours, considering the sheer number of days Karen had been there, was amusing.

"Do you want me to come over and take your mind off of the delay?" he asked.

Luna's heavy sigh was practically felt over the phone. "No. I'm fine." Her voice sounded muffled.

"Where are you right now?" he asked.

"In the backyard. Today was such a beautiful day. Not too cold, the sun was shining. I'm looking out over the lake."

He imagined her holding the phone to her ear, her head leaning to one side with a quiet smile on her face. That was the view he wanted. "I seem to only be there when it's dark, snowing, or raining. I don't think I've really taken in the view."

"You will."

Nate leaned into her promise.

"Where do you want to go in celebration?" he asked.

"Of finishing the case?" she asked.

"I was thinking more about having your house back to yourself, but sure. We can call it a closed file celebration."

"A furniture store."

Nate started laughing. "A what?"

"I'm painting and redecorating the room my mom was in."

"I was picturing soft candlelight with epic views. But if you're looking forward to the meatballs at the IKEA cafeteria . . ."

There it was . . . the laugh he wanted to hear more every day.

"Those are pretty good," Luna uttered.

"But hardly a celebratory meal," Nate expressed. "Okay . . . furniture store and food. I can come up with something." An idea already started to form.

"Guess who made a visit yesterday," Luna said.

"Considering the number of people that we both know is less than ten, I don't have a clue."

"Ethel."

It took Nate a second for the name to register.

"We . . . you've officially given her the name?"

"Had to," Luna exclaimed. "Asking Ethel if she's the one flipping the lights on and off keeps me from freaking out."

Just hearing about it ran chills up his spine. "When did this happen?"

"Yesterday. I was in the attic, quite literally cleaning up the mess my mother made up there. I came across some photographs that were better off in the trash when Ethel started her light show."

"Are you sure that wasn't a coincidence?" he asked.

"No. But considering none of the digital clocks in the house were flashing and in need of being reset, I have to think the attic lights were isolated."

"A bulb burning out?"

"Why didn't I think of that?" Sarcasm laced her words. "All bulbs that are dying like to do so with company. The light in the stairway must have been talking to the bulbs hanging from the rafters."

"I get it."

"The lights did pull me out of my memory lane funk."

"That's good."

Nate could tell by the noise behind Luna's voice that she was walking. "I'm trying to keep in mind what Jorden said about Ethel being a good thing."

"The medium?"

"The woman who doesn't want to be a medium. The woman who doesn't fully believe she's a psychic. Things I didn't put much weight into until we met her. She predicted my mom coming and turning my life upside down. Not by name, but close enough."

"Is your life upside down? I know your mother's a lot, but . . ."

"Sometimes it feels like it is. She's certainly opened old wounds that I thought were healed."

Nate leaned his head back on his sofa and stared at the ceiling. "Wounds can't heal if someone is still dripping poison into them." And if there was one thing he'd noticed from the Canning family dynamics, Karen had a vial of poison in her hand, or more accurately, on her tongue, at all times.

"That's so true."

Nate sighed. "She'll be gone soon, hon. Then we'll go to LEGOLAND for furniture and put this behind you."

He heard a door close and Luna laugh.

"I'll call you tomorrow and hopefully be able to plan that date," she said.

"Okay . . . try and get some sleep."

"I will. Good night."

Nate looked at his phone.

His home screen was a picture he'd taken of a sunset somewhere in middle America on his drive to Washington state from DC.

He needed a picture of Luna.

Luna holding her black cat and talking about ghosts.

No one could have ever convinced him that this would be his life.

Yet here he was . . .

Nate pulled up the images that had been shared between Clarissa and Tony on their trip to Leavenworth.

One captured Luna waving a finger puppet of a shark in his face.

Tony and Clarissa had started singing "Baby Shark." The earworm didn't go away until they drove home.

Nate set the picture as his wallpaper and lock screen and then put his phone aside.

He needed to come up with something much better than IKEA and meatballs.

Luna deserved more than that.

CHAPTER TWENTY-EIGHT

When it was clear that Ben wasn't going to make it that night, Karen insisted on a last-night-with-the-girls drink.

They opened the bottle of wine Ben had gifted to Luna and drank it with a meal thrown together with leftovers and a salad.

Luna and Miley had planned on date night with the Hallmark Channel . . . but that would wait another day.

"I know you want me gone," Karen pointed out.

"No one in their thirties wants to live with their mother. It's not just you," Luna said, doing her level best to avoid anything controversial.

"I guess when you put it like that it doesn't sound so bad," she said.

"My mother would drive me nuts if she came for a month," Miley told her.

"I don't think I ever met your mother," Karen said.

"You haven't."

"Is she a difficult woman?"

Miley shook her head. "We have different views of life. She's quick to tell me hers are all right and mine are all wrong."

Karen tapped Luna's forearm. "See, it's not just me."

Before Luna could comment, Miley diverted. "I'm just saying that there is a reason adult children shouldn't live with their parents."

"A visit isn't the same," Karen said.

Luna held the stem of her wineglass and looked up at her mother. "That's true, Mom. And when the visit is expected, it's a lot easier to prepare. Please don't take this the wrong way . . ."

Her mother turned her full attention to Luna.

"The next time you come to visit, let's make sure it's good for all of us."

"You know I didn't plan this."

"I know," Luna said. "But at some point on the bus coming over, you could have called."

Karen sighed. "You're right."

Luna waited for the *but.*

It didn't come.

She let her point go and finished the rest of her wine.

Miley yawned and pushed her empty glass aside.

"I'm keeping you up," Karen declared.

"It was a busy day. Two traumas, one heart attack, and a whole bunch of stupid crap." Miley pushed her chair back.

Karen poured more wine into her glass and then acted like she was going to put more into Luna's.

She waved her mother off. "I'm good."

"My bags are all ready to go. If Ben gets here before you're out of bed, I'll just sneak out."

Miley opened her arms.

Karen leaned over and hugged her. "Thank you for everything."

"Safe travels. Let us know when you get there," Miley added.

"I will."

Luna took her glass along with Miley's over to the sink and set them to the side.

"I need to get some sleep, too, Mom." They'd done the long "last night" thing the evening before.

Karen shoved to her feet and once again opened her arms. Luna stepped into the hug and closed her eyes.

"I do love you, Luna."

"I know." As much as she could anyway. "I love you, too."

Her mother patted her back a few times before pulling away. "I'll clean this up before I go to bed."

"Thank you," Luna said.

"And I'll let you know that I got home safe."

Luna wasn't convinced that she wouldn't wake up if she heard her mother leaving, so she left her goodbye for later.

"Good night," she said instead.

"Good night, baby."

As Luna took the stairs to her room, Midnight following from behind, she couldn't help but think that if every night that her mother had been there was like this one, it would be so much easier to deal with her.

Luna left the door to her room open a crack so she could say goodbye in the morning.

She fell asleep almost as soon as her head hit the pillow.

She was running, holding her breath and knew if she just concentrated hard enough gravity would defy itself and Luna would take flight. She had to prove the power was in her. Everyone was watching, whispering behind their open hands hiding their sinister smiles.

Every muscle in her body ached. Why was this taking so much effort? She'd flown hours before, she knew it. The knowledge of how to do it again was right there . . . just out of reach.

I can do this.

Why can't I do this?

Dreaming. I'm dreaming. But that doesn't mean I can't fly.

Luna felt the edges of sleep tugging her deeper into the dream.

Am I awake?

It felt like she was awake.

Miley was calling her name. "Show them you can fly."

I can't.

Show them!

Luna erupted from her dream, muscles aching, heart racing.

"Luna!"

Miley stood at the foot of her bed, a bathrobe covered her frame, the belt tight around her waist.

It was still dark.

Her gaze drifted to the clock at the side of her bed.

Just after midnight.

"What?"

Miley looked over her shoulder. "You can't hear that?"

Luna ran her hand over her face to push the fog away.

Voices.

The muffled sound of her mother.

And a man saying, "Am I being too loud?"

Luna tossed back the covers; the cool air of the room circled around her. "Who is that?"

"Ben."

Luna checked her clock again. "It's after midnight. What the fuck. How long has he been here?"

"No idea. They sound drunk, though."

She grabbed her bathrobe that had been tossed over the chair in the room and shoved into it.

She and Miley both paused when the voices stopped.

Hoarse, angry whispers . . . that's all they heard. Whatever was being said wasn't pleasant.

"It was too much to ask that Karen leave quietly," Luna said under her breath.

She looked around for her slippers but gave up once she heard Ben's voice carry up the stairs.

Miley followed Luna.

Midnight stood on the stair landing, hair up . . . but didn't look as if she was going to get any closer to the middle-of-the-night chaos.

The closer their feet brought them to the kitchen, the louder the voices grew.

The vibration of an angry man's voice had Luna's legs faltering.

Luna stopped Miley in the hall. "Hang back just enough so you can call the police if he gets ugly."

"You're serious?"

Luna nodded once. "I'm going to tell them to leave." As calmly as she possibly could.

Her arms trembled; her brain told her to stop. *You've been here before, you fucking idiot. When will you ever learn?*

Luna silenced the voice in her head and stepped into the kitchen.

The island had a second bottle of wine on it, and the nearly empty handle of vodka that her mother had bought earlier in the week. Beside that was the fallout of what looked like a bag filled with hamburgers and french fries versus a mass of teenage boys all competing for the burger with bacon.

"What's going on?" Luna asked, announcing herself.

Ben turned around, exposing her mother.

Her mascara was nothing but black patches under glossy eyes. That half-hooded kind that said she was beyond hammered.

But Karen wasn't who Luna focused on.

It was Ben.

Red faced, eyes half mast. His clothes were dirty like he'd just come off a field where he'd been standing behind a tractor collecting the dust it kicked up. There was very little of the man Luna had met a few days before. No kind smile or platitude. No humility or respect.

This man she'd seen before on every face her mother brought home.

This man was unpredictable and likely empowered by alcohol.

"I told you . . . you were going to wake 'em up," Karen shouted at Ben.

"Shut up!" he sneered.

Luna jolted.

"I'm sorry—" Karen started.

Ben took hold of her mother's elbow and Karen stopped talking.

"We were having ourselves a little party." Ben licked his lips, stumbled forward a couple of steps. "You should join us."

Bile rose in Luna's throat.

Her eyes drifted to Miley.

Luna moved to keep the island between them. "We were trying to sleep."

Ben opened his arms wide, letting Karen go. A crooked smile spread over his face. "What are two young girls like you goin' to bed so early for?" Alcohol brought his Southern accent closer to the surface. He reached for the bottle of vodka. "Let me get you—"

Karen reached out. "They don't want a drink."

Ben slapped her mother's arm away. "Was I talking to you?"

"This isn't how we live in this house, Ben. Miley and I both have early mornings. I won't tolerate midnight parties."

Ben's robust laugh echoed in the kitchen and likely to the foundation of the house itself. "Well, la-te-da. Aren't you full of yourself."

Luna was a hundred percent angry, and fifty percent scared out of her mind.

Miley shifted back in the hall and out of sight. *Call the police,* Luna screamed silently. This wasn't going to end well.

"I'm going to have to ask you to leave." Luna cursed the wave in her own voice.

Karen's eyes grew wide. "We'll be quiet. You guys go back to bed."

Ben snagged the bottle off the counter and splashed a heavy shot in a glass. "Speak for yourself. I don't have to be quiet. This is your house as much as it's hers," Ben said to her mother.

Anytime Ben took a step closer, Luna took one in the opposite direction. "This is my house. And you're not welcome."

Ben leaned on the island, shook his head. "Now is that any way to respect your mama's visitor."

Luna stopped looking at Ben and stared at her mother. "Mom, you both need to go. Now."

Karen stared at her as if she were crazy. "Neither of us can drive. We'll sleep it off and—"

Luna clenched her fists at her sides.

"We ain't fucking leavin'," Ben yelled again. "You got mail coming here with your name on it. You don't have to leave. I told Karen weeks ago to change her address. Your mama's dumb, but she knows enough to listen to me. Squatters have rights."

Luna stared at her mother. "Seriously?"

"Just a phone bill. I'm not staying."

"This house is worth twenty times what that shack in Alabama is. We ain't goin' nowhere."

Her mother stepped closer to Ben. "Let's just go to bed, Cody."

"I'm. Not. Tired."

Luna stalled. "Cody?" she repeated.

"Benjamin Cody," he sang into his glass before tossing it back with a shout.

"*Alabama* Cody?" Luna asked her mom. The one she fled Alabama from, Cody?

Karen attempted to blink the fog from her eyes. "It's not what you think."

As always, her mother's chronic deceitful nature astounded her. "I'll call you an Uber," Luna said.

Cody laughed. "Is she stupid? I thought you said she was a bitch, but she was smart."

Luna ignored the pain his words were meant to inflict and searched for an out. One that would remove her from the kitchen and away from the garbage that was standing in her way.

By now Luna was between the island and the kitchen sink. Her mother on one side, Ben . . . no, Cody on the other.

Cody had inched his way to Luna's exit to the rest of the house.

Miley wasn't anywhere to be seen.

The police.

Luna needed to get out of the kitchen and wait for the police.

~

When the phone wakes you up in the middle of the night, it was never for anything good.

Nate dragged the phone to his ear without looking at the screen. "What's wrong?"

"Get over to Luna's." Ash's words rushed together, his voice a mix between frantic and worried.

Nate sat straight up. "What's going on?"

"Mom brought a man over. They're drunk, refusing to leave. She's scared, Nate. Nothing scares Miley."

Nate's feet hit the floor, and he started grabbing clothes and hopped into them. "Is someone hurt?"

"I don't know. Fuck. I should have listened to Luna."

My gun . . . where is my gun?

Nate's gaze fell on his dresser.

He grabbed his gun, his car keys, and a coat as he ran out the door.

"Were the police called?"

"Miley called me first. She thought I could talk to my mom. Whoever is there is yelling loud enough to wake the neighbors. By now Miley should have called 911."

"How fast does Seattle respond to domestic disputes?" Nate asked.

"Not fast enough . . . fuck, fuck, fuck."

Nate thought of the shotgun that was under Luna's bed. He couldn't imagine the fighting was going on in her bedroom. "Does he have a gun?" Nate asked.

"He's a truck driver. How many truck drivers carry guns?" Ash asked.

"A lot," Nate declared. Truck stops where long-haul drivers slept weren't filled with the best of humankind.

"Hurry."

The apartment door slammed behind Nate as he ran down the hall. "I'm on my way."

CHAPTER TWENTY-NINE

"Fine," Luna sighed, hoping she sounded resolved. "Stay up. I'm going back to bed."

"Hold on now." Cody leaned one hand on the counter, the other wrapped around his empty glass.

Does he know the glass is empty?

"What did your mama tell you about me?"

She looked at Karen, then back at Cody. "That you were her boyfriend." Which was true.

He tapped the glass on the counter several times, his eyes dug into hers. Then turned to Karen. "If that's all you said, why did you call me Ben? I don't go by Ben."

"I call you Ben," Karen said.

Luna felt her pulse in her throat. She started moving toward her mother. "This is between the two of you. I have to work tomorrow."

Karen's eyes kept twitching.

Nystagmus.

A word Luna wouldn't know if not for Miley.

Luna had seen it on her mother's face more times than she could remember . . .

Luna tried to fake a smile and failed.

Seeing her mother this intoxicated, up in the middle of the night fighting with a man she said hit her, was the last straw.

I'm the bitch, Luna mused.

Karen told Benjamin Cody that Luna was a bitch.

Of all the things said so far that night, that was the one thing Luna believed.

None of it mattered. Luna needed to remove herself from the situation and throw her mother out later.

"Go to bed, honey."

Luna couldn't stomach it. "Don't," she said, shaking her head. "Just, don't."

"What did you say, Karen? Did you tell her what a mean and fucked up man I am and how you love it so much you keep begging me to come back?" Cody laughed, went to take another drink. "Fuck." He glared at the empty glass, moved closer to Luna, and grabbed the bottle of vodka again.

Luna took his distraction and attempted to move around her mother.

One side step and Cody stood between Luna and the exit to the hallway.

She stopped short of running into him.

He was too close.

So close she smelled his breath and the odor of his skin. A mix of pure grain alcohol, bad teeth, and grease from a stale hamburger.

Her words felt strong, her back was shaking. "I'm going to bed."

Cody looked her up and down.

Luna fought the urge to pull the ends of her robe closer together.

"You look like your mama."

Luna swallowed back the bile. She stepped to the side to move around him.

Cody blocked her.

Behind her, Karen said nothing.

Dirty fingers reached toward her, touched the edge of her robe.

Luna looked at his hand, then back to his face and hoped she looked strong. "Back off."

This was not going to happen. Not again.

Not in her house.

He didn't move.

"Ohhh, there she is. Karen's little *bitch*." His words were slow, his eyes barely focused.

That was her advantage, she thought.

He was drunk.

Slow.

Luna took a calculated step back, never lowering her eyes.

"Don't push him, Luna."

"Get him out of my way, Mom."

Cody smiled and set his glass down.

"Let her go to bed, sugar. It's late," Karen said from behind Luna.

"Why would I do that? The fun just started."

Luna felt her feet falling into quicksand.

This was fun to him. This was fun to everyone like him.

Her breath started to come in short spurts.

Cody took a step closer.

Her body wanted to move, her brain said the minute she did he would give chase. As all predators did.

Retreat wasn't an option. Maybe threats would work.

"We called the police," Luna said in a volume just above a whisper.

"Excuse me?"

"The police are on their way," Luna said louder. "If you leave now, you might be able to get away before they show up."

Cody laughed. Slow at first and then so full he tipped his head back to suck in air. "And when did you call them? Between the sink and the stove?"

Luna moved beside her mother.

Karen was looking beyond Cody to the doorway. "Miley," she whispered.

Cody stopped laughing.

"Let's just go." Karen stepped closer to Cody.

Cody swung to look in the empty doorway.

Luna shouted so he wouldn't leave the kitchen in search of her friend. "I triggered the alarm. The police will respond. My brother will be called."

"You're lying."

The lights in the kitchen flickered.

Luna stepped back.

It was a warning. Ethel was warning her.

"You're not the first angry man my mother has brought around. I triggered the alarm before I walked into the kitchen."

Karen rushed to Cody. "They'll send you to jail—"

Cody shoved Karen aside.

Her mother stayed on her feet but only because she was close to the wall.

Luna expected the violence but found herself jolting anyway.

Cody turned and lunged toward Luna.

She jumped back, felt her feet tangle beneath her. She caught herself from falling by grasping at the counter she knew was behind her.

Something sharp pierced her skin.

Cody's fingertips grabbed her robe and started to pull her closer to his putrid breath.

One of the empty wine bottles was a foot away, she reached for it.

For a drunk man, Cody moved fast. Those hands on her robe pulled her back and slammed her against the counter.

The wine bottle was forgotten.

"Get off me." She slammed her fists against his chest, but he was too close to do any harm. She thrust her knee, aiming for his groin.

He shifted, laughed, and brought his booted foot on top of her bare one.

Someone was screaming.

Luna was pretty sure it was her. Only just like the dream she was pulled from, this didn't feel real. If she could just wake up, everything would be okay.

Cody's body pinned her to the counter, one of his hands held one of hers down, the other fisted and hit her jaw.

She clawed at his face, drew blood.

"Bitch!"

Cody captured her neck and started to squeeze.

"Let her go!"

The sound of a shotgun being cocked echoed in the room.

The lights flickered again.

Cody's grip on her neck loosened enough for Luna to scrape at his fingers.

He looked behind him.

Out of the corner of Luna's eye, she saw Miley, the shotgun in her hand.

"Let her go!"

His fingers slid from Luna's neck.

She sucked in a full breath.

Cody was laughing. His body pressed so close to Luna she felt every move his laughter created in his body. "You're going to shoot me? And hit her?"

Karen moved in front of Miley. "Put the gun down."

Lights flashed again.

And there were sirens.

Sirens coming closer.

"Get out of the way, Karen," Miley yelled.

Karen waved her hands in front of her.

Luna felt the moment Cody's attention moved from her and onto the noise coming from outside.

He crawled over her to push the kitchen curtains aside to look out the window.

"Fucking bitches."

Luna looked for a weapon.

Anything.

She saw a scented jar candle and grasped it.

Without hesitation, she swung it with as much force as she could toward Cody's head.

She grazed the side of his temple enough to hear a crack.

Cody stumbled as the back door of the house burst open.

That's when she heard him.

Nate.

In a deadly voice she'd never heard before and hoped she'd never hear again.

"Body bag or jail, motherfucker."

Cody must have been holding on to her, because when Nate's words registered, Luna fell to the floor and was free to get away.

Sirens and flashing lights screamed into the driveway.

Cody slowly put his hands in the air.

Miley dropped the gun and ran to Luna's side.

Three squad cars, an ambulance, and a paramedic truck were skewed all over Luna's driveway.

Nate glared at Benjamin Cody while one of the officers finished taking Nate's statement.

"He's on probation for armed robbery and aggravated assault. He's already spent five years in the state penitentiary."

"How long will he go away for this?" Nate asked.

"Not long enough," the officer admitted.

Nate's finger itched. He should have taken the shot.

"He could have killed her," Nate said, his voice low. "His hand was around her neck."

"It's a good thing you showed up when you did, then."

Nate looked the officer in the eye. "Luna's brother is Portland PD."

"Good to know," the officer said. "Most of us know Miley. She makes our job easier when we roll into the ER. We'll keep an eye on this place. Make sure this asshole knows we're watching."

Nate stuck out his hand. "Thank you."

The squad car carrying Cody away backed out of the driveway.

Luna sat on a gurney, her eyes tracking the police car as it left.

Nate walked over and stepped in front of her view.

She looked up slowly and tried to smile.

The light from the ambulance was enough to show the red blotch where she'd been hit. Miley was cleaning a cut on Luna's hand while the medic was wrapping her foot in gauze.

Nate hadn't been able to talk to her yet.

He'd kept his gun on Cody, and after a short, tense moment when the police arrived and weren't sure who Nate was, the officers took Cody into custody and rushed him out of the house.

Miley held Luna while Karen sat in the corner and cried.

When the paramedics arrived, Nate and Miley walked her out to the ambulance where she hadn't moved since.

Nate saw the cut on her hand. "That's going to need stitches," he said.

"I'm not going to the hospital," Luna told him.

Miley looked up at Nate with a shrug. "It's a straight cut, it needs glue. I can do it. But you should have that foot x-rayed."

Luna glanced at her friend. "If something is broken, it can wait until tomorrow, right?"

"Yeah but . . . he was choking you," Miley argued.

"Good thing my roommate is an ER nurse. I have faith in you."

Nate placed a hand on Luna's shoulder.

"Hey, Miley?" one of the officers called out. "We need your statement."

Miley looked at Nate. "Talk some sense into her?"

Miley walked away.

"Can you give us a minute?" Nate asked the medic.

Once they were alone, Nate took Luna's uninjured hand in his.

She rested her head on his shoulder.

"Talk to me. Why don't you want to go?" he asked softly.

Luna nodded toward her mother.

Karen was already loaded in the back of the ambulance.

"I need to be as far from her as possible."

"Did he hurt her?" Nate hadn't seen any evidence of injury on Karen.

"I don't know. I heard the medics talking to Miley. Between the alcohol and hysteria, they want to take her in for a psych eval."

"That sounds reasonable."

Luna shook her head. "I can't do this again with her. I don't have it in me. She'll play the victim. Get everyone to feel sorry for her." Luna stared up at him, wetness pulled behind her eyes. "Then a year from now look at a picture of her and Cody and tell me how good-looking he was. How tonight wasn't that bad." Luna started to cry. "I can't . . . I can't."

Nate gathered her in his arms.

Luna buried her head into his shoulder and cried.

"Shhh, it's okay. You don't have to go. I'll take you to the doctor in the morning."

Luna nodded and kept crying.

His heart was breaking for her. There was so much more here than physical pain. Injury deeper than any blade could cut.

Nate coaxed Luna off the gurney and helped her back into the house.

Later, Nate lay beside Luna long after she'd fallen asleep. She'd stopped crying once her mother was taken away. Gave her statement to the police like a seasoned pro and let Miley glue the laceration on her hand.

He heard a motorcycle in the drive and slipped out of Luna's bed to talk to Ash.

When he stepped into the kitchen, he saw Ash holding Miley.

Nate hung back.

In all the chaos, Nate hadn't thought about how Miley was holding up. This had to have been hard on her, too.

Ash noticed Nate and slowly pulled away. "He won't be back," Ash told her. "I'll make sure of it."

Miley followed Ash's gaze and centered on Nate. "How is she doing?" she asked.

"Sleeping."

"Why don't you go to bed?" Ash asked her. "I'll finish this in here."

Miley had been cleaning the mess in the kitchen. Or maybe just looking at it since most of it was still there.

Broken glass, blood on the counter, empty wine bottles.

Miley nodded and turned to Nate. "You're staying, right?"

"Of course."

"Watch her. If she has trouble breathing, we have to take her to the hospital."

Miley had already told him this. Her biggest concern was swelling from Cody choking her.

"I will."

Nate watched as Miley left.

Ash was studying the wreckage of the fight, running both hands over his head.

"I should have shot him," Nate said.

"It would have been hard for them to live in this house if you had," Ash replied. "How is she really?"

"Sleeping but shook up."

Ash nodded. "Where's my mother?"

"In the hospital."

Ash looked up.

"She's not hurt. Psych eval . . . maybe alcohol poisoning, but from what Luna tells me, that would be hard for her to achieve considering her tolerance."

Ash pinched the bridge of his nose.

"She's not coming back here," Nate said. "Her bag was packed. I'll take it to her myself if I have to."

"I'll do it."

"Good. You don't want me to. I'd remind her who the victim was here, and how she's not fit to call herself a mother. I protect the people

I love, even if it's against family. I'd crush her spirit so far down, she'd be on a 5150 as a danger to herself before I left."

Ash kept nodding. "I understand."

"I'm sure you do," Nate said. "She's also your mother, so . . ."

"I'll make sure she gets back to Alabama, or wherever, far away from here. If Luna asks, tell her I dealt with it." Ash's shoulders slumped. "I thought maybe she'd changed."

"Really?" Nate asked. He found that hard to believe.

Ash shook his head. "Hoped."

Nate could live with that. "I'm going to get back to your sister."

Once Nate left the kitchen, he heard Ash not so quietly explode.

CHAPTER THIRTY

Luna turned her head from side to side taking in her reflection in the mirror. Her jaw had hurt for a week. When the bruising was at its worst, she didn't leave the house. The last thing she wanted was other people staring and wondering who was beating on her.

The last of the yellow green hue was gone, the laceration on her hand had closed, but was still a red mark on the side of her palm.

She'd caught it on a knife but hadn't thought quick enough to grab it.

Then again, who was to say that Cody wouldn't have used it against her.

She called the scar her reminder. Something she'd see every day to remind her to never trust her mother again.

Her foot took the biggest hit.

Dirty cowboy boots versus bare feet were not a great combination. Luna still wore a hard sole shoe to keep from bending the fracture of two bones in said foot two weeks later. A course of antibiotics took care of whatever festered on the bottom of the boot that did the damage.

It took two days for her to get out of bed, and everyone in the house treated her like a porcelain doll that was going to break.

No one brought up Karen. Not what happened to her, if she'd gone home . . . nothing. And Luna didn't ask.

All she knew was that when she walked by the guest room her mother had been using, all her personal belongings were gone. Soon after, Ash and Nate were purging the room of furniture and prepping the walls for paint.

What had started out as eliminating the room of cigarette smoke and bad perfume turned into something entirely different.

Luna compared it to selling off everything associated with her first marriage. From the clothing she'd worn, to the chair she sat on, Luna sold it all. She wanted to smile when she saw the room, not be reminded of Karen.

Now Luna stood in front of her bathroom mirror and assured herself that the bruises were all gone.

Harper and Ash were both over, Miley was off work, and Nate was doling out tasks while he made everyone dinner.

Luna was the last one to make her way to the kitchen and hesitated when she heard her name whispered.

"Is Luna sleeping?" It was Harper asking the question.

"She's restless," Nate said.

"Has she said anything since that night?"

"No," Miley answered Harper. "Not to me."

"Me either," Nate added.

"I'm worried."

"Our sister is stronger than you think," Ash whispered.

Luna looked down at her feet.

One foot in a therapeutic shoe, the other slid into a canvas tennis shoe.

She knew her family's concern was out of love. They'd been respectful of the time and space she needed. They needed to know she was okay.

Luna lifted her chin, pasted on a smile, and walked into the kitchen.

"You don't need to worry."

Every eye in the kitchen turned to stare.

Miley spoke first. "It's hard not to, Lu. You haven't been yourself."

"I know. I also haven't had a moment alone since . . . Cody." She winced. "I don't want to say his name."

"Don't, then," Miley told her. "How about 'that night.' You haven't been alone since 'that night.'"

Luna nodded her approval. "I try not to think about it. Now that my face doesn't look like I was left in the boxing ring with someone who had to prove themselves, it'll get easier."

"No one wants to pressure you into talking," Nate said.

Luna took a few steps closer to him and placed a hand over his. "We can't exactly ignore the elephant in the room, though . . . can we?"

He shook his head.

"No," Miley muttered.

Luna looked at her best friend, tilted her head to the side. Miley looked tired. The kind that came from too many hours of work and no sleep. "How are *you* doing? I wasn't the only one here that night."

Miley blinked a few times, her nose flared. "Uhm . . ."

A knot caught in the back of Luna's throat when she realized that Miley was going to cry.

Luna closed in on her friend and pulled her into her arms.

Miley's arms tightened. "I thought he was going to kill you."

"Not with you here," Luna tried to laugh. "Holding a gun."

They pulled apart enough that Luna could see the pain on Miley's face.

"I keep having the same dream." Miley bit her lip. "I pull the trigger, and I hit you."

"Oh, God," Harper whispered.

Luna placed her hands on each side of Miley's face. "But you didn't. And I'm here. No one got shot."

Miley nodded.

They hugged again.

All this time Luna didn't want to talk, she hadn't thought of what Miley was going through. Now she felt selfish for her silence.

They both sat at the kitchen table.

Harper had found tissues and handed one to Miley.

Luna looked at Nate. "Do you have the same dream?" she asked.

"No." He shook his head. "I regret not shooting him." Nate turned back to the stove and removed whatever was in the pan simmering from the heat.

Luna looked at Ash. "And you?"

"I wasn't here," he said.

"I know but . . ."

"I wasn't here. I should have been." His words were angry.

"How were you to know?"

Ash looked her straight in the eye. "You knew. You knew Mom would pull something like this. You said it. And I didn't listen."

"You can't blame yourself for that, Ash. That asshole was here three days before and we were so excited that Mom was leaving that we let him stay. That's on me."

"No, it's not. Miley told me the reason you didn't tell me was for fear of how I would react. And you're right. I wouldn't have let any man Mom brought over stay. If there had to be a fight, it should have been with me, not you."

"And I didn't want you to get into anything that could cost you your promotion. So, we're even. You want to protect me, and I want to protect you. We're not the problem here." Luna paused and looked at Harper and Ash. "Mom is."

"I could have told her to stay with me," Harper said. "She wouldn't have brought over a man with Jerry there."

Luna couldn't argue that. "If she ever shows up here again, you'll get your chance."

Nate moved to Luna's side and took a seat beside her at the kitchen table.

She held out her hand for him to hold.

"She won't," Ash said.

"She will." Luna turned and looked him directly in the eye. "You said you should have listened to me, so hear me now. She will show up again. It might be five years from now . . . two. The difference will be me. I will not open the door for her. Six feet of snow, pouring down rain . . . I don't care. I have given her too much of my life to mess up. How she hasn't scared you off yet, I don't know," Luna said to Nate.

"I don't scare easy." He lifted their joined hands and kissed the back of hers.

Luna leaned into him.

"Is she back in Alabama?" Luna asked.

"Yes. I bought her a one-way plane ticket," Harper said.

Luna nodded several times. "Good. I wouldn't ask either of you to stop having a relationship with her for my sake. I will ask that you respect my decision to cut her out of my life. Don't invite me over if she's visiting. Don't tell me if she asked about me. The only thing I'll ask is that you let me know if she's in town. So that I'm not taken by surprise if she has the audacity to show up. She'll never willingly break this cycle of abuse. That is entirely up to me. I refuse to become her. And I'll no longer accept her in my life." It felt good to say that out loud. The morning she'd woken up broken and bleeding, she knew her relationship with her mother was forever changed. But telling her siblings made it real.

Harper released a sigh. "I'll call her and tell her."

"No," Luna said. "That isn't your job."

Nate placed both of his hands around her one. "Hon . . . you've asked everyone how they're doing. How are *you* doing?"

She couldn't bring herself to lie. They all deserved better than that. "I feel numb. I don't even feel angry anymore. Just numb."

Miley leaned forward. "That's not good, Luna."

"I know. I've avoided therapy. Told myself I was fine when I wasn't. I don't think I can do that anymore." Luna looked at Nate. "I don't want to mess up the good things in my life by burying all this. Right now, I don't trust myself to not screw things up." She felt like crying again, which was better than numb.

Nate pressed his lips close to her ear. "I'm not going anywhere," he whispered.

She wanted to believe that.

She wanted to trust again.

She wanted to let herself love again.

"I'll talk to the social worker at the hospital, get some resources," Miley told her.

"Thank you."

Luna looked between the faces of her family, friend, and lover. All of them there for her, for each other. These were the people in her life that counted. The ones she could count on.

Her mother was never that person and never would be.

Luna turned to Nate, felt a genuine smile on her face. "What's getting cold over there? It smells delicious."

He winked and said slowly, "Swedish meatballs."

"From IKEA?" she laughed.

"I found their recipe." Nate released her hand and went back to the range.

Miley leaned over. "He's one of the good ones," she whispered.

Luna felt her friend's words deep in her chest. "I don't want to fuck it up."

"I won't let you."

Luna sat under the covers of her bed, knees pulled up to her chest.

The sound of the shower had turned off and she could hear Nate moving around in her bathroom preparing himself to go to bed.

When Harper made her excuses and left for home, Luna and Nate worked their way upstairs.

Miley and Ash were still up talking.

It always seemed that her brother and her best friend grated on each other's nerves, but something had changed since "that night." They were softer to each other, kinder.

So much had changed . . . in all of them.

"Someone is deep in thought." Nate's words pulled Luna out of her head.

She smiled and looked him up and down.

Hair wet from the shower, bare chest . . . and gray sweatpants.

"How many pairs of those do you own?" Luna made a scene of letting her eye linger below his waist.

"Before or after I knew about your fetish?" he asked.

"It's not a fetish. It's a preference."

Nate strolled up to the bed, sat on top of the covers, and leaned over her until his lips were a breath away from hers. "The way you go on about my choice in clothing edges on fetish," he whispered.

The fresh scent of soap mixed with Nate filled her nose and made her shiver. They had fallen asleep in each other's arms every night since . . . but Nate hadn't so much as kissed her briefly. The way he touched her, at least when he was awake, was mindful and soft. Like he was afraid she would break if he held her too tight.

Except in his sleep. There his arms held on as if she were a life raft and he'd drown if he let go.

"My obsession has little to do with the sweats and everything to do with the man in them."

"Is that right?" he whispered, smiling.

She brought her hand to his face and looked him in the eye. "I won't shatter, you know."

He dropped his forehead against hers. "I know," he said on a sigh. "I don't want to hurt you." He ran his thumb over the fading bruises on her face.

She slid her good leg down on the bed, and carefully maneuvered the one wrapped in yards of elastic bandaging to stabilize her foot to follow.

Luna did everything she could to stop her wince when her foot caught on the blanket and shot pain up her leg.

She felt Nate flinch.

"Like that," he said.

Maybe she would shatter . . . a little.

"Maybe it is too soon," she agreed.

He pressed his lips to hers, but instead of deepening that kiss, he settled next to her, dropping his cheek onto her chest.

Scooting down until she was flat, Luna held him close and enjoyed the soft motion of his hand drawing up and down her leg.

"It kills me to see you in pain," he told her.

"It feels worse at night," she admitted. "But it's getting better."

"If I had just gotten here a few minutes earlier—"

"Stop," she interrupted his thoughts. "You kept things from getting worse. Focus on what you did do, not what you couldn't change."

Nate squeezed her.

Luna ran her fingers through his hair. She thought about what he'd said in the kitchen, about how he regretted not squeezing the trigger. Hair on her arms rose with the thought. "I'm glad you didn't kill him," she said quietly.

Nate stiffened.

"If you ended up in jail, or—"

Nate lifted his head from her chest. "It would have been justified. He was strangling you."

"But we would have had to defend you, and there's no telling what the courts would say. Or my mother in that asshole's defense. It's better this way. We both know that."

Nate offered a non-convincing nod and drew away long enough to slide under the covers and pull her into his arms.

"I won't let anyone hurt you again," he swore.

She smiled. "Are you going to be my personal bodyguard?"

"If I have to."

She liked the sound of that. Her eyes started to drift closed. "You know . . . eventually you are going to have to go home," she said.

"I know. But not tonight."

"Not tonight," she agreed.

"Or tomorrow."

She giggled.

"Sometime next week," he concluded.

Luna snuggled even closer and attempted to place her bum foot in a position that felt comfortable. "Maybe next week."

Nate reached over her and switched the light on the nightstand off before wrapping her in his arms for the night.

"You're going to have to kick me out of this bed." His words were so quiet, she barely heard him.

Just as quietly she replied, "I'm going to need two good feet to do that."

She felt his lips on the side of her temple. "Get some sleep. I've got you."

And he did . . . heart, body, and soul.

With a little coaxing, Jorden agreed to visit the house on Queen Anne Hill. Ethel, who seemed to be around every corner when Karen was in the house, had been rather silent since "that night." Once Jorden heard that, she agreed to come over.

The sun hadn't quite set, but the full moon was still visible, not that anyone needed to see it to partake in a letting go ceremony.

And that's what Luna wanted. What both Miley and Luna wanted.

A bonus was Harper joining them.

Something Luna had noticed happening more often.

"What is Jerry doing tonight?" Luna asked her sister while the three of them prepared for Jorden to arrive.

"He said poker."

"Is he any good at it?" Miley asked. "Or is poker night code for the guys all sitting around drinking and bitching about their wives?"

Luna laughed. That she could see.

They were in the kitchen preparing a simple dinner. The kind with a salad, fruit and cheese plate, and wine. Although Luna was happy with sparkling water. Something she'd taken to since "that night." Even without a threat, it felt right to keep a clear head.

"Probably the latter," Harper replied.

"What could he possibly have on you to bitch about?" Luna asked.

"My discomfort with his unemployment."

Luna stopped arranging cheese on the plate and looked at her sister. "Not again."

Harper released a long, frustrated breath. "I'm over it. He keeps chasing the big gold ring with these start-ups and ends up with the plastic booby prize. I told him, if sixteen-year-olds can figure out how to make six figures on the internet, someone with his degree should be able to do the same."

"What did he say to that?" Miley asked.

"That he was better at doomscrolling social media than he was posting on it. Sometimes I think I'm married to an overgrown high schooler. One waiting for the perfect summer job that doesn't actually require him to work."

The sound of a car driving in suggested Jorden had arrived.

Luna wiped her hands on a kitchen towel to greet their guest.

"Maybe he can be a professional poker player," Luna teased.

"Bite your tongue. It's one thing not to make money, it's something else entirely if he is actively losing it."

Luna stepped out the side door as Jorden was exiting her car, a large bag in her hands.

She paused and looked up at the house. "Wow."

"Thank you for coming."

Jorden turned, looked behind her. "This is fantastic."

"It's hard to take credit for something you inherited," Luna told her.

They hugged in the driveway. "It's been yours for a while now, you can take credit."

Luna hadn't thought of it that way. "Good point."

Jorden hesitated for a split second as she walked into the house but didn't linger.

"I don't believe you've met my sister, Harper. Harper, this is Jorden."

"I've heard a lot about you," Harper said.

"All good I hope."

"We don't know any of the bad bits yet," Miley joked.

"Hi, Miley."

Miley gave Jorden a hug.

"Would you like a glass of wine?" Luna asked.

"Sure." Jorden walked around the kitchen island looking at the walls, the ceiling, then her gaze caught on the unused greenhouse. "Is that what I think it is?"

"A giant terrarium? Yeah."

She walked closer, reached for the doorknob. "Do you mind?"

"Go right ahead. We don't really use it," Luna admitted.

"Why not?"

"We don't cook enough to use that many herbs." Luna handed Jorden a glass of wine and studied the room with her.

Jorden looked as if she was walking into Alice's Wonderland. "Herbs are used for more than cooking. Not to mention flower starts and fresh vegetables all year round. Lavender and sage, rosemary . . . I would grow everything in here," she cooed.

"Eye of newt?" Luna teased.

Jorden laughed. "Mustard seed, and yes, that, too. Did your grandmother use it?"

"Some. Not as much as she got older."

"Someone loved it, once upon a time."

Luna tried to see the space as Jorden did. Long rows of empty tables, a utility sink, open shelves, and windows everywhere to provide solar heat. "My boyfriend likes to cook. Maybe he'll talk me into using the space."

Jorden smiled at her. "Boyfriend, huh?"

"Something good came out of the last few months," she reported.

"The work guy?"

"Yeah."

"Good. You deserve it."

Instead of sitting around the kitchen table eating, they took the food into the living room where they could curl up on the sofa and plush chairs and have a proper "girls' night."

"Before we get into the 'how is the new boyfriend working out' conversation, I have to say this. Luna, I wish I could have seen the real danger you two were in. Maybe it—"

"Jorden, please. As soon as my mother showed up, I should have seen it. I knew what she was capable of bringing in, you didn't. Like you said, the cards only tell me what my subconscious already knows."

"It's not your fault," Miley said.

"Oh, I'm not taking blame, I just wish I could have given you a sterner warning. How are you doing since?"

"I wrote a Dear John letter to my mother, and I start therapy tomorrow."

Jorden lifted her glass of wine. "And how was that? The letter?"

Luna considered the question. "Freeing. I told her I was done. That nothing she could do or say at this point would change my mind. She can't twelve step her way back into my life. She's proven to me from a very young age that she only ever considers herself and that I would no longer expect any different from her. And since she is not the kind of person I would choose to have in my life, I no longer want her in it at all."

"Wow," Jorden exclaimed. "Do you know if she received the letter?"

"Oh, she got it," Harper moaned. "She called me, completely hysterical. Couldn't understand why she was being blamed for Cody's actions. I let her vent for ten minutes before I cut her off and told her that Luna was serious, and Ash and I supported her decision."

"What about you?" Jorden asked. "Do you feel the same way?"

"I do. It's different, though. It's hard to explain." Harper didn't elaborate.

"You don't have to."

A flash of sorrow crossed her sister's face, one that had Luna questioning what Harper was thinking about.

"How is Ethel?"

Luna and Miley both stared at Jorden.

"What do you mean?" Luna asked.

"She was here that night." Jorden paused. "Was it raining?"

"No. It was cold but not raining. Why do you ask?"

Jorden looked at Miley. "I sense lightning. Or a power blip."

Luna huffed. "That seems to be her thing. Everything happened so fast that night, I don't remember."

"I recall looking at your mom and wondering if she was standing next to the light switch, so yeah, something had to have been happening. Like Luna said, it was all a blur," Miley said.

"You guys are talking about her like she's a real person," Harper argued.

"She was," Jorden told them. "And she's family."

Luna leaned forward and lowered her voice. "Is she here . . . now?"

Jorden nodded.

"That freaks me out," Harper said.

"She's good energy. There's nothing for you to worry about," Jorden told her.

"Easy for you to say until you hear footsteps and no one is there." Harper shivered.

"I thought you didn't want to be a medium," Luna said.

"She's not talking to me," Jorden denied. "I just . . . sense her. I also sense some of your mom's bad energy. And Joe . . . who is Joe?"

"You must be talking about Grampa Joe."

"He could still be alive," Harper said.

"Maybe. He lived in this house, yeah?"

"Longer than most of Nana's husbands," Luna laughed.

Jorden set her wine down and pulled the bag she brought with her onto her lap. "You want to keep Ethel and Joe's energy, but let's see what we can do about telling your mother's to take a hike."

"Does this really work?" Harper sounded doubtful.

Luna pushed some of the plates on the coffee table aside to give Jorden room to light her candles.

"It can't hurt," Luna said.

A soft meow brought their attention to Midnight, who stood at the entry to the living room.

"Awhh, and who is this?" Jorden asked.

"Midnight. I know, the most unoriginal name . . ."

Taking Jorden's beckoning fingers as an invitation, Midnight slowly walked over and accepted her pet. "Aren't you beautiful."

"Do you have cats?" Miley asked.

"No. It's hard enough dating when men think you're a witch, having cats would be the icing on my forever celibacy."

That had them all laughing.

"This we need to hear more about," Miley said.

Jorden stopped petting Midnight and proceeded to set a candle in the middle of the table. "It's not in the cards for me. Men, I mean."

"I thought that the day I walked into your shop. And now there's Nate."

Jorden lit the candle. "And the cards predicted him. My cards"—Jorden put a hand on her chest—"not so much."

Miley leaned over and picked up the tarot deck Jorden had removed from her bag. "You need to teach me how to read these. I bet I can predict your future man."

"Predict, not conjure," Luna laughed.

"Make sure you conjure a man with a steady income," Harper added.

"And a big dick." Miley removed a card from the deck and looked at it. "Would you look at that." She turned the card around.

The card had a man sitting in front of a reflecting pool waving his hands around while streaming sparkles whipped up from two bowls.

"The magician," Jorden whispered.

Miley squirmed in her seat. "Steady income and a big dick . . . What else should we ask for?"

"Muscles," Harper chimed in. "And tall."

"Opposite of Jerry?" Luna asked.

"Jerry isn't short."

Luna started to laugh. "The dick must be questionable."

"Humor," Jorden added. "He has to have a sense of humor."

Miley tucked her feet under her and shuffled the cards. "If we're going to conjure a unicorn, then he should have a hedge fund."

EPILOGUE

The family therapy practice was in an old bungalow home turned into office space on a street not far from the crystal store Luna had told Nate about. The side yard of the house had been turned into a small parking lot fit for only four cars.

Nate asked if he could drive her for her first day.

His reasoning . . . "What if you're upset when you leave? You don't want to drive when you're crying, or angry."

The expression on Luna's face said she didn't buy it, but she agreed to him driving her anyway.

"This isn't a onetime thing," she told him.

"But it's a first-time thing, and after the first time, you'll know what to expect."

Ten minutes before her appointment time, they sat in his car in a lot that didn't have any other vehicles.

"Do you think she lives in there?" Luna asked, looking at the house.

"I doubt it. Maybe she parks on the street."

"Looks safe."

"Getting mugged on the way to therapy would be bad."

Luna laughed.

God, he loved that sound.

"How was the meeting with the Woo-Woo Club?"

"It was amazing. We conjured up the perfect man for Miley and Jorden."

"I need to hear all about this."

Luna shook her head. "Not from me. What happens in the Woo-Woo Club stays in the Woo-Woo Club. Oh, except about Joe."

"Joe who?"

"Grampa Joe. Jorden seems to think that Joe's energy is still in the house."

"Are he and Ethel having a thing?" Nate chuckled.

"Wouldn't that be cool. But no. Before she left, she said something about Joe keeping secrets. I didn't tell her anything about his possible Mafia ties."

Nate stopped laughing. "That's scary."

"She's legit, I'm telling you."

"I keep meaning to look him up."

Luna glanced up at the house again. She was nervous, Nate didn't need to be part of the Woo-Woo Club to sense that.

"I'll be in there for an hour."

"I'll research Seattle's Mafia, see what good ole Joe was up to," he said. "Oh, by the way, I talked to my parents last night. They're coming to town in a couple of weeks. They want to meet you."

Luna looked surprised. "You told them about me?"

"Of course. I told them about you weeks ago. They assumed my happiness had to be about you. I told them you were stealing my heart. Naturally they want to meet you."

Luna blinked . . . twice. "Stealing your heart?"

He reached for her hand. Felt fear in her question. "I'm not sure what else to call it. I wasn't expecting you. You could say I was actively trying to avoid a relationship until I got a foothold on this PI thing. But then you tripped me, and coffee flew everywhere."

Luna closed her eyes, smiled, and lowered her head.

"I've had women try and get my attention before, but that was a new one."

"You make me laugh," she told him.

He kissed the back of her hand and waited for her to look him in the eye. "I'm all about smearing your lipstick, Luna. Not your mascara. Unless you're someone who cries when they're happy."

"I am happy." Her soft smile gave him hope.

"So am I. Stupidly happy. And you are stealing my heart. I need you to know that. If you ever want me to walk in there with you—" He nodded toward the therapy office. "I will. I want us. I want you. No matter what it takes, or how long it takes."

Luna sniffled and leaned toward him, lifting her lips to his.

He kissed her slowly, lovingly. And when it ended, they didn't pull away.

"Wait for me," she whispered.

"I'm right here," he said as he gently placed his palm on the center of her chest.

She pressed her hand to his. "I gotta go."

Nate stole another kiss and pulled away. "Go. I'll be here."

He watched as one of the bravest women he'd ever met stepped out of the car to face her demons.

Before she got far, she turned around.

Nate lowered the window. "Yeah?"

She was smiling. "Do you have a hedge fund?"

He laughed. "What? No . . . why?"

"Woo-Woo Club."

He rolled his eyes. "You're going to be late," he told her.

She waved before disappearing behind the door.

~

Luna stepped into the bungalow to what would have been a home foyer, on the side of that was a living room that now housed two large sofas and a giant coffee table filled with magazines. Who read paper magazines anymore? *Seattle Living*, *Psychology Today* . . . not one celebrity tabloid or fashion trope that would have a patient comparing themselves to the unachievable.

Someone thought that through, Luna mused.

There was a fireplace where one should be, only this was filled with fake plants.

The space felt like a home that no one lived in.

She heard footsteps on the creaky old stairs and for a brief second wondered if Ethel had followed her.

"Luna?"

She turned. "You must be Rachel."

Rachel nodded and they shook hands.

"We have our offices upstairs."

"Okay." Luna was led into a revamped bedroom. Carpeted floors, a wall to wall bookshelf, a single chair, and a sofa. Off to the side of that was a similar space, this one with a desk and the kind of lounge sofa depicted in every movie where a patient would lie down and tell their life story.

Luckily, that wasn't where Rachel encouraged her to sit.

Rachel took the chair opposite the sofa where Luna sat and took in the room.

Soft paintings, and windows that did a good job of providing natural light. And there was a box of Kleenex on every flat surface she could see.

"Would you like some water?" Rachel asked.

Luna shook her head but then said, "Yes."

Water would be good. Just walking in the room had the back of Luna's throat aching.

Rachel handed her a mug and sat back down.

Rachel was a small woman, casually dressed with short, wavy salt-and-pepper hair. She smiled with her eyes . . . yes, her lips, but it was her eyes that Luna noticed. Not the color, or the shape . . . but the kindness.

"This is a beautiful old house," Luna told her.

"Isn't it? We really like it here. It's much more comfortable than an office building."

"That's true," Luna said.

Rachel took a tablet and held it in her lap. "I read over your intake form. This is the first time you've sought therapy?"

"Outside of a high school counselor, yes."

She was quiet for a moment.

Where should she start?

"What brought you to therapy at this time?" Rachel asked.

"So many things."

"Let's start with one. Ask yourself what it is you want to achieve with therapy. What do you want out of your time here with me?"

Luna's thoughts drifted to the man waiting in the car.

"I met someone who I'm falling in love with." Her throat started to close up. "And I can't help but feel like I'm going to fuck it up and drive him away."

"Tell me about him."

Luna smiled through the tears that were already there. "He . . . he's a unicorn. Kind, caring, there when you need him. Funny . . . he makes me laugh. Loving. Smart. Good-looking but not arrogant." She thought about that for a second. "Well, maybe a little arrogant, but not in a bad way. Protective." Luna nodded with that one. "Very protective."

"He does sound like a unicorn," Rachel said.

"Not married, not gay, doesn't live in his mom's basement, has a job, no kids, and he cooks. I'm not talking warms up food in the microwave but actually cooks."

"Wow. So, what's wrong with him?"

"Nothing."

"Trustworthy?"

Luna nodded. "Yes," she said quickly.

Rachel was silent for a moment.

"Some say that when a stranger hurts you, you go through life not trusting others. But when someone close to you hurts you. Someone who should love and protect you, hurts you, you go through life not trusting yourself." Rachel paused.

Luna stopped staring at her lap and looked up.

"Who was that person in your life?"

Emotion so thick it gripped her neck and chest like a vise crushed in, and the tears started to fall.

"My mother," Luna whispered.

Rachel took a deep breath, her kind smile was gone and replaced with cautious understanding and compassion.

"Tell me about your mother."

I REFUSE TO BECOME MY ABUSER

By Catherine Bybee

When passion meets persistence, changes are made.

I refuse to become my abuser. My pursuit of this passionate plea has taken me to the top of my tower. The one I built myself. The one where I sit quietly, and not so quietly, and write these words. The one where I create worlds where others like me can escape and envision as their own. Where they are respected, loved, safe . . . and know that when the last page is turned there is a cloud lined in silver on which they can land.

These worlds are not real.

Utopia does not exist.

Even in seemingly perfect worlds there is pain and tragedy. Trauma and hate. Crippling anxiety and fear that stops all forward momentum to a better life.

I refuse to become my abuser.

I will not allow the insecurity of others to silence my voice. Not anymore. Silence is the quiet approval of others' actions. Silence is permission. Silence is how evil becomes power.

Opening the pages of your past when others scream for you to slam the book shut, is a story worth reading. Not to sit in pain and wallow, but to unpack the clothing others told you, you should or shouldn't wear. The impossible dress that signifies the standards of beauty this world covets. The pants you're told not to wear because your place is to let others tell you how to live. The shoes you have worn in battle that you've been told to ignore.

In my quest to not become my abuser, to find my voice . . . the tomb of my history must be read . . . must be written by this victor.

Victory is not only survival. Many survive and hold no victory. They are alive but believe the whispers of their oppressors, they obey in advance with their silence. They move through their days, as I have in the past, following the path of least resistance.

Moving around, over and under, but never through.

I will not become my abuser.

I will fight the current until I walk freely upstream.

The only voice I will silence is the one that lives in my head that others have put there.

That voice has served her purpose.

She has kept me safe, kept me alive and whole. She was a dressing pressed upon my bleeding soul in my field of battle, wearing the shoes, the pants, the dress. Living in quiet, screaming agony at the abuse of others.

Learning from the past and moving on is not my answer. Digesting the parts that fuel me and getting rid of the waste . . . that is my answer.

I will live my life out loud.

My life. The one I built from the tower I sit on.

I will be the shining, and sometimes tarnished, example of the victory of my life.

I will be the one abusers fear.

For the only power they have is what I give them.

I will not become my abuser.

AUTHOR'S NOTE

The first time anyone suggested that I write a book, I couldn't have been over fifteen years old. It was my neighbor . . . the mother of a friend who watched in silence at the life I was living. She would quietly whisper words that kept me going. "Your life won't always be like this." "All of this is temporary." And of course, "One day you could write about your childhood and have a bestseller."

My story isn't unique. In fact, it's old . . . tired. Told over and over by so many children of narcissistic and abusive parents. One day I will write all of the pain of my past, but until then I will sprinkle out the parts I can stomach. Like this one, where the names have been changed to protect the innocent . . . and not so innocent. And dare the ones that hurt me the most to come my way. I will not be silenced into submission. Like the poem said, I will not obey in advance.

I write these stories with my past woven in, not in search of sympathy, but in hopes that others can read between the lines and find hope.

Refusing to become my abuser was my first step in breaking a cycle that statistically I was destined to follow. I have built a life that I am incredibly proud of, against the odds. But not without falling into the trap of inviting the wrong people into my life that I thought would fill the void my mother left behind. All because I hadn't yet worked through the childhood I wanted to ignore.

It's through years of therapy and unmasking the truth of my past that I can confidently say that my abusers no longer have any hold on my soul.

Needing and seeking help to face the demons that keep you up at night and scared is incredibly brave.

If anything about Luna's story struck something inside of you, dear reader, a hurt you have not faced, a past you desperately don't want to repeat, I encourage you to find someone to talk to.

A therapist, a doctor . . . a helpline.

I've said this before, and I will say it again . . .

Some people are meant to be a chapter in your story, not the whole book.

There is no shame in walking away from people that have caused you pain . . . even if you call them family.

Catherine

PS . . .

The ghost on Queen Anne Hill was real. The footsteps running up and down the stairs to the attic . . . the pots and pans on the kitchen floor . . . all of it. Years after we moved out of the house, I remember rushing home from school to watch *General Hospital* with Luke and Laura hiding in a mall . . . the news broke in to talk about an unsellable home that was being demolished.

It was that house on Queen Anne Hill . . .

Why was it being demolished?

Because it was thought to be haunted and no one ever lived in it for long. Leaving the house to ruins.

The running theory in my family was that it was the mother of the abusive pedophile we called our stepfather, rolling over in her grave every time he did something vile.

Ethel was a very active spirit.

ACKNOWLEDGMENTS

As always, to Amazon/Montlake for publishing this book and all the others. For giving me a place to tell the stories that I need to tell. To my editors Maria Gomez and Lindsey Faber, who always keep it real when editing books that are pages from my past, thank you. To my line editors, copyeditors, beta readers, and Audible talent . . . thank you for all that you do.

Jane Dystel, I never take you for granted. Thank you for helping me build my tower.

To Kari . . . for inspiring the idea of an ex-government criminal fraud investigator by example. I still can't believe you're the one who ended up wearing a gun on your hip.

And now to Rachel.

If it wasn't for your help over the years, I wouldn't have been able to write this book, and likely the ones that will follow. I know our work isn't yet done . . . but boy have we come a long way. The memory of me talking to you that first day and telling you that "I don't want to spend all this time going over ancient history" and that I'd "'worked through' my stepdad and mommy issues." And you just smiling and nodding like you agreed, will never go away.

You have helped me find my voice, my purpose, and the love for myself that I have denied for so many years. You have given me permission to walk away from people who only know how to hurt me. And grace when I still hold on to those I can't let go.

Since you're my therapist, I am unable to return the favor, but I hope that in some way, your time with me has given you something. If nothing else, know that I am better for having known you, stronger. And that in that strength I'm able to reach readers who may just read the pages of this book and take the steps they need to for a better life.

Your reach will go far past our zip code.

Saying thank you isn't enough, but I'll say it anyway.

Thank you.

Catherine

ABOUT THE AUTHOR

Photo © Catherine Bybee

Catherine Bybee is the *New York Times*, *Wall Street Journal*, and *USA Today* bestselling author of nearly fifty novels that have collectively sold more than eleven million copies and have been translated into more than twenty languages. Raised in Washington state, Bybee moved to Southern California in the hope of becoming a movie star. After growing bored with waiting tables, she returned to school and became a registered nurse, spending most of her career in urban emergency rooms. She now writes full-time and has penned the Heirs series, Not Quite series, the Weekday Brides series, the Most Likely To series, the D'Angelos series, and the First Wives series, among others. For more information, visit www.catherinebybee.com.